MASQUERADE

Book Three of
The Dragonfly Chronicles

ELERI DRAKE

McCollum Creative Endeavors, LLC

McCollum Creative Endeavors
P.O. Box 1712
Apex, NC 27502

Cover design by Najla Qamber
Editing by Melinda DeJongh
E-book ISBN: 978-1-962436-04-5
Print book ISBN:978-1-962436-05-2
Manufactured in the United States of America

*First Edition published by The Wild Rose Press under the name Heather McCollum, December 2011
*Second Edition, November 2025

For more information about Eleri Drake and Heather McCollum books, please check out her web site. https://www.heathermccollum.com/eleri-drake/

Eleri Drake Website

CONTENTS

DEDICATION

To Skye, Logan, and Kyrra.

May you each find someone who loves you for who you truly are.

And may butterflies always guard your backs.

TRIGGER WARNINGS

I want you to thoroughly enjoy this time travel, fated mates continuation of the Dragonfly Chronicles series, so please be aware of the following. There are no rape scenes on the page, but there are threats of cruelty, sexual assault, drowning, and death by fire. There are also mentions of child abuse, domestic violence, and incest.

FOREIGN WORDS IN MASQUERADE (SCOTS GAELIC)

bana-bhuidseach – witch

daingead – damn it

Dhia – God

Diciadain – Wednesday

fuil air son buaidh – blood for victory

mac an donais – damn it

mattucashlass – double sided blade

mo ghràdh – my love

olc – evil

siuthad – go on

OTHER BOOKS IN THE DRAGONFLY CHRONICLES

Prophecy – Book #1

18th Century Scotland
Forbidden Love * Dark Prophecy * Telepathy

Prophecy
Buy Links

Serena Faw must shut out the barrage of thoughts from everyone around her. Her telepathic powers reveal the darkness and true intentions behind every false smile. When her adopted brother is accused of murder, the only man who can help her is the one person she cannot read. Can she trust the Highlander with the life of her brother? Can she trust him with her heart?

Keenan Maclean, the younger brother to the new chief of the Macleans, has grown up in the shadow of a dark prophecy. It is said that one Maclean brother will live, wed to a witch, and one will die. Keenan has grown into a fierce warrior while accepting his fate to defend his clan and die with honor.

Serena and Keenan hunt a loyalist murderer before the Battle of Culloden while trying to deny the attraction growing between them.

Despite the prophecy's warning that she heralds his death and Keenan's need to protect his brother and family, the passion becomes too great to ignore. Will their lives be the penalty for their forbidden love?

Magick
Buy Links

Magick — Book #2

10th century Denmark
Enemies to Lovers * Redemption * Healing Magic

Fury and guilt assail Hauk, a fierce Viking warrior, after he allows false healers to "cure" his family to death. When he's ordered to capture the Great Witch of the Woods in Northumbria for his king, he doesn't anticipate that his hatred for all things magick would be challenged by a long-legged beauty with sparking green eyes.

Strong-willed and daring, Merewin doesn't cower from the warriors who storm her homeland, stealing her away to a land across the sea. But when she learns that her purpose is to heal a child with her magical healing powers, her fear of failure wages war against her resilient spirit.

Strong wills clash as Merewin and Hauk battle their instant attraction. Can Hauk trust a healer with his remaining family? Can Merewin conquer her own pride to love this powerful man who possesses an unacknowledged magick of his own? In the end Merewin and Hauk must put their faith in each other and in their love. For love is the only magick that can heal someone's soul.

PROLOGUE

On the Border of Alba and Strathclyde
On the Western Sea of Scotland, 1005 A.D.

"Katell, come here. You're next to go!" Gilla, the great Wiccan Priestess of the Western Mountains, Keeper of the Earth Mother's magic, tugged her four-year-old daughter from behind her twin.

Katell flinched as another tree shook the house. "No," she whispered.

"Now! You must go now!" Gilla hugged the child in weakening arms and pushed a blue moonstone into her palm, closing her small fingers around it. Katell trembled, making Gilla's stomach twist. *Earth Mother, please protect my bairns!* She couldn't stand to think of them twisted and broken like her mate, Druce.

"My wards are falling," she whispered, forcing herself to breathe. Soft words blew gently across her daughter's coppery blond curls. Thatching rained down from the ceiling of their once warm cottage. "You both must be brave," she said, eyes level with the other twin waiting in silence. Gilla pulled Katell back by her shoulders and kissed her cheek, sticky with tears.

"Mama, come hide with me!" Katell pleaded.

Gilla yanked the yellow sash from her waist. The cloth's soft folds were embroidered with golden and blue butterflies weaving and dancing along its length. She tied it around her daughter's palm, wrapping the stone against her skin so it couldn't be lost. "Nay, my dear heart, I must stay." Tears ran freely down Gilla's cheeks. This was too hard. She was too weak. What does a mother say to her child when she knows she won't ever see her again? How does she explain that sending her away will keep her alive? Her two eldest girls may have understood, but to a four-year-old, this was abandonment.

Gilla brushed at Katell's tears with a thumb, wishing, so hard it hurt, that she could brush away the fear in her bairn's eyes. "As long as you escape, dear heart, as long as you are safe and alive, then so am I." Gilla grabbed the precious girl to her chest, gasping at the pain that swelled in her heart. "Even if you don't see me, I am always with you, loving you with all my heart."

Katell sobbed, pressing into the folds of Gilla's luminescent gown as if trying to crawl back into her womb.

Gilla breathed deeply to refocus her will, reinforce her strength. Her remaining magic held the demons outside the stone sentries standing in a circle around their cottage. "Dear Earth Mother," Gilla prayed out loud to the cold, dirt-strewn room. "Give me the strength to save my children, to save the world." She ended on a whisper barely heard above the dark howl that thrashed around the eaves. She kissed Katell's small head, inhaling her sweet essence as her eyes squeezed more tears from them.

"Tha gaol agam ort, dear heart."

"I love you too, Mama," Katell's muffled answer choked on another sob.

Gilla stroked her light auburn curls. "My skittish foal, you've always liked to hide. I will gift you with my water magic." She pulled Katell's bound hand and brushed it against her lips.

"I freely gift you with my power to hide, to change shape. On the currents of my blood, on the currents of my love, on the currents of my power given by the Earth Mother, send her now within my thread of glamour."

Gilla blew out the power that lay within her chest, blew it steadily out of her in a thin stream. If the stone had been uncovered, Gilla would have seen the coils of power snake within, flooding the stone and her daughter's small body with magic. The sudden weakness at the loss of another magic thread made Gilla sway.

Katell gasped and looked down. "The rock's hot, Mama."

Gilla nodded. "That's a good thing, dear heart. Always keep my moonstone close to you." Katell formed a little fist around the stone tied to her by the sash. "Go now." Gilla kissed her cheek that melted away into energy beneath her lips.

"Mama?" Katell called, fear pinching her young voice. The child's gaze darted to her twin, standing alone, waiting. "Goodbye."

Her twin twisted her hands in front of her. "Love you, Katell."

"Go, dear heart, and live," Gilla called as she watched her four-year-old thin out into a thread of blue energy. The thread elongated, darting upward toward a hole in the once-resilient roof that Druce had built for them. *Oh Druce. How will I beat them without you?* She wouldn't, but saving their bairns would be enough.

"Mama!" She heard the echo as the thread shot through the evil wind.

Gilla rubbed her tear-streaked face and turned to her last daughter. "Come, Sweetheart." She opened her arms as the little girl rushed to her. "Let's send you away from this terror," she whispered and withdrew another stone from her pocket. Once she sent the last of her magic away, Gilla would be powerless against the demons. Her wards would fall and she would die. At least the pain would stop.

⋯⟨O⟩⋯

Lambeth Borough, London, England
3:18 AM on 13 January 1999 AD

Drakkina, an ancient Wiccan priestess who now only existed in spirit form, floated in the shadows near the old stone building with its mighty cross. Dragonflies flitted about her silver hair that hung loose, unaffected by the chilled night wind.

"There," she said, spotting a glimmering blue thread coiled up in the sky. If she still had a heart, it would have beat faster with relief.

The thread swelled as it shot downward toward the sleeping city, silently expanding into the shape of a young girl with auburn hair. Gilla's magic, taught to her by Drakkina, set the child down gently on the stone steps. "Saint Mary's Abbey," Drakkina read from the carved letters above the door where the little girl stood, turning slowly with round eyes, her thin arms clasped around herself. A doe-eyed sculpture of the revered Mother Mary looked down at the child as if she would scoop her up.

"Mama?" the girl cried, gaze darting into the darkness. Drakkina floated out of the shadows. Something in the little voice beckoned, a pain that caught Drakkina's breath, if she had breath. Drakkina wanted to comfort her. *How odd.*

"Daughter of Gilla, you will be safe here."

The child ran up the steps to the heavy wooden doors and pressed herself against them as her eyes tracked Drakkina. "Are you a demon?"

Katell rubbed at the birthmark Drakkina knew sat upon her upper arm. It was Drakkina's mark, the mark of the dragonfly. Each of Katell's siblings had one, like a homing beacon. The ancient magic of the dragonfly sat at the heart of Gilla's and Drakkina's powers.

Drakkina reached out but pulled back when the child shrank in panic. "No, child. I was a friend of your mother's. I taught her all about magic."

The child shunned her touch. No matter. It would require a huge amount of Drakkina's power to make herself feel corporeal enough to touch the girl, to give her physical comfort. Instead, the Wiccan spirit smiled, the gesture feeling odd on her face.

"You will live here, or near here." Drakkina looked up at the huge stained-glass windows of the stone building. Certainly, there must still be foundling sanctuaries this far into the future.

Drakkina turned back to Katell. "The demons won't find you here," Drakkina murmured more to herself than to the child. "Their God will protect you," she said, feeling the low vibration of holy magic about the place.

Drakkina threaded her powers outward to scan the slumbering building. Women under holy oaths slept or turned in their beds or shuffled to the privy. Depictions of ancient heroes and martyrs stared out from stained glass windows near the pinnacle, just under the large cross. Feelings of tradition, holy love, and comfort assured Drakkina that this was a good place. Gilla had aimed well.

Katell shivered and rubbed her bare arms. Of course, the child was cold. Drakkina's consciousness didn't feel heat or cold. She frowned. Nor hugs or hand holding.

"Time to get you indoors." Drakkina motioned. "Sit on the steps, Katell." She waited for the child to move away from the doors and willed her powers toward a window on the third floor. Fourth one to the right felt full of compassion. *Tap, tap, tap.* She heard the small pebbles she'd hoisted hit the glass. *Tap, tap, tap.* They clinked sporadically until a face appeared. Drakkina focused on the streetlamp, bending the downward ray of light from its path until it fell across Katell, making the child blink.

The face in the window disappeared, and a light switched on somewhere within.

Drakkina smiled. "Sister Susanna will love you, Daughter of Gilla."

"Are you leaving me?"

Drakkina faded from the child's sight as one of the large doors swung inward and a young woman in a terrycloth robe stepped out.

"Child? Where have you come from?" she asked, looking up and down the deserted street where the winter wind blew brittle leaves between car tires. "Where is your mother?"

Tears washed down Katell's rosy cheeks. "Far away."

The young nun removed her robe and draped it around Katell but continued to stare into the darkness. "We will find her, child."

"Are you Sister Susanna?"

The nun's gaze flew back to her. "I am... But how...?" She let the question hang there.

"You will keep me safe?" Katell asked desperately.

The nun looked stunned, but then as if waking up, she smiled, lips a strong line on a wise-beyond-her-years face.

Good, she's also intelligent, Drakkina thought. She wouldn't waste too much time looking for a mother who couldn't be found.

"I'll keep you safe, little one," the young nun promised. "Let's go inside now and get you some hot cocoa."

"Hot co...coa?" Katell repeated.

"Now tell me," Sister Susanna said, as she guided Katell through the heavy door. "Do you have a name?"

Drakkina couldn't hear the child's small voice but watched from the shadows as a dozen butterflies flitted through the night to follow the child, stopping only when the door shut them out. Drakkina smiled. "Gilla's love will always follow you, Katell."

CHAPTER ONE
FOR THE CHILDREN

London, England
9 June Current Day

"Rich, sexy as hell, and smart enough even for you." Lisa Gibson set her phone down in front of Kat, tapping her short fingernail next to it before dropping into the kitchen chair.

"Exactly how sexy is hell?" Kat asked and sipped the hot cocoa in the cheery morning sunlight beaming through the window of the small breakfast nook. "And what do you mean, smart enough for me?"

"Hell is sizzling," Lisa said, making a sizzle sound as she touched her curvy bum clad in jeans. She snapped the phone back up and waved a picture of an attractive man at Kat. "He must be smart to care about all those artifacts. And you, Kat Lambeth, don't suffer fools."

Even on a day such as this, her best friend and partner, Lisa, could make Kat smile. Hot cocoa and sun: she needed all the calming influences she could muster before reading the latest letter from the mortgage department of Barclays Bank. She closed her eyes as she pulled in a steamy sip, nearly hot enough to burn, but not quite. Just as she liked it. As the chocolate warmed the center of her belly, she watched several butterflies circle the window outside. She waved her fingers at them.

"I wonder if he's single." Lisa set her phone before Kat again, and the article title caught Kat's attention. *Artifact Collector Showcases Priceless Scottish Pieces.*

She had studied history at uni, specifically the Elizabethan era in the late sixteenth century, and loved exhibits with artifacts. She set her cup down, picking up Lisa's phone. And priceless usually meant a price so high that one shouldn't ask. It wasn't for sale. At least through legal markets.

"Why can't I meet a man like that?" Lisa lamented. She grabbed a fresh scone from Kat's plate and bit into it.

The man stared right out from the screen as if looking into Kat, seeing all her secrets. She shivered. *Don't be ridiculous.* There was the barest hint of a grin that did not reach those dangerous eyes, as if the photographer had begged him for a smile and he had conceded. His hair was dark brown and wavy with a casual cut.

"I bet he has a sword like Adrian Paul in the old *Highlander* television series," Lisa said.

Kat rolled her eyes. "Great. An immortal LARPer."

Although Lisa was right. The man was gorgeous in a wild, dangerous way. Like a beautiful lion before it attacked. Handsome, but different from the classic womanizer type. Rough around the edges, like he had a story but would never tell it.

"He looks like some knight from long ago." Lisa sighed dramatically. "He even has a battle scar."

Kat pulled her hair over to cover the right side of her face. Even though she used glamour magic to smooth the puckered skin from her childhood burns, the old habit of hiding them remained.

"A battle scar?" Kat squinted and saw a raised white line on his jaw where the short beard he wore didn't grow. "He probably got into a row defending his rugby club."

"That's still a battle scar," Lisa said.

Kat read out loud. "And you can meet Mr. Sexy as Hell," she said, pointing to the location of the exhibit, "at the Courtauld Gallery in Somerset House." She traced the route on the tube in her head. "It's right along the Thames in Covent Gardens."

"His name is Toren MacCallum," Lisa said, and stood to turn on the hot water for her instant mocha infusion.

"It's open from eleven to seven all this week," Kat murmured. Holy Mary, this week was busy. Could she fit a heist at the exhibit into her schedule? How much money would a priceless artifact bring? If she found the right collector, plenty. Exactly what she needed if she were to keep Sister Susanna's Home for Children out of the Bank's apathetic hands.

Kat couldn't help but think about the thick envelope sitting up in her room. The last letter from the bank had mentioned lawyers if they didn't make up the mortgage payments for the last two months. Homeless children or not, those blackhearted bankers would close their doors and the children would be split up. The kids also needed shoes, that meant twelve pairs, before the school term started. And then there was the bus that wouldn't start. They needed the money.

Kat's phone dinged. It was her calendar, and it read *Kyrra Boswell-YMCA*. "Shoot." She glanced at her watch and stood. "It's Saturday. I have a swim lesson for the tadpole group at the Y."

Lisa's pierced eyebrow rose. "You're leaving me with just Edith to help?"

"Most of the kids are sleeping in."

"Most, huh? That leaves five who are already up and about." Lisa jerked her chin toward the door, where a little face, set in a crazy array of angelic curls, peeked in. Lisa crooked her finger at the girl, who ran to hop in her lap. Lisa kissed the top of the girl's head and handed her the remains of Kat's scone. "Like this little pixie."

"I'm...no...pixie," the four-year-old said between bites. "I'm a fairy princess."

"I stand corrected," Lisa said.

Kat smiled warmly at Clara, who perched quite like a princess in Lisa's lap. The children made all this worth it, every terrible call from the bank, every threatening letter from the mortgage company, every crime she had to commit to keep the lending hounds at bay.

Kat bent to kiss Clara's curls. The aroma of sweet, clean, loved child made up for all the loneliness, exhaustion, and worry. "The fairy princess of Sister Susanna's Home for Children." Kat nodded. "Sounds right."

"I thought that was you," Lisa said, the grin teasing in her round face with dimples.

"I passed that baton when we bought this place."

Kat and Lisa had been raised together as sisters behind these loving walls. As teenagers, they'd helped the nuns with cooking, cleaning, and childcare. They almost gave up their scholarships to uni to run the home for the aging nuns. It really had become their home.

Four years had passed since they graduated from Oxford, Kat on a swimming scholarship and Lisa on a football scholarship. The two had returned for a visit to find the orphanage bankrupt and being auctioned by the Bank of England. And the church wasn't swooping in to save the home this time. The children were in jeopardy of being split up. Ten kids had already been worked into the foster system with a dozen still at the home and the nuns desperately trying to keep them together.

If a child was adopted it was sad to see them go, but the separation would lead to a happy, loving life. But it was utterly cruel to tear a child away from the only family they'd ever known to send them to another institution. No matter how many times Kat heard from "experts" that kids were resilient in the face of change, she had no intention of seeing what was left of her family torn apart.

So Lisa and Kat threw in a bid for the building. With help from their GoFundMe page, bake sales, car washes, and the local Catholic church, they were able to scrape up enough money for the down payment. After six months of licensing classes, inspections, and jumping through every government hoop, Lisa and Kat finally rounded the corner. The orphanage was theirs, along with the children, ages four to fourteen. They had named it Sister Susanna's Home for Children after the kind nun who had loved them so well until she'd been reassigned to an abbey in Wales.

The new owners immediately hired help and wrote to every institution they could to beg for funding. They were barely successful. Local churches provided Christmas gifts and school supplies, but wages for an extra carer and a cook were high.

Kat glanced at the door to the large living area that was still quiet. "Where's Jimmy, Fairy Princess Clara?"

"Asleep," Clara answered and cuddled into Lisa's shoulder.

Lisa and Kat frowned at one another. Clara's twin brother was loud and ready for the day before the day was ever ready for him.

"I'll check on him," Kat said and stood. She padded down the hall, her bare feet gently slapping the polished wood floors. She met two ten-year-old girls on the stairs, high-fiving them as she raced past.

"Miss Edith is making pancakes in half an hour," Kat whispered loudly to a group of kids. They cheered in whispers, a rule before 9:00 AM on the weekends. They hurried into one of the two multi-stalled bathrooms Kat's diamond heist had paid for last year. Kat made a sign of the cross and sent a prayer for forgiveness to the ceiling. Not for the crime, but because she knew she would do it again just to see the happy tears in Lisa's eyes despite her fretting about the cost of remodeling the chipped and leaking bathrooms.

Kat cracked Jimmy's door, and his open eyes turned to her. "Miss Kat," he croaked. "My stomach hurts, and my throat." Kat sat down on the plaid comforter to kiss his forehead. *One hundred and two.* Her guesses were always accurate after kissing so many feverish foreheads over the last four years.

"You're hot, too," Kat said, and smoothed back his hair. "Probably strep throat." Kat managed a calm smile, but inside she shrieked. Strep throat through a group of twelve children was daunting. "Are you hungry? Miss Edith is making pancakes. I can bring you some." Jimmy shook his head no.

"Okay." The boy was really sick if he didn't want pancakes. "I'll get some medicine that will make you feel better, and we'll have Doctor John come out." Luckily the elderly doctor made house calls for the home.

"Grape? Not the awful grape, but the good grape?" he whispered.

Kat nodded. "Good grape, no cough medicine in it."

He nodded and closed his eyes with a grimace when he swallowed. She retrieved the grape-flavored pain reliever from the medicine lock box in her own bathroom and returned to Jimmy's side.

"Good grape?" he asked again.

She nodded, and he opened his mouth. He took it down and swallowed some water while making his "I'm in pain" face. Kat tucked the blankets around him. "If you feel better, I'll make sure there are some pancakes saved for you."

"Thank you," he whispered.

"Sure thing, Jimmy. Stay in bed and don't lick anyone."

He giggled. "No licking." The words came out croaky.

She returned the medicine to its box and washed her hands. Kat checked the hallway to make sure no one was calling for her. Silent for the minute. She locked her bedroom door and went to the chimney against the far wall. Unplugging the hole where a stove pipe used to connect, her fingers went to the hidey-hole up and to the right. Kat grabbed the velvet bag, withdrawing it without so much as a smudge of soot on her arm. She rolled the bag into a pool towel and threw it into her duffle bag along with a swimsuit and tight-fitting white leggings.

Glancing at her watch, she yelped. "Crap!" After fourteen years living with nuns and four years running the orphanage, the worst swear words that came out of her mouth were mild. She made a mental note to color up her swearing for the meeting today.

Kat raced past Lisa who was using the kiddie step up stool to reach the mugs on the top shelf. "Call Dr. John. I think it's strep. I gave him grape pain reliever."

"The yuck kind?" Lisa asked.

"No, the plain pain reliever. After breakfast send Edith for some more. Have everyone wash their hands."

Lisa nodded, and Kat could see her making a mental list while she brushed another girl's hair.

"And save Jimmy some pancakes in case he feels like eating." Kat grabbed her keys from the hook by the front door.

"Pancakes!" all the kids in the room called out since it was after nine.

"Okay, everyone," Lisa said in her announcement voice. "We are all going to wash our hands. Now. And then we are wiping down everything with Clorox wipes."

Kat shut the front door, turned the key, and looked up at the gray storm clouds. *At least that's working in my favor.* She jumped into her old blue hatchback. The rain frizzed her hair, but it also strengthened her magic. Water was her element, and today she would need some extra umph. She clutched the blue moonstone, the one her mother had sent with her, that she wore on a chain around her neck for luck.

As the car raced toward the M25, Kat listed her to-do's out loud. "Nine-thirty sell jade pendant to Mr. Pinkas, swing by two post office boxes and my gym locker to hide money, teach swim lessons at twelve-thirty, and try to scope out the artifact exhibit. Then pick up antibiotics that Dr. John will probably call in for Jimmy." She groaned. The kids also had a football game that night.

At least it was Saturday so she didn't have to talk to the bank. Even when she got the money, she couldn't go plop it down on Roger Hamilton's desk. She had to deposit it into several different banks, a little at a time to make sure it didn't look like she was acquiring large sums of cash illegally, which of course she was. Life would be easier if she had a Swiss bank account. *I'll look into that on my day off.* She laughed out loud. When did she have a day off?

Kat's hand signed the cross at the thought of the cash. She'd never stolen anything before, not even offered streaming login passwords at uni. But now she was on her way to sell a third piece of stolen jewelry.

"The rich, selfish sons of biscuits don't need all of it anyway," she whispered, and swallowed the guilt with the acid from her stomach.

Kat's first heist was a pair of diamond earrings. It had taken her several months to figure out how to sell them. The second piece she'd lifted was a moon rock for some private collector. For this last heist, she'd snuck into an exclusive gem collection in Edinburgh. For the ancient jade pendant, Mr. Pinkas would give her enough money to get the bank off her back and buy school shoes and a new outfit for each of the kids.

Kat's heart pounded. If she could just get used to the illegal aspect of the whole thing. It had all seemed so romantically Robin Hoodish when she'd first thought it through.

Kat's stomach clenched as she rolled past the dead-end street. Mr. Pinkas's black sedan sat at the end. Her hand automatically squeezed her moonstone pendant. Its magic made it possible for her to understand other languages, and other people could understand her even if they didn't speak the King's English.

Kat drove a few blocks past and parked on a residential street that was clearly declining. Before she stepped out of the car, she took several gulps of water from a warm bottle, ignoring the slight taste of plastic. Kat scrunched down in the seat, checking that no one was near. She let the liquid splash around her tongue and down her throat as she closed her eyes. She pulled the little pockets of magic that lay within the water inside her body. The magic pulsed, danced inside the water molecules. The more she drank, the more water magic enhanced her, helped her to change.

She envisioned a young grandmother she'd seen in her *Aesthetica* magazine, and the magic slid across her skin. Kat appeared as a fifty-year-old Black British woman in the rearview mirror. Magic draped her in a worn pink jumper and khaki skirt with practical shoes. She stepped out of the car and looked at the street lined with row houses.

Children jumped rope on the cracked sidewalk, their voices calling commands and rhymes amidst laughter. The ancient sycamore tree shaded them with its towering canopy. *Nine-forty in the morning and already too hot.* Kat fanned herself with what would look to the outside world like a church bulletin. Several gold and blue butterflies flittered down to her, but Kat shooed them away. "Not now, my little friends."

Girls lounged on a front stoop trying to look five years older than they were. Several boys, really young men, swaggered by with their name brand T-shirts belying their family income. No one gave her a second glance as she ambled toward a single house. No one saw her step past the house down an alley where she changed into Rocko.

Rocko, thick-necked and broad-shouldered, wore a mustache and tattoos circling his arms and down the side of his mobster face, complete with a poorly healed broken nose. He wore a Millwall Football Club T-shirt and jeans. His trainers were made for running, but his scarred fists were made for fighting.

Rocko had to be tough enough that no one would challenge him. Because Rocko only had the strength of a weak, though plucky, young woman. One who was desperate to help her children.

It took Kat a couple of minutes to tame Rocko's heart enough to perfect his swagger, sneer, and accent. Kat's moonstone looked like a skull etched in bronze on Rocko. Four or five butterflies hovered just overhead. Her friends definitely didn't fit in with Rocko's air of danger. "Visit later," she whispered, and they drifted up on a current of hot air.

Butterflies followed her everywhere, and not just the yellow and blue ones. Perhaps it had something to do with her magic. When she'd arrived at Saint Mary's Abbey at the age of four, she'd been wearing old-fashioned clothes, ancient in fact, as she'd discovered from her studies. And her hand had been wrapped with a butterfly embroidered sash. It and the stone were all Kat had of her birth mother. Even her memories were hazy, if she could count them as memories at all. Impressions of warm hugs and the smell of baking bread were all she had left of her home before Saint Mary's Abbey. That and the feel that part of her was missing, a sister.

Kat tucked her water pistol in her pants and kept the jade pendant in its bag stuffed into a slim pocket of her leggings. The water gun looked like a Browning Hi-Power Mark III pistol, and it was loaded. With water. Not much help, although she could always use the water to increase her magic. With enough magic coursing through her, if someone frisked Rocko, she'd feel like Rocko to them with thick muscles, corded abs, and an adequate knob.

Kat narrowed her eyes until they went slightly out of focus. Her eyes adjusted so that when she looked down at her chest, her D-cups disappeared behind a barrel chest and T-shirt. "There you are, Rocko," she whispered, feeling more confident that she'd seen him. She spit on the ground. "Let's go get twenty grand," she grumbled in her deepest, snarliest voice. It still sounded too high to her. It's a good thing Rocko didn't talk much.

CHAPTER TWO
DRAGONFLY AMULET

"Damn ye old crone," Toren swore as he walked through the labyrinth of war artifacts on display in the rented gallery at Somerset House. While trying to locate information on the family he'd left when the witch had taken him from his century five years ago, he'd come across the hidden cache of weapons his father had told him about, weapons to defend his clan. Instead of fulfilling his responsibility, Toren had been sucked away, leaving his people at the mercy of their enemies, leaving his sister and brother to die without progeny. His clan's castle on Craignish Peninsula was merely a ruin in the twenty-first century, which shredded Toren's heart every time he thought of it.

He'd used some of the gold coins he'd been holding at the time of his abduction to renew his identity by obtaining a passport, false birth certificate, and driver's license. He'd remained in the area of his clan on the western shores for over a year, searching for anything to lead him back to the witch who'd ruined his life and destroyed his clan. His focus had been intense, and he'd tapped into some of the magic that ran through his maternal line.

Which, he believed, is what led him to the dragonfly amulet, set in a necklace, that he'd found near his birthplace. He'd meditated in a nearby circle of standing stones that his mother had said resonated with magic. Sitting on a granite slab in its middle, his senses had led him to the artifact as if in answer to his prayers.

This necklace would bring the witch, he was certain. She'd been wearing it when she'd worked her black magic on him. If the old witch had used magic to recreate the necklace on her spirit body, then she'd be more than interested in the real thing.

After a second year of collecting artifacts, anything that reminded him of home, he'd started to move within the collector circuit, trading, selling, and buying relics from all periods. Now that he had the dragonfly amulet, he had started showing his finds, like a fisherman throwing a line and hook out into the sea.

A Celtic cross from tenth-century Ireland sat on display with crosses from fifteenth-century Scotland. Tapestries had been hoisted onto the walls while a suit of authentic armor stood guard just inside the doorway. Safe within display cases, Viking brooches unearthed from Denmark lay against recreated clothing the Vikings would have worn. Daggers and swords lined the walls, each piece bathed in soft museum light, waiting for the doors of the exhibit to open.

"Come find this, ye witch." He stooped to inspect the rubies and onyx gems in his prize piece, the ornate dragonfly necklace that sat on a pedestal with a flimsy piece of clear plexiglass surrounding it. *Bait.* Toren stood to his full height in the middle of the light-infused display room of Courtauld Gallery in the north wing of Somerset House. "I am waiting for ye, bana-bhuidseach," he said, the words snaking out from between his clenched teeth. "Come find me!" he yelled abruptly to release some of the swelling frustration within him. His voice echoed in the open, museum-like room.

Toren breathed deeply, focusing, letting the fury subside until he once again looked halfway civilized. He glanced in the full-length mirror that had once belonged to a Welsh princess. His black Armani trousers and casual button-up shirt fit his shape well. He even admitted that they were comfortable. But he would give his own sword to again wear the clothes of his homeland, in his proper century.

At the open doorway his young archeologist assistant, Kyle Jansen, cleared his throat. "Mr. MacCallum?" When Toren turned to the man, Jansen hesitated. "I...I'm sorry to interrupt."

Clearly Toren hadn't rid his face of his restrained fury. He tried to smile, but the effect only made the poor archeologist take a step backwards into the tiled entry.

"What is it, Mr. Jansen?" If the man continued to call him Mr. MacCallum, then he'd return the formality.

"The security guards are here." Jansen motioned to two medium-built men in their blue, modern uniforms. "I was about to pull back the barrier rope. There are a few people already waiting in the gallery entry."

Toren motioned toward the corridor beyond the room. "By all means, let them enter." Not that he expected the witch to come in to see the exhibit, but word would get out. If she listened at all to the goings-on of mere mortals, she'd hear of the necklace. He'd put pictures of it on his computer machine that would send it around the world. Through his study of Celtic magic, Toren had learned that power hummed under his skin. It had taken him a year to tap into it, binding the necklace to him. If she took the necklace, he could track her.

Toren strode past the security men into the side room where a broad selection of wines sat along a mahogany bar. He nodded to the barman and poured a draught of thirty-year-old Glenfarclas whisky. He threw it back quickly and breathed, feeling the fire of Scotland burn along his tense nerves. The musical laughter of some woman came from the entryway as the soft score of Celtic music began over the speakers. Perhaps he'd go have a look. A lass was a lass, and he needed a release.

Lady Madeline, as Kat liked to think of the seventy-year-old woman she currently portrayed, sipped from her water bottle as she exited the Temple tube station. Screwing the top back on, she strode toward the huge neoclassic building complex made of white marble and slipped behind the thick trunk of an oak tree just outside the courtyard.

She had stashed her twenty-thousand pounds, given her swim lesson to a group of nine-year-olds, taken Amoxicillin back to the orphanage for Jimmy, and changed into her tight-fitting white leggings and white vest that hugged her body over a sports bra. What a bloody busy day, and it wasn't over.

Kat leaned against the tree and finished the water bottle, setting it on the ground since she didn't see a rubbish bin. "Apparently I'm also a litter lout." She breathed deeply, calling upon her power. It trickled up through all the water molecules embedded in her body. As the magic resonated in concert with her thudding heart, she imagined the humid, hot summer air wrapping around her like a blanket, blending her into the scenery. Within seconds, Kat's body faded to nothing.

Kat looked down at what should be her hand, but it was gone. She smiled. Nothing could beat the comfort of being totally invisible. She didn't have to disguise a voice or change her walk. She breathed deeply and rolled tight shoulders, enjoying the feel of being totally alone, totally masked from the world.

Kat walked along the cobbled courtyard, mindful of the sound of her footsteps that could still be heard. But the outdoor space was vast, and no one was close. Her tight clothes clung so she'd be less likely to brush against someone. Perhaps she could take something today, not have to come back. During the day the heist might be easier. No alarms and laser lights like the debacle in Edinburgh when she'd taken the jade pendant. Kat's heart beat hard as her adrenaline raced. Edinburgh had been way too close.

Inside, Kat crept along the wall, following the signs toward the Courtauld Gallery. Entering the rooms, she avoided two stout guards. There were about twenty people milling around with wine glasses in their hands as they peered at the properly lit exhibits. Lacquered chests, polished steel blades, and ancient ivory combs graced the amazing collection. Who was this sexy Highlander who collected everything Kat loved?

Ancient tapestries covered the walls in muted colors that Kat could imagine being bright when they were first needled. If Kat hadn't been on a mission, she would have spent time studying each piece. Medieval and Renaissance Britain were her favorite periods. She'd written several papers in school regarding costume and weaponry.

Kat glanced in a warped mirror set in one corner. No Kat. If she could go through life invisible, she would. The freedom was so enticing. She could pull her underwear straight, adjust her bra, pick her teeth, even pick her nose if she wanted to.

A group of society ladies sauntered toward the door. "Magnificent," a redhead whispered with a sly leer at her friend. "I may just come back later to see if I can entice him out of that Armani."

"Evelyn." The perfectly blond woman next to her whispered, her face aghast. "What are you thinking?"

"Who can think around those warrior pheromones he's giving off," she said dramatically, fanning herself with the program.

"God, he smells good," a petite brunette said breathlessly on the other side of the trio. "But that's as close as I'd like to get." Evelyn's brows rose. "He's scary," the brunette defended. "Did you see that scar on his jaw?"

Evelyn laughed. "I like mine scary. I'm sure I could wrap him around my pinky," she taunted, holding up the digit that was manicured into a talon of lustrous coral orange.

Kat stood against the wall beside an exquisite suit of armor. She began to hedge the room, her gaze scanning the displays. Many of the items were behind glass. Kat rubbed her arm absently as she studied the beautifully savage swords. Her hand hovered near a glimmering blade. It seemed to call to her, as she studied the finely wrought edge.

Who once held you? Loved you? Whose life did you save, and how many lives did you take? She stepped backwards and grazed a man standing there. She jumped silently and side-stepped away.

It was Roger bloody Hamilton, the loan officer at the bank, her enemy. She nearly snarled but kept quiet while she shot silent daggers at him. He glanced around and rubbed the spot she'd touched. Dismissing the contact, he swilled some wine and loosened his necktie. Could he feel her hatred? One minute he was threatening to take away her children, the next minute he was looking down her blouse.

Kat rubbed again at her arm and glanced down at the strange warmth. It was her birthmark, the one shaped like a dragonfly. For years she'd tried to envision it as a butterfly since they followed her everywhere, but its wings were different. And right now it tingled. Why?

Kat crossed away from Roger. As she moved, she sensed something, like the hum of harmonic bells vibrating, similar to her magic. Kat felt the power draw and direct her toward the center of the hall where a plexiglass cube was lit on a tall stand.

On a bed of white velvet sat the source. A necklace. Rubies and black onyx were surrounded by diamonds that caught the light as they alternated along the thick gold chain. In the center sat a large onyx surrounded by rubies, with a teardrop pearl hanging below. But the most interesting part of the necklace was the medallion affixed to the top of the center onyx. Etched into the medallion was a dragonfly. Kat watched it closely, and the wings flexed. She blinked and stooped, bringing her gaze almost level. No alarms sounded; only a flimsy barrier of plexiglass stopped her from touching it. The dragonfly's wings shuddered as if coming to life. Kat rubbed her arm where the birthmark tingled.

"There's magic in you," she whispered. As if denying the statement, the image settled back down into the etching. Definitely magic and somehow linked to her. Maybe it could help her figure out who she was, what she was. "Do you know my real last name?" she whispered, but the image remained within the confines of the metal. The abbess at Saint Mary's Abbey had given Kat the last name Lambeth since that was the borough where she'd been dropped on the doorstep.

She pinched her lips tight and frowned at it. *It's calling to me.* She made the sign of the cross and stamped down the guilt that bubbled up in her all the time now. She could still sell it for the children, but first she wanted to study it.

Kat straightened and glanced around. She needed a distraction. Walking back to the swords against the wall, she veered to where battle pikes leaned in a corner like a huge set of pick-up sticks. Roger walked past, and she allowed a small smile. *And you will do.*

Toren stood at the back of the room. He took a drink of glistening fresh water, enjoying the clear unfettered taste. *Hard to find this back home.* He looked at the people. Small clusters moved amongst his pieces, chatting more about each other than the history before them. The socially elite were easy to pick out with their guarded smiles and judgmental whispers. He already had three phone numbers from eager ladies bored with their safe lives. The upper class liked intrigue here in the twenty-first century as much as at court in the sixteenth.

He stilled as his gaze followed a woman in white, keeping to the periphery of the room, as if she were avoiding people. She wore a tight-fitting white suit and spoke to no one. Graceful movements reminded him of a cat walking along a windowsill. Stepping away from the wall, she threaded around attendees to the center pedestal, and Toren set his water cup down. The cat-like woman bent over to stare at the dragonfly necklace, giving him a perfect view of an exquisitely rounded arse. Toren's gaze roamed her curvaceous figure in the strange clothing. Lean muscles accentuated the length of her legs.

At home I'd have to handfast or marry her to see so much. His gaze traveled to the soft flare of her hips. Her golden-brown hair had an auburn cast to it that would probably shine with fire in the sun. It was caught up in a fastener, but if she let it down, it would probably fall past her shoulders. The lass's nose nearly touched the faux-glass box.

Toren spared a glance at his guard near the doorway. The man looked straight past the woman. Toren frowned. His assistant had insisted on paid guards, though Toren was certain he could do a better job.

The woman turned, and he stopped, only then realizing he'd taken two steps in her direction. Her eyes were almond shaped and framed by dark lashes. Nose perfect, cheek bones high. The skin across her left cheek looked as soft as satin. It was the other cheek that caught him off guard. Puckered skin ran from the hairline at her temple, across her right cheek down to the soft point of her chin. It was a bad burn. Was this why she skirted around the others? Did people here mock her? Anger filled Toren's chest.

Inhaling, a deep need to shield her filled him. "My sword is yers," he whispered the pledge. The words had tumbled up from him without conscious thought. Anger trailed them, anger that he would pledge to a stranger so easily. He shook his head as if to break a spell placed upon him, one that tethered him to her.

The woman picked up a pike from the display in the corner.

"What in bloody hell are ye up to?" he said aloud. The guards were useless.

Mouth tight and eyes fastened across the room, the woman wove deliberately around several people. No one questioned or even acknowledged her as she walked like a mythical spear maiden. Even if she weren't dressed in clinging white fabric and carrying a deadly pike, the men in the hall should be drawn to her lushness. Toren shook his head, wondering if he'd ever understand moderns.

She glared at a brown-haired man of medium build in a gray suit who seemed not to notice that one of the bite-size tomatoes he'd bit had squirted on his tie. As he moved around the hall, she pursued him.

Should he intercede? She was armed and clearly furious with the man. Toren crossed arms over his chest and quirked one eyebrow. Perhaps ignoring a lass like that should be a crime. He grinned and waited to see what would unfold. This was the most interesting exhibit he'd had all year.

The woman glided around people and still no one raised their eyes. It was as if she invoked some spell to turn them away.

Toren frowned. Maybe she was akin to the crone who'd sent him here. His gaze flickered to the group filing in when a lady laughed overly loud. Glancing back, he saw the woman in white lower the pike in front of the man's shins.

"Bloody hell," Toren swore as the man tripped over the staff. Red wine flew through the air. The woman hefted the pike up high with both hands and stabbed its blade down into the polished, wooden floor.

"Mac an donais!" he swore and reached for his weapon, but he only grasped air and expensive trews. "Daingead!" He'd stopped wearing a sword when it caused more trouble than it was worth in this land.

The woman released her hold on the pike, and the whole room suddenly seemed to notice it quivering there. Chaos broke out. The screams brought curious onlookers. A sea of people surged toward the impaled floorboards.

"It just appeared there!" a woman screamed.

"Ghosts?" one elderly man yelled, pivoting with wild eyes.

"It's possessed!" another woman shrieked.

The two guards shoved through the mass. "Move out of the way!"

Toren's height allowed him to see above the tangle. The mystery woman grabbed a carved stone fertility goddess from a pedestal and swung at the plexiglass cube over the dragonfly necklace. It toppled easily, and she snatched the necklace, turning to run.

"Nay!" he yelled above everyone. "Stad! Stop!"

The woman turned and their eyes locked. Surprise and horror crossed her face.

"Stop, ye in white!"

She spun and ran straight for the exit. The alarm built into the plexiglass box around the necklace had shrieked to life, adding to the chaos.

Toren grabbed a thirteenth-century short sword. "Caraich! Move!"

People screamed when he jumped forward with the sword. It took him a full minute to press, dodge, and threaten his way through the crowd without injuring anyone. One of the guards met him at the exit door and followed him down the hall.

"Ye didn't even see her take it," he yelled as he rammed the outer door to run out of Somerset House and across the stone courtyard. "The pike was a distraction." Toren growled low in his throat, a primal fury. How could he have been so unprepared for the attack? Bloody hell, he'd just stood there watching!

Toren caught sight of the woman in white as she ran out of the gates and turned left down the Strand. He was as strong as ever from eating healthy foods and training with weights in this century. "Ye're mine," he said as he ran after her. She turned left onto Temple Place, which led to the River Thames. The wide river would hem her in, block her escape, but she didn't stop. Throwing her arms over her head, she dove.

"Daingead!" He dropped the sword and ran toward the snaking body of water. It had been a cesspool of garbage and sewage in the 16th century, bringing disease and possible death to those who swam in it. He'd read about cleanup efforts, but he still couldn't see through the surface to spot which way she'd gone. He swam out, kicking off his shoes, the current sucking them away immediately. He treaded water, watching for her head to bob up. She'd looked fit. She wouldn't dive into the massive river if she couldn't swim. His guards stood on the shore, and Jansen hopped up and down on the terrace on the backside of Somerset House.

Toren ran a hand over his sopping face. "Sod it."

Somehow she'd gotten away with the one thing he could use to bargain for his life back. He'd let his guard down and a mere lass had stolen it.

He scanned out over the flowing water. No ripple gave her away. "I will find ye," he swore and trudged back to shore, thankful that he'd woven a thread of tracking into the necklace.

Kat stripped off the stained white suit as the hot water from the showerhead cascaded down her body. June was hot, but the Thames had felt cold and tasted briny. She sneezed and spit. Breathing through water was one of her gifts. She couldn't drown in her element, but sucking in the salty water had irritated her nose and throat.

The man had followed her into the water. She'd heard his curses, felt his wrath. He'd wanted her, wanted the necklace that she now held in her palm. As the shower washed away bits of debris, she studied the gems that sparkled in the light from the transom window, but it was the medallion with the dragonfly that hummed with power. Kat ran a thumb over the etching, its wings, its slender body.

"Dragonfly." She mouthed the word. "What are you?"

It didn't change, although her birthmark tingled. The necklace looked familiar, like it belonged in some ancient portrait. Kat had studied many portraits, but she didn't remember any with a dragonfly. The museum plaque had said it was found in western Scotland in a circle of stones. She'd always wanted to journey up to western Scotland. In fact, she felt drawn to it. But life had been too busy and money too sparse for her to plan a vacation.

Kat set the necklace on the side of the tub and let the hot water rinse through her hair.

Toren MacCallum had seen her. How? No one else at the exhibit had. Had he seen her before she touched the necklace? Maybe the necklace's magic negated her own. Kat groaned. Had Roger seen? Kat was surprised the police weren't already knocking down the washroom door.

She looked toward the ceiling. "I promise, God, I won't steal anymore unless it's absolutely necessary to keep my kids together and well cared for. I swear." The memory of Toren MacCallum's rage would remind her over and over again why she wouldn't be stealing again anytime soon. His eyes had sparked with cold fury, as if she were sprinting away with something crucial to life.

She closed her eyes, remembering. His broad shoulders, hands fisted, jaw rock hard. He was well over six feet tall and broad enough to worry Rocko. Lisa had been right, though, he looked like some ancient warrior. His Armani trousers couldn't hide the power he could wield.

Kat shivered and looked at the necklace under the thin fall of water. It glistened in her palm, and she wrapped her fingers around it. A warrior like that wouldn't give up until he reclaimed what had been stolen.

CHAPTER THREE
HOCUS POCUS FEE FIE FOX

"Bloody hell, Kat, we have an emergency!" Lisa cried, running into the dining hall decorated with balloons and rainbow-colored streamers, her hand across her full bosom stuffed into a *Six: The Musical* hoodie.

Kat whirled around, heart pounding so hard she couldn't breathe. She nearly turned invisible right there even though Lisa knew nothing about her powers.

Kat swallowed, her stomach clenching. She caught the back of a chair to steady herself. "Lisa, I can explain," she started, certain she'd see police storming in with Roger from the bank on their heels.

"The blasted magician isn't coming!"

"What?"

Lisa threw her hands out. "The birthday party, the magician. The kids will be so disappointed." Lisa threw herself dramatically into an overstuffed chair in the corner. "I'm disappointed too," she mumbled.

It took Kat several long seconds and another glance out into the long hallway to realize she wasn't being filmed for the latest COPS reality show. "The magician from Olive's Party-rama?"

"Has the flu." Lisa pouted. "Probably has the wankered flu."

Each quarter of the year, they celebrated that quarter's birthdays with a huge party for all the kids. If some didn't know their birthdays, like Kat, they celebrated the day they came to Sister Susanna's Home for Children. She moved around the room twisting errant crepe paper streamers and re-sticking balloons while her heart returned to a normal beat.

"It's fine, Lisa. We'll find someone else to entertain."

"Who? At the last minute?"

"Let me call Olive's," Kat said, her mind already conjuring up the image of a magician. "You make sure the cake is ready while I ask for a replacement."

"Good luck," Lisa grumbled and pushed out of the chair.

Kat dashed around the house, finding odds and ends that she could use. A large cardboard box out by the garage, an old shower curtain, a sparkly princess wand, a bucket, and some newspaper. She set things up in the main room on a table. Kat stapled the shower curtain to the top of the box and filled the bucket with water. She dragged in one of the new plastic kiddie pools. The kids trickled in and stayed to watch the set up.

"What are you doing?" Grace, an outspoken eight-year-old, asked.

Kat smiled. "It's a surprise." She winked.

"We're having an indoor pool party," Scott, a rough and tumble five-year-old, hoped out loud. "I'll get the hose."

"No," Kat said, "it's for the magician."

"So they're sending one?" Lisa asked, walking in, her gaze sliding across the props. "But...he doesn't have his own stuff?"

"He's coming right from his house and won't have time to pick up anything." Kat looked at Lisa. "And they were so sorry, they aren't charging us." That perked her friend up. And if this worked well, Kat might have another way to bring in money. Although a hundred and fifty pounds for a party was nothing compared to what she could make from a jewel heist.

Heaven help her.

———◆———

Toren stepped off the curb across from Sister Susanna's Home for Children as the Uber car pulled away.

An orphanage? What the bloody hell?

The binding spell on the necklace indicated the piece was inside. He shook his head, mentally reeling in his aggressive look. If there were nuns and children here, he couldn't bully his way inside, at least not like he'd considered with a den of thieves run by a sultry mistress who had the courage to walk in and steal from right under his nose.

Toren crossed the street and jogged up to the double doors. He knocked, but no one answered. A few windows were propped open trying to catch the breeze. Laughter filtered out.

So how does one lay siege to an orphanage? He tried the door handle, but it was locked. Toren walked around to the side yard, where another door stood ajar.

Inside the laughter grew louder. Pictures of grinning children lined the walls, all framed and arranged in vivid colors. He peered around the open doorway into a room full of young lads and lasses staring at a large cardboard box.

The box shook as if someone were inside. A voice called out from behind a curtain. "And now, my new assistant, Princess Clara, will pull back the curtain after I say my magic words."

A girl in a pink fluffy dress and gold ringlets stood giggling beside the box, her cherub's face pinched in barely suppressed amusement.

"Now, Logan, are you still behind my magic box?" the deepened voice called out. "So that I cannot escape that way?"

An older boy, probably ten summers old, poked his head around the cardboard corner. "Still here. You can't get out this way."

"Then," the voice drawled dramatically while the box shook. "Hocus pocus, fee fie fox, make me disappear from this box!" Suddenly the shaking stilled.

"Open the curtain!" some of the kids yelled.

The little girl pulled back the curtain to gasps and laughter.

"Where'd he go? Logan, did he get out the back?" one child yelled, standing up.

Logan ran around front to look. "No, man, he's gone!"

The kids clapped and ran around the room hunting for the magician while an attractive, very curvaceous, dark-skinned woman tried to calm them down. Toren slid back so they wouldn't immediately see him, but he could keep his eyes on the open box and the woman standing in an orange bathing costume silently inside. His lips parted, and he held his breath as he took in the strange scene. Children laughed and ran around while the woman stood waiting and quiet where everyone should be able to see her.

"Mr. Magician!"

"Where is he?"

"Is there a trap door under the box?"

Just like at his exhibit, no one seemed to see her. While everyone was distracted with their hunt, the woman in the box tugged the half open curtain closed, and the box began to shake again.

"Look!" a child yelled. "The box!"

The little princess shrieked and rushed behind the woman who'd helped calm things down.

"Logan, pull back the curtain," another boy yelled.

Logan yanked back the curtain, and the woman jumped out, her arms raised high.

Everyone gasped and clapped.

In a deepened voice, she said. "Ta Da! And now for my last trick."

The kids moaned.

"Ahh," she continued. "But I hear there is birthday cake after my act."

The kids cheered and plopped back down to watch.

Toren stood stone still, watching, half confused and half wondering what she'd do next to make these children so happy.

The woman stepped into a plastic tub with fish painted on it. He'd seen the strange container on the TV flat-screen before, especially when hawkers tried to sell it in the summer months.

"Now, Miss Lisa," the woman said in a deepened voice. "You will dump that bucket of water on my head." The room erupted in laughter.

The young woman known as Miss Lisa stepped up on a chair. One of the older lads lifted a seemingly heavy bucket from its spot. "It's half full of water," the lad said, and handed it off to her. The children in the room shifted and squirmed with obvious excitement.

"When I say three, Miss Lisa, dump away." The woman's expressive eyes turned back to the children, and she moved her eyebrows up and down making them giggle. "Watch closely, children. Water doesn't stick to me."

Curious whispers filled the room as large eyes stared at the woman in the fish tub.

Toren couldn't take his gaze off her. Once again he was seeing more of her beautifully sleek, full-bosomed body. But he was more drawn to the spirit in her face that transformed her into the most beautiful lass he'd ever seen.

"One, two, three…"

Miss Lisa poured the bucket on top of the woman's head. The water drenched her fully and filled the tub at her feet. The kids gasped, clapping wildly.

"How'd you do that?" was accompanied by, "I don't believe it! He's all dry."

To Toren, the woman was completely soaked and looked chilled. Her nipples stuck out, causing his groin to tighten. He readjusted his offending member and tried to focus more on the absolute bizarreness of the situation instead.

She took a bow, stepped out of the tub, flourished a black cape which she tied under her chin, and waved goodbyes as she walked out the back of the room amidst cheers. Some of the kids pointed at the wet footprints she left behind. "Look! Look!"

Toren pushed away from the corner and headed down the corridor. He wouldn't let her escape again. He flattened himself against the wall, waiting.

The woman crossed to the kitchen in front of a full mirror facing him. The reflection in the mirror was someone very different, a man with a mustache and black hair without a drop of water on him.

A prickle ran down the muscles of Toren's straight back. Sorcery? He knew enough about the black arts to respect them, but the woman didn't look anything like the witch who'd stranded him here. This woman was young and beautiful, but she definitely possessed some sort of magic. And she currently possessed his necklace, which he must reclaim.

Toren followed when he heard the back door click shut. Quickly, he slid out the screened door after her. The wet footprints were easy to follow behind a squat little building at the rear of the orphanage. He rounded the corner and stopped.

The wet woman gasped when she saw him, her gaze darting as if seeking escape. The cement block building on one side, the fence behind, and prickly bushes on the other side made a getaway improbable.

Fear ripped across her face, making her eyes wide.

He relaxed his stance. If she were afraid, she wouldn't talk to him. That was why he felt compelled to lessen her anxiety. Not because he felt any softness toward her after watching her make the children so happy.

"How do ye do that?" he asked casually.

The woman's eyes grew round. "Do what?" she asked in the deep male voice.

Should he reveal that he knew her secret, that he could see through the charade? Caution was usually the best approach with a cornered animal. Plus, knowing an enemy's secret when they didn't know you knew their secret was a powerful weapon.

He jerked his thumb back towards the orphanage. "Inside just now. How did ye do the water trick?"

Toren found it amazing that her eyes could grow even larger, her wet lashes sticking together in a fan over the blue orbs.

"You were inside?" she asked in her male voice. "You aren't allowed inside the children's home without permission and without logging in with one of the house coordinators."

"I obtained permission."

She frowned. "You lie." She shook her head. "You didn't alert anyone that you were inside."

"I called ahead. No one answered when I knocked, and the back door was unlocked..."

"I know you are lying!"

He tipped his head to the side. "How would a magic man know who calls the home?"

"I..." Her perfectly formed lips gaped open and then closed. She glared. "I know the women who run the house."

"Good," he said. "I have a need to find a lass who works here."

The woman's breath caught. "Why?"

Toren looked into her stormy blue eyes. "She has something of mine." He paused, watching the striking woman sweep a wet length of hair over the scar on her right cheek. 'Twas from a burn long ago from the looks of it.

"She's left town."

"So ye know which woman I'm looking for?"

The kitchen door squeaked open behind him, but Toren didn't take his eyes off his prey.

"Kat! Kat! Where are you," the lady named Lisa yelled and walked toward him. "Oh... Can I help you?" she said to his back.

Reluctantly, Toren turned to her.

The pretty woman gasped softly and blinked. "You...you're the art collector."

"Artifacts," he corrected and made his jaw loosen enough to smile.

She smiled back, bringing out the dimples in her cheeks. Then she glanced beyond him.

"Mr. Reynolds, do you need anything else? I was told your services were free today because you were filling in for someone, but I'd like to give you a tip. You truly made the day special for the kids."

"No need for a tip, Miss Gibson. I'll be on my way." She stepped widely around them.

"Miss Gibson," Toren said quickly. "I have an invitation for your associate."

"For Kat?"

The woman trying to hurry away without looking like she was hurrying away stopped at the edge of the orphanage and picked up a bag. She bent to unzip it and rummage around inside, but Toren would wager she had merely stopped to hear.

"There was a woman yesterday at my exhibit. Golden auburn hair, amazing blue eyes, taller than ye."

Lisa laughed. "That's Kat. She's beautiful and also highly intelligent, determined, and an all-around fabulous person."

"And she has a very loyal friend." He tipped his head to her.

Lisa smiled, hand flapping back toward the house. "She's wonderful with the kids. They'd all be split up without her, sent to different foster homes."

"She is named after the feline?"

Lisa sniffed a laugh. "True she can be quiet as one, but she spells it K-A-T, short for Katell."

"Kat," he repeated her name slowly, feeling it on his tongue. "Aye, a good name for a lass who moves like a cat: graceful, silent, and a master at escape."

"So...you two know each other?" Lisa asked, her eyes narrowing.

"She came to my exhibit yesterday. And there was...an incident."

Lisa bit her bottom lip as if to stop another laugh. "She snuck off to that exhibit after all."

"She seems to have an interest in artifacts," he said, still keeping track of Kat, who hovered in his periphery.

"She graduated from uni with a degree in medieval and renaissance history."

He tipped his head slightly. "And she works in an orphanage?"

Lisa wrapped her arms around herself. "It wasn't our first choice, but when we came home to see the place," she said, waving a hand behind her toward the home, "it was about to be shut down. We couldn't let that happen to the children, so we bought it."

"Ye and Kat?"

"Yes." She nodded with a sad smile. "We were raised here."

"She's an orphan?"

"We both are. So it made sense that we took over, but it hasn't been easy."

It made sense only if one was willing to give up their lives to honor the past.

Lisa's gaze slid up and down Toren, her easy smile thinning as if suspicion had seeped through the cracks of her teeth. "You said you had an invitation for Kat."

Had he scowled? That usually chilled smiles, so he forced one. Lisa actually took a step back as if he'd snarled instead. He grabbed the back of his neck. "Apologies. I am quite busy organizing my charity dinner party tomorrow evening and would like Kat to attend."

The eyebrow with the little ring pierced through it rose. "What a wonderful idea. Which charity?"

He'd advertised that the money would all go to the local children's hospital. But then Kat had allowed water to be dumped over her head just to make her children laugh.

Toren cleared his throat, making sure his voice carried to the masquerading woman. "That's why I want her to come, and ye, too," he said catching her small hand in his. "Sister Susanna's Home for Children sounds like a worthy cause. I would like to split the money raised, which I'd intended for the children's hospital, with your home." Though he held Lisa's hand, his eyes moved back to his prey.

Kat stopped puttering and turned towards him. The bag fell from her hand to land amongst the pebbles. She stared, perfect lips parted.

"The orphanage is a very worthy cause," Lisa said breathlessly, stretching up and down on the balls of her feet. "Wait until I tell Kat. She'll be so relieved."

Toren glanced down at the woman's happy brown eyes. "She worries about money?"

"We both do. The grants have run out. The church has cut their charitable donations, and the government doesn't seem to understand why we won't just close this place and split up the children, sending them to bigger institutions or into the foster system. No matter how many ways Kat explains that this is their home, their family." Lisa shook her head. "Kat will be very excited to hear about your generosity. Thank you." She smiled up at him, once more trusting.

"'Tis dinner and cocktails at eight o'clock on the morrow in the Somerset House on the Thames. Ye'll tell her?"

"Certainly."

He bowed slightly, which caused the woman to beam like he'd gotten down on a knee and kissed her hand.

Kat grabbed the sack and stalked toward the buildings that must house the automobiles.

"Mr. Reynolds," Toren called out.

She turned and cleared her throat. "Yes?"

Toren pointed overhead where a swarm of blue and yellow butterflies gathered. "They seem fond of ye."

She stared for a moment but then flourished her cape and forced a smile. "They're attracted to magic. Good day." She walked stiffly away. The butterflies hovered around like another cape, some landing on her wet hair.

Toren glanced up to the windows of the orphanage where he sensed the necklace lay hidden. "They aren't the only creatures attracted to magic." He knew now that the third window to the right on the second floor belonged to Kat.

Fury, dark and palatable, stretched and quivered within the swirling mass of thirteen intertwined souls. Bound for thousands of years, the demons fought against each other and against their impenetrable walls. Lust, greed, envy, hatred—foul emotions simmered together, moved together, searched time and space together. They had ripped the magic from the Warlock, Druce, but still needed his soul mate's half to break their bonds, releasing them. So they moved slowly from year to year across the globe searching for Druce's daughters.

Their mother, a crafty Wiccan, had hidden the girls throughout time just before they had crushed her useless human body. Regret that he didn't move quicker against Gilla nibbled at Semiazaz, but he hid the weakness. At least Druce's magic allowed him to thread through time, searching for the dragonfly power.

A tickle trailed down through Semiazaz's chest to where his gut used to live when he had a corporeal body. He paused to concentrate on it for a long moment before calling out in a deep voice. "Wait!" The word radiated throughout the oily pool, causing the chaos to organize along the perimeter into individual souls. He coalesced into his familiar image of a wise, tall man with a long white beard. "Feel that?" He rubbed a gnarled hand over his imagined chest.

The souls shuddered and lashed out.

"Kill!"

"Crush!"

"Vengeance!"

"Die!"

"Quiet!" Semiazaz's voice crashed through the chaos. The jagged fragments of hatred and bloodlust quelled into a low murmur.

"A tremor from one of Gilla's daughters. Her magic, it sings to me." His shadowy essence smiled.

"How is it we hear her now?" Bast, a cat-like Egyptian demon hissed from where she materialized near the edge of their prison. Her sinewy body was wrapped tightly in white linen with a blue collar around her neck. An ornate, golden headpiece perched upon her head, giving her the appearance of an Egyptian god.

"Something joins with her own magic, something powerful," Semiazaz said as he studied the direction from which it came. He inhaled. "There, in London of the twenty-first century," he murmured. Then louder to the group of swirling violence and fury, "we move now, together, concentrate on the vibration!"

The dark storm lengthened, thinning into a dull gray thread, and shot up and through the layers of temporal dimensions toward the magic that called to them.

CHAPTER FOUR
KNICKERS

"But you *have* to go," Lisa pleaded. "I don't want to go alone. And anyway, he seemed more interested in you than me. Why didn't you tell me that you went over to the Courtauld Gallery yesterday?"

Kat sneezed and blew her nose with gusto. "I dropped by after my swim lesson." She cast a pallor over her face with her magic to make her sick excuse more believable. "We talked briefly, hardly at all. I'm sure he's not interested in me." Kat wiped a red, drippy nose. "And I'm too sick to go. You go."

Lisa sat on Kat's soft double bed with the blue quilt she and Sister Susanna had sewn together. "Aren't you excited that he's giving half the money from the dinner to us, to the orphanage? I did a search, and each plate costs three hundred pounds, Kat, and there are three hundred seats so that means ninety thousand pounds which means forty-five thousand pounds to us!"

Kat rolled her eyes. "I'll believe it when I see it."

Lisa stared at her with an open mouth. "Why would he say he was going to give it to us, if he wasn't going to?"

"Some people are cruel."

Lisa's face pinched like she'd smelled something rancid. "What people? Terrorists, people who abuse puppies, those types, but Toren MacCallum doesn't kick puppies."

Kat rubbed her ear lobe. "You gathered that from talking to him for what, two minutes?"

"Five minutes," Lisa said, "and we were alone in an alley, and he didn't even look at my beautiful baps." She spread her fingers across her breasts as if showcasing them.

Kat waved her hand. "Whatever. You go. Represent us well, and we'll see if Laird MacCallum comes through with his money."

"You know, he could be a real laird. I did a search. Most of the MacCallums have died out. Maybe he's a long-lost descendent of the sixteenth-century clan."

When Kat didn't respond, Lisa huffed. "Eat the chicken noodle soup and take meds. I'll let you know how it goes." She hurried out the door, tugging on her little black dress.

Kat watched from her window until she saw Lisa leave, walking toward the tube station around the block. Kat felt guilty for making her go alone, but she needed to get in and out without having to worry about her friend being implemented if she were caught.

Lisa had arranged for two trusted women to get the kids under control and into their beds so Kat didn't have to worry over them. She pulled on black leggings made of warm, woven material and a tight-fitting black sweater. Although it was June, a cold front had come through, and the sweater-like leggings would keep her warm, plus they had pockets. She whipped her hair back into a high ponytail. Sliding out a drawer, she pulled out the dragonfly necklace and laid it on a bandana.

Drawing close to it, she listened for the slight hum it gave off. Radiation? Some cosmic energy trapped inside? Magic? Whatever it was, it was too much trouble. "Somehow, he found me because of you," she whispered. Her finger hovered over the dragonfly etching and lowered onto the cool stone. A buzzing vibrated through her fingertip, and she yanked it back. She stared at the image, but it didn't change. "And I have a feeling he won't give up until you're returned." She hoped once he had the artifact back he wouldn't try to prosecute or drag the orphanage into this mess. Kat wrapped up the necklace. "You're going home. Tonight."

She didn't dare let the necklace touch her bare skin. Somehow Toren had seen her when she'd stolen the piece. But yesterday he'd only seen Mr. Reynolds the magician. The magic within the necklace must have made her visible to him when she'd touched it at the Courtauld Gallery. In the chaos, no one else had noted her fleeing. She wouldn't make the same mistake twice. She'd return it to the gallery while Toren was busy with guests. The party was a perfect diversion.

If only she could keep thoughts on the plan and not on the way the muscles of his chest filled out the black T-shirt he'd worn yesterday or the way his jeans molded to his gorgeous ass. Her cheeks warmed, and she turned invisible. Silently, Kat hurried down the steps and out the kitchen door to the garage where she let her body materialize again before walking onward. Fifteen minutes later she sat on a plastic seat on the tube, but she couldn't stop thinking about him.

Hell's bells. When he'd leaned against the garage, his powerful arms had bulged. A Celtic tattoo encircled one chiseled bicep. His muscled chest tapered into narrow hips and thighs. She sighed, feeling her stomach tighten and a rush of heat pool down between her legs. *I really need to shag.*

Unfortunately she never had. Being twenty-six and still a virgin was too weird to explain even to Lisa. She couldn't let anyone near enough to her that they could feel the ridged scars on her face. Call her old-fashioned, but to trust someone enough to sleep with them meant trusting them to see her for who she was. A girl with a monster's face who was odd beyond the realm of reality.

Uni had introduced her to many pretty guys who were all smooth lines and just up for a chase. There were even a couple of bum holes who hadn't taken "no" very well, and she'd had to vanish, hoping they were drunk enough to think she'd run out of the room. Then she'd made it her mission to track them while cloaked in magic to catch them in the act. Two were still incarcerated.

But twenty-six was old enough and finding a man to trust was probably impossible. Perhaps she would hide her scars through the whole interlude or tie the man's hands so he couldn't stroke her cheek. It could be her kink. Yes, it was time to become a woman after Eve, as Sister Susanna had called it.

Toren MacCallum seems warrior enough to break through my shields. But she'd stolen his treasure, and he'd probably have her jailed if he caught her.

With a big huff, Kat cleared her head. She would consider her options for sin later. Currently she had a reverse heist to pull off. She flashed a sign of the cross and sent up a guilty prayer for help.

Kat rode the tube, getting off at the Temple station a quarter mile from Somerset House. She drank a twelve-ounce bottle of water to fuel her magic and checked to make sure the wrapped necklace was still secure in the slim, stretchy pocket of her leggings. Rain pattered on the pavement when she emerged, but she continued toward the huge riverside building that glowed like a sparkling chandelier in the darkness.

As Kat crept closer, she heard laughter and string instruments playing with a piano. Thunder rumbled overhead, and she glanced up at the black sky. No moonlight showed through the cloud cover. Kat held herself invisible anyway.

Lightning arced downward several miles away as expensive cars rolled up, stopping for valets to take them off for parking as the guests hurried inside.

Kat climbed a set of service steps onto the terrace overlooking the Thames, droplets of rain stinging her face. As lightning continued to discharge, she crept up to a window that had been left partially open and peered inside.

Toren stood along one wall, eyes searching the crowd. Was he looking for her? His gaze shifted to the window. Kat gasped and threw her shoulder blades against the building. Could he feel that she was near? Or perhaps the necklace, she thought, and looked down at the bulge in her pocket.

She froze as he neared the open window. Could he see through her magic when she had the dragonfly close? "Looks like a storm is blowing in." His rolling burr raced down her spine as he lowered the window.

Breathe, he can't see me.

With another rumble of thunder, the clouds opened, dumping their deluge. She ran through the downpour toward a lit gazebo, rounding the white post under the cover. Hair soaked, she breathed hard and plucked at her sweater that seemed to hold water like a sponge.

Kat's adrenaline hummed so that she barely registered the chilly rain against her skin. She wiped her hand down her face and watched the hired help dash out the doors toward her on the gazebo. Kat flattened against one side of the railings while they retrieved the hors d'oeuvres that were set up on tables there under tiny white fairy lights. Water from the roof slid down her back, making her gasp, but no one seemed to hear her in the commotion.

Kat must get inside and leave the necklace somewhere safe where Toren would find it. If someone else stole it after she returned it, he'd never believe her. "Back in the gallery," she whispered to the tempest as she hurried towards the door that was closing behind the last server.

Breathing through her mouth to be as silent as possible, Kat stood in a short corridor that must lead to the kitchen. *Drip.*

She looked down. "Cripe!" she whispered at the small puddle that was forming under her. She rubbed her foot through it, but more water dripped from her sweater and ponytail, adding to the wet mess. A narrow Oriental rug ran down the length of the hallway, and she stepped onto it. Outside, lightning lit the sky across the Thames. She shivered and rubbed her arms, but that just made more water drip from her sweater like a sponge being squeezed.

Kat could hide herself, but she couldn't hide the water falling off the sweater and the leggings. *Dang it all.* Could she weave through rooms of people without leaving a trail or dripping on guests?

She squeezed her ponytail over the rug. The sweater was soaked. Her thick leggings held the rain against her cold legs. Why had she worn the sweater-like leggings? There had been no call for rain that evening and she'd felt cold. Now with the wetness against her skin, she was even colder. She could make herself look like she had warm, dry clothes on, but she certainly wouldn't feel them.

The hallway was empty, but she still moved toward a recessed corner. She might be invisible, but the clothes wouldn't be once they weren't touching her body. Kat yanked the wet sweater over her head and balled it up to stick in a large flower arrangement on a long skinny hallway table. She rolled the clingy leggings down her thighs and hid them behind the urn on the table. She took off her shoes, leaving her in hot pink socks that were thankfully dry so they wouldn't leave a trail.

She looked down at her matching pink cotton underwear. *Not even the right day of the week.* She knew the word "Wednesday" scrolled across the back of her knickers, a gag gift from Lisa on her last made-up birthday. Her wet black sports bra clung to her breasts, her nipples erect with the chill, although the air inside Somerset House was warmer than the cold rain. Her moonstone hung low, nearly slipping into her cleavage.

Kat drew the knotted bandana from the leggings' pocket and tied it to her bra strap. Looking down the hall, she ran through the building schematic in her mind. Thank God for tourists who film every step of their tour through Somerset House and the gallery in the north wing.

I'll run in, put the necklace in the upstairs gallery with his artifacts, and run out. That's it. Quick, in and out. She remained close to the wall as she tiptoed down to the catering kitchen where the sound of clinking cookware and glasses mingled with calm orders.

"Do not overcook the asparagus. Bright green, not mush. Drop them in ice water now."

"A hoity guest says the cheese is dry."

Someone snorted. "Not as dry as her twat."

Kat flattened against the wall as someone strode through the door, then scooted inside. It was a gauntlet of silver pot handles, bustling caterers, and balanced trays of glassware. The aromas were fabulous, and Kat's stomach growled. She pressed a hand against it and worked her way through the least traveled areas of the room, doing her best imitation of Catwoman.

When the door to the hall opened, she didn't have time to reconsider. She scooted past the glass-laden server and slid out the door. Her breath caught at the number of beautifully clad people chatting in the hall before the rooms set up for dinner, and she flattened against the wall. *They can't see me. The necklace isn't touching me.*

Laughter, some sort of mellow Celtic music, and tinkling glasses bled out of the rooms, but here in the hallway people looked at paintings and sculptures on pedestals that normally filled Somerset House. But she needed to get to the north wing, to Courtauld Gallery where Toren's artifacts were kept.

Kat took several long, deep breaths in an attempt to get the tingly, numb feeling to leave her chin and hands. Some jewel thief she was turning out to be. She couldn't even return an artifact without hyperventilating.

Kat's gaze ran down the length of rug on the polished floorboards. There was a back staircase that way, and she began to walk-run toward it. But she came up short when Toren MacCallum stepped out of the connected rooms with Lisa chatting to him.

He wore another expensive suit that fit perfectly over his broad shoulders, definitely custom-made. *Magnificent.*

Roger followed them out, calling his name while Lisa looked like she might spit at the little man. Roger nodded to Lisa, and Toren's gaze turned directly on Kat. Frozen in fear, she held her breath for several seconds until his gaze slid past her and on to others in the hallway. *He can't see me.*

A group of servers came forward, arms laden, as someone on the microphone inside called people to sit for the first course. Kat hurried toward the staff, making sure to remain as flat as possible against the wall when they passed. The back staircase was in the darkened corner. She reached it, turning the knob only to find it locked. "Bugger," she whispered, turning to search the emptying hall.

The only other quick way to the north wing above was the curving staircase inside the rooms. Kat turned and took a full inhale, the cool wood of the door against her back, reminding her that she was standing in nothing but her knickers. *Holy Mother Mary!*

She'd come on the night of the dinner because there would be people opening doors and noise to hide her movements. She didn't want to get caught by Toren MacCallum in a gallery that would be mostly silent on an average day. But having to prance around hundreds of people while wearing practically nothing, despite them not seeing her, made the whole thing worse. *I can do this.* She took a moment to stand tall in the Wonder Woman pose that Lisa said gave a person confidence. Unfortunately, the concentration made her suddenly appear as Wonder Woman.

Kat squeaked, cloaking herself in invisibility again, thankful no one had been looking down the dark hallway. She hurried back to the open doors of the interconnected rooms, stepping inside. She dodged people hunting for their place cards at tables. Once she reached the curving staircase, she ran up them past a podium set a third of the way up. Focusing, she tried to ignore the people behind her as her bum proclaimed the day to be Wednesday even though it was Monday. Her moonstone thumped against her chest as she ran, and she grabbed it. *Mother help me.* It was a prayer to the Virgin Mary and her true birth mother who had gifted the stone to her.

Kat reached the top landing and glanced back over one shoulder. Her hand clutched at the banister to keep her from falling back down the stairs, right into Toren MacCallum who climbed the stairs below her.

Shooting down the hallway, her gaze snapped side to side. Which way was the gallery? She nearly squeaked when she saw Toren reach the top of the stairs. If he hadn't glanced at his watch and adjusted his tie, Kat would swear the man was following her.

A placard with a man and woman on it indicated a loo, and the door was open. Kat slipped into it, standing in the dark corner against the ornate wallpaper. He was too close for her to shut the door without him noticing. *Go away*, Kat screamed in her head.

But the giant Scotsman walked right into the bathroom. He shut the door behind him and flicked on the light.

No escape. Kat shrank into the corner. Should she turn around to give him some privacy? Kat didn't dare move for fear he'd hear her rub against the wall.

Toren's hand deftly unbuttoned his pants. Kat closed her eyes as he pulled himself out and proceeded to piss. He lowered the lid and flushed, went to the sink and slowly washed his hands.

But once again the ornery man didn't obey her silent pleading. He stood before the mirror adjusting his perfect tie. "She's not coming." He huffed a little sigh and spoke to his reflection. "I wager she's just a thief. I'll have to expose her tonight." He shook his head. "I only hope Lisa and the orphans will survive this," he murmured and opened the door.

Shock paralyzed Kat where she stood in the corner of the bathroom, listening to Toren's shoes tap down the hall. She swallowed hard past the wretched acid of pre-vomit in her throat. "Sweet Jesus." He was going to tell them she was a thief. Kat felt the racing panic of her heart. They'd take away her children and the house. Lisa would never forgive her. The littles either.

Kat's feet flew. She ran back down the hallway to the stairs where Toren stopped before the podium.

"May I have yer attention, my good ladies and gentlemen," he said raising his hands. "I have an announcement to make this evening."

I have to do something. She yanked on the knot holding the wrapped necklace to her bra strap. If she could just give it back to him.

"Tonight ye all came to this dinner to benefit children. Half of the donations collected tonight and this week through the gallery will go to Great Ormand Street Hospital for Children as advertised, and the other half will fund Sister Susanna's Home for Children, an orphanage in desperate need of basic provisions for the residents." The people below clapped politely. "The children and I thank ye." More applause. "But I have an announcement to make this evening, and I hope that it won't harm the children in any way."

The git was going to hurt the children by exposing her.

"There was an incident on Saturday," he started.

"Sure was," Roger called out from below and muted laughter filtered upward.

Kat looked to her left where an oval mirror stood framed above a bowl full of roses. With a quick change of the magic flowing around her, she reappeared in a gold sparkly cocktail dress. She imagined her wet, curling mass of hair into a tight French twist and her makeup perfect.

Kat hurried down the stairs to stand next to Toren and placed her hand on his arm. When he looked down at her there was no surprise in his eyes, only a glint of humor.

She pushed the bandana into his hand. "Please," she whispered near his ear. "Here is the necklace. Let me explain." She glanced out at the multitude. "Privately."

"And here is the lass herself, Kat," he said, and the people clapped again, waiting expectantly for his announcement. He lowered his voice. "I don't know yer last name."

"I...uh, I don't really have one." Why the hell was she telling him anything? *I must be in shock.*

He stood tall beside her, speaking out to the crowd. "Kat has a degree in medieval and renaissance history, specializing in artifacts like the one that was misplaced on Saturday."

"Please," Kat breathed quietly. "It's in there, don't—"

"Kat has agreed to help me in my research," he continued.

"I, uh…" Kat looked down on the people who were nibbling the dinner rolls and sampling their salads. Lisa stared open mouthed.

"Don't fash yerself, Ms. Gibson," Toren said, nodding to Lisa. "It won't take much time away from the children."

Lisa smiled and nodded, but her eyes sent daggers at Kat as if she'd kept a secret. It was a promise of a fabulous tongue lashing full of every curse Lisa kept inside, stored up from when she was around the children.

"Was the necklace found?" one of the ladies below asked, causing murmurs to sound like the rumble of thunder that still rolled outside.

Toren opened the bandana and pulled out the necklace. He held it up and everyone applauded. "It is a beautiful piece, but it looks even more beautiful against the skin of a woman." He stepped behind Kat at the top of the grand staircase. His fingers grazed her skin as he pulled the chain she was already wearing up and slid the moonstone around to her back.

"No, I couldn't wear it." Kat made to move forward, but his hand on her shoulder and the three hundred sets of eyes below stopped her. That was six hundred eyes. The necklace would counteract her magic, and she'd be standing in her knickers and bra before everyone, her facial scars exposed too.

"Of course ye can," Toren countered. His breath hovered at her ear, causing ripples of awareness to run down her entire body.

"No…no I couldn't. I don't want—"

"Hush now, lass, it will look lovely against yer softness." His fingers moved along her naked neck, and she felt the heavy coolness of the necklace rest against her skin.

Kat closed her eyes, humiliation flushing her.

Instead of the gasps, or even stunned silence or screams, more polite applause sounded. Kat opened her eyes. Several people meandered toward the bar to refresh their drinks, while a few chatted with the person next to them in hushed tones. One woman even yawned. Lisa smiled and raised her glass in salute.

A bell sounded.

Toren raised his hand. "It seems the second course is about to be served. Enjoy." The crowd turned to their plates as an army of servers walked out with trays full of dinner plates.

The necklace hadn't revealed her? But hadn't it the other day? Wasn't that why Toren had been able to see her?

Thunder boomed outside and the lights flickered off, then on again, sending gasps through the audience followed by a light chord of laughter.

In the brief darkness, Toren's warm, solid hand wrapped around her own. In mute confusion over everything, she let him turn her to him. "Ye look lovely tonight."

She followed his gaze down her length and exhaled with relief that she still saw the gown embracing her body.

"I am Toren MacCallum, but ye already know that."

Kat swallowed and nodded. She'd had only a brief encounter with him yesterday, and he'd smelled wonderful then. But now, the combination of masculine warmth and a fresh-showered pine smell, underlined with the hint of expensive whiskey, flooded her senses. Thunder once again vibrated through the room, but she ignored it, shaking his hand. "Thank you," she said. "For not—"

"I need an assistant," he said briskly. "My last one did not work out." He touched the necklace at her throat. "I will pay ye well."

"I couldn't, I mean I have other—"

"I'll pay ye enough that ye'll have no need to steal again." The eyes that met hers were hard, unreadable, undeniable.

She breathed as evenly as her rapid heart would allow and wet her lips. Her voice remained low. "I don't steal things for *me*." She glanced down at her feet that looked like they were in Jimmy Choo pumps. "It's for the children. Like Robin Hood."

"Ye can work for me, help me, and I will make sure ye have all the funds ye need for the children."

"I...can't."

He moved closer. "Ye can." There was curiosity written in the strong planes of his face, curiosity mixed with determination born out of some other emotion. Could it be pain? "And ye will," he whispered, his focus dropping to her lips. He was only a breath away from her when the lights flickered out again.

Lightning and thunder cracked at the same time, filling the open rooms with sporadic light. It was hard to hear him above the gasps and thunder, but he moved his lips near her ear.

"Tell me first." His thick burr rolled through her revved body. "Who is Wednesday? And why are ye wearing her undergarments?"

CHAPTER FIVE
UNNATURAL STORM

Kat's face snapped up to his gaze. As lightning lit her lovely face, huge eyes stared back, frozen. Her lips parted as if gasping, but no breath seemed to flow freely between.

Fok. What the hell was wrong with him? Toren had given it all away, the secret that he should keep from the enemy. But this lovely lass wasn't the witch who'd stolen his life away. Kat had magic, but she'd just been drawn to the dragonfly for its uniqueness and expense. He could have let her leave after returning it. Instead, he'd made her a research assistant to replace Jansen. What would he do with her? Have her research black magic to find the one who'd trapped him in the twenty-first century?

Toren stared at her statue-like features, so delicate and even more interesting with the scar running down the side of her cheek and jaw. In the dim illumination from the emergency lights along the stairs, he watched her hand rise to it as if checking that the puckered skin was still there. She swayed slightly. If she lost consciousness, would everyone else see her in the small coverings that served as underclothes in this century? Pale, smooth skin with two strips of fabric covering her breasts and cunny?

He steadied her in the continued darkness. "Ye have nerve, lass, so don't pass out now." The lights flicked back on, blinding Toren for a second.

Kat twisted her wrist and yanked, freeing herself. *Daingead.*

She raced down the steps, her minimally covered breasts jouncing up and down. Would they pop free of the stretchy black material containing them? Toren walked down the stairs. He could catch her, but she needed some space. He'd give her ten feet.

Toren strode across the interconnected rooms, ignoring the questions thrown toward him from his guests. He wouldn't lose his quarry this time.

"Ladies and gentlemen," his event planner called, thankfully taking over since that was what Toren paid him to do.

Toren paused outside the rooms, his eyes searching the darkness pooled at the end of the corridor. "Ye won't get away this time." A door slammed in the kitchen, and he surged forward to push through the swinging door. Several servers gasped, and he wove through them and steel counters to reach the backdoor to the terrace.

Rain pelted him and the wind roared, snapping tree limbs. Toren's large stride easily caught up to Kat in the gazebo that looked ready to be blown apart. She was bent over a mound of wet clothing.

"Bloody piece of crap!" she yelled at the uncooperative black breeches as she tried to shove her foot into one side. She was a damp, beautiful she-cat, bedraggled by the rain and situation yet still ready to fight.

"What are ye doing?"

"Leaving!" she shouted above the wind.

"With my necklace, again?" he said stressing the last word.

Her hand landed on the heavy dragonfly amulet hanging around her neck but then dropped it. He couldn't see her face except when the lightning flashed, but he could tell she was glaring. "You saw me without clothes the entire time." Accusation laced her words as if he should feel guilty for the strange ability he had to see through her tricks.

"Aye," he said simply.

"And yesterday at the orphanage?"

"Aye."

He watched her stamp her feet in temper. The wind buffeted the gazebo and the two potted trees on the terrace. "So why tell me now?" she asked over the sound. "Why not continue to pretend?"

Crack! A tree limb fell, hitting the terrace's stone floor. Toren leaped towards Kat, shielding her body from the rain-soaked wind. He looked down at her. "Because I need yer help."

"Bollocks," she snapped.

"Ye have magic." He touched a curl that seemed to snake around his finger on its own accord. *What am I doing?* He dropped it.

Kat pursed her lovely lips, refusing to answer.

Toren caught her chin in his grasp and leaned in toward her body. "I feel it," he said. The pull to her was more than lust because he'd felt that before. This was deeper, even if he couldn't put a description to it. It felt...imperative to touch her.

Kat's lips opened, but she said nothing as they stared at one another. He leaned toward her mouth, those lush lips calling him as if she were a siren singing her song, luring him into a glorious death.

"No time for kissing." A voice split through the storm, a voice Toren hated so much that the fire raging down the length of his body turned instantly to ice.

Toren spun around but kept Kat shielded behind his body. "Bana-bhuidseach! Witch!" he yelled at the ghostly image hovering in front of them.

"Call me what you will, but I'm here to help." The apparition looked the same as when he'd seen her five years ago. She was a crone, but her age shifted continuously. Her long white hair tangled with her flowing silvery blue robes as she floated. The dragonflies encircled her like a battalion ready to attack.

The witch slid to the side to see Kat. The evil crone would have to go through him to reach her.

"Katell, Daughter of Gilla, the demons are coming for you," she said indicating the storm roaring around them.

Toren turned to Kat, staring into her wide eyes. "Ye know this witch?"

Kat shook her head with force. "No," she yelled above the wind.

When he pulled away from Kat and the witch could see her fully, the apparition gasped. "My dragonfly! You're wearing my dragonfly!" She held out a long, sharp finger toward Kat's neck. "Take it off. 'Tis what's bringing them to you!"

"Who are you?" Kat asked. "What demons?"

"The ones who killed your parents, girl." The witch glanced around at the thrashing trees. "There's no time to explain, take it off!" She jabbed her pointer finger at the dark river. "Look, they come."

Toren stared out over the Thames where a funnel cloud spun upriver towards them, destroying rowboats, piers, and motor crafts. "Kat, give me the necklace," he said. She extended the long pale column of her neck so he could work the catch on the chain. It released, and he balled the necklace, sticking it into his jacket pocket. He'd rather go to Hell in that bloody tornado than hand it over to the crone. His gaze turned back toward the river. "It still comes."

"Because 'tis too late," the witch yelled. "They know she's here. I must hide her." The witch's head whipped back and forth as if she sought a hole to stuff Kat into.

He glanced sideways at Kat who wrapped her arms around herself against the cold wind in the scraps of her soaked undergarments.

Toren shucked off his suit jacket and draped her in it. She fisted it closed in front. A brief smile touched her lips. A thank you, perhaps.

Her gaze moved to the witch. "You knew my parents?"

"I am Drakkina. I taught Gilla and Druce." The witch's words flew, her eyes still wild. "Gilla sent you with her magic to hide you from them." She jabbed a long finger at the cloud. "You can't let them take you. There's more than your life at stake."

In the frantic flashes of lightning, Toren studied the funnel cloud on its race up the wide river. It did seem to be headed directly toward them. There was something unnatural in the way the cloud sparked from within its swirls. The air smelled like stagnant death. Not the tangy scent of fresh blood during a battle, but the smell of death two days later, when the unclaimed, partly eaten corpses begin to rot. His warrior's instincts thrummed, putting him in full alert. There was more threat here than a mere tornado. "They want her magic?"

"Yes, yes! The dragonfly, combined with her own magic, called to them when it touched her skin," the witch spat. Her eyes bore into his, wide with hysteria. "They'll kill her for it." The crone closed her eyes for a brief moment as if trying to concentrate. "I will send you away like Gilla did."

She opened her pale blue eyes and looked straight at Toren. "Guard her, give me back my dragonfly, and I will leave you alone in the century you desire."

"I don't trust olc magic."

"My magic is not evil," she replied.

"Then I don't trust ye."

"You have little choice. Give it to me!"

"Nay!"

"There's no time," she said, throwing a wrinkled hand out to the funnel closing in on the shore. It turned toward them from the middle of the Thames.

"Hide her without taking the necklace from me," he demanded.

"Stubborn troll," she spat, then shook her head, pale eyes full of white anger. "Take it with you but give it back if you want me to leave you alone. And don't touch it," she yelled to Kat. "They'll find you if you touch it."

The tornado raced close enough that Toren could see the water being sucked up into the giant swirling twist. And he could almost make out voices in the mist. Toren pulled Kat into his chest, shielding her from the debris flying across the terrace, pummeling the gazebo. Under the roar Toren could barely hear the witch's chant.

"On the currents of my blood, on the currents of my yearning to save your humanity, send them, Earth Mother, now, within my thread of power." The witch looked at Toren. "Return the Highlander to whence he came." With that she blew out a long breath that seemed to raise the temperature of the air around them. Then the crone began to waver before his eyes. "Hold her tight," she called. Toren wrapped himself around Kat.

"Everything looks blurry." Kat clung to him as fiercely as he clung to her.

It wasn't just the witch that wavered. Everything did. And then Toren felt the melting, the same feeling he'd had five long years ago when the witch had stolen him from his time, from his world, and thrust him with no explanation into the twenty-first century. "I think we are about to fly," he said near Kat's ear.

"Fly?" she squeaked.

Toren felt her fingers grip his back like a terrified, feral cat. And then they softened, stretched thin into two threads coiled together, snaking up through the maelstrom to leave the world behind.

Their bodies elongated, twisting and thinning into threads, his thread and Kat's thread, separate but twined so tightly that they couldn't fall apart. They flew upward, snaking through a crack in the dense, sticky clouds. They soared, unable to talk, unable to do anything but hold on to one another with their whole bodies, their souls. Toren sensed fear from Kat and tried to push a feeling of calm toward her strand. It felt just like it had five years ago, when the witch had snatched him away from his business at the English court. The moon and stars, the sun and sky blinked past him so fast that they blurred together making him dizzy and furious.

Once again he was not in control. *Bloody hell!* He should be the only one responsible for his destiny. And yet this crone, who was somehow connected to Kat, could change everything in his life with mere words. The more he thought of the bizarre circumstances, the more white-hot fury built inside him. Worry, fear, and the beginning of anger resonated from Kat's thread. She was apparently picking up on his emotions.

The flashing slowed until it finally stopped. They were still coiled together as threads when they descended over Hampton Court, entering through minute cracks in the roof, down through the rooms, until they came to rest in an antechamber, their forms quickly expanding back into flesh and bones. Kat gasped and coughed as if her lungs weren't working correctly.

Toren glanced around. They were alone, dressed as they had been when the crone manipulated them. He wore his well-tailored twenty-first century suit, and Kat was draped in his jacket over slips of underclothes.

"She's done it," he murmured, his mind racing through memories of that night five years past. He stood exactly where he'd been when the witch had snatched him away in a similar thread, totally at the mercy of her magic.

"What has she done?" Kat asked, her voice full of numb bewilderment.

"Sent me back to the moment she took me."

Kat clutched his arm. "Back in time? To when?"

Toren turned to the damp woman. "Dress yerself, mistress," he said, his burr thicker than she'd ever heard. "Ye're about to meet Elizabeth."

Kat swallowed. "Elizabeth who?"

The double doors began to open, and a loud voice proclaimed. "Laird Toren MacCallum of Craignish to see Queen Elizabeth, Sovereign of all England and Ireland."

CHAPTER SIX
THE VIRGIN QUEEN

Kat's lower jaw dropped open. Who? When? How? The questions banged into one another in her mind like crazed fun fair dodgem cars.

"Clothe yerself." Toren's insistence broke through the mental fog.

Kat poured magic around her and Toren, covering them in Elizabethan court clothing. So her degree was of use despite what Roger at the bank thought. She laughed slightly, but it sounded croaky, on the edge of hysteria.

Kat leaned into Toren and touched his arm. Her nails dug in enough to catch his eye, and she tried to keep the panic out of her voice. "As long as I touch you, they see you dressed also in Elizabethan clothing. I can place the spell around us both even if you can't see it."

"We can't be separated?"

As the doors began to swing inward, Kat spoke low over the heart hammering in her ears. "Not unless you want them to see how demonic tornados trash Armani suits." How utterly impossible that she was still able to joke in a moment like this. She must be dreaming. But if this was the dream she'd conjured with Mr. Sexy as Hell, she needed to do a much better job at it.

She'd had the melting, twisting-into a thread nightmare since she was a kid, but she'd never ended up at Queen Elizabeth's court before. Maybe a tree branch had struck her unconscious. Should she play along until the Yellow Brick Road appeared and she could skip to the Emerald City looking for a balloon to take her home? *I'm bloody losing my mind.*

Kat willed her feet to move forward at Toren's tug. *Breathe, must breathe.* Little stars sparkled before her eyes. *No fainting. Absolutely no fainting.* The scent of wax candles burning and dried flowers filled her inhale. Kat glanced around at the amazing statues and tapestries. The details were perfect, the colors vibrant, and a chill ran down her bare spine. Too many details for a dream. She had to concentrate on her costume, down to the smallest detail. She'd chosen a gown she'd studied at uni, outlining every pearl and stitch of green thread in a paper that earned the highest mark.

Toren and she walked between several small groups of men through another doorway where a length of carpet covered the wooden floor, leading to a throne. Kat swallowed past a tongue that stuck to the roof of her mouth and let Toren lead her toward Queen Elizabeth I.

The famous Tudor monarch had red hair piled up on her head. *Probably a wig.* What year was it? *It could be her real hair.* The white makeup caked on her face made her look like a china doll. Elizabeth wore a blue gown with bees embroidered over it, and the ruff at her neck gave her the look of a floating detached head. The queen's scrutiny enveloped her.

Toren bowed low and Kat tried to imitate the deep curtsies she'd seen in the Elizabethan movies she loved so much. "Yer Majesty," Toren murmured.

Elizabeth flipped her hands. "Rise, Laird MacCallum," she ordered sharply, her etched coal eyebrows drawing together. "Who is this woman?" she asked disdainfully. "And why is she wearing my favorite gown?"

Shoot, shoot, shoot! The dress she knew the best had of course been one of Elizabeth's. Kat took two deep breaths and started tweaking the glamour she'd poured over herself. The dress had been cream silk, so she changed it to a peach velvet. The embroidered leaves she transformed into miniature green butterflies, and the pearls became French knots in white.

Kat bowed her head. "Forgive the similarity, Your Majesty."

"Similarity? It is exactly…" Elizabeth's voice trailed off as she studied the gown again. The silence stretched while Kat stared at the chipped Heavenly Pink nail polish on her big toe. "Yes, I see now. It is similar, but not the same."

Kat raised her gaze to the stately woman.

The queen looked at Toren. "I was told you had a gift to present. Am I to assume that this woman is your gift?"

Toren hesitated. He must have had something to present when the witch, Drakkina, had taken him. Why had she taken him? No wonder the man acted like a legendary Highlander. He was a sixteenth-century laird.

"Nay, Yer Majesty. I am to present ye with this necklace," he said, holding the chain of the dragonfly necklace. The pendant dropped down to swing in the air. "From Clan MacCallum to pledge our allegiance to ye."

Holy Mother Mary. The witch would be completely livid! Would she zap him somewhere else if he didn't hand it over? Where was Drakkina anyway?

Elizabeth nodded. A groom took the magical necklace and held it out for the regal queen to study it. "'Tis unique, exquisite. I send my thanks to your family." Her gaze shifted back to Kat. "But who is she? I had not heard that anyone besides your brother and sister had accompanied you to court."

Again, Kat held her breath, waiting for Toren to fabricate something. This was his century after all. Did he expect her to give a plausible excuse for her appearance?

Kat felt Toren's arm tense under the thin black dress shirt. He placed his large hand over hers. "Yer Majesty, I would present to ye my betrothed, Mistress Katell..." Bugger, she hadn't told him the closest thing she had to a last name. "Mistress Katell Diciadain," he said and bowed once more.

Kat curtsied, bowing her face toward the ground while still holding tightly to Toren.

Elizabeth flicked her hands again to get them to rise. "Diciadain? I have never heard of that family. 'Tis a Gaelic word, is it not?" She squinted her eyes. "A day of the week I think?"

"Aye."

"Her name is...Katell Wednesday?" the queen asked, one coal eyebrow rising.

Kat glanced down at her day of the week knickers and grimaced.

"Aye, it translates that way," he answered.

The queen leaned back in her throne, both thin eyebrows raised, her lips pursed into a perfect red circle. "Either you are lying to a queen and ready to forfeit your head or you are fooled by her beauty and ready to believe whatever she says." Elizabeth leaned forward. "She does speak, does she not?"

Kat curtseyed once more. "Yes, Your Majesty," Kat said using her best *Pride and Prejudice* accent. "I just find myself without a tongue when I am nervous."

Elizabeth smiled. "You admit that you are nervous?"

"Immensely," Kat said without hesitation.

The queen weighed her. "'Tis good that one of you is telling the truth." She frowned at Toren.

"Forgive the abrupt announcement," Toren said. "I had met Mistress Diciadain when I journeyed through the Lake Country several months ago. Her family died of the sweating sickness, leaving her alone. During my time helping her we developed an attachment."

"Well she is quite comely," Elizabeth assessed, as if speaking about good horseflesh. Would the queen ask to inspect her teeth?

"I see why you might be enthralled." Elizabeth looked Kat up and down again, and Kat hoped that her costume was authentic enough to pass inspection. "Tell me Mistress Diciadain, your accent is quite strange. From where does your family hail?"

"The Diciadains moved..." Toren began, but Elizabeth held up a ring-bedecked hand. She rarely wore gloves, preferring to show off her long, slender fingers that held a fortune in rings.

"Even though I seldom tire of listening to your rolling, deep timbre, I must insist on hearing from the lady," she ordered without moving her gaze from Kat.

Kat inhaled slowly. In the sixteenth century, where would she come from with an odd accent? She felt the weight of her moonstone necklace, but it would not make her able to speak another language unless the queen spoke to her in another language. Kat bowed her head. "My father sought wealth in the Caribbean, Your Majesty. He traded merchandise along the routes."

The queen's eyebrow rose. "Your father was a pirate?"

"Nay, Your Majesty. An honest merchant trying to find honest fortune without a benefactress."

She nodded. "A pirate, but perhaps a polite pirate." The queen smiled sarcastically at Toren.

"You wish to wed a pirate's daughter?"

"Aye."

"That may be difficult as I already have a petition sent to me this morning for you to right a wrong and wed another."

Kat glanced at Toren from the corner of one eye. Right a wrong?

Toren opened his mouth, but Elizabeth waved her hand again. "We will talk of this predicament alone. You are my favorite laird." She smiled like a Cheshire cat. "But honor, duty, and justice are essential to my throne." Elizabeth looked at Kat. "I will talk with you later, Mistress Diciadain."

"My lady does not know the labyrinth of yer palace. I would escort her to her quarters," Toren said.

"And exactly where would those quarters be?" the queen asked. "With you?"

The woman was as quick and clever as history remembered.

"Nay, with my sister, the Lady MacCallum," he answered.

"Soon to be Lady Campbell," Elizabeth added.

Toren's hand tightened over Kat's. "That is another discussion I wish to have with ye, Yer Majesty."

Elizabeth stared at Toren for a moment and then signaled to a guard holding a pike near the double doors. "Take Mistress Diciadain to Lady MacCallum's quarters."

Kat's fingers bit into Toren's arm. She couldn't let go of him or her magic would dissolve around his body. "No," she stammered.

"No?" The queen's eyes snapped.

Blood drained out of Kat under the blade of her glare. Even sitting, Elizabeth Tudor was a force so strong as to make men tremble.

It wasn't difficult for Kat to give way to the stars that floated before her eyes. Her penchant for hyperventilating could be helpful in this sixteenth-century nightmare. Kat grabbed hold of Toren's arm with both of her hands and let her knees buckle underneath her imagined gown. Down she went in a mirage of skirts and embroidery. Her body hit the stone, but the imagined velvet was silent.

Kat vaguely sensed Elizabeth rise. "I had hopes that this woman would be different." Toren scooped Kat up into his arms without even a grunt or groan. "A woman to match you, Tor, must be strong of spirit, not one of these bird-witted maids."

"Yer Majesty," Toren murmured, and bowed his head before backing out of the room. "I will return quickly."

Kat listened to his heels clacking against the floorboards while she let her breathing even out. "Bird-witted," she whispered against his chest.

Toren turned a corner and lowered her feet to the floor. He grinned, and the lines of his face relaxed. "A bird-witted maid isn't able to devise a plausible lie when a queen is shooting daggers from her eyes. I may have to call ye Kat the Pirate."

"Better than Mistress Wednesday." Kat pointed at the script on the back of her knickers. "The days of the week knicker set was a joke gift from Lisa because I kept forgetting what day it was." She looked down the hall. "Are you really taking me to your sister?"

Toren's smile faded. "I have a need to see her safe and well. And there aren't many places to put a lady without quarters. I'd rather keep ye in mine, but that would ruin ye."

"I can't believe you gave the queen the necklace. You know Drakkina will come for it soon."

Toren frowned. "I had no choice. I was holding a small fortune in gold coins when the witch took me the first time five years ago. Because of my disappearance with the gift, my family suffered and died out as far as I could tell from the old records in yer century."

"You looked up your family records." She trailed her fingers over the white plastered stone walls and shivered. Even with his jacket around her shoulders, the drafts were cold against her bare legs.

"Aye, in Scotland. I went to where Craignish Castle once stood. 'Twas nothing but rubble."

Kat squeezed his arm, looking at him. "You were in my time for years?"

"Five." He peered down the hall. "I'll get the necklace back. Until then, we behave naturally."

"I'm...to behave...naturally? In the sixteenth century?" Her brows rose high on her forehead. "In Queen Elizabeth's court?" Kat glanced around. She took a step back into a sculpture on a pedestal and spun around to steady a marble woman in a toga holding a bow. The cold ached up through Kat's bare feet on the floor. The smell of oil burning in the lamps around them tickled her nose. This was as real as it got. "I'm not going to wake up, am I?" she whispered.

Toren looked back at her. "Rocks yer world, doesn't it." The modern phrase sounded odd coming from him even though he was dressed like a damp twenty-first-century man. There had been so many clues that he wasn't from her world, but she'd had such limited time to notice them.

"Picked up some of our slang during your five years."

"A warrior absorbs everything about his environment if he wants to survive." His gaze scanned down one length of the hallway and then the other.

At the distant sound of footsteps Toren pulled Kat down the corridor. She had long legs but still trotted to keep up. After so many turns that Kat knew she'd never find her way out, Toren stopped before a heavy oak door that appeared to be just like all the other doors along the hall.

"How do you keep track of where your room is without numbers on the doors?"

"One must be more observant in this time. The sixteenth century doesn't have commercials yelling at ye nor signs flashing in red telling ye what to do and what not to do."

"Perhaps that's another reason for the low life expectancy in your century."

Toren gave a slight grunt in response as he maneuvered her through the door.

The room was chilled and had a hollow feeling, although a bed and other pertinent furniture sat about: a clothes press, privacy screen, two chests under two windows. The fire had burned down in the hearth.

"This is your sister's room?" Kat asked, turning to touch a single finger to a colorful tapestry. Toren grunted a reply that she assumed was a "yes" or an "aye" as he stirred the coals in the hearth. He bent his face and blew on them.

Kat traced the colorful threads in the tapestry, relishing the fact that it didn't stand behind glass and no guards were there to ask her to step away. She leaned into it, smelling the dyed wool, and then pulled back to study the scene that dripped with authentic history. "Lovely," Kat breathed and walked to the small, raised bed, clutching Toren's jacket closed around her shoulders with one hand. Her fingers brushed the soft curtains flanking it. "Although I don't think your sister will want to share such a small bed with me."

"Ye will sleep with me." Toren glanced out the window.

"Uh, I believe that would ruin me," Kat said as she tried to ignore the sudden thumping of her heart. Her gaze roamed down the damp slacks that hugged Toren's gorgeous bum.

"Ye will be safer there."

Safer? Kat wasn't so sure of that. "But your sister?"

"Briana will say what I bid her to say." A hint of disgust edged his words. "One thing we MacCallums are is obedient. All the way to our demise."

"But what will she think of me?" Back in the sixteenth century, the sin of fornicating out of wedlock hit right up there with thievery for a woman. Maybe even murder to some.

"As much as I admire the Wednesday undergarments, it is time for ye to dress."

Toren opened the wardrobe containing gowns, and all thoughts of her near-naked and exposed self fled as Kat hurried toward the court costumes. "Holy Mother of Jesus." She passed the sign of the cross before her chest. "Look at these gowns." She whirled to Toren, pure excitement in her eyes. "Do I get to wear one?"

A thoughtful grin replaced his ornery frown, making him look not only civilized but once again sexy as hell. "What exactly would ye give me to divest my sister of one or two of her ensembles?"

His low voice tickled shivers along Kat's skin. The blush that always stood ready flooded her. She threw her magic naturally into her skin to shield it.

Toren's hand moved to her left cheek. "She weaves her way through a ballroom of people in nothing more than scraps of cloth and doesn't blush. But a few words..."

"Oooo!" She pivoted back to the wardrobe. "I was invisible then."

"Not to me," he said, and Kat could feel his hand as it skimmed the length of her wild curling hair.

Was that his breath she felt? Kat took a shallow inhale that hitched in time with her heartbeat. "It's not fair that you can see through my magic," she murmured, and ran a hand down a velvet cloak. "Why is that?"

Toren shrugged. "I won't apologize for being able to see through the tricks of a woman." His cold tone sucked away the warmth Kat felt.

She turned her attention on the glorious fabrics. Her fingers paused on a deep blue, the nap of the cloth so soft. She pressed the neighboring gown back to look down the length of the velvet gown.

"This one looks warm," she said and drew it out. "Would she mind if I borrowed it?"

"Ye are a thief, yet ye worry about someone's feelings over taking a gown?"

Kat turned, her gaze slicing through him. "Robin Hood robbed from the rich and gave to the poor."

Toren eyebrow rose. "If he was more than a mere story, he was still a thief."

"Perhaps his actions weren't justified until my century," she said.

"Romanticized."

She sucked in a breath with annoyance. "Robin Hood was justified and therefore not a thief and neither am I. When I return to my century, I will find another way to keep the children together. And yes, I'd worry about your sister recognizing her dress and accusing me of stealing."

"I will speak with her." He stepped away. "Pick one or two more. I will have ye fitted for a wardrobe tomorrow."

She blinked. "A wardrobe? How long do you think we'll be here?"

"Ye may leave as soon as the crone shows up. I plan to stay. This is my time, my life."

Kat spun back to the court costumes. *What do I care if he stays?* This was his century after all. Lisa would be disappointed that they wouldn't get the funding if he disappeared. Maybe he would let her take an artifact or two back to sell.

Toren walked to the door, and Kat's heart jumped. "Where are you going?" The Elizabethan court was much more intriguing when viewed at a safe distance across a page of history text. In the sixteenth century, people were known to disappear from court. "How will I get this gown on by myself?"

Toren glanced over his shoulder, eyes raking her nearly nude body. "I think I would just hinder yer efforts, mistress."

Kat felt a blush. She automatically threw up a shield to hide it and then frowned. Why didn't her magic work on him?

"I must find appropriate clothing and then my sister. She can help ye dress."

"What...what do I tell her?"

He kept his voice neutral. "Go with the pirate tale."

"Right." Kat's mind whirled. What exactly had she said? "Pirate tale," she murmured, as the door shut soundly behind Toren.

CHAPTER SEVEN
A COURT OF LIES

"A second claim, Laird MacCallum," Elizabeth drawled. "Any other women tucked away, panting for the chance to wed with you?" Elizabeth reclined before a well-stoked fire. It didn't bode well for Toren that she was calling him by his formal title.

"Since I wasn't aware of the first claim, I am unable to say for certain, Yer Majesty."

She stared at him for a moment and tapped a slender finger against ruby lips. She looked to her trusted advisor, Lord Cecil. "I will deal with this matter myself as it is a delicate situation needing the heart of a woman. I trust that you can enact my orders from earlier today regarding our fleet. I agree that Spain is planning to act soon."

"Your Majesty," William Cecil murmured, and bowed. Several guards followed him out of the double oak doors leaving only two ladies-in-waiting and two male servants.

"Come closer, laird. Let me take a better look at why these ladies fawn over you. It can't all be from that devilish Highland brogue."

Toren lowered in a crouch before her chair so their faces were level. Otherwise he would seem to loom over her. Elizabeth was a fair and just monarch except when she felt cornered or bullied. Then she could turn ruthless, very much like her father.

"May I ask," Toren said slowly, his flirtatious eyes finding hers. "Who is the other lady who has petitioned for my hand in marriage?"

Elizabeth's brow rose as she stared into his eyes. "You have no idea?"

"Nay, Yer Majesty. I was unaware of any other interest."

A small frown creased her brow. "Do you lose track of those women you've bedded then?"

"Nay, Yer Majesty. I believe my duties to family have left me rather virtuous and chaste these days."

"Fie, I smell a lie." She smiled. "A man like you does not stay chaste for long." Her smile turned bitter. "Lady Margaret Maxwell has brought evidence of your seduction."

Lady Margaret Maxwell, the little mouse who skittered away every time he entered a room? "And what evidence could she possibly have since she has never been alone with me, Yer Majesty?"

"Her father said that you would deny stealing her virtue." She moved her hand, indicating he should stand again.

"Her father." That explained it all. Hughe Maxwell would use his only daughter for gain. "When did this supposed thievery occur?" Toren stood with his hands clasped behind his back.

"Six years ago."

Toren tried not to laugh. Six years ago, when he'd last been forced to attend the Maxwell's low country Christmastide feasts with his family.

"And why would her father petition now for me to marry his daughter?"

"It seems she can no longer care for your child without your assistance."

The words, spilled so casually, struck hard against Toren's gut. Child? There was a child in that hellhole, being raised by the devil's daughter.

"I have no child."

"So you deny that the child is yours?"

"Vehemently." Toren couldn't keep the anger out of his voice. "I have no knowledge of a child, especially from my seed. I maintain that I have never compromised Lady Margaret. In fact, I don't believe we have even shared but a few words in all the years I spent under her father's roof."

"The act of creation does not require the sharing of words," Elizabeth said.

Toren frowned. "I haven't shared anything with Hughe Maxwell's daughter."

"Your word against Maxwell's."

"A son or a daughter?"

"A daughter. A bit over five years old now."

"And why can she not raise the child without me?"

"Apparently her father feels the child is touched by the devil and that if you take the sacrament of marriage with his daughter, the devil's mark will go away. He's giving his daughter one year to marry someone, preferably you, or else he will send them both from his home."

"Devil's mark?"

"Some sort of defect on the face, very red. I've seen it, quite unsightly. Unfortunately, people like to label anything unusual as the devil's work."

Toren stared at the flames in the hearth. "So I am to sacrifice and marry her and make everything proper and blessed."

"We all sacrifice," she said, her face serious.

Toren met her sharp gaze. "I am not the father."

Elizabeth indicated a chair before the fire. Toren sat but did not relax. The clever queen was like a viper lulling its victim with gentle words. She touched his arm. "I did not think you were such a lecher as to deflower a woman of stature and leave her encumbered, Toren."

"What does Lady Margaret say about all this?"

"Not much. She's...rather timid."

Toren snorted. "Does she seem the type of lass I'd pursue?"

Elizabeth squinted as if inspecting him, weighing his seduction tastes. "Nay," she drawled out. "I do believe you would hunt down a little more headstrong prey."

Thank the good Lord that Elizabeth knew him well enough. Did she know Maxwell too? Toren's father had sent him to live in the Maxwell's Lowland Scottish barony as a lad of ten to learn culture and the English language in a more sophisticated household. His father was convinced that Queen Elizabeth would make King James of Scotland her heir, and that Toren must learn English etiquette to be accepted in a royal court. What Toren had learned instead was that the world was a cold, lonely place where tragedy and blame could occur at any moment.

"If I do not marry her, what will happen to the child?"

"Exactly my concern." Elizabeth glanced over at Toren. "You do not worry over the lady's welfare?"

Toren swore in Gaelic. "She's survived as her father's daughter all these years. She is meek and respectful and has a lovely face without blemish. The child is the one in jeopardy."

Elizabeth watched the flames, suddenly melancholy. "'Twould seem the plight of many children. 'Tis the way of this world." After a moment she shook her head and motioned to one of the attendants to bring forth a chess board with ivory and ebony pieces. They set it up quickly and Elizabeth moved her ivory pawn. "So then, tell me of your Lady Wednesday."

"Diciadain," Toren corrected and moved his pawn out onto the board.

"'Tis not a real name."

Toren didn't say anything but moved his knight to capture the queen's pawn.

"Aggressive advancement can feel victorious," she said. "But can prove foolish in the end." Elizabeth moved her bishop into a threatening position against the daring knight.

"I find that it is often best to make the first move. I'd rather attack than be stalked."

Elizabeth leaned back in her chair and took a sip of wine. "That mouse who fainted before me hardly looks like one who would dare to stalk you." Kat may not have stalked him, but she had come for the necklace, risking so much.

Toren moved his knight out of harm's way by taking another of the queen's pawns. "Looks can be deceiving," he said, a smile in his voice.

The queen waved to a servant who brought Toren a goblet of wine. After several more moves she casually stole his damaging knight with her queen.

"Errant knights should be wary of ivory queens," she said, eyes glinting dangerously.

Toren leaned back in his chair and let the mellow wine sweep through him, relaxing him enough to concentrate on the game, both the one on the board and the one in the room. He breathed deeply.

The queen had all the power, and she could smell a lie as surely as she could steal his pieces. She practiced the art every day, all day. As a child she learned to use her wits and play the world's game in order to survive. And now that she had the vast power to conquer anyone she saw as an enemy, she used those wits as a warrior would use his sword. Her battlefield was in state rooms and great halls instead of outdoors in fields.

"She has no real name, no family. She is orphaned," Toren supplied.

Elizabeth leaned back in her chair, moving a pawn to a vulnerable position. A gift? Toren took it. It was the polite thing to do.

"And you will rescue her." The queen nodded. "Like you rescued your brother from your father's wrath."

Toren raised an eyebrow.

"Of course, I know of this. My counselors keep me abreast of all who enter my court." She took a drink and moved her queen back into a non-threatening position. "I know that he planned to banish the lad from your clan because he refused the match he'd set." The fire crackled, sending sparks up into the dark hearth. The tiny fire stars dissolved into the darkness. "And that you challenged your father over his threat."

Toren didn't say anything but moved a pawn forward where it would be trapped. His queen was now vulnerable to Elizabeth's bishop.

Elizabeth gaze snapped from his foolish move to his face. "You would rather commit suicide on the playing field than discuss family matters." She pursed her lips for a moment before snorting softly. "I'm much the same." Instead of stealing his queen, she moved her bishop and took another pawn.

"Will ye try to stop me from wedding Kat?" He didn't really plan to marry Kat, but the proposal gave him an excuse not to wed Margaret. And the idea of courting the beautiful, mysterious wildcat from the twenty-first century not only warmed his blood but made him feel alive without the need of fury.

"Kat?" the queen laughed. "I have a dear friend named the same. Does yours have claws?"

"Aye. She has spirit, though she hides it."

"She wasn't really fainting, then."

Toren exhaled through his nose. "She seemed hearty once we quit the room."

The queen laughed and moved her bishop in an aggressive move against his other knight. "Still, marrying a woman without a name, without a dowry. 'Tis a good thing your father's dead as he would never have allowed it."

Toren moved, taking her bishop. Elizabeth sat upright, not expecting the bold action.

"'Tis a good thing my *Catholic* father is dead, else ye and I may not be having a friendly game before the fire."

Elizabeth frowned, her eyes sharp. "He was an open supporter of my cousin Mary while she lived."

Toren met her eyes. "I support ye, Elizabeth, King of England and Ireland." His words were serious and heavy with the oath.

She leaned forward studying him. "I see it in your eyes, my Highland knight, and I feel it in the weight of your gift," she said, pulling the necklace from where it lay against her cinched bodice of blue velvet.

The dragonfly center sparkled in the firelight, its wings almost coming to life. Toren blinked, and the image stilled.

He breathed in fully. "I'm pleased ye like the gift," he said. *Daingead!* She was wearing it. How many hundreds of other pieces had she received as gifts and had tucked away in some dusty room? But she wore the dragonfly necklace, which made it impossible to reclaim.

Elizabeth inclined her head toward the board and moved her queen in line with Toren's king. "Check."

Toren didn't look at the board but studied the strong, intelligent woman before him. She had a king's heart, a commander's intellect, and her father's passion. Her interference or favor could change the course of history. "Will ye forbid me from marrying Kat?" Did she think he'd missed her failure to answer him before?

Elizabeth's eyes flashed as they came to rest on him. "It seems, my Highland knight, that you make your own decisions, regardless of authority."

"I do not wish to make myself yer enemy, Yer Majesty."

Her eyes narrowed. "But you will bloody well do as you like."

She would know if he lied and could throw him in the Tower if he agreed. It was best to hold his tongue. Instead, he moved his king out of check.

Elizabeth quickly moved to match him. "Check," she said. Toren moved out of check again, and she followed. "Check." She chased him for two more moves until finally leaning back in her chair. She ran a hand along her cheek. "I grow weary of stalking you."

Toren reached across the board to his ebony king and laid it down at her ivory queen's feet. "Then I surrender." He bowed his head in what he hoped looked like supplication.

"God's teeth!" Elizabeth yelled, making his gaze snap up. "If you imagine that I would believe your surrender in this matter so quickly, you must think me quite the fool." Her words seethed, but her eyes twinkled, and a small grin played on her painted lips.

"Yer Majesty—" Toren began, but the queen threw up a hand to stop him.

"I will make my opinion known after reviewing all the testimony. Your Mistress Kat Wednesday or Lady Maxwell." She steepled slender fingers before the embroidered bodice of her royal dress. "'Tis your word against Maxwell's, and the child must be protected if possible."

She nodded at an attendant, who quickly took the chess game away.

"And then it will be up to you, my Highland knight." She raised her goblet of wine in salute. "To rescue the one who needs it most."

CHAPTER EIGHT
NOT A HUGGER

The half scream, half gasp made Kat jump and spin around, gown clutched in front of her chest. A tall, attractive, brunette woman stood staring at her.

"I knew I'd run afoul one day," she said, her Scottish accent evident. "I counted the wrong number of doors. Please forgive me. I must have the next room."

"Wait," Kat said, before the woman could exit. "Is this your gown by any chance?"

The woman looked closer, then glanced around the room, and blinked at Kat, a look of horror on her pretty face. "This is my room," she said. "Aye, that is my gown." She looked Kat up and down. "Who are ye and why are ye donning my gown? Where are yer clothes?" She glanced around the room. "Did ye walk here naked?"

Had Toren told Kat his sister's name? Brie or Briana or Briannan?

"I am Kat. And you are Toren MacCallum's sister? Briana?"

"Cat? Like the beast?" the woman asked.

"No. Nay. It's spelled with a K."

"Oh. Is it short for Katherine then?"

"No, Katell."

"I've never heard of that name before. What is yer family name?"

Kat wasn't quite sure what to say so she went with what Toren had started. "Diciadain."

Toren's sister stared at her with amusement. "That isn't a family name, 'tis a day of the week. Today actually."

"It's Wednesday today?"

"Aye."

They stared at one another for a long moment. "Have ye come to steal my clothing then? Or perhaps jewels?"

"No." Kat clutched the gown before her. "Your brother brought me to your room and said that you wouldn't mind if I borrowed one of your gowns until a wardrobe could be made for me."

"Tor is having a wardrobe made for ye?"

"Yes," Kat said guardedly.

"Why?"

Kat's mind churned for an explanation that made sense. "Because we are betrothed?" she asked, more than stated.

The sister's eyes widened. "Oh bloody hell. Did my brother beget a child on ye, too, then? First Lady Maxwell and now Lady Wednesday."

"Diciadain," Kat said, although her mouth went dry like sandpaper tossed about in a desert wind. "And I cannot claim the title of lady."

Toren's sister pivoted to pace. Her hands emphasized words sporadically. "I know that he is brawn and that the ladies like his strength and bluster, but really, he should know something of restraint. There will be illegitimate MacCallums running all over the country at this rate." She threw her hands in the air. "Ruined women are unable to make a suitable match. At least he says he will do right by ye." She looked at Kat.

"Ye are more beautiful than Lady Maxwell." She smiled, her emotions flipping so quickly Kat was having a hard time following them. But the one thing she'd gleaned from the rapid fire was that Toren MacCallum was a player.

Briana frowned. "I do feel sorry for the little Maxwell child, what with that problem with her face."

"Problem?"

"Aye, they say 'tis the devil's mark on her, red as a berry and big, right up to her pretty blue eye." Briana looked at Kat's middle. "Ye sure are a slender thing for having carried a bairn. A daughter or a son?"

"What?"

"Did Tor father a daughter on ye or a son? Or are ye just now with child?"

"I have no child, of my own that is," she added, and then wished she hadn't. Her children were all in the twenty-first century. Her heart pinched with homesickness. They weren't even born yet. Their ancestors weren't even born yet. Yet Kat grieved for them. They would be split up if she didn't return. Lisa wouldn't know how to hold the orphanage together.

Briana's mouth fell open. "No child? But ye said that Tor had begot a child on ye?"

"Actually, *you* said that."

"And ye agreed."

"I believe I just stood here in my underwear."

Briana looked her over again. "Pish, we should get some clothes on ye. Did my brother steal yer clothes? I'll box his ears if he did."

Kat held up her hand. "No," she said, her mind and mouth finally falling into sync. "My clothes were ruined when I fell into a pond, and my trunks never arrived. Your brother gave me a short cloak to wear."

Kat pointed to Toren's ruined Armani jacket on the floor. "And he brought me to your rooms, knowing that your kindness would allow me to borrow a gown until more could be made." Kat inhaled, thankful that she'd been able to make up a plausible lie.

"Ye poor dear." Briana hurried over to help Kat into the blue gown. "Of course, ye can borrow the gown, though yer bosom will be near to popping out the top. Tor probably likes that. Men have such a fascination with breasts." Briana rattled on as she fastened the back of Kat's gown.

Kat wasn't sure if Toren liked her breasts or not, although his eyes had lingered there several times. The thought irritated her as it should any modern woman still trying to put the patriarchy in its place, but it also sent a languid warmth through her that she decided to ignore.

Briana had been correct. Kat's breasts did push up rather dangerously above the neckline.

"Aye," Briana said. "Necklines seem to plunge lower each season. Soon we'll be parading around court with our breasts open to all." Briana tucked a thin silk handkerchief into the top of the gown to try to hide the swell. "Well Tor may like it, but he won't like other men liking it."

Kat stared dumbfounded in a polished glass that served as a mirror.

"Ye look beautiful Mistress Diciadain."

"Please call me Kat," she whispered as she stared at the Elizabethan court woman reflected back at her. Her fingertips ran over the lovely gold butterflies stitched around her tight waist.

"Then you can call me Briana." She bent to look closer at the butterflies. "I don't remember the embroidery, but it is lovely."

Had her butterflies somehow followed her into the sixteenth century? She hoped they had, but they wouldn't be much help stuck to a gown. Kat stroked the velvet fabric that lay in soft folds over the French farthingale. A padded roll worn about her hips held the heavy skirt in a cylindrical shape.

Briana had convinced her to take off the Wednesday panties, holding them up as if they were a drowned rat. They were soaked, anyway.

Kat's fingers roamed the fine hand stitching on the sleeves as Briana tied them in place at her shoulders. It made her historian's heart beat with joy.

"Now for yer hair," Briana said. She dragged a bone comb through Kat's tangled hair. Kat watched, but her fingers itched to hold the ancient relic. If she wasn't worried about getting back to her children, Kat would be hastily studying all the authentic pieces around her: the wash basin and clothes press, the finely made furnishings and that incredible tapestry on the wall.

"'Tis such a perfect shade. Do ye dye it?" Tor's sister asked.

"No."

"Ye have no need to. How lucky."

Rap. Rap. "Milady?"

"Do come in, Lilly," Briana called, and a slender woman in a simpler dress came in through the door. Her hair was pulled back and tucked tightly under a cap, and her eyes widened in her round face.

"Mistress Diciadain, this is my lady's maid, Lilly. She does wonderful weavings with hair."

Lilly curtseyed and then came to take the comb from Briana. Tor's sister chattered on pleasantly while her maid worked a string of pearls in an intricate weave over a pad she'd inserted under Kat's hair on top of her head. "Ye are a beauty, Kat. No wonder my brother has asked ye to marry him so quickly. Before any other at court could even meet ye." She giggled and pressed her hand to her breast.

"Are you here to meet someone?" Kat smiled. "I can't imagine you will stay a maid for long, unless that is what you want."

Briana's smile dissolved like a thin wafer in a puddle of rainwater. "I am betrothed already, to Laird Fergus Campbell of Glenmore. My father set up the match before he died."

"I'm sorry about your father. Toren didn't mention that he'd died."

"He was...not an easy man."

Kat studied the woman's reflected face. "And...you don't want to marry the man he chose for you?"

"I can tie the last ribbons, Lilly. Thank ye," Briana said to the maid, who quit the room. She turned back to Kat. "Nay, I do not. There are rumors."

"Bad rumors?"

She nodded. "Also...well, there's no happiness in his gaze when he looks at me." She moved her hands in the air before dropping them to her lap. "I know how that sounds. Foolhardy."

Kat shook her head cautiously so as not to dislodge any of the amazing hairdo. "Not foolhardy. A woman's instincts mean more than rumors in my book."

"Ye have a book?"

"No," Kat said. "I mean to say, that your intuition regarding someone is usually more accurate than what people may say."

"My father didn't agree, and he made the match anyway."

"But he has died."

"Tor has kept the match to strengthen our borders."

Anger welled up in Kat. Brothers were supposed to look out for their little sisters. "You told this to Toren, and he still says that you need to marry this man?"

Briana nodded.

"We'll have to do something about that," Kat said and squeezed Briana's hand. Living in the twenty-first century for five years had hopefully taught Toren something about the rights of women. If not, Kat would make certain he understood that Briana didn't have to marry anyone, especially a known brute with dead eyes.

Toren stood amongst the spineless Englishmen talking about the political implications of Spain's aggression and the threats of revenge for Mary Stuart's execution last year. They certainly spoke with strength, but could they wield a sword with such power? However feeble the men were, the topics deserved attention.

But after years in the twenty-first century, he was no longer the sixteenth-century laird come to pay tribute to the resplendent queen of England. Curiosity and determination to find his family had sent him in search of historical references to his time.

Toren knew the Spanish would attack, but the poor weather would hold them back. He knew that Elizabeth would speak of God having a hand in saving them. He knew she would die without a direct heir, and King James Stuart would take the crown. His ideas and input on the varied conversations around him mattered little. He couldn't jump in as a soothsayer, telling everyone what would happen and the ramifications. He would be leading his people, his clan, based on information he wasn't supposed to know. Bloody difficult to explain.

So his mind drifted to an unknown future. Kat, her golden auburn hair, so soft and full. A proper diet, healthcare, and a natural radiance made Kat exude vigor and strength unlike so many who were weak in his century. The fascination and adoration he'd seen in her blue eyes as she studied the tapestries and his sister's gowns had pulled Toren in. Could she ever look at him that way?

Foolish knave. It was ridiculous to feel jealous about artifacts that weren't even artifacts yet. Toren took a drink from the wine he held while he half listened to Lord Farley talk about another Catholic threat.

"You, Laird MacCallum, will be making quite a good connection with the Campbells once your sister and their chief are wed." Lord Jenks nodded toward the arched doorway where Briana entered, her gaze scanning the Great Hall.

"Where is Laird Campbell?" Toren asked.

The oil lamps and candles lit the stuffy space as the sun descended beyond the paned windows. Five years of electricity made the everyday ways of his natural life dark and dingy. The smells of unwashed, heavily perfumed bodies in the smoke-laced rooms of granite and wool tapestries combined in an unpleasant way. The aroma of tallow warred with the smothering scents of sweet marjoram and nutmeg.

Another woman walked slowly into the room behind Briana. *Kat.* She wore the blue gown she'd picked from the clothespress, and it seemed that Briana had found her. Pride expanded in his chest as he watched Kat smile at something Briana said, as if she weren't nervous or out of place. The court was made up of beautiful people, but she stood out with her tall, curvy frame.

"Campbell's been to court. Saw him at dinner earlier this day," Farley said, and several agreed. "Her comes your sister now."

"What new lady has graced the court with her beauty?" Jenks asked, as all the men turned toward Briana and Kat. Kat's movements were graceful despite wearing something that must feel cumbersome and foreign to her. Women in the twenty-first century grew up wearing very little, giving them freedom to do whatever they desired. He'd never before thought of the ensembles of his time being cages, but they were, keeping women from escape or self-defense. They couldn't run or swim or climb in them. Were they intentionally made to keep women in their place?

Kat tilted her head slightly while examining another tapestry, and several of the men also tilted their heads. *Bloody fools.* When she turned toward them to follow Briana, the men straightened like peacocks. They would never be able to win the modern wildcat, even if she had studied his century at university.

"Tor," Briana said in greeting as she walked closer.

His dear sister. Just as beautiful and young as when he'd been swept away, and she'd disappeared from history. Without thought, Toren pulled her into a hug.

She was stiff in his arms. "What are ye doing, Brother?"

To Briana, he'd seen her just that morning, but to Toren, it had been five long years of searching, five long years of thinking he'd never see her sweet genuine smile again. Toren closed his eyes as he smelled her familiar lavender scent.

"I'm greeting ye, Sister." He pulled back and looked into her eyes. "Ye're a beauty, Briana. We are blessed to have ye as a part of our clan, and I am blessed to have ye as a sister." The words were long overdue.

Briana's face pinched with confusion even as her eyes welled up with tears. "Why thank ye, Brother."

His eyes lingered for another moment before sliding past her to Kat, who had been surrounded by the gentlemen. He lowered his voice. "Did Kat tell ye about the favor I need?"

"To clothe the nearly naked woman in my room?" she whispered. "Yer betrothed? Or second betrothed?" She tapped a thin finger to her lips as if contemplating his scandalous situation.

"I am not betrothed to Lady Margaret, and her daughter is not my child."

"And are you also not betrothed to Mistress Kat?"

His gaze raised to find the woman in question staring at him. The soft light flickered over the court gown and woven hair. And her eyes were full of excited curiosity even if she seemed overwhelmed by the men who were raking her ripe figure with their gazes.

"Bloody hell," he murmured and left his sister.

"Tor, ye didn't answer me," Briana called.

"Give my lady room to breathe, gentlemen," Toren said, breaking through the little boundary around Kat.

"Your lady?" Farley asked with indignation. "Lord Maxwell will have something to say about that."

"I am free to hear his words whenever he wishes, but the rumor he has started is not true in any way," Toren said. "And this is no place to bring them up around Mistress Kat nor Lady Briana." He put his arm out, and Kat rested her gloved hand on the blue jacket that seemed to be a perfect match for her gown. He guided her with his sister toward the opposite side of the hall.

"I must greet Lady Tilly," Briana said and pulled away to hurry forward.

"The artifacts are incredible," Kat whispered even though no one stood nearby.

"Here, they are modern pieces. Rich because they are at court, and in the current fashion."

"Like your costume," she said, touching the edge of his blue sleeve. "Each little stitch done by hand. And it is cut to fit you so well."

"My tailor is a member of the Tailor's Guild here in London."

"I always wondered how men could look masculine while wearing hose." She glanced down at the silk hose he wore with breeches as one did at court. "Very nice calves, McCallum."

"'Tis too cold here to go prancing around nearly naked, like most do in yer century."

"Oh but we are much more comfortable."

"Agreed." He'd grown accustomed to cotton trousers and soft shirts, not to mention the stretchy soft material his undergarments were made from. Boxer briefs or trunks were a definite improvement over the loincloths or braies of his century.

"So you don't wear a kilt?" she asked. "Well, they don't call them that yet. A plaid?"

"Not at Elizabeth's court," he murmured, walking slower so Briana made it to the wine station before them. "Now try not to act like..." He hesitated.

"A woman who has rights, good hygiene, and a need to cover my fanny? I mean really, it is drafty underneath all these layers." Kat swiped a hand before her petticoat.

He snorted a small laugh. "Nay, I was going to say not to act like someone from over four hundred years in the future."

Briana watched Toren as they stopped near her, a hand before her like a shield. "Ye aren't going to embrace me again are ye?"

Kat's head tiled slightly as she studied the pair. "He's not a hugger?"

"Someone who embraces often," Toren explained.

"Nay he is not a...hugger," Briana said.

"There has been much turmoil with Maxwell's suit," Toren said. "I was overcome."

"What about the turmoil of Fergus Campbell's unwanted suit," Kat said, frowning at him. "Will you be overcome by that?" Briana made a garbled noise. "And then there is the turmoil of you being betrothed to two women," Kat continued, "and your sister thought I might also be the baby mama of one of your children." She moved her hand in a small circle between them and looked at Briana. "Perhaps all that turmoil brings out the hugger in your brother. It's all so overwhelming."

Briana blinked, and the silence stretched as his sister seemed to be deciphering everything Kat had said in her modern monologue.

"I...I am not certain I understood all ye said, Mistress Kat," said Briana as she fiddled with a pearl necklace around her throat, "but what I did sounds true."

This was court, and running down a list of his faults would not help his family survive whatever it was that destroyed it in history. His gaze flashed cold as he met Kat's. She just raised her eyebrows and feigned ignorance.

"Lady Alexandria has just come in," Briana said. "I must see how her mother is doing in Sussex." She nodded to them both and walked toward a lady about her own age with dark hair and pale skin that made her eyes look more sunken. How much healthier would they all be if they ate vegetables and fruit and took the vitamin supplements he'd seen on the television flatscreen late at night?

He turned his gaze back to Kat and frowned over the lowness of her bodice. Leaning close to her ear, he whispered. "Are ye using magic to cover more of yer bosom?"

"No," she said, irritation evident.

His chest tightened and he stared down at least one young courtier who kept looking over toward Kat. "Use yer magic to make it look higher."

Kat stared up into his scowl. "I'll have you know that in a few more decades, the style of necklines will dip to the nipple. Making this neckline quite modest."

His gaze moved down to her bodice. "Yer nipples," he said and swallowed hard.

"Perhaps I'm the one to start the trend," she said, but he could see the blush spread across her bare chest where a thin neckerchief just hid her cleft. Kat turned slightly so the right side of her face would be in shadow. The upswept hair style was lovely, but it didn't hide the scars. With the leers from the men in the hall, Toren knew she must be hiding them with her magic.

Briana and Lady Alexandria walked toward them, polite smiles intact, although Toren saw the hungry look in the lady's stare. She'd fallen into his bed once and he remembered it being a pleasant night, but that was all.

"There you are, Tor," Lady Alexandria said, her curls pulled high over her head like a pile of dark grapes. She gave a cursory glance at Kat but ignored her.

"Lady Alexandria," he said gruffly, "how fairs yer mother?"

A look of true sadness softened her face. "Not well. I will return to her bedside after speaking with the queen about a family issue." Lady Alexandria finally turned her attention to Kat. "Family is so important. And what of yours, Mistress Diciadain? Do you have any family?"

It was likely a ploy to get Kat to admit that she wasn't connected to anyone powerful. Toren glanced at her, ready to support whatever lie she said to anyone except the queen.

Unshed tears made her eyes look like they were made of glass, reflecting the low candlelight in the room. The woman had stolen from him, run across a ballroom nearly naked, held her own against his fury, and come up with a plan on the spot under the hostile scrutiny of the most powerful woman in Christendom. Yet, a question from a lady had brought tears.

"Excuse me," she said, turning to stride away from their small group.

CHAPTER NINE
HOMESICK

Kat strode toward the alcove that led to the stairs beyond. *Do you have any family?* The woman's question had been asked to make Kat feel unworthy or small in this grand court. But Kat had been made to feel less-than most of her life. That wasn't what had made Kat's eyes sting with tears she'd had to hide behind a thread of magic. All thoughts of exploring the artifacts surrounding her had washed away with a wave of homesickness.

Princess Clara and sick Jimmy, her preteen girls acting ten years older in the new full-length bathroom mirrors. Would Joseph pass his math test without her? She'd been gone half a day, but that was over four hundred years in the future. So they couldn't miss her, right? Not like she was missing them, anyway.

"Ye're sad." Toren's words slid along her back from behind.

She turned, her hand pressing against the rough plastered wall outside the Great Hall. Inside the chairs around a central dining table were quickly filling with velvet and lace, starched neck cuffs and opulent jewelry-laden courtiers. A quartet of musicians began playing a light tune in one corner.

In the alcove, Tor stepped next to her without touching.

"We left my home on a Sunday night, so it could be a Monday night at home," she mumbled and blinked to clear her eyes. "Movie night."

Toren said nothing, just waited. Kat curled her fingers against the wall. "The children know to get their schoolwork done as soon as they get home. Then we all get in our pajamas around five o'clock, make popcorn, and watch a movie together on pillows and blankets spread in the main room. Tonight we were to watch *Mary Poppins* at the first showing and then the classic *Jaws* movie at the second showing for the older kids."

Kat watched Briana sit down opposite a man who looked remarkably like Toren, but without Toren's large biceps. Instead of his serious face, the younger man had an easy smile.

"It makes Mondays more bearable," she said.

"Ye haven't missed it yet." Toren stared outward next to her. "The movie night won't happen for several centuries."

The bizarre timeline and the fact that all her children's ancestors weren't even born yet didn't help. They seemed even farther away.

Briana, the younger man, and Lady Alexandria all turned in their direction. Briana waved them over with an impatient smile.

"Perhaps food will help," Toren said, putting his arm out. "It has been centuries since ye've eaten."

She snorted softly but took his arm, letting him lead her across the room. Her magic easily hid the redness she could feel in her eyes, and she raised the line of her bodice an inch. *For myself, not because Toren wanted me to.* Investigating genuine Tudor food would hopefully take her mind off her children, her family.

"Briana, do me the honor of introducing me to yer new friend." The man across the table said and stood.

"She is mine, Eagan." Toren's voice ripped through the polite conversation along both sides of the table, and everyone looked toward them.

Kat threw up another layer of magic to hide the heat climbing her neck like stinging ants. She would have smacked Toren's arm, but the move would probably cause a scandal in this setting. She'd have to remember to smack him later.

A teasing grin quickly covered Eagan's surprise. "Welcome to the queen's court, Lady Mine. Please excuse my very loud brother." He winked at Kat. "He tends to growl."

Several guests tittered, hiding their smiles behind goblets and bites of food.

"Actually," Briana chimed in, "Tor's betrothed has an unusual name, Mistress Katell Diciadain."

Eagan froze for a few seconds, and then his brows rose. "Betrothed? To Mistress Wednesday?"

Kat felt the burn of thirty pairs of eyes on her.

"Wait until Maxwell hears of this," one man said.

"Wait until Elizabeth hears," a woman whispered in the silence.

Toren slammed his goblet down on the oak table. Briana and Eagan looked unfazed.

"I have spoken to the queen, and she is investigating Lord Maxwell's absurd claim. Mistress Diciadain and I were betrothed before I heard of Lady Maxwell's petition." Toren's gaze moved down the row of shocked onlookers. Perhaps such juicy gossip wasn't usually thrown out to the ravenous courtiers.

Toren's eyes held the glint of a caged tiger Kat had seen at the zoo when she'd taken the children last spring. It had walked along the perimeter, its great tail twitching. Just like the big cat, Toren watched his peers, daring them to poke a finger between the bars.

"A toast then," Eagan called, breaking the stillness. He raised his goblet. "To ye, Brother, and yer lady love." He smiled at Kat. "Slainte mhor!" he called in Gaelic. "Good health!"

Briana raised her goblet but whispered in Kat's ear. "Pish." She shook her head. "My brothers always cause an uproar when they're forced to attend court." Most of the table mumbled good wishes and drank long.

The gelatinous meats made Kat reach for the warm yeast rolls and fresh butter instead. She found it difficult to eat with so many curious eyes, and the food was more like a display in a museum than appetizing. And then there was Toren. He sat next to her, his hard thigh pushing against her own through the layers of petticoats, making her heart speed. His elbow brushed against her full sleeves from time to time, and Kat noticed every single touch.

He spoke occasionally to Eagan across the table. Briana chattered pleasantly. Each time Kat leaned a bit forward to reach for something, Toren's words halted. At one point, Kat laughed at a witty retort by Briana to a brotherly insult from Eagan. Toren's breath caught in his throat, and he coughed.

She turned to him. "Are you choking on a chicken bone or something?"

"Yer bosom," he murmured.

Kat glanced down expecting her nipples to have popped out, but the lace kept its place just above indecency. "It is covered."

"Barely."

"Only to you," she whispered back. "To everyone else it sits halfway to my neck."

"Are ye certain?"

"Everyone would be staring at me if it wasn't in place."

"Not with me next to ye." He paused to watch the gazes of several men "Ye could be sitting here naked next to me, and they wouldn't dare to stare," he boasted darkly.

Kat couldn't think of a retort with Toren's rock-hard thigh pushed against her leg. Her leg pushed back with equal pressure, and her body warmed. It must be her lack of sexual release that revved her body into humming every time Toren touched or even looked at her. He was like a hero in the romance books she'd devoured over the years.

Kat sat there wishing for a cold swim and a bowl of cookie dough ice cream. She took another sip of the dry wine. *Feck it.* She could have him in this century. Why not be rid of her virginity? Sex would no doubt involve face touching, and she hadn't allowed anyone to get close enough to feel her scars. But Toren saw them no matter how much magic she used. Would he be interested in sleeping with someone like her? A scarred twenty-six-year-old virgin?

Toren leaned slightly towards her ear. "Ye look flushed." His voice held concern.

"I'm not used to drinking alcohol," she murmured.

"The water is unsafe, especially to yer twenty-first-century gut."

"I know, but by the end of dinner, you'll have to carry me to your sister's room."

Toren placed an orange and several other juice-filled fruits on her plate. "As much as I wouldn't mind carrying ye to *my* room," he said stressing the word, "I would not have ye ill." His breath moved along her earlobe, tickling the sensitive skin.

She kept her chin forward so that he couldn't view the right side of her cheek and jaw. With his gaze searching her face, she felt more naked now than when she'd been in her Wednesday knickers and bra.

"How is it that you can see through my magic?" she whispered.

He shrugged and turned back to his plate, taking a bite of the venison pie that he'd heaped there.

Kat glanced down at the mountain of food. "Hungry?"

"It's been five years since I've feasted on food with true flavors." He took a roll and broke it open to spread some fresh butter on it. "Nothing but flour, water, yeast, and sweet churned butter."

Kat watched him savor the simple roll. The sweet butter caught on his upper lip, which he licked. Kat swallowed hard and looked away. "You missed all this," she said indicating the Great Hall.

"Nay." He shook his head slightly, speaking low. "Not the court, but the century, aye, some of it." He took a drink of the wine, a smile on his lips. "Although I'd almost give up this century for a lifetime of steaming hot showers."

Kat smiled and took a bite of orange, enjoying his relaxed banter much more than his frowns and growls. Food certainly helped Toren's attitude. The man got hangry.

"What are ye two whispering about?" Eagan asked, glancing between them with an odd expression.

Toren just grunted and continued to delve into his plate. Eagan looked at Kat. "I don't remember the last time I saw my brother smile." Eagan tipped his head toward her. "Mistress Diciadain, ye are a most remarkable lass."

Dinner concluded after rounds of wine, grease-laden food, and courtly conversation that kept Kat and Toren mostly silent. Kat had stuck to eating the few vegetable and fruit dishes and bread. The several goblets of wine made the world a bit unsteady, and before she knew it Toren was walking her down the many corridors to his sister's chamber.

"...ten, eleven, twelve—"

"What are ye counting?" Toren asked, his arm under her hand like a rock holding her out of the sea.

"Shhh. Thirteen, fourteen..." She stopped counting when he stopped walking.

"This is Briana's chamber. She has agreed to let ye share with her to keep yer reputation pure."

"Fourteen doors from the archway," Kat said glancing at the wall opposite. "Across from the picture of an odd little man feeding grapes to a...toad."

Toren looked at the oil painting and then nodded to Briana's door. "After living in yer world, I do believe numbers on doors would help greatly."

Kat let the wall hold her up as she studied Toren. The wine had relaxed her immensely. Was she drunk? She hadn't been drunk since uni.

Tor's small smile gave his dangerous features a seductive cast in the glow of the sconce. Kat reached up and touched his cheek, avoiding his scar. He smelled of wine and spice and warm man. His body, tall and solid, filled the space between them.

"Ye can touch it, lass." His deep voice sent a chill down Kat's body, hardening her nipples.

She cleared her throat. "Touch it?" Was he talking about the erection Kat assumed she'd see straining his breeches if she looked down? Or was the wine making her feel heat in his words and touch?

Toren took her cold fingers in his warm hand. She held her breath as he raised them to his jaw to touch the scar there. "It pains me none now."

Kat inhaled deeply, keeping still for a moment. Her finger trailed down the thick white line etched with smaller lines where a needle had sewn the flesh back together. She marveled at the strength she could feel underneath and in his solid jaw. Toren made a small growling sound and pulled back. He glanced up and down the stone corridor, then pushed open his sister's door and pulled Kat within.

It was obviously empty, and they'd left Briana chatting happily below. Toren pressed Kat against the inside door, blocking any other from entering, and stared down at her. He searched her face, and the silence between them became too much for Kat.

"How did you get it?" she asked, her gaze falling on his scar.

The fire in Toren's eyes died to cool apathy, and he stepped away from her light touch. Toren turned away, and Kat felt his distance like a blast of cold wind. He walked to the dying fire and rekindled it with the iron poker, throwing on some peat squares that sat nearby. "The man I lived with, Hughe Maxwell, believed in harsh punishment."

"You received that as a child?"

He turned at her horrified tone. "A child by yer century's standards, a young man in mine."

"And you, as a young man, deserved a slice across your cheek that required stitches?"

He shrugged. "It taught me much."

"Much about what?" Kat couldn't keep the anger from her voice. A boy could marry as a man as early as fourteen in Tudor England. But he was still a child, making child mistakes.

"About whom I couldn't trust." He grinned then, though his eyes remained cold. "But that was long ago." He walked back. Toren's body shadowed hers. Raising his hand, he caught a curl along her cheek, sliding his fingers over it. The fire crackled behind. "I would rather speak of now, lass."

His fingers barely touched her, but the effect of his closeness was like a shock on her system. One moment she was filled with anger at the obvious injustice of his upbringing, the next she was washed in his scent, in his presence. She wanted to protect the boy he'd been and yet welcomed his protection in this amazingly bizarre world she'd been thrust into. Her emotions tumbled about, loosened with the glasses of wine.

"Then speak of now," she said, her words breathless.

His fingers dropped to his side, and he stared deeply into her eyes. "I feel a strange pull on me, and I know ye possess magic. Have ye bespelled me? Made my body heat just looking at ye?"

She stared, trying to comprehend his words. They weren't coming from a modern man who threw around words like 'bespelled' to be whimsically romantic.

He continued when she didn't respond. "My heart beats faster when ye speak, as if ye were a siren singing me to my death."

"You are... accusing me of casting a love spell on you?" Kat's breasts pressed against the lace edge of her neckline with each of her deep breaths.

"I have never wanted to kiss a woman more than I do now." His ruggedly handsome face was so close to her own.

"I have cast no spell," she whispered. "I don't even know how."

"May I?"

She wasn't quite certain what he was asking. Did men ask to merely kiss? But Kat decided right there that whatever he was asking, she wanted to say yes.

"Aye," she said, using the archaic word that seemed right. If she had fallen into one of her old romance novels, then she would play the part.

Toren stepped into her, his warm, powerful body against hers. His lips pressed against hers, moving from sweet to seductive in seconds. Kat instinctually tilted her face, the kiss sweeping her away. His arms encircled her, holding her steady as her insides melted into hot liquid, sliding down to pool in her abdomen and aching between her legs. A dampness grew, making her wish she'd saved the Wednesday underwear instead of going authentically naked under the petticoats.

Kat placed a hand on his chest to steady herself and felt his rapid heartbeat against it. Her fingers curled into the fine linen of his tunic under his open jacket as she slanted against his lips. He made a growling sound in the back of his throat. The knowledge that she was affecting him filled her with confidence, and she wrapped an arm around the back of his neck, kissing with wild abandon. Her fingers splayed through his hair, and she felt him dislodging the pins from her own hair until its weight pulled it down.

She stroked his broad shoulders, running her hands along the muscles of his biceps. They were solid and smooth, like an Olympic swimmer. Not like the steroid-induced bulk of some weightlifter in a gym.

"Aye, lass," he said and moved his hand to the low neckline, his warm fingers caressing the bare skin there and then sliding up her neck. "Ye've bewitched me." He didn't sound angry about his conclusion. Quite the opposite, and his words fed the trail of fire from her ear down through her core.

This was it. She wouldn't stop him. For once and for all she'd give someone her blasted virginity. So what if the wine was peeling away her inhibitions. She'd decided to do this with Toren before the wine.

Toren's hand moved up to cup both sides of her face, his open palms on her cheeks. She felt it against her right cheek. Instantly Kat yanked back from his grip, her flaming body going cold, leaving only the ache of loss instead of passion.

"Och lass, do the scars still pain ye?"

Kat turned away even though there wasn't anywhere she could go with his body all around her. *Trapped*.

Anger flared up inside. "No, they don't hurt." She answered and combed hair over her shoulder into a protective shield. She pushed against his arm, and he let her leave the circle he'd created. "I just don't..." She hesitated, not wanting to look at him. "I don't want you touching them."

"Ye hide them." He waved his hand. "With yer magic, so others don't see them."

"But somehow you can," she said, her frustration making her words into sharp chips. Why was she angry? Toren was probably the only man who saw them and still wanted her.

"A burn when ye were a wee lass?" He took a step closer.

She sighed softly. "Yes." The irony wasn't lost on her. She'd been ready to give him her body, but she was reluctant to talk about her foolish scars.

"Who did this to ye?" he asked. His jaw seemed to harden as if he would pledge to duel some villain for the misdeed.

The years of regret held a grip on Kat. Why had she pulled the pan with the sizzling grease down from the shelf? Sister Joan had warned her to stay away. The nun had put it up high to keep away from the children while it cooled.

"No one did this to me," she mumbled. "I was a stupid, curious kid who wanted to cook her own eggs."

"It could have killed ye." He leaned forward to see past her hair, but he kept his distance.

"My century has better medical care."

Toren crossed his arms over his chest. "When did ye start hiding them?"

Kat used her thumbs and forefingers to yank up the too-low neckline and strode to the small cut window. She couldn't see past the thick glass to the night beyond. Instead, it acted like a mirror, reflecting her scarred face, warping it even more in the old, wavering glass.

"Long ago." She remembered precisely when she'd begun the glamour that made the scars look like they were healing away to nothing. She'd just turned ten and had asked Sister Susanna to teach her to tame her red-gold hair that curled every which way.

A new boy, Kevin, had arrived at the orphanage soon after she'd left the hospital. He was already a teenager and wore his dark hair so that it draped over his eyes like he didn't care what the world thought of him. In a black tee and jeans, watching him skateboard before the children's home, he'd looked like a hero to Kat. Her crush on him had been immediate and intense when he'd smiled at her.

Sister Susanna had fashioned a beautiful French braid one day in Kat's hair, and Kat had walked toward Kevin's room in hopes he'd happen to see. Coming up to the open door she'd overheard him talking with an older girl about Halloween costumes they wanted to make.

"I want to get that gnarly looking gross stuff to stick on my face," he'd said. "So I can look like some burnt-up dead guy."

"You mean like Kat." The older girl had laughed, causing Kat to pull back into the shadows and turn on her invisibility.

Kevin laughed. "Yea, like Kat," he'd said.

Their cruel words had jabbed deep into her heart, like shattered glass. Each time she repeated them to herself the shards had pushed deeper still until they'd become a part of her.

Kat spotted the light from a lantern outside as it bobbed along the cobbled pathway, and she concentrated on keeping the old tears of a foolish ten-year-old at bay. "A long time ago, when I didn't want to look like a monster anymore."

Kat felt his nearness even though he made no sound. His hand caught at the loose curls falling between her shoulder blades. "A monster," he said, without pity or surprise. Slowly he turned her towards him until she had to look up into his face or look like a coward. "Monsters, lass, are scarred on the inside." He ran a thumb over her bottom lip without looking at nor avoiding the right side of her face. "I've lived with them." He shook his head slightly. "Ye're not a monster."

Kat reached up and rubbed her upper arm where it tingled through the heavy brocade. She glanced at the spot where her dragonfly birthmark sat.

"Where is it?" the powerful voice echoed in the sparse room.

Toren whirled around, blocking Kat's body with his own. "Witch!" he growled.

CHAPTER TEN
WITCHY VISIT

"Be gone," Toren yelled. "Ye will not take me again."

Kat peeked from under Toren's arm to see the Wiccan priestess, Drakkina, floating like a ghost near the door. Ethereal dragonflies flitted around her long floating hair. Her smooth cheeks pulled down into a frown, making the ageless face wise and angry like some furious goddess.

"Where is my dragonfly?" Drakkina glanced around the room. "And put that dagger away before you cut someone. It won't do any good against me," she said, dissolving in the air and reappearing closer to them. She peered around Toren's massive frame, but he moved to block Kat.

"Step down, warrior." Drakkina's voice seemed to fill the room. "I'm not sending anyone anywhere." She squinted her eyes, "not right now, anyway."

"Foking hell," he said.

Drakkina ignored him and moved around to look at Kat. "Katell, I must speak with you, but first, where in the name of the goddess is the necklace?"

Kat felt more than saw the muscles in Toren's back clench as the apparition addressed her as if they knew one another.

"Who are you?" Kat asked, although she remembered the woman from her dreams.

"Come child, pay attention when I tell you something," the old woman admonished. Her form had solidified since she'd lowered to the floor; the swirls of her dress still moved on a nonexistent breeze across the stone.

Kat looked at Toren, whose face was pinched in fury and suspicion. "I've seen her in dreams." She shook her head. "That is all." Yet his gaze still asked if she were some type of traitor.

Kat looked back at the woman, pulling the details from the dreams that were too clear and memorable to be true dreams. "You are Drakkina, and taught my parents how to use their magic," she answered. She stepped to the side of Toren, and he didn't stop her.

"So I am," Drakkina answered, her eyes scanning the room.

"Why are you"—Kat moved her hand around to indicate all that had happened to them—"involved with us?"

Drakkina looked at her. "You won't tell me where my dragonfly is until I answer your questions."

Kat gave a little smile.

"Damn stubborn children," Drakkina murmured. "All of you take after Druce. Gilla was much more compliant." Drakkina crossed her arms. "You need to know, anyway. I was but waiting until I thought you were old enough to comprehend the gravity of the situation."

"What situation, bana-bhuidseach?" Toren ground out, his body in a primed state, ready to strike.

Drakkina narrowed her eyes at Toren. "I prefer Wiccan Priestess, Highlander. Always suspicious, these soul mates."

"Soul mates?" Kat asked.

"The situation?" Toren asked at the same time.

Drakkina looked between them and smiled. "Yes, you two will do well together, I think."

"Ye talk in riddles," Toren said, sheathing his blade and pulling Kat into his side.

Drakkina frowned again. "I will explain, but there is not much time for questions." She looked at Kat. "That tornado was a tempest of pure evil." She moved her arms like a tumbling storm. "A conglomeration of thirteen demonic souls seeking to break free of their binding and steal magic to increase their power. A storm like that killed your father and mother, Katell. Do you remember the night Gilla sent you away? The night you arrived at the orphanage?"

Kat's hand instinctively clutched around the moonstone resting against her chest. "I...remember darkness." She looked back up. "And melting, like when you sent us here."

Drakkina nodded. "I sent you two here the same way Gilla saved you on that night, threading you through time. If she hadn't sent her magic with each of you, the demons would have absorbed it when they killed her."

It was one thing to suspect her mother had died, but the conformation made Kat's chest tighten. "What would the demons have done if they absorbed her magic?" Kat asked, clasping the moonstone hanging around her neck. She had only the faintest memory of her strong, beautiful mother. And where were her sisters?

Drakkina's voice deepened. "Life for humans will become like the Hell your people fear if they capture Gilla's power. Combined with Druce's magic, the demons could control time."

"Do you know where my sisters are?" Kat asked.

Drakkina frowned with fierce intensity. "Do you know what controlling time *means*?"

"Probably stealing people from their natural time and throwing them somewhere else without their permission," Tor said. "Perhaps *ye* are a demon."

Drakkina waved her hand. "When I scry the future in the great oracle, one probable outcome surfaces. The demons will collapse all the times on top of one another." Her voice grew darker, more ominous, sending chills through Kat. She wrapped her arms around herself.

Drakkina's body faded and grew solid again as she spoke. "All the people who have been will suddenly populate this little planet. People piled on top of one another, fighting for resources. Most will be consumed by the evil. Those who survive will hide in darkness and fear in a timeless plane of existence until they too are captured and consumed. Then the demons will populate this world with their own and humankind will cease to exist, except for the few they keep around to play with."

"By consumed," Kat asked, swallowing the bile at the back of her throat, "you mean eaten?"

"Eaten, played with, tortured, raped, used in some way," Drakkina answered slowly.

"What about God?" Kat asked. "If these"—she moved her hands around—"demons are pure evil and are swallowing up everyone on Earth, wouldn't God step in?"

Drakkina looked at her. "As I understand it, your God of Light gave up His right to interfere when He gave you all free will."

"So God just abandons us," Kat said and crossed her arms.

"Perhaps, perhaps not," Drakkina said cryptically. "He's allowed you and your sisters to survive and eventually fight for the Light. He's allowing me to guide—"

"How do I fight these demons?" Toren asked, frown still in place, eyes narrowed as if he judged the truth in the threat to be genuine.

Drakkina shook her head. "It's not time to fight them, warrior, but one day it will be. And I need the combined strength of Katell's sisters with their soul mates to conquer them. They must be conquered with something stronger than steel blades."

"What do you mean by soul mates?" Kat asked, glancing at Toren, whose hands were fisted.

Drakkina paused as if to choose her words carefully. "Each of Gilla's children has a partner, one they are destined to be with. Their love together is stronger than either one of them alone. I must find each of you and make sure you find your soul mate so that you will be ready for the final battle against this unimaginable evil."

Kat swallowed hard. "And...and you think Toren MacCallum from the sixteenth century is my soul mate?" The last two words came out a bit breathless. "Which is why you stole him from his home and sent him to mine," Kat finished softly.

"He can see through your magic, can't he?" Drakkina said.

Kat's heart pounded. "Yes."

Drakkina exhaled with great relief. "Then I wasn't wrong, he is your fated partner. It's been the same with all your sisters. Their magic does not work on their soul mates."

"Mother Mary," Kat said, looking at Toren, "It's my fault she stole –"

"Baa!" Drakkina shouted, waving her hands. "There is no fault, there is only what must be done." She looked at Toren. "The fates split the two of you." She threw her hands out to either side, floating a bit off the ground. The dragonflies buzzed around as if they shared her annoyance. "I've learned it's best not to interfere in love, but four hundred years is a big chasm for mortals to cross to find one another."

"Ye plucked me away from my clan, my family." Toren's stony voice rang through the room. He didn't yell, but the anger behind his words made Kat's heart pound. "Mac an donais," he swore and ran a hand through his hair. "Why didn't ye tell me to go find Kat? Ye landed me in Oxford with no direction."

"She was attending college there," Drakkina countered.

"Ye could have given me her name."

"Serena and Merewin taught me it was best to let things happen naturally," Drakkina said, crossing her arms. "I believe they're right. Soul mates are drawn to one another."

"Naturally?" Kat asked with a frown. *This is ludicrous.* "How could moving someone over four centuries in the future be natural in any way?"

"I returned him," Drakkina said defensively.

Kat rubbed her hands over her face. Perhaps when she opened her eyes again, she'd wake and be back in bed at the orphanage. But when she opened her eyes, she was still in Briana MacCallum's room in a Tudor-era palace.

"And me with him," Kat said. "You've taken me from my home and family."

"You're an orphan; you have no family," Drakkina said, flipping her hand in the air.

Kat's eyes narrowed as rage bubbled up past her bewilderment. "I have twelve children and a friend who is as close to me as a sister back in the twenty-first century." Kat felt tears well up, angry tears. "I love them, each one of them, with all my heart."

"How could you love twelve"—Drakkina paused—"no, thirteen people with all your heart? Love is rarer than that."

"You couldn't have found me a soul mate in the twenty-first century?" Kat's fists balled up against her gown.

"The Oracle showed me him." Drakkina pointed a long finger in Toren's direction.

"You need to return me." Kat loved history, but being forced into the past without a way to return made her stomach roll with homesickness and fury.

"You two will learn to love one another," Drakkina said.

"You know nothing about love." Kat glared at the wavering apparition. "I know every one of those kids; I know their hearts, their fears." She thumped her chest. "I know their loneliness. And I love every single one of them." Kat ignored the tear that had escaped. "If you ever want to see that necklace again, old woman, you better send me back to my children."

Toren probably thought she was a child throwing a tantrum, but she didn't care. She would go home to her kids, no matter what. Soul mate or not, end of the world or not.

End of the world. The steam flowing through Kat tamped down, and her shoulders sagged. If the witch was right, the end of the world meant the end of her kids, end of her family in any century.

She exhaled, studying the woman who had come to her in dreams. "Couldn't you just pull each of us from our centuries so we can be together when the time comes to fight? Leave us in our homes until then. A long-distance soul mate thing," Kat said and glanced at Toren who resembled a god carved from smooth marble. Hopefully the dimness of the room hid her blush.

Drakkina looked between them, her solemn face breaking into a slight grin. "I believe you know less about loving a man than I do, daughter of Gilla."

Rap! Rap! Someone knocked on the door. Drakkina's body faded. Only her voice remained in the cold room. "Bring the dragonfly to me and you can go home."

"Briana," a man called from outside the door. "Are ye in there?"

"Eagan," Toren said as he approached the door. He glanced back over his shoulder. "Shield yer bosom," he commanded and pulled the door open, allowing his brother entrance.

Shamed and still angry, Kat turned entirely invisible and moved to a corner.

Eagan walked in and looked around. "Here alone, Tor? I thought ye'd be wrapped around yer betrothed."

Toren glanced at Kat. She held a finger to her lips, and he turned back to his brother. "Is that why ye came pounding on the door? To catch some illicit—"

"There is talk that ye've broken Briana's betrothal with the Fergus Campbell," Eagan interrupted.

Toren swore and grabbed the back of his neck, pinching there as if his muscles ached. "She doesn't want to marry him."

"We all know she doesn't want to marry the Campbell, but ye've always supported Da's command that she marry to secure the boundaries."

"Do ye back me in this, Eagan? It will mean unrest, possible war with the Campbells."

Kat couldn't see Toren's face as he stared into his brother's eyes. She was a fly on the wall in her invisible state, listening and hoping Toren was being truthful.

Eagan snorted. "Give me the word, brother, and I'd be happy to relieve the Campbells of some of their cattle." But then his smile fell when Toren didn't say anything. "Ye're serious, Brother?"

"Aye."

Eaden whooped. He grabbed Toren's shoulders. "Bless ye, Brother! Ye've saved Briana." He pushed against Toren as if to shake him, but Toren's large frame barely moved. "Ye've really saved her, Tor."

Kat's heart squeezed. Toren wouldn't trap his sister into a loveless, possibly brutal marriage. Despite his outward steely composure, the man had a tender heart. *Soul mate? Could he be?*

Toren crossed his arms. "I've come to that conclusion, too. No good will come of Briana's union to the Campbells, but I didn't want the whole court talking of it, especially before ye could get Briana home and alert our men."

Eagan frowned. "I thought she would be here. Perhaps she's with yer Kat?"

Kat squeezed her moonstone absently. Could Briana be in danger?

"I've just seen Kat, and Briana wasn't with her," Toren said. "Check the feasting hall, perhaps she lingered over the wine. I will walk the grounds." Toren threw the door wide to find a liveried servant with his knuckles raised to knock. Toren stopped, and Eagan nearly ran into him.

The man dressed up like a peacock in the colors of Elizabeth's household lowered his hand, his other behind his back. "Her Majesty Queen Elizabeth requests the presence of Toren MacCallum. Now."

CHAPTER ELEVEN
TAKEN

Toren exhaled. "Eagan, check the Great Hall and walk the grounds. I must deal with this Maxwell issue now it seems."

"Or lose yer head." Eagan grabbed Toren's arm. "Is it true, what Maxwell says?" His voice was low so the servant who had walked farther down the corridor couldn't hear him. "That ye fathered Margaret's child?"

Toren turned at the anger he heard under Eagan's words, his gut tightening. "Nay, I have never bedded Margaret. He lies about it, and she is too much the mouse to correct him."

Eagan's stance relaxed a bit. "He speaks as if it's a known truth."

"When has Maxwell told the truth when a lie better suits his purposes?"

Eagan frowned. "I hate that Margaret lives under the tyranny of that man."

"She should speak up, refute him. I did."

"And ye have the scars to prove it," Eagan said, shaking his head. "Margaret is a gentle lady."

Toren searched his brother's eyes. "Ye care for her? For Margaret Maxwell?" The servant cleared his throat down the hall. "Bloody hell. Later we will talk. Go find Briana."

Eagan strode past Toren down the hall.

Toren glanced back over his shoulder into the room. Kat stood near the bed. "Stay here. If anyone comes, turn invisible, unless 'tis Briana." He turned back around, then paused in the act of pulling the door shut. He looked right at her. "Do not let the witch take ye."

Without waiting for a retort or curse from Kat, Toren shut the door and walked briskly after the servant. He'd never felt so powerless, even under the rule of Hughe Maxwell. How could he keep Kat, or himself, in this century? How could he protect them from the witch? And then there was the world the crone foretold. How could he protect his clan and his world from the evil that hunted Kat for her magic?

"Daingead," he murmured, the word lost under the sound of his boots along the corridor. She'd been the reason for his abduction, the reason he'd lived five long years desperate to find a way home.

He rubbed a hand down his short beard. Without his time researching in the twenty-first century, he'd never have discovered that his sister was to be murdered by her Campbell husband before he took over the MacCallum holdings. He'd been taken from his time, but he'd seen what the future held if he followed his father's dictates upon his death. This was a second chance.

Kat had lied to him, stolen from him, tried to trick him. She had spirit and passion. He'd seen her warrior strength in the actions to save her orphanage and in trying to outwit him. And the love she felt for her children had been evident in her earlier tears and passionate speech to the crone.

And she was to be his soul mate? His partner to battle against these demons. Toren breathed deeply, annoyed at the tightness he felt in his chest. How to save his clan and protect the world and Kat? And just as important, how could he keep Kat here with him in his century?

———◦———

"Are ye certain of this plan, Maxwell?" Fergus Campbell twisted the leather strap between his large, dirty hands and slapped his leg. A whimper pulled his gaze to the corner of the dark horse stall.

"She's waking," Hughe Maxwell said. "You must get her out of London, back to your own land before Toren and Eagan catch on that she's missing." His words were clipped with irritation. The man should already have the MacCallum chit on her way out of London.

"Ye think I don't know the danger I'm in with those two?" Fergus asked. He swore and slapped his leg with the strap. "I had it all laid out in honest fashion, a betrothal worked out with her father and then Toren." Fergus spit on the dirt again, his fist slamming into the wooden stall door. "And suddenly Toren changes his mind," he growled low, his barbaric temper about to explode. "The bastard is going against the dying wishes of his father."

"What did you do to make him change his mind?" Hughe asked, accusation tempered by his lowered voice. The idiot must have done something, given the girl a fright or gotten drunk enough to brag about his infamous past.

"Nothing!" Fergus hit the wood again, grimaced, and looked at his bloodied knuckles.

"Fool," Hughe said. "Get control and take the girl away. Now."

Fergus eyed the whimpering woman in the dark corner. "I could hit something softer," he murmured.

Hughe grabbed his arm, shaking some sense into the tall, slender man. "Not until you are away."

Fergus shook Hughe's hand off his arm. "MacCallum suddenly decided I might be dangerous to her. That's what my paid contact heard when listening outside Elizabeth's privy chamber."

"Someone must have seen your temper or heard of it," Maxwell said.

Fergus kicked the stall door. "And now I've abducted his sister. He'll be after me." He rubbed palms against his coat, his red face distraught. He glanced at the doors to the barn as if expecting one of the MacCallum brothers to be standing there ready to skewer him.

Hughe snapped in front of Fergus's face to get his attention. "Listen. You took her because you love her and when you caught the news that the betrothal might be negated, you couldn't help but steal her away and marry her before God."

Fergus looked heavenward. "They won't believe it."

Hughe's voice lowered into a calm, severe command. "You agreed to the plan, Campbell, for the good of us both."

Fergus shifted back and forth as if he needed to take a piss.

"Stick to the plan, Campbell," Hughe said. "You marry Briana, and I will see Toren MacCallum married to Margaret. With a foot in the door on MacCallum land and Briana held within your walls, we will undercut the strength of Toren and Eagan. Clan MacCallum will be undone, and you will have their grazing pastures all the way to the sea."

"And ye will have the rest," Fergus said. His eyes glanced to the back of the stall where Briana MacCallum lay bound and gagged.

Hughe heard her scratching around as if trying to find a weapon to hold with her tied hands.

"I would think that the grazing lands and a lovely wife will see you happy enough," Hughe said. The temperamental young man nodded absently, and Hughe noticed that he adjusted what was probably an erection under his breeches. Briana MacCallum wouldn't be a virgin for much longer.

"Take the girl," Hughe said, "before her brothers find her and hang you from the rafters. I will stay behind and act helpful, sending them in the wrong direction. And I need to press Elizabeth on my claim to see MacCallum wed to Margaret."

"Ye're a colder bastard than I, Maxwell, throwing yer own daughter to the enemy ye plan to destroy. What will become of her then?"

Hughe barely thought of his daughter, so meek and such a disappointment. "She's obedient, I raised her that way."

"I guess it is a good thing she survived the fire then, so ye could use her. With yer son ye wouldn't be able to get a foothold into their clan."

Hughe slid his dagger free and with a snap of his wrist, launched it through the air. *Whump.* The six-inch blade stuck into the wooden support next to Fergus's shoulder.

"Dhia, Maxwell!" Fergus croaked, jumping sideways.

Hughe Maxwell's kept his voice as flat as week-old death as he walked forward. "If she had died instead of Edward, I would not be at war with Toren MacCallum." He looked hard at Fergus while he yanked the dagger free of the wood. "Do not speak of my son, Campbell. Get your bride and head for the outskirts of London. My men wait there to escort you north."

"Where my men wait," Fergus mumbled under his breath, as he walked into the stall. Fergus's voice strengthened, and Hughe could hear his leer. "Och but 'tis good to see ye, Briana lass," he drawled out to the bound girl in the corner. "And just how I like ye. Tied up and helpless."

"Stay here," Kat mimicked Toren's command in a childish voice. "Bollocks! Briana's missing, Drakkina is demanding her necklace, and you're off to talk with one of the most fascinating monarchs in history, the history that I spent four years of my life studying!" Kat let anger roll out of her in the empty room as she paced.

At least she thought it was empty. Her birthmark didn't tingle or burn alerting her to Drakkina, so the witch must have moved on. Where to exactly, Kat had no idea. "Some temporal realm," she said flippantly, as she fought with the ties holding the large sleeves up on her shoulders. She grunted in frustration. Elizabethan clothing was exquisite, but not practical when one had to be literally tied and sewn into it, especially when one was raised in twenty-first century casuals.

At least she knew how the costumes were put together and could untangle herself from the layers. She found a small tailoring knife near the clothes press to snip the threads that the maid had sewn to hold her outer and inner petticoats in place. Reaching underneath, Kat untied the farthingale, letting it fall from her hips with the two heavy layers. She stepped out of the voluminous puddle that looked like a small mountain rising from the floorboards. Untying the corset, Kat took a full breath. How she longed for her Oxford sweatshirt and joggers. She'd have to make do with the white linen smock that served as underwear in the sixteenth century. If Eagan returned, she would just make herself look dressed. Only Toren would see through her magic.

Kat found a warm cape in the clothes press and slipped it on, buttoning it before the polished glass mirror. Her fingers rose to her face, feeling the slight puffing of her dimpled skin on her right cheek that ran across to her hairline. He'd touched her ugliness when he'd kissed her. No one had touched her scars before. The few relationships she'd attempted were with men who seemed more inclined to running their hands across her chest than across her cheeks. Yet Toren had cradled her face in his hands, even with the rough skin.

Kat picked up the mound of damask and velvet, shaking each layer and smoothing them back into the wardrobe. Checking the trunks, she saw there were no breeches or hose, and her modern bra and Wednesday knickers were gone. She'd have to stay in the smock that looked like an old-fashioned nightgown and the cape. A pair of boots sat on the bottom of one trunk, and she pulled them on. They were just a little tight. She picked up the tailor's knife since there were no other weapons, although she certainly couldn't use it to kill anyone. What ramifications would occur if she killed someone whose great, great, great, great grandbaby did something important in history? She decided to leave the small blade behind.

Kat stepped out into the candlelit corridor and glanced both ways. *Empty.* Which way to go? She wasn't the best with direction and decided to turn the way Toren and Eagan had gone. Silently she counted the doors running down the hall but stopped to inspect one of the vibrant hanging tapestries. "So much more beautiful in full color," she whispered at the heavy stitching.

Kat paused at a dark staircase that wound downward. "Once more unto the breach," she quoted Shakespeare in a whisper. She would sneak around invisible, looking for Briana and listening to anything she could. Kat felt the rough wall as she descended, guarding her footing on the narrow rock slabs. There wouldn't be a handrail for another four hundred years.

She stopped and inhaled. *I'm standing in history.* A flutter of excitement tingled out from her middle. She reached a landing. Voices floated from the right, and she turned that way, keeping concealed. She was thirsty and would give anything for a bottle of water. Hopefully there was enough liquid in the fruit to keep her invisibility functioning. Or else she'd be the start of a ghost rumor at Hampton Court.

"The Spanish decided to wait out the winter, but it's already April. Elizabeth must dispatch the troops." A male voice spoke softly but with a vehemence that stopped Kat. They were discussing the Spanish Armada! Kat had written a paper on the famous sea battle. She'd love to pop in and tell them exactly what would happen, though perhaps that would change history, which she definitely didn't want to do. And they'd probably burn her for being a witch once events started to happen as predicted.

A second well-dressed man whispered back, moving his hands in a flurry of concern. "She says she doesn't want to pull her people away from their lives until she must." As long as nothing interfered, all would be well, and the English would win. Kat knew this, but Elizabeth didn't. She was a very brave woman and was always who Kat picked when asked who from history would she wish to spend a day with.

Despite the late hour, there were small groups of beautifully dressed people chatting in the halls. Some minstrels played in one large room where people danced. Kat stood at the arched opening into the room, entranced by the simple yet beautiful music, all played without synthesizers or amps. To get a taste of this back home she'd had to seek out Renaissance Faires that were often more touristy than accurate. *What a wonderful time period to visit.* Although she wouldn't want to live for long without hot showers, toilets, tampons, ibuprofen, and clean water.

"Sara, child where are you?" A richly garbed woman rounded the corner opposite the room, her head swiveling left to right. She had blond hair piled high on her head and wore her velvet gown gracefully. It was obviously tailored to fit her trim body to perfection, unlike the borrowed gown Kat had worn. "Where has that child gotten herself?" she murmured.

The clipping of a strong pace made Kat jump, and she turned to see Eagan striding toward the woman. "Lady Margaret," he said, and bowed his head. "Have ye seen my sister, Briana? She did not return to her rooms after the evening meal."

Margaret? This was the daughter of the devil? The one who supposedly had Toren's child?

"Nay, Master Eagan," she answered and glanced downward. Was that a blush? Blinking, she raised her gaze to his. "Have you seen my daughter, Sara? She's run off again."

Eagan grimaced. "Nay, I haven't." He lowered his voice. "Lady Margaret...why do ye say that Tor fathered the child when ye know that he did not?"

Seems that Toren's brother was as direct as Toren. Kat held her breath waiting for a reply.

"Excuse me, but I must find my child." She turned, striding away.

"He will not marry ye, Margaret," he said to her retreating figure as she all but scampered down the corridor calling Sara's name. "But I will," Eagan said softly as she moved out of earshot.

Kat's mouth dropped open. This was better than any period drama she'd streamed.

Eagan moved farther into the room, making inquiries about Briana. Kat stood still for several more minutes while her mind whirled around the social predicaments of Toren's family. And what about this devil that helped raise Toren? Where was he and what part did he play in this lie?

She pulled away from the archway, ready to look for Briana in the gardens. Being invisible kept her safe and allowed her to enter restricted places. She turned toward where she thought the front of the palace must be. She'd visited Hampton Court often, dreaming about the people who had walked the halls. Although this Hampton Court smelled a bit more "lived in." Fresh air would be welcome.

Kat turned down a short flight of stairs to a servant's door, and there on the bottom step sat a little girl leaning against the wall.

The girl turned in her direction at the sound of Kat's unconcealed footsteps. Kat let go of her shield, else she'd frighten the child who had obviously heard her. "Hello there," Kat said from two steps up. "Good eve," she corrected, remembering that hello wasn't used in greeting for another three hundred years.

The little girl scrambled to her feet. She was dressed like an adult so she must have been at least five years old. A raised reddish birthmark sat below her left eye. It looked like a strawberry hemangioma. Lizzie, one of Kat's children at the orphanage, had come to Sister Susanna's with one on her cheek. The doctors had told her it would eventually fade away, and it did, but not until Lizzie was eight and a half.

The child pulled her hair to fall in front of the quarter-sized birthmark. Kat squatted down so she was on the child's level. "Would you happen to be Lady Sara?"

Sara looked up, but she kept her focus downcast. "I am Sara, milady."

Kat smiled warmly. "Your mother is looking for you."

Sara nodded but gazed down at the steps before her. "I don't know how to find my mother," the child confided, glancing upward through her hair.

"Well then, we can stay together until we find her," Kat said and held out a hand. "My name is Kat"—she hesitated—"Kat Diciadain, but you may call me Kat."

Sara smiled timidly, still hiding half her face behind a swath of hair she seemed to have pulled free of her braid. The child touched Kat's hand with her small fingers. They were cold and thin. Kat wished she had some hot cocoa to give her. Sister Susanna had convinced Kat that all the wrongs of the world could be solved with a simple cup.

Sara stumbled as she walked up the steps.

"I can't imagine that you can see with your hair before your eyes. It is so dark here," Kat said, but Sara didn't do anything except lean more into her as they made it up the rest of the steps. "I don't mind your birthmark."

Sara paused and looked up at her. "Birthmark?"

Kat pushed back Sara's hair and looked at the hemangioma. It was red, even in the muted candlelight given off by one of the hallway sconces. "I've seen one before," Kat assured her. "And it faded away by the time the girl turned nine years old. How old are you?"

"Five years," Sara said, touching the raised mark. "My grandfather says I'm cursed." Her small voice caught at Kat's heart, and she bent down level with the child's eyes.

Kat pushed back her own hair and released the glamour she used to cover her scars. "People used to not want to touch me," she said while she tried to sound confident. Sara looked at her closely, studying the puckered skin. Would this child recoil from her like so many others? Kat's stomach tightened into a ball. "Unfortunately," Kat continued, "my scars won't fade away like yours will." Kat stood, turning her right cheek away from the girl. "I know, they make me ugly."

"I think you're beautiful, Mistress." The little girl tucked her hair behind her ears so she could see and clasped Kat's hand firmly. She allowed a small smile. "Do people stare at you?"

They continued walking to the corridor. "No because I cover my scars up," Kat said. Here she was trying to help this little girl understand that her birthmark didn't make her less of a person when all her life Kat had hidden her own scars because they made her ugly.

"With your hair?" Sara asked.

"Sometimes, but I also use heavy make...face paint to cover the scars so that they aren't that noticeable."

"My mother will not allow me to paint my face," Sara said.

Kat thought about the heavy paste favored in Elizabethan times, some of which included lead. "Your mother is right. You're too young, and like I said, your mark will fade within a couple more years."

The little girl huffed. "Years are long."

Kat squeezed her hand gently. "I know, but it will fade. And then people will only notice your kind heart because you'll remember what it's like to look different. You will be kind to those who suffer the same."

It was true. Kat knew firsthand what it was like to suffer stares and whispers. Those without magic to hide their scars were the brave ones. Kat's face flushed hot. Sara was forced to be brave while she hid.

Kat and Sara wandered down the long halls looking for familiar paintings and statues. The child talked of painting birds and flowers. Through their wanderings, Kat never saw Briana. When they approached others, the child would naturally quiet as if she were used to blending into the shadows. Kat also cloaked both of them with invisibility.

After a few times, Sara stopped and turned to Kat. "How do you do that?"

Sara had noticed? Since they were linked, the child should not have seen that she'd turned invisible.

"Do what?"

"Walk us right past people. Not one said a word to us. No stares, not even nods."

Kat breathed out a silent sigh and patted Sara's hand. "It's late. Everyone must be too tired to notice us."

That seemed to satisfy the girl, and they continued until Kat heard Margaret's desperate voice calling softly around a corner.

"Sara...Sara, where are you?"

Sara turned toward the voice and let go of Kat's hand, running down the hall. "Mama!"

Kat stood back silently watching. Should she leave or disappear? Margaret grabbed the little girl up in her arms. "Where have you been? You scared me half to the grave," she scolded but hugged Sara tightly. It was quite obvious that Margaret loved her little girl, legitimate or not, and with the devil's mark. "You didn't show your face to anyone, did you?"

Sara looked down at her feet. "I met a lady. She helped me find you." Sara turned to where Kat stood, but Kat had faded to invisibility. "Mistress Kat?"

Kat didn't say anything.

"Kat?" Margaret said and peered down the hall. "Did she say that she was friends with the MacCallums?"

"She did not say, Mama. But she did say that she knew a girl like me, who had a mark. And it went away when she turned nine years old."

Margaret smiled at her daughter. "Wouldn't that be wonderful." She pulled Sara into a hug. "We will beseech the Virgin Mother about it." She squinted to see down the dim corridor, her doe-like eyes raking along each stone. "Come, 'tis late." They turned and walked back down the other hall, and Kat listened to their footfalls fade to silence.

"Kat!"

Kat jumped at the deep voice. She whirled around and pushed against the wall, her heart pounding.

Toren's long legs ate up the distance between them. His thundering halted before her and he placed his hands on either side of her shoulders, palms against the wall. "When I say to stay in the room that is what I mean." His words were like weights bearing down on her. Toren grabbed her arms, and she jerked. But despite the fury in his voice, his hands were gentle. He dropped them and pulled his short cloak from his shoulders, draping it over her as if to hide the fact she was roaming the halls in her smock and robe. The added warmth from his body heat engulfed her, covering her with his fresh scent. "I find ye half dressed, alone in a dark, dangerous castle."

"There is no danger for me," she retorted. "I blend in with the walls, remember." She stared up at him and hoped her eyes weren't large with fear. She didn't fear him, but surprising her had set her heart racing. "Only you can see me."

"Ye weren't in Briana's room. Ye weren't in my room."

"Since I don't know where your room is, that was a very unlikely place to find me."

"Bloody hell, I thought the witch had stolen ye."

"I tried to find Briana and ended up finding Sara."

"Sara?"

"Your daughter."

"Daingead, Kat. Ye know that's a lie. I've never bedded Margaret Maxwell," he said as if he were tired of explaining. His jaw clenched, and he rubbed it as if it ached.

"I made certain Sara found her mother."

"Ye met Lady Maxwell?"

Kat shook her head. "She never saw me." Kat paused. "Margaret's quite lovely." She tilted her head, studying Toren.

"She's scared of her own shadow." He looked like he wanted to bite into an adder and shake it in his jaws.

"Sara doesn't seem too timid. I wonder who the father is?"

"'Tis not me."

He was still riled. Kat put her hand on his forearm, squeezing. "I believe you, but I hate to leave her in her grandfather's home. He told her that she's cursed."

Toren stared down at Kat's hand and then his gaze rose to hers. "Would ye have me wed her so I can save the child?"

The thought soured in Kat's stomach. "I didn't say that."

"We do not live in yer century, Kat, where government and lawmen can come and take a child out of a terrible home. In the sixteenth century, a child is just thankful to have food, a roof over its head, and a household free of plague. They may suffer silently, but they live."

Kat knew he was right. She'd studied history and knew the horrors children could face without an advocate. But it still made her sick to think of the children in poverty with no one to care for them. She glanced down. "At least Margaret loves her."

Toren pulled Kat along the hall. She wasn't sure where they were going, but she hoped it was a room where she could sit down. She was suddenly very tired of this long adventure. How many hours had passed since she'd woken in her sunny room at the orphanage?

He finally stopped before a door, and she realized she hadn't counted. It wasn't Briana's. "Where are we?"

"My room." The room seemed larger and had a big low-standing bed, its headboard pushed against one wall. A fire smoldered in the hearth, barely feeding the room with any warmth.

Toren left her sitting on the edge of the bed. Exhaustion pushed her over on one side. "I'm just resting my eyes for a minute." She blinked heavily, watching Toren toss some fuel on the fire and stir it up. She should see what fuel they were using. Peat, twigs, and wood? It was all so interesting. She yawned so wide it squeezed tears from her eyes. The comfortable weight of sleep pressed down on her, and she sighed into the soft throws.

CHAPTER TWELVE

MORE, BUT NOT THE MERRIER

Toren strode back into his room, exhaling his unacknowledged relief that Kat still slept there with him in the sixteenth century. He watched her slumber in the low wash of firelight as he stripped away the English clothes. The shadows cut across her face, and her chest rose and fell. She was beautiful, her hair fanned out across her cheek, her delicate hand relaxed against the coverlet. She shouldn't be here with the danger around him, but they were linked by the necklace and the witch, Drakkina.

Toren threw his tunic on over his head and grabbed the long length of plaid that he'd stored away in his clothes chest. Quickly pleating it on the floor, he wrapped it around him and secured it with a thick leather belt, throwing the sash over one shoulder. Och but it felt good to be back in his real clothes, the smell of clean wool and leather as strong a memory as Briana's homemade tarts.

Briana. Daingead. He must find her.

Toren bent over the gorgeous, magical lass in the bed. Kat's lips were parted just a bit, her dark lashes fanned against ivory skin. He wouldn't wake her. He'd just leave, let Eagan guard her until he brought Briana back.

Toren inhaled her scent—warm woman, spring flowers. "Slàinte mhór, lass," he whispered and began to turn. Kat pushed up immediately and glanced around. "What? Who needs me?"

"Hush, lass," Toren replied. "Go back to sleep."

Kat looked at him and then around the room. "Where am I?" Kat rubbed her eyes and shifted her legs off the side of the bed. The thin smock rode up her shins nearly to her thighs. Sleek muscles moved under her soft skin, showing her athleticism. No wonder she'd been able to swim away from him in the Thames.

"Hampton Court in the time of Queen Elizabeth. The first." He walked back over, exhaling. "I didn't mean to wake ye," he said with what he hoped was a soothing voice. He lifted her legs back up onto the bed. Aye, her skin was soft and warm. How would those legs feel around his waist?

"And the year?" she asked sliding her feet back to the floor, the smock once more sliding up too high.

Toren squelched the eruption of fire that her legs had kindled within him. He didn't have time for this. Every minute meant that Briana rode farther away. "1588."

"I was hoping that was all a dream," she mumbled. Kat's gaze traveled down him. "You've changed."

"I must leave. Briana has been stolen."

Kat pushed off the bed past him. "Stolen? Are you sure she's not just lost? This is a big place. Have you looked in the stairwells?"

"Fergus Campbell took her. Elizabeth's guard witnessed it."

"Fergus Campbell. The man Briana doesn't want to marry?" Kat asked, glancing around. "Do I have any clothing?"

"The olc, bloody folking betrothed," Toren said in a low, controlled voice. If he could control his voice, maybe he could control the fury that threatened to send him into a berserker rage. The bastard had stolen his sister. He'd only just seen her again after five years of believing he'd lost her forever. And now she was gone and in the clutches of a future murderer. "Eagan will bring ye gowns on the morrow."

"On the morrow?" Kat imitated his Scottish accent. "I won't be here on the morrow."

He looked directly into her narrowing eyes. "Ye aren't coming with me, Kat. Eagan will care for ye here until I return." He waited for her shouts, perhaps stomping, or a tantrum. Isn't that what women did when they didn't get their way? "Once I find Briana, I will take her to Craignish and then return for ye. Ye'll be safe here until then. Explore the century but stay out of trouble."

"Can Eagan protect me from Drakkina?" she asked calmly.

Toren frowned. "Can anyone?" He could if he made it home to Craignish, where he had magic that would tether him to this century. Then Kat would be here with him, because the witch wouldn't dare pull them apart after her foretelling.

He'd always felt the buzz of energy around the circle of ten large stones to the west of his home. He'd come to understand and manipulate some of the power, which was why his binding spell on the dragonfly necklace still told him its location. His mother's ancient texts outlined some complex binding rituals. One of them would show what he needed to do. Then he'd return to convince Kat that she would be happy here. She loved history. Now she could live within it.

Kat hurried to the clothes press and pulled the heavy oak doors open. She grabbed a pair of his riding breeches and a shirt. They would be huge on her.

"Do you know which way he went?" she asked as she turned her back to him, stripped off the thin chemise and threw his large shirt over her head. Words left him at the sight of her naked back and sweetly rounded arse, her straight spine, her shoulder blades. Toren scrubbed his hands over his face. This was no time to ogle Kat, nor have this conversation.

She looked back over her shoulder and frowned. "You don't know which way they went?"

"Maxwell says he went east to go across the channel to Calais."

"East," Kat said. "Do you know where my knickers and bra ended up?" she asked. "I didn't see them in Briana's room."

Before she could finish her sentence, Toren strode across to the mattress where he'd concealed his modern clothes along with Kat's undergarments. He tossed her the skimpy piece of Wednesday embroidered cloth and her bra. "I said, Kat, ye aren't going with me."

Kat caught the scraps of fabric. He watched as she drew the pink cloth on under the edge of his tunic and then shimmied into the britches, hoisting them high. The cuffs still hit on her lower calf instead of at the knee.

"He kidnapped her because he heard you were breaking the engagement?" she asked.

Kat tucked the black bra under his shirt and slipped her slender arms inside the tunic sleeves. After a moment of elbowing and tugging, her arms pushed back out through the arm holes. "That feels better." She looked at him. "Do you have a belt of rope I could use to keep these up?"

Toren's anger simmered. "I don't have time to deal with ye. Ye're staying here."

She spun around, her stubborn jaw jutting slightly forward. "Will he hurt her? What is his plan, marriage against her will?"

"Aye, he'll hurt her. Aye, he'll try to marry her." He shook his head. His sister was terrified of the man. And marrying Fergus would see the end of her and his clan. "I must get her away from him before 'tis too late."

Kat met his eyes. "Then you're taking me with you because I can get her away from them when you cannot," she said succinctly, her tone taunting him to ask her how. But he knew what she was thinking.

"I have no need to hide," he said low, and she broke the stare for a moment as if he'd slapped her, her cheeks darkening in the low light.

A knock broke the silence and Eagan walked in. "Yer horse is ready. Send word when ye find her, and I'll bring Mistress Kat with me. We will meet at Craignish Castle."

"Aye," Toren said, still watching Kat as she picked up a short, woolen throw. He walked toward the door and Kat followed.

"Guard her well." Toren commanded Eagan.

"Where is she?" Eagan asked and Kat grinned, though the humor did not reach her eyes.

"He cannot guard me, Toren."

Her voice made Eagan turn in a circle. When he came back to her again, his eyes opened wide. He bowed. "Mistress, I didn't see ye there."

Toren growled low in his throat. "I don't need ye, woman."

"I can be of great use, Toren; or do you think Briana would prefer to see her brother battle fifty Campbells to the death before her betrothed forces himself on her?" Kat's harsh words dropped Eagan's mouth open. "I can move in there silently. I can cloak Briana too. Bring her out."

"I fight in the open."

"Then ye'll die in the open, ye cocky arse," she said with a poorly imitated burr. "And seeing as we're supposed to be together and alive to save the gosh darn bloody world," Kat said, moving her head and hands together in a gesture that held the sarcastic, condescending attitude that he'd witnessed often in her century, "I think I am going with ye, milord or milaird or whatever you are." Toren glanced at his brother, who stood with wide eyes and an open mouth.

Toren cursed, his eyes on Kat. "Ye'll follow me anyway."

"And only you will see me." She smiled darkly.

"Daingead," he swore in Gaelic. "Eagan, find her some smaller trews to ride in."

Eagan found his tongue. "If she goes"—he shook his head slightly—"then I go."

Toren glared at both of them. "Then we ride immediately."

———◄O►———

Toren and Kat stepped out into the predawn chill where Toren's bay horse, Apollo, awaited. Jogging, Eagan led two more from the silent stable.

"She doesn't know the way of riding, Eagan. Kat will ride with me," Toren said, as they walked across the courtyard. Out of the shadows of the stables came another cloaked figure, a woman.

"The horse is not for Mistress Diciadain," Eagan said, his words hard, defensive, guilty. "I came upon them trying to leave on their own."

Kat halted next to Toren as the woman walked awkwardly across the hard-packed ground, awkward because she carried something of good size. Kat's inhale brought his attention back to her. "It's Margaret and Sara," she said softly.

Anger jerked up through Toren in time with his heartbeats. "This is no place for a Maxwell, especially a woman and a child."

Margaret took a step back and lowered the child. He should have left by himself without saying anything to anyone. He'd already have Briana back by now.

"Tor." Eagan stepped between them. "They have nowhere else to go."

"The child is not mine," Toren said. "Her father lies."

"And he threatens," Margaret said, raising her head in an awkward show of defiance. "I will no longer live in fear for my child."

Kat moved around him and squatted down before the girl. "Good morn, Sara, we will get to see a beautiful sunrise, don't you think," she said in a positive tone. Kat glanced upward at Margaret Maxwell. "I am Kat. You have a lovely little girl."

Margaret blinked as Kat straightened, obviously not used to any kindness. It squeezed Toren's heart even though he chose to ignore it.

Sara smiled warmly at Kat but didn't say anything. Margaret would infuse the child with her own timid character if that was all she was taught.

"I believe I have you to thank for finding Sara," Margaret said. "She should not have put you to such trouble."

Kat smiled at Sara. "It was no trouble to make a new friend."

Toren turned to Eagan. "They aren't coming. This is a rescue, not a ride in the country."

Margaret raised her eyes to Toren. "My father lied. Campbell heads to the north where his men await at the border. I overheard his plans."

"I had surmised that they were not headed to Calais."

"But you did not know which way he went." She lifted a small fist to her chest.

He narrowed his eyes. "Why help us?"

Margaret stroked Sara's hair and looked down at the top of her daughter's head. Her voice seemed to shrink in the large expanse of dimness. "I've always done what I need to do to survive." She pulled her daughter closer. "But I do not know if I can protect her...from him. 'Tis why she ran off earlier, away from his rage." She pulled Sara deeper into the folds of skirts. "I cannot protect her alone." Margaret's voice caught and tears sparkled in her eyes.

"Ye know I was not to blame for Edward's death," Toren said, watching her closely.

Margaret gave a brief nod but would hardly meet his eyes. "I know—"

"But ye said nothing when the blame fell on me?" Toren pressed, as he kept the pain buried deep where it had lived since the night of the fire.

Margaret's voice was tortured. "I've always done what I need to do to survive. I keep out of everyone's way, and I keep quiet."

Kat glared at him and patted Margaret's arm. The firm set of her jaw told Toren that she had already made up her mind. She would protect the child and mother. He should jump on his charger and take off, leave the rest of them to figure out what to do with themselves. His hands fisted.

Eagan moved to stand beside Margaret. "Now that she's told ye his plan with Campbell, he will kill her and Sara if we leave them here."

Daingead! Toren wouldn't have the death of a woman and child on his soul. "Ye're responsible for them, Eagan. And when we find Briana, ye will take Margaret and her daughter back to MacCallum land. We will decide what to do with them after that."

Eagan nodded solemnly.

Kat bent down and whispered something to the girl which made her smile. He had the uncomfortable feeling that Kat was making fun of him. He scowled and moved to his large charger. "Kat," he called, and swung up into the seat. "Unless ye wish to run along behind, ye best come over here. Now."

Kat frowned as she approached the wrong side of the horse.

"Other side, Mistress Diciadain," Eagan said, helping Sara up to Margaret who had already mounted.

"Please call me Kat." She walked behind the horse to the other side. Toren rolled his eyes. He'd have to give her a lesson about horses and safety when he had a chance. Luckily, Apollo wasn't one to kick outside battle. He reached down and clasped her waist. She gasped as he pulled her up and quickly settled her before him, throwing a woolen robe in front of her so that she was blanketed up to her adorable stubborn chin.

"Will Sara be safe riding with her mother?" Kat asked, as she batted at the blanket. He pulled it back up, tucking her in like a child, just as he knew Margaret would do with Sara.

"The child will be safe. Margaret learned how to master a horse at an early age, much earlier than you would have mastered driving an automobile."

The others fell in line behind Toren out through the gates, Eagan in the rear. Toren had left a message with Elizabeth's advisor, alerting her of the need to leave hastily. As for the reasons, he'd kept them fairly ambiguous. This was a Highland matter, and he would deal with it as a Highlander, not some English courtier.

Toren tapped the charger gently, though the steed snorted and danced, just waiting for him to let up on the reins. Toren felt much the same way, but they should clear the castle grounds and the city gates first.

Toren inhaled the sweet fragrance from Kat's hair, so contrary to the pungent smell of too much humanity living together that weighed down the stagnant night air. The lass fought to stay upright and wiggled between his loins. He wrapped an arm around her waist, hoisted under her breasts and pulled her back. His lips grazed the soft skin near her ear. "Stop wiggling yer sweet arse against me lass or ye'll make this a damn uncomfortable ride." She stopped immediately. "Just relax back. Apollo's step is steady and true, and I won't let ye fall."

"Apollo? The sun god?"

"My horse." He inhaled her sweet scent. Just holding her was making this a damn uncomfortable ride. Perhaps he should bed her and be done with it. From the brief kiss they'd shared, he was fairly confident she would agree if he asked.

He glanced at the other two horses. Margaret held tightly to her daughter. Her lowered eyes darted to Eagan while he openly watched her. Was she acting coy, or fond of Eagan, or just guilty? That one was hard to read.

They rode out through the gates where Elizabeth's sleepy guards noted their passing. The peace a couple hours before dawn was broken only by the occasional drunk or courtesan wandering to their homes or a place to lay their heads.

Toren's eyes watched the sides of the road. Maxwell may be using his daughter, allowing her to overhear his plans. Even if her intentions were pure, Lady Margaret could very well be leading them into a trap.

◆◇◆

"Why do we even bother to follow the amulet?" Bast, the Egyptian demon of pleasure purred her apathy from a throne in the dank mist as she licked her sleek black forearm. Her body, a cross between a voluptuous dark-skinned woman and a short-haired cat, lounged against a golden pillow. It was all a show, as she didn't have her body, nor gold, nor anything close to a throne. "We've lost it and the girl, and I tire of searching. Can't we just wait to feel a tremor again?" She hummed nonchalantly, her tail flicking back and forth in subtle irritation.

Semiazaz glared at his companions. Thirteen of the most feared demons known to mankind sat on imagined cushions and thrones in a damp circle of mist. Semiazaz's white beard snaked down into his gray robes. Razor-like nails bit into the arms of the imagined throne holding his body a little higher than the rest. "Bast," he called across the circle, his breath clearing a path through the mist directly to the cat-like demon.

Her golden orbed eyes met his.

"How long have you sat upon that throne, washing imagined specks of dirt from your imagined body? A thousand years, two, three?" Bast's body seemed to grow larger, but it was merely an illusion. "I believe it could be five thousand years by now," he said.

Semiazaz's cold eyes surveyed the occupants of their dank prison. They were trapped together. Together! The foulest word in his black heart. They were never apart, never alone, never at liberty to do anything without the others.

Thirteen headstrong demons forced to be in constant awareness of one another. They all sat as far apart as the binding spell would allow them. Their bodies, once young, virile with power, had withered away, leaving only their demonic souls knotted together. They could move, but only as one. They could destroy, but only as one entity.

A thousand years ago there had been a chance to harness the powers to break the bond that the white Wiccan, Drakkina, had bound them with when they began to form their coven. The most powerful coven outside of Hell.

Semiazaz's eyes moved continuously. Would anyone strike? Jagged grumblings swirled in the mist of the otherworldly abyss where they lived between times. His voice grew until it echoed, covering the murmurs of caution and approval. "We act now! The dragonfly amulet is out there. We felt it when one of Gilla's daughters touched it! It can give us back our bodies, real"—he stood, his hands fisted—"real bodies, not these illusions." He moved his hands around and through the image he projected. "We would at least be able to feel again," he said, looking once again to Bast.

A ripple of thunder cracked above them, bringing Semiazaz's attention to Bechard, the demon of tempests. "Yes?"

Bechard stood, armor-like chest bronzed, long blond hair pushed behind his pointed ears. Black, veined wings stood out from his back, and his large maw stretched, exposing three-inch teeth. It was a wonder the creature didn't cut his own tongue off with those teeth.

"Why bother with corporeal bodies?" Bechard said, his voice deep like thunder. "We need the witch's magic, the match to the power we stole from her mate. That will free us, free us so that we may play within this world again. We will take over whatever body we want once we are free. Why waste time—"

"It is not a waste," Semiazaz cut in. Would they never agree? Five thousand years of forced sameness, moving constantly together, and yet they still argued. The blackness of their souls warred against each other, vying for leadership. Bickering, taunting, brandishing pretended power. "The power in that amulet will not only give us corporeal bodies, it will strengthen the powers we stripped from the warlock. To break free, with that amulet we may only need to capture the magic from one or two of Gilla's daughters. How is that wasting time?"

"I agree with Semiazaz." A horned female demon named Deumis spoke. "Moving systematically through each mortal year, searching across the globe for the purity of Gilla's magic." She snorted. "That's a waste of time."

Fire crackled throughout the sphere of souls. Barely contained raw anger seeped from the demons, ricocheting off each other's energy. "But we've lost the amulet!" another demon called.

Semiazaz held up his hands to halt the snarling and snapping around him. He grimaced in disdain. *They really are beasts.* But he needed them. Without full cooperation, they were just a stagnant mass of hate-filled gas. The cacophony ebbed as he lowered his hands. "She sent the girl with the amulet into another time." He looked around the circle. "The amulet draws the dragonfly magic. Once the girl touches it again, we'll know exactly where she is. 'Tis near her."

"What if she doesn't touch it?" Bast asked softly. "Drakkina would have warned her by now."

Semiazaz moved his eyes to Bast's form. "We know where in time Drakkina sent the amulet, so the girl must be there too. Even if Gilla's spawn doesn't touch it, I have been able to feel it." *In those rare quiet moments.* He smiled. "Can't you?" Silence descended as curiosity overrode their combined venom.

Bast gasped and stood. "Yessss." She turned to him. "How?"

"Proximity. The amulet's magic is so strong it seeks the girl. When the girl uses her magic in the same plane of time, they resonate together even if they don't touch."

"Let us thread," Bechard roared. The others screamed, tumbling about the prison. Their illusionary bodies disintegrated as their souls raced amongst each other like frantic sharks smelling blood.

"Calm," Semiazaz called over the chaos whipping about. He shut out the cacophony as he concentrated on the girl's magic. "Once we're there, we'll find my Drakkina's ward and take Gilla's daughter's magic and her life force."

He raised his hands high and looked out at the ravenous demons, some of them drooling over the mere idea of sucking energy off the girl. "Everyone concentrate on the thread." The swirling energy funneled into one long black thread, twisting like a tornado.

"You won't win this time, Drakkina," he murmured. The thick thread elongated and shot off into the gray mist of the temporal plane toward 1588.

CHAPTER THIRTEEN
SAFE PLACE

Kat grimaced as she came down hard on the saddle. She'd ridden a horse once before when Lisa had arranged for their Girl Guides group to go on a trail ride. But that was years ago, and she'd forgotten how to rise up and down to protect her fanny and bum, both of which would be quite bruised before the end of the day.

"Isn't there a way to make Apollo ride smoother, like a canter or something?" she asked, jouncing in front of Toren's chest. How did the man protect his groin with all this bouncing? And while wearing a kilt that rode up his knees? She could feel the muscles of his thighs pressing around her hips.

"Once we are out of the city, we will race and it will be smoother," he said. "Ye should try to sleep."

She snorted and turned in her seat to glare at him. Toren, with all his godlike gorgeousness, just stared out over her head, but she swore she saw a faint tip to the corners of his mouth.

"Are you laughing at me?" she asked.

He glanced down at her. "I am barely talking to ye."

"Horseback riding is not one of my numerous skills." She turned forward, letting her gaze slide over the waking city. "I'd like to see you drive a bus of kids hyped up on sugar through the city without crashing and burning," she murmured. "I rule at that."

Several dark windows came alight as they made their way out of London proper. The smells were pungent in the city, with open sewers being emptied into the Thames and animals kept behind clustered homes and shops, but it was much quieter than modern London without cars and air traffic. Carts rattled over cobbled streets, and the sound of their horses clopping permeated the air around them, but not much else.

The warmth of Toren's chest pressed against her back, and she felt his breath on her ear just before he spoke. "What are some of yer other skills, Kat?" The tone was slow and almost seductive. But then he pulled back.

Kat inhaled through her nose and grimaced at the smell of the open sewers. "I am a very good swimmer. I can sew Halloween costumes, braid hair, and make a delicious chocolate cake. In fact, I can do a lot. There hasn't been much use for horseback riding in my life. Now ask me to get you from one side of London to the other the quickest on the tube, and I'm an expert."

She heard what could have been a muted chuckle and turned to look, but Toren continued to stare out at the street. So she returned to staring straight ahead, holding to the pummel while tightening her legs. Ahead was an empty road and pre-dawn shadows.

Toren's arm snaked around her middle, and he pulled her back into his parted legs. Kat's stomach flipped at the feel of what must be a sizeable knob hard against her backside. "Excuse me?" she said.

Toren's mouth returned to her ear. "We're clear of the city," he said. A tingle rushed down her neck. His lips were close enough to skim the sensitive spot below her ear.

"Hold on, lass. Time to race."

Kat didn't even feel him give the horse a signal. There was no "giddy up," no kick of spurs as a forewarning, and Apollo plunged down the dark road.

Kat found her breath and inhaled. "Holy Mother!" Wrapping both hands firmly around the saddle pommel, she was thankful for Toren's arm seat-belting her to him. The horse's gait was like a rolling wave. Its muscles flexed beneath them as its hooves churned the pebbled dust. Kat caught a glimpse of Eagan and Margaret riding to their left across the road.

Margaret held Sara wrapped in a blanket. Kat couldn't even see the girl tied tightly into her mother's waist. Hopefully Sara was used to this mode of travel and was asleep. A child definitely needed sleep. Even though slumber was impossible, the breakneck speed kept Kat's thoughts more on survival and less on the rock-hard chest she pushed back into.

They galloped in silence until dawn tinged the eastern sky. Kat swiveled her head in the opposite direction, toward the northwest. Since she'd landed in London as an orphan, she'd always known which direction was northwest. The pull, like some homing beacon, hadn't changed since landing in the sixteenth century. Did it have something to do with her mother's magic?

Kat absently rubbed the spot where her birthmark warmed. Drakkina would know. Where was she? Would she be furious they'd left the amulet with the queen? Questions pounded through Kat with each rolling stride of the horse. They rode for what felt like hours until she tilted her head back so she could see the rugged jut of Toren's chin. "Are we there yet?" she asked, knowing he wouldn't get the modern reference.

Toren looked at the other riders and held up his arm. They slowed the labored horses. "They need to refresh," he said and turned the horses off the main road into a leaf-shrouded grove of black alder and oaks. Toren lowered her to the ground. He held her up at first, and Kat fought to keep her groans inside as she shook one leg and then the other. "I'm okay," she said, and he left her to remove the bit from between Apollo's teeth.

Eagan helped Margaret dismount with Sara. The child slept as Margaret carried her to a dry place amongst the ever-lightening trees. It was obvious that she loved her daughter.

As Margaret bent low over the child's small head, perhaps inhaling her little girl fragrance, Kat's stomach twisted with a new wave of despair. All her little girls back home and all her little men. She would kiss them each goodnight, even the ones who thought they were too old for her tucking in.

Lord how she missed them. They were all different with different needs and insecurities from varying backgrounds. But they all could count on Kat's love, no matter how many bad words they used or things they broke. Kat caught a stray tear from her lower lid. If she didn't return, would they just think she'd left them by choice? Would they wonder if she'd been murdered? Or would her entire timeline disappear, leaving Lisa and the children with no knowledge of her?

Kat blinked back tired tears and bent forward to rub the backs of her abused thighs. She was definitely not a long-distance rider, or any rider for that matter. Kat ran her thumb and fingers down her hamstrings and calves, bending completely forward until her nose rested on her knees and her hair hung forward. If she had half a chance she'd run through her familiar yoga moves to loosen up. Kat raked fingers through the tangles in her hair and let her arms shake the soreness out of her shoulders. Slowly she rolled up one vertebra at a time like the lady on the yoga program insisted. At the top, eyes still closed, she rolled shoulders back, stretching out chest muscles, and then slowly opened her eyes.

Three pairs of eyes watched. Margaret and Eagan stared open-mouthed.

"Just stretching some of the kinks out," Kat said. "I don't ride very often."

Kat saw Toren in her periphery. Standing behind, he'd gotten a good show of her bum as she'd stretched in the breeches. His mouth wasn't hanging open, but his look affected her more. He didn't look surprised since he'd lived in her century for five years. Instead he looked hungry, like a man who stared at a luscious meal. He waved his hand toward his brother and looked away.

As if released from a spell, Margaret and Eagan began to remove their horses' bits.

"We have a long way to go," Toren said. "We will rest for a few hours and continue during the day."

"Are we going to your home in Scotland?" she asked.

"Once we rescue Briana."

Kat followed him, lowering her voice. "But the necklace?" He fully knew that the Wiccan spirit could mess with their lives if they pissed her off. Kat definitely didn't want to snake through time again unless she was headed to the twenty-first century.

Toren led the horses farther into the dense woods, away from his brother and Margaret. Kat followed, questions on the tip of her tongue. Then she heard the clear tinkling sounds of water. They walked up to a creek, making Kat so thirsty she nearly fell on her knees and started slurping. Instead she watched the horses drinking greedily and would have salivated if she'd had any saliva left. She hadn't eaten much at dinner and had drunk too much wine since there was little else. Even eating fruit, it was a wonder she could keep up any sort of glamour at all.

"Is there anything for two-legged beasts to drink?" she asked. The water looked so cold and clear.

"This water is safe," he said and stepped upstream of the horses. He scooped up water in his hands and drank, then splashed some over his face. "I know the source and 'tis safe enough."

"Safe enough?" Kat questioned half-heartedly and dropped down to cup some of the best-tasting water she'd ever gulped. Cold, fresh, totally wet, Kat sucked down the offering, praying that Giardia bacteria didn't exist in the sixteenth century.

Toren filled several wine skins with the water and threw them back over the horses. He walked up behind her.

"Once Briana and Margaret and the child are safe at Craignish, we will return to England for the necklace." He glanced around the clearing. Kat straightened and followed his searching gaze.

"Do ye sense the witch here?" He was close to her, looking down into her eyes.

Her birthmark didn't tingle or burn. "No." Her heart beat hard with his nearness, which was silly considering she'd ridden up against him for hours. "I hope she doesn't show up before we—"

Kat barely had time to gasp as Toren pulled her toward him, his hands on her shoulders, his face full of raw intent. It was the look that had passed over his face after he'd watched her stretch. Hunger and barely held control. The raw truth of it raced straight through Kat, making her knees feel weak.

He pulled her into his arms, intent so obvious it enveloped her, pouring heat through her veins in response. But he paused as if letting her decide to react. To strike him or push him away or break free of his hands, which loosened on her arms like manacles unlocked.

Without a word, she reached up to capture the back of his head, pulling his face down toward hers. The warmth and scent of him was familiar. He was a mountain to hold onto in the darkness. He accepted her magic, and he was the only person who knew she didn't belong here. Her fingers caught in his thick hair, while the dawn light seemed to hold off, giving them privacy. She closed her eyes as his lips descended, his arms sliding completely around her. She felt as if she were slipping into safety, into a warm, comfortable place where she might belong.

She slanted her face so that they fit perfectly close together. His tongue glided along the small part between her lips, and his thumb pushed her chin down to grant him entry. He growled low as he tasted her.

Kat's legs wobbled, and he molded her against his body. Without the cumbersome petticoats Kat could easily feel his hard length. A rush of languid heat pooled in her pelvis as she was sucked into a whirlwind of passion. She answered him with a soft moan and moved her hips against him. His hands caught up in her hair and slid down to hold her face. He pulled away slightly, but she could still feel his breath on her damp lips.

"Ye should not have come, lass."

It took a moment for the words to penetrate the sexual haze engulfing Kat. "What?"

Toren stepped back and squatted next to the creek to splash cold water over his face again. Without the finery of Elizabeth's court trapping the man, he had transformed into a warrior like the muscled immortal from the TV series. But the sword that hung at his side was real, not some Hollywood prop. Everything about Toren MacCallum was real and hard and full of pent-up passion.

And here she stood, her mouth still damp from his kisses, her hair tangled from the wind and his fingers, and her ill-fitting boy's clothes hanging off her. Worse yet, she couldn't hide her ugly scars from him. Kat rubbed the cuff of her tunic across her mouth and turned away.

"We will finish what is between us," he said as if that solved everything. "But I would not have it here in the dirt."

Kat frowned, turning back. "So you didn't want me to come on this journey because you're afraid you won't be able to control yourself?"

He pulled the tethers to lead the horses from the creek since they'd stopped drinking. "I am always in control."

"Always in control," she said and harrumphed. "Perhaps that's your problem."

Toren glanced at her while he checked the horses' hooves. "I'm The MacCallum now. It is my duty to be in control."

A moment passed while Kat watched the casual way he walked around the huge animals, checking their feet, inspecting their bridles. "Then why shouldn't I have come if you aren't worried I'll drive you insane with lust?"

Toren grunted. "'Tis dangerous."

"More dangerous than staying at Elizabeth's court? I don't think so."

He turned, frown set. "Ye are not as likely to get a blade through yer middle at court."

"There are a lot of other dangers at court. Remember, MacCallum, I know history."

"There's also the fact that ye're slowing me down," he replied.

Kat stood tall, hands on hips. "Slowing you down? I didn't make one bit of protest until I thought your horses were about to collapse." Then she saw the grin. It was more in his eyes than along his lips. She huffed.

"You're baiting me, Highlander." Was it because she'd come too close to the truth? Had he felt just as out of control during the kiss as she had?

She rubbed her face with clean hands and tried to squelch the yawn that bubbled up and out. "I will be an asset when we reach your sister," she finished behind her hand as the yawn nearly cracked her jaw.

"Ye need to rest."

"So do you," she said. "When was the last time you slept? I know what lack of sleep can do to a person. There are clinical studies. Someone who goes thirty-six hours without sleep functions at the same level as someone who is legally drunk. I don't want to be caught in a battle against thirty outraged Highlanders with a chief who is sloshed."

"I will rest before we catch them."

"Which will be when?"

"We are close to the pass where Campbell would have met up with his men. He would rest then, not knowing that we pursue." He glanced at the rising sun splintering through the trees. "We will rest a few hours, until the sun is high." He looked at Kat. "Ye can walk in amongst the Campbells unseen in the bright sun?"

"And walk out with your sister," she boasted. *Leave me behind indeed.* She was the most valuable player in this mission.

"She will be bound. Ye'll have to cut her ropes," he said, and tossed a dagger he'd drawn. It stabbed the ground next to Kat. She yanked it out, feeling very much like a warrior princess. She just needed some black leather. She also needed a sheath for the razor-sharp weapon. What would she do with it, tuck it in her pants?

"You can hold it until I go into the thick of things." She handed it back, handle first, careful not to slice her palm. He slid it within its sheath. She looked around at the dense blackberry bushes across the narrow stream. "Where exactly do we rest?"

Eagan, Margaret, and Sara walked through the trees. Kat smiled at the girl and tried to make eye contact with her mother. Margaret gave another timid smile and hurried Sara toward the stream where they all drank.

"Umm...that's kind of where the horses drank," Kat said and waved them up stream. "Up there is probably...tastier." Margaret and Sara moved upstream while Eagan wiped his arm across his mouth and looked at his brother. He too had changed into a great kilt.

"We will set our camp back here by the creek. 'Tis more hidden," Toren said, and jerked his head in the direction of the blackberry bushes. "Just until the sun is high. Then we'll surprise them north of Fallows Pass."

"We attack in the daylight?" Eagan asked. "Two of us against thirty or more?"

"There'll be no attacking," Kat said, glancing through the thick bushes. How exactly were they to get back in the clearing without the blackberry thorns ripping them to shreds?

"I have a plan," Toren said over her words. Eagan nodded and walked back to the horses, totally trusting in his brother and chief to come up with the best plan. Kat had read about the importance of hierarchy in the clan system and how chiefs had to prove themselves worthy. Toren must have proven himself very worthy.

"How do we get in there?" Kat asked, pointing at the brambles.

Toren pulled the two horses behind him and walked to the far end of the bushes. Kat watched him closely, but right before her eyes, he disappeared. "Toren?" she called.

"Follow," he instructed.

"There's a path," Eagan said and moved upstream to escort Margaret. He picked Sara up in his arms.

Kat walked to the place Toren disappeared. The way the brambles grew on a diagonal hid the path that had been forged through them. The bramble branches were cut along the path, but buds sprouted from their severed ends.

Kat walked into an open meadow encircled by blackberry bramble. Giant oak trees anchored the perimeters of the spherical field like stately sentries, and knee-height, pocked standing stones stood at their bases. The tickle of magic ran under Kat's skin. *Strange.* She turned in a circle as she stared up at the clear dawn sky that filled the ring left open by the green oaks. She closed her eyes and inhaled, feeling the magic of the water in her body, the magic of the place resonating.

"What is this place?" she asked, breathing deeply, eyes still closed.

"A hiding place I was drawn to on my way south five years ago." Toren's voice was close.

She opened her eyes. Hundreds of butterflies fluttered down around her, their yellow and blue wings whispering. Toren stared. Kat smiled at her friends. They made Kat feel like her mother was close.

Margaret's gasp and Sara's squeal of delight turned Kat's head where they stood with Eagan, staring in wonder at her fluttery friends. With a shake of her hands, the butterflies lifted upward and caught a stray wisp of wind. They drifted into the woods.

"They must like this meadow," Kat said. If she wasn't careful, she'd end up being burned as a witch in this century. Of course she was, but not the evil, steal-your-baby or dry-up-your-cow kind of witch. Although, if Toren was a devil, she had contemplated fornicating with him in the woods.

She moved her hands around, feeling the warmth of her blush. "We rest now, all of us." She pointed at Toren. "Including you."

"I'll take the first watch," Eagan said.

"Why can't we all rest?" Kat asked. "The sun will be high in just a few hours. We all need sleep."

Toren stepped closer to Kat, his voice low. "This place may resonate magic to some degree, but it won't keep others out." He turned away as if that were the end of the discussion. Kat took several steps to keep up with him.

"But I can," she said. "I can keep others out."

Toren pulled the heavy blankets from the backs of the horses and began to lay down pallets in the shade of the trees.

Kat caught his arm, ignoring the steely muscle beneath the fabric. "I've done it before. We'll be totally guarded. No one will be able to get in here," she whispered. When he picked her up and set her on one of the rocks, she lost her patience.

"Stop placing me about like I'm an errant throw pillow," she snapped. She lowered her voice. "I wouldn't have stood for it even if I'd been born in the fifteen hundreds."

He opened his mouth as if to say something but closed it. He sat down on the pallet.

Kat stood, spreading her arms. "Where exactly do you think we will be able to hide once they realize Briana has been taken?" She dropped them to her sides and walked over to stand before him. Placing her hands on her hips, she stared down. "Are you expecting to hightail it all the way up to Scotland with an army of peeved Highland bad guys chasing us? That's a long way." She wasn't sure of that, but it seemed so riding horseback. "We need to have somewhere to hide where they can't find us no matter how hard they look."

Toren watched her closely. "Ye can make this place invisible?"

Kat leaned closer and matched his softer voice. "I've put glamour spells around small places where I've needed to hide things." She blushed and then pushed the guilty feeling away as she remembered the stash of money she had shielded in the gym locker. "The magic in this area," she said waving to grassy space, surrounded by brambles and oaks, "will enhance my power."

Kat walked over and placed her palm on the oak behind the rock where she'd sat. Closing her eyes, she concentrated, but there was no tickle of magic in the tree. When she slid her hand to the rock however, it flowed easily up into her.

She smiled. "It's the rocks."

Eagan walked over to them. "What's the lass doing?" he asked Toren.

Toren watched her. "Do ye remember Ma?"

Eagan nodded slowly. "A wee bit."

"Kat has a touch of the wisdom."

Kat closed her eyes, focusing her magic on the crystals embedded in the rock. She tweaked the words she used to hide objects and repeated them in her mind until her haphazard thoughts came together into a single thread.

Hide, be invisible, only people full of honor, full of heart may enter. People with a true need to hide will be protected here, invisible from the world, invisible from every entity worldly or unworldly. And any of my blood. Upon my blood and with my magic.

Kat imagined the threads peeling out to form an invisible web around the meadow, interwoven like a reed basket. She tied off the weave and turned to see everyone watching. But she moved to the next stone, which was nearly covered with moss and stray daisies. Twelve stones in all. At some point, Toren handed her a flask of water, and she guzzled it down.

By the time Kat laid hands on the last stone, she swayed on her feet. This stone was several feet high, and she leaned over it, concentrating on the weave over the entire field. *Hide, be invisible, let only those with need and true hearts enter.* She recited the words through a numb mind. With the last bit of strength, Kat tied off the flow of magic around the large stone and collapsed over it.

She felt Toren's arms lift her away from the hard granite.

"Lass?"

"We can *all* rest now," she said through slurry lips. Toren carried her to a pallet, and Kat felt like she was floating. He settled her on the blanket and covered her. Just before blackness overtook her, she felt Toren lower himself and lay out against her back. His arm pulled her into his warmth. Kat smiled inside because her lips were too exhausted to move. Now they could truly rest. It was a good thing he'd brought her along.

CHAPTER FOURTEEN
RESCUE MISSION

"Achoo!" Kat woke with a sneeze and rubbed her nose. Something flitted across her hand, and she swatted at it. She opened her eyes to find dozens of butterflies perched on her, some fluttering above.

Eagan, Margaret, and Sara stared at the spectacle. *Holy Mary.* Her friends weren't used to her sleeping outdoors and the magic of the meadow must call to them.

Go, please. Kat pushed the thought out toward her little friends. "Thank you," she said as they alighted and moved upwards.

Sara's eyes were wide as full moons. "How do you call them? Even in your slumber."

Kat sighed and ran fingers through tussled hair. She was sore but felt much better than before the nap. "It's sort of a family trait."

"I thought ye didn't have a family," Eagan said, eyeing the fluttering wings that were flying well past the oaks into the blue sky.

"Everyone starts off with one. My mother knew she was going to die, and she didn't want me to be alone," she said glancing around for Toren. Where was he? "She sent her sash with me, and it had butterflies embroidered on it." The three stared with brows pinched in confusion. Kat pushed herself up. "It's complicated."

Eagan gave Kat a faint smile. "My ma had a touch of magic. The kind that runs through things of nature."

Margaret turned to look at him with stern assessment.

"She was a good Christian woman," Eagan defended. "She just had a way of influencing natural things. It was a gift from God."

"I like your butterflies, Mistress Kat," Sara said.

Kat smiled. "Thank you."

Toren walked back inside the circle through the brambles and directly to her. "Ye are thirsty." They had only been back in his century for a day or so, but already his thick Scottish accent rolled across his tongue. She was grateful for the moonstone to help her understand.

He handed her a flask, and she drank the bladder dry. "I scouted ahead," Toren said.

Kat handed back the bladder. "Instead of sleeping?"

"I saw tracks just off the road," he continued despite her fiercest glare.

"You are human, Toren," she said.

Eagan snorted. "He's always pushed himself hard, and now Briana is in jeopardy."

Toren's voice was even, and his gaze rose to meet Kat's. "Because I allowed her to be at risk. I will correct my mistake."

"Not if you work yourself into a grave," she said.

He turned back to Apollo. "We ride."

Kat sat behind Eagan this time while Toren scouted farther ahead. He followed the trail he was convinced was Fergus's fleeing path from London.

"He won't charge into Fergus's men on his own, will he?" Kat asked Eagan. "You know, lose his head with fury and bellow a battle cry and charge in to save his sister."

"I have not seen Tor lose his head before," Eagan said. "When he has a plan, he sticks to it unless the circumstances change."

"Could the circumstances change?"

"Circumstances always change," Eagan said, a smile touching his voice. Kat noticed that Margaret smiled where she and Sara rode next to them, but her eyes stayed forward.

The plan was for Toren to find the Campbell camp up ahead and ride back to get her. Which was not what Kat had wanted. It made better sense for Toren to take her with him. So if the circumstances changed, she'd be there to cloak them. Kat huffed loudly.

"Be sure, Mistress Kat," Eagan said. "Tor's plans usually work out perfectly."

"Hmmm...usually." Kat swayed along with the slow-moving beast, her ears tuned into the world. No planes roared overhead, leaving white trails amongst the clouds. No hum of an unseen highway muted the sounds of nature. Twittering birds hunted for food. Small animals scampered around the trees as they rode along the wide path they called a road. Time stretched lazily onward with laborious seconds as Kat waited. She tried to relax in the quiet, but the wondering put her on edge.

Margaret watched Eagan under lowered eyes. Sara sat behind her mother, hugging her gently, her head moving from side to side to spy wild cornflowers and buttercups. Who was Sara's father? She couldn't ask in front of the child even if she were on close terms with Margaret.

Sara, with her slightly sloped nose and pale skin and hair, looked nothing like Toren or Eagan. It was as if the child had taken on all of Margaret's physical characteristics and none of her father's.

Several miles along, the sound of hooves pounded from a bend up ahead. "Into the woods," Eagan said and grabbed Margaret's reins to pull them both off the road.

Kat kept one hand on Eagan's back and reached over to Margaret's horse. "Both of you, hold my hand."

"I don't understand," Margaret said, her eyes round with building panic as she watched the road from behind some trees that couldn't possibly hide their large horses.

"Hold on," Kat said, throwing her open hand out toward them. "I am...I'm frightened." The girl and her mother grabbed her hand, and the three held together so that the cloak of invisibility that Kat threw up covered them all. Kat felt like a fool, throwing one leg out to touch Margaret's horse while her other leg remained pressed against Eagan's. But the effort would keep them hidden. If it was Toren, he'd see through the magic.

The hooves thundered like a deep heartbeat, and Kat held her breath. She let it out, releasing her magic when she saw the large Highlander pushed forward over the neck of his warhorse.

Toren's determined stare met her eyes, and he reined in. Apollo's nostrils flared as he sucked in large pulls of fresh air. The other horses shied and nickered off to the side as Eagan fought for control.

"They prepare to move on," Toren said, his gaze going to Kat.

She held her arms out to him, and he pulled her from Eagan to sit in front of him. The strength of his arms sent a sizzle along her skin. She felt dizzy and mentally shook herself. She must concentrate on the plan. But Toren wheeled Apollo around, making her head spin more.

She let out a little groan. "You're going to make me sick up."

"Take them"—Toren's head nodded toward Margaret and Sara—"back to the blackberry grove. We'll bring Briana. They won't find us there."

"Tor," Eagan said hesitantly. "They are at least two score in number from the tracks, and ye take a woman into battle?" He paused. "And send me to hide in blackberry bramble." Eagan's chin rose a notch as he stared his older brother and laird in the eyes. "I am going with ye."

Tense silence came between them, and Kat was glad to be still for the moment while she roped in her anxiety.

"We've only come a few miles," Margaret said. "I know the way back to the grove. Sara and I will wait for you there."

"I have a plan, Eagan." Toren's voice sat low, crouched as if ready to jump and conquer any weakness.

"Circumstances change," Eagan said with much less humor than when he'd discussed the topic with Kat. "And I don't know why ye'd risk yer lady."

"She fits into my plan," Toren replied, without a hint of giving ground.

"Ye would use a lady in yer battle plan?" Eagan sounded aghast, astounded, and very judgmental.

Kat felt Toren's body flinch behind her back as if his brother had delivered a blow. "She...the lady has certain abilities that will be of use," Toren said, and pulled his horse around to cut off the conversation. "I do not answer to ye."

"I'm coming," Eagan ended, and glanced at Margaret. She shooed him with a hand and turned her horse around. She took off in a canter, not even waiting to see if Toren would demand Eagan stay behind.

Kat understood pecking order among boys. She grew up with ten or more of them and had been raising six. Normally she'd encourage them to go play an aggressive game of basketball or assign them kitchen duty until they worked things out. But she didn't have time to positive parent two stubborn Highlanders in the sixteenth century. Kat turned her face to Toren. "Let him come. If something happens, we'll want the extra sword." She uncorked the refilled bladder of water and drank long gulps to prepare.

He exhaled. "And in one battle the MacCallums of Craignish will be no more."

His words rang eerily against her heart. She couldn't let that happen.

He pressed his heels into his horse's sides. Kat pushed back into his rock-hard chest as they rode, trying to redistribute the jouncing of her poor gluteus muscles. It was like leaning into a rock cliff. Toren hadn't relaxed one bit since Eagan's defiance and had kept the place ahead of his brother along the narrow road. Poor Eagan was probably swallowing his brother's dust. She gave Eagan credit for not trying to ride next to Toren. The man knew something of diplomacy.

Toren slowed his horse and veered away from the dusty road down a path that wound into a glade of trees and low bushes. They followed the trail around large boulders outcropped amongst the old-growth oaks. Lord help her, Kat was completely lost.

The thickness of early spring foliage hid the camp from sight, but the woodsmoke in the air showed they were getting close. Toren made a motion with his fist, which stopped Eagan next to him. They dismounted, and Toren lifted her down.

His lips brushed her ear, sending shivers along the exposed skin of her neck. "Yer invisibility doesn't hide sound. Aye?"

"Correct, yes" she whispered. He took her hand while Eagan secured the mounts with loose knots around stumps. They walked slowly and silently through the woods until she heard the low murmurs of men, broken by an occasional curse or throaty chuckle. Kat's chest tightened. This was the closest she'd come to a battle, a bloody Highlander battle at that. Reading about one in a book was very different from living through one in flesh and blood. The air was chilled, and the wind whipped hair before her eyes. There were warriors ahead with swords, and probably no issue with ravishing a woman without consent. A cold sweat broke out on her brow, and she almost turned invisible right then and there.

Toren signaled for them to stop. They stepped closer to peer through the leaves, conscious not to kick anything that would alert the small army of their presence. Distant thunder sounded like a growl from some cosmic wolf.

The Campbells were obviously not too worried about anyone nearby. Their cook fires smoked, their unchecked voices carried, and their mood was far from wary. They wore dirty, rumpled versions of ancient kilts. They gathered bundles together, and a few rubbed down the horses, inspecting their hooves.

"They're about to leave," she whispered. The sun had begun its decline somewhere behind the clouds racing in. A rotted tree had been chopped into stumps that the men used to form a circle around a central fire pit. One large Campbell with a swath of crusty mud on his cheeks kicked ashes over the smoking cinders and grabbed the blackened spit that had roasted some animal. The others packed up bed rolls and weapons. One man stood near a tree taking a piss.

Kat jumped as Toren's hand moved around her shoulder. His finger pointed to a familiar form against the base of a tree on the far side. Briana sat with hands behind her, most likely tied. Her gaze followed the men with a frantic fluttering. Her eyes were red and her cheeks streaked. She sat in a torn and muddied gown without the comfort of even a blanket. A tall, dark-haired man paced before her. Briana turned away from him when he spoke until he gripped her face, forcing her to look at him.

"I will kill him," Eagan whispered.

This was no bride eloping with her love. This was a hostage situation. Kat's anger took root, building along her spine, dissolving her fear. She pulled at the water in the air, small molecules of humidity, and wrapped them around herself, preparing to vanish.

Toren's lips brushed warm against her ear. "That's Fergus Campbell," he said in a clipped whisper. He pushed the hilt of his dagger into her palm. "She's bound. Use this."

Kat gripped the dagger. She pulled away and took a deep, centering breath. The buzz of magic hummed as she concentrated on the water molecules infusing her body. And she cloaked herself in glamour magic.

Eagan inhaled quickly, eyes wide and searching.

A gust of wind whipped the unfurling spring leaves overhead. "You might want to explain the plan...and me, to your brother," Kat whispered and crept through the bushes. She attempted not to touch anything that would give her away, but it was difficult with so many leaves and branches to snake around. Luckily the wind continued to rise, muting her stray sounds.

Her twenty-first century nose wrinkled in offence at the smell of old sweat and manure. Kat walked up to a horse who nickered and sidled away. Animals could sense her even if they couldn't see her. *Hello diversion.*

The horses stood tethered. Kat tested the blade along the leather straps that dangled down from one horse. The blade sliced through easily, and the animal shied to the side, pushing the next horse over and so on like dominoes. Kat walked before them, slicing through any hanging strap she saw. Meanwhile, her invisible movements among the beasts unsettled them.

One of the men held his hands out in a calming gesture. "What's spooking ye?" He patted one mare's forelock. "Be there fairies about?" He spat on the ground and farted. *Such talent.*

Kat moved swiftly toward the sword that the man had been cleaning. She slid it along the ground until it lay hidden in the bushes. It would help their cause if she could hide and cut as many things as possible before racing off with Briana. Kat darted around the men, pulling swords and satchels away from the camp out into the bushes and slicing bags of oats and leather straps. The dark clouds moved overhead. The weather was a diversion in itself. With all the swaying of trees and branches and dust blowing around the camp, no one noticed her invisible sabotage.

"Men, we ride before the storm," Fergus Campbell yelled.

Holy Mother!

Fergus turned towards Briana. Kat ran to intercept him, one long leg sliding across his path. He tripped over it and fell forward. Kat leapt up and waved her hands overhead at the already spooked horses, screaming in a high pitch like she imagined a banshee would.

The front horse reared up, its hooves churning in the air as it backed into the animals behind it. They all started screeching and stomping their legs. Kat rushed again and even swatted a few of the calmer looking ones. The horses jostled against their severed ties and burst apart, running frantically in all different directions. Kat jumped to the side as nearly every Campbell ran after their mounts and into the woods.

Kat hurried to the other side of the camp where Briana sat watching the scene, her hair flying about in wild disarray. Kat came up behind her, her voice near the captive's ear.

"Briana, it's me, Kat."

Briana turned in the direction of Kat's voice. "Where are ye?"

"I'm here, just...camouflaged."

"What?"

"Don't move. I'm cutting you loose."

"Take me away from here," Briana choked and stood gingerly as the bindings fell away. "Tor?"

"He and Eagan wait in the woods for us."

"Fergus Campbell will kill them."

"Not if they don't see them."

Briana turned toward Kat, her eyes sliding over the empty space where Kat stood. "Where are ye?" Briana asked, her eyes widening.

Kat reached out to touch her. As soon as she made contact, Kat allowed her invisible shield to coat Briana which made her visible only to the frightened woman. Briana gasped and tried to take a step back, but Kat held tight.

"How...how is it that ye appear?"

Kat shook her head. "There's no time," she said glancing around. "It's part of my gift, to hide, a gift from God so I can help those in need." She led Briana slowly through the camp. The Campbell men ran about the clearing after horses, the wind blowing now with intensity. Several had realized their swords were missing.

"You must keep in contact with me." Kat pulled Briana's hand. "They can't see you now."

Briana took a slow step. "They don't see me?"

"Not as long as we stay connected," Kat said above the rush of wind that yanked her hair free of its confinement. It flew around to mix with Briana's hair in a whirlwind of dark and auburn curls. Kat jumped against Briana to avoid Fergus Campbell. He ran to the tree, picking up the frayed ends of the ropes.

"She's escaped!" he roared.

"Keep moving," Kat ordered as she awkwardly danced Briana through the turmoil. They dodged two men running with swords without breaking apart. They jumped together over a dead branch that fell to the ground. They stood to catch their breaths for a moment in the cooling fire pit. Which way was the fastest and least obstructed route to Toren? Men and beasts ran everywhere. Complete pandemonium swirled about them and the storm seemed like another foe.

"Briana, run when I count to three!" Kat yelled above a crack of thunder a second after lightning zapped across the sky. Kat saw Toren and Eagan crouched through the trees on the far side, ready for them. Toren's eyes met hers. They beckoned, almost begging for her to come to him. "I'm coming," she whispered. "One," Kat called out loud.

"One," Briana repeated.

"Two," Kat said.

"Two." Briana grabbed a handful of torn petticoats in her hand.

"Three," Kat said and took a huge step.

"Stop!" Drakkina's voice shook through Kat. "Stop, Katell! Uncloak yourself! Stop using magic! Now or you'll die!" Drakkina's ethereal body floated above them.

"Three," Briana repeated and tried to step after Kat but ended up bumping into her instead.

"The storm is not natural. It's the demons. They've followed your magic," Drakkina said.

"But I don't have the necklace," Kat yelled back.

"What necklace?" Briana asked bewildered.

"They've tracked the deep magic of the necklace to this year, but they're here and can feel you using magic." Drakkina stared down at Kat. "They will do anything to possess you." Drakkina's words blasted cold fear through Kat's body. "Uncloak now, and I'll draw them away with my magic. They'll think I'm you."

"I can't!" Kat yelled, surveying the Campbell warriors finding their swords. Surprise and embarrassment blended together to increase their fury as they dove into the brush in search of their captive. Any moment now they would find Toren and Eagan. "I can't!"

"You must!" Drakkina yelled back, her smooth visage pinched with frantic appeal. "Or they'll take you."

"Look around me. They," Kat said, pointing to the large men roaming around them, "they will take me if I uncloak!"

"With your magic and the dragonfly amulet, the demons will take the world," Drakkina countered.

Kat closed her eyes. They were dead either way.

"What are ye doing, Kat?" Briana asked, pulling on Kat's arm. "Who are ye talking to?" she said looking up nervously at the whipping trees. "I see Tor. He's motioning for us to come."

Kat opened her eyes and looked into Briana's wild ones. "I'm so sorry," she said and uncloaked them. "Circumstances have changed."

CHAPTER FIFTEEN
BATTALION

Toren's blood pumped where he crouched in the thick, barely budding bushes, Eagan beside him. The storm didn't seem natural, like the one back in Kat's century that the crone said was caused by demons. The hair on the back of Toren's neck stood erect.

Toren's eyes fastened on Kat. Terror flitted across her face as she spoke into the empty air before her. Fear and regret lay heavy on her features.

Toren's instincts whipped him around in time to slice through the Campbell who crept up behind them.

"Och!" Eagan yelled and stood. "They were gone, Tor, but now look!"

Toren pulled his blade free and turned back to the chaos in the clearing. "Ye can see them?"

"Now I can."

Toren jumped out of the bushes into a run. "Then so can the Campbells."

Toren and Eagan made it to Kat and Briana at the same time as Fergus Campbell.

Briana screamed as blade clashed against blade next to them. Kat grabbed Briana against her side.

"Run!" Toren yelled and Kat propelled Briana to the side away from Toren and Fergus, but three other Campbells ran to their chief's aid, blocking the women.

"We can't!" Kat yelled back.

"To my back!" Toren ordered and Kat yanked Briana behind Toren's back. Eagan, who had been fighting two Campbells, moved in front of the women so that he and Toren sandwiched them.

Slash! *Clang!* Slice and lunge. Toren fought from where he guarded Kat and Briana. Eagan did the same. Long minutes passed until Fergus stepped back, sweat running down his grimy brow. He held his sword ready but wiped his other arm across his forehead.

"Ye cannot win, MacCallum," he sneered and motioned to another Campbell to take his place while he rested.

Toren raised his sword to deflect the blow from another man.

"I will keep sending in replacements until you fall down in exhausted defeat." He laughed. The wind whipped around him, swirling dirt and leaves. "Then I'll slaughter ye before yer ladies." Fergus motioned toward Eagan who also fought a fresh Campbell. "Oh and also yer brother there. I'll force yer sister to marry me, and ye and yer brother will be dead." He stood up and grabbed his sword, ready to jump back into the fight.

Toren funneled the rage that surged inside him into his sword arm. He was well trained and seasoned, but could he outlast thirty men? Perhaps his earlier words would ring true. Perhaps in one fell swoop, the MacCallums would perish this day.

"Nay," he said and brought his sword down low in an arc. Fergus jumped back but not before the tip of Toren's blade cut through Fergus's leather tunic and shirt, baring the man's stomach. A thin line of blood cut across the white skin.

"Bloody shite!" Fergus cursed and glanced down at his middle. A distracted second, Toren would take it.

Toren lunged forward, his sword plummeting down. Fergus unfortunately used his instincts too and turned. Toren's sword sliced into Fergus's arm. Not a mortal wound but damaging.

Fergus dropped his sword and jumped backwards, holding his bleeding upper arm. Toren moved forward but two Campbells blocked his advancement. "Finish them!" Fergus spat out as he tied a strap around the useless arm.

"Kat," Toren said and felt her against his back. "Ye cannot cloak us?"

"No, the demons are here. If they take me, they could destroy the world."

"The storm," he answered noticing now that the storm had vanished.

"Drakkina is leading them away from us," she whispered. "If I cloak us, it will call them back."

Toren watched a small cluster around Fergus regroup.

"Toren...I'm so sorry," Kat said.

"We aren't finished yet," Toren replied as five Campbells advanced on him with swords drawn and death in their eyes.

"Five to one," Toren yelled to Eagan.

"Six here," Eagan answered.

Toren could hear his sister's shaky breaths behind him.

"Sweet Jesus Christ, help us," Kat prayed out loud in a calm voice. "Holy Mother Mary, help us." Pride filled Toren as he deflected the first blow. Aye, his lass had spirit and courage.

"Fok!" the Campbell yelled and pulled back. "Hamish, ye almost sliced my arm off, ye fool."

"Feel free to maim each other." Toren worked his shoulder in a circle to relieve the ache as the five constructed a quick plan on how to attack and not kill each other in the process.

The first butterfly hardly caught Toren's attention. Its delicate wings glided on the newly stilled air to sit on one Campbell's head. Blood thrummed through Toren's ears as he prepared to take down as many Campbells as possible. Maybe he could distract the men long enough for Kat and Briana to run. If they could reach the horses they might have a chance.

Two butterflies landed on a second Campbell. He brushed at them with his hand and Toren lunged.

"Arrr!" the second Campbell screamed as Toren's blade sliced down, severing his arm. He dropped to the ground, and another man dragged him back. Toren held his bloody blade before him, his face chiseled of stone.

Four yellow and blue butterflies landed on the next challenger. The man ignored them and danced around Toren, jabbing chaotically. He was either drunk, untrained, or scared to death. His wrinkled red eyes squinted at Toren with rage. Drunk then.

Toren let the man plow ahead towards him and sidestepped the lopsided attack, giving him a powerful kick in the arse. The Campbell flew halfway across the clearing. Toren turned expecting the next attacker.

Instead, the Campbells had stilled, their eyes round with confusion and horror.

Toren followed their gazes upward as a dark cloud blocked the red-tinged sky. He took an involuntary step back, bumping into Kat and Briana.

Even Eagan stood staring as the shifting, fluttering mass of butterflies descended across the clearing, engulfing everyone except Eagan, Toren, Briana and Kat. Butterflies everywhere. Thousands covered the stunned Campbells.

The delicate creatures didn't just alight on the men; they attacked the men. Campbells gagged as butterflies dove into their mouths. They spit out curses with glittery wings. They swiped at the winged beasts that swooped into their eyes and tried to squeeze up their nostrils.

"Toren?" Eagan asked in an awed whisper.

"Go," Toren commanded and grabbed Kat's arm. He was about to throw her over his shoulder like Eagan had done with their sister, but Kat's long legs were already leaping over fallen, butterfly-covered, thrashing men as she raced for the horses.

"Go, go, go!" Briana yelled as Eagan threw her up onto a horse.

"I'm going!" Eagan hoisted himself up after her, looking back at the clearing. "Bloody hell!"

Toren leaped up onto Apollo. He leaned down and caught Kat around the waist, lifting her easily before him. He jerked the reins, wheeling the charger toward the clearing. Throaty garbled screams and thrashing mixed with Gaelic curses. And over all of it came the odd, dizzying flutter sounds of thousands of butterflies as men writhed on the ground, scraping at their faces in desperation. The men were suffocating under the battalion of butterflies.

Toren turned his horse down the road toward the warded clearing. His arm wrapped around Kat's middle, pulling her into him. "Yer friends," he said against her ear.

She nodded, her head bumping into his chin. "I hope they…" her words held worry. "Butterflies are so fragile. They're my friends."

"'Tis a battle of blood, Kat. They are sacrificing to save ye," he rasped, bent over the charger's neck as the animal flew along the path.

When they came close to the blackberry bramble, Toren slowed Apollo. Eagan did the same and came alongside. Briana sat in front of her brother, staring out at the growing twilight.

Eagan looked at Kat and then at Toren. "Are ye a witch?" Eagan asked.

"'Tis a gift from God," Toren said, his words firm. "Like mother's gift."

"I'd say Kat's gift is a bit more useful." A smile spread across Eagan's face.

Kat sat silently in Toren's arms, and he pulled her in even though she was stiff.

"Perhaps we should change the MacCallum crest from the stone fortress to the butterfly." Eagan chuckled. The four wound their way to the path through the brambles.

------------◄O►------------

Kat sat with her knees under her chin as she stared out at the darkness from the middle of the clearing. Her butterflies had sacrificed themselves for her. They were just little insects, but they had died to save them. Where had they come from? Not from the twenty-first century, surely not. They were sixteenth-century insects. Did they even have butterflies in sixteenth-century Scotland? They must since she'd seen the insects depicted in clothing of the time.

Her mind spun between relief, sorrow, and guilt. She'd been certain they would die. Or Toren and Eagan would die and then Briana and she would suffer rape and torture. Kat raised a trembling hand to the right side of her face, to the puckered skin. She couldn't use her magic, or she'd draw the demons. Even though the ancient magic and the additional magic she'd tied off in the stones hid the meadow, she wasn't sure it would hide her if she covered her scars.

Darkness helped shroud her, but in the dawn light her companions would see her ugly face. Would they say anything or act as if it were the most natural thing? Which was worse? Kat shivered.

Toren strode to Apollo who was munching from a bag tied to his halter. Toren pulled a woven blanket from a satchel and shook it while walking back to Kat. "Ye're cold." He settled it around her, covering her to her neck. Kat burrowed down into the heavy cloth, into the darkness as if to hide away from Toren witnessing the others' reactions or non-reactions.

His intense gaze made her squirm. She nodded toward the dark forest. "Will they follow us?"

"Aye, those who survive," he said, with calm certainty.

"When?"

"As soon as they can." He straightened, looking around at their little camp. Margaret and Eagan lowered a blanket over a mossy patch for Sara's bed, and the girl sat down upon it. Briana was washing her face with water Toren had brought back from the stream in a bladder.

"Yer wards still protect this place even if ye can't use yer magic?"

Good question. Kat had warded the gym locker and safe deposit boxes to hide her heist money, making them virtually invisible to people. Once she tied off the power, it was no longer from her, of her, it was from the universe, from the energy and magic that flowed through the earth and water. She'd done the same with the clearing, using the water magic inherent in the brook that flowed nearby, weaving it with the earth magic around the deep roots of the oaks and the foundations of the stones that surrounded the place.

Kat nodded on an inhale. "It should. The Earth protects this place now, not me." She could feel its hum, a soft breeze without wind, a warm glow without sun, a mixture of woven magic that recognized those who should enter and those who should stay out.

Eagan walked over, and Toren nodded toward a blanket on the other side of the fire. "Ye sleep," Toren said. "I'll take the first watch."

Eagan grunted. "If you command it, Brother. But I swear as soon as I close my eyes, I'll have nightmares about butterflies flying up my nose." He glanced toward Kat.

Kat pushed the tip of a stick in the dirt. She sat with her legs crossed, the right side of her face turned slightly toward the cold darkness.

"What are ye drawing?" Briana asked. "It looks like a dragonfly."

Toren snorted behind her. "I'll be walking the perimeter inside the trees." Pebbles crunched as he stalked away.

"It is," Kat said, pulling her eyes away from Toren's broad shoulders.

"I'd think ye would be drawing a butterfly," Briana said, and nibbled on a bannock that Eagan had handed out to each of them after they'd started the fire. "Ye have a gift with them." Briana looked over at Margaret. "Ye should have seen it." She shook her head. "Thousands of them descended like yellow and blue leaves on the Campbells, fluttering and then diving into their eyes and mouths. Never seen anything like it before. They *attacked* the Campbells. We don't even see butterflies up here until summertide."

Kat watched the dirt as she moved the pointy tip of the stick through the soft silt in the glow of the fire. The right side of her face and her back felt the bite of cold but the front of her was hot. "Butterflies have always followed me," Kat said and shrugged her shoulders. "They come when I need a friend."

"Or a regiment of warriors." Briana said.

Kat nodded but kept her gaze on the ground. This way, in her own thoughts, she didn't have to turn toward Margaret and Briana. Silence stretched while they ate the bannocks, the rabbit Toren had snared, and the fresh blackberries that grew throughout the brambles encircling the clearing even though they weren't in season.

"Sara says ye hide yer face," Margaret said, her voice cracking through the silence like an axe through a frozen pond.

"Mama," Sara squeaked, sitting up from her pallet behind her mother and looking at Kat. "I meant that ye're able to hide, unlike me."

Kat's mouth relaxed. "Sara, you will grow out of your birthmark. I've seen it before." Kat's gaze moved to Margaret. "I knew a little girl with the same type of mark, and it disappeared completely by the time she was nine."

Margaret nodded and then leaned forward trying to catch sight of Kat's right cheek. "She says ye burned the whole side of yer face."

Kat felt the flush. It was familiar but this time she couldn't hide it, couldn't use her magic. She stared down at the dirt again and nodded. Maybe the ladies would just let it drop.

Briana stood and walked to her other side. So much for relying on sixteenth-century manners. "I've tended more burns than I can count," Briana said and squatted down on Kat's right side. Her hand touched Kat's shoulder. "May I see?"

Kat looked up and exhaled. "Sure." What else could she say? She turned her right cheek to the fire.

Briana didn't touch the skin. "Looks old, well healed. Ye were just a lass when it happened."

Kat nodded. "I was little and foolish."

Briana straightened. "Aren't we all when we're wee lads and lasses." She laughed and glanced at Sara where she watched from her position lying on her side.

Kat didn't turn away when Margaret leaned almost into the fire to see Kat's scars. "Oh they are well healed." She nodded again. "A blessing that."

"Do they pain ye?" Briana asked. "I have some salve that some say helps."

"No," Kat said and moved her gaze to Briana for the first time since she'd been inspected.

Briana smiled. "Ye certainly are a beauty even with the burn. I can see why Tor is so caught up in ye."

Margaret smiled timidly and leaned forward, whispering. "He stares at you all the time."

Kat's stomach flipped a little. "Stares at me?"

A mischievous glint lit Briana's eyes. "Aye. I've never seen him do that with a lass before." She sat back and wiped her hands together. "Oh many a lassie has followed my brother with her gaze, but none until now has he noticed for more than a night of fun."

"Briana," Margaret whispered, warning in her tone.

The flutter in Kat's stomach tightened, and she frowned. "He has a lot of those 'nights of fun' then?"

Briana waved a hand. "Och, Kat. Do not listen to me. Nay, he does not." Briana reached over to squeeze her fingers. "Kat, there's something new in my brother," she said, her voice low and serious. "Something I've never seen in Tor before."

Muted anger and hopeful excitement clenched in Kat's chest, but she quickly soothed it away with a deep breath. Why would she care if Toren looked at her? He was attracted physically like others before. And just as with other men, it was best not to let him too close. He certainly didn't want to take on all her baggage—the children, the witch, saving the world. And then there were her hideous scars. Unfortunately for him, his reported soul mate was marred.

Kat watched Toren stalk along the perimeter of their warded meadow. He stopped near Eagan who lay asleep on a rolled plaid. Eagan shifted, his hand flying out to swat the air before his face, eyes still closed.

Toren turned toward the darkness. His back was broad and strong, his stance full of determination, full of duty. Even if Briana had noticed him looking at her, he couldn't take on all of what Kat was. She was too much for any man and, at the same time, not enough. She touched the puckered skin of her cheek.

He had his family to protect just as she did back in the twenty-first century. Finding the dragonfly necklace and sending Kat home would be second to taking his family to safety. As it should be.

"Are ye truly betrothed?" Briana asked, her voice low.

Kat shook her head and met her gaze. "I think I'm just an interesting problem for him, a complication."

Briana laughed softly and pushed a long stick into the fire. "I wouldn't expect an easy woman to capture my brother's interest." Briana smiled. "Complicated suits Tor," she said and laid her head down on her dirt-smudged arm.

Margaret and Sara cuddled together under another plaid, and Kat heard them whispering their nightly prayers together. Kat wrapped a wool blanket around her shoulders, still sitting before the fire. Her eyes grew heavy as she watched Toren pace like a large cat with silent, powerful strides. He stilled every few paces, listening and peering into the dark.

Toren turned towards her as if he felt the questions in her stare. She couldn't look away from his dark orbs. His stare, his stance, made it difficult for Kat to draw in a full breath of the crisp cold air.

"Sleep," he said, his voice soft but carrying.

Kat turned away and lowered to spread out on her side. Her hand caught her moonstone, gently squeezing it. "Then stay out of my head," she whispered, and closed her eyes, shutting him out.

CHAPTER SIXTEEN
CRAIGNISH CASTLE

Misty sunlight and angry voices roused Kat from her sleep. She blinked and jumped. Briana's face sat so close to her own, Kat couldn't focus on it. Kat rolled back, but Briana followed.

Briana leaned so close to her ear that her lips touched. "Don't make a sound." The terror in Briana's voice froze Kat. "The Campbells are out there." She pointed with one long finger at the bushes where Eagan and Toren stood, their swords drawn. Kat saw Sara and Margaret clutched together near the far side of the circle.

"As long as we stay in the circle, they can't find us," Kat said and sat up.

"Are ye certain?" The desperation in Briana's tone tickled doubt along Kat's skin.

"Yesterday, I...God gave me a gift to hide us, and I used it to hide this clearing. As long as we stay within it no one can see us."

"But ye are not using yer power now," Briana whispered, pointing to her cheek. "I can see ye."

Kat's palm automatically covered her scars. "I tied off my magic into the natural magic elements already here. The oaks, the rocks." Kat nodded to emphasize her words, but Briana's eyes remained large. Kat took her hand and squeezed reassuringly. If they were in the twenty-first century, Kat would help Briana find a good therapist to work through what she'd gone through. But there was nothing like that here, only the care of friends.

"Their trail ends here," a rough voice called on the other side of the blackberry bushes where Eagan and Toren stood guard.

"Then where the bloody hell are they?" That was Fergus Campbell, and he was furious.

No one answered, but Kat watched the bushes all around their circle rustle and sway as the men searched the underbrush. *Let the wards hold!* A chill raced along Kat's neck as if she'd heard those frantic pleas before. The crashing, swearing, and shuddering bushes continued for countless minutes. Toren and Eagan stood back-to-back watching the perimeter brambles jostle, their swords balanced, ready to strike. It was as if all in the circle held their breaths. The birds had silenced, and the tree leaves overhead ceased to flutter as if they were suspended in time and place.

"They must have moved off the road and into the forest to hide their tracks. Them MacCallums know the way of hidin'," another man added, his brogue so thick that Kat wouldn't have understood him without her moonstone.

"They aren't here. Daingead!" a man cursed. "Just these devilish thorns."

A roar of fury echoed off the trees followed by Gaelic words flung so hard Kat cringed, and Margaret covered Sara's ears. "To London, then!" Fergus shouted. "They would put Briana before the bloody queen's nose and demand retribution. Maxwell must have another plan," he said, his steps fading.

Margaret Maxwell's eyes were enormous as she watched Briana. "The sins of my father are great," Margaret whispered. "I am sorry." Kat wondered if Margaret even noticed that she pulled Sara closer into the protection of her own body. Kat's chest grew tight at the thought of them living under Maxwell's rule, what Margaret must have endured to keep her daughter shielded.

An unease sat amongst the three women until Briana exhaled. "They are his sins, not yers. Sara and ye are welcome with the MacCallums."

"Aye, ye are welcome," Eagan added as he walked up and reached down to help Margaret stand.

Margaret's gaze moved to Toren. Her eyes shone with unshed tears. "I am grateful for my daughter's protection." She bowed her head.

"We head out now," Toren said from the far perimeter.

Rocking onto her knees, Kat rose and smoothed her shirt front and breeches while the ladies dusted their gowns. Although the stable boy outfit she wore was much more practical, Kat yearned to swish the Tudor-era skirts. Even dusty and torn, the gowns were certainly more attractive, not that she was trying to attract anyone.

"'Tis good we ride in the opposite direction to Craignish," Toren said.

"So north of here?" she asked. Although he'd said it before, it still felt risky. Drakkina could pop back in at any moment to demand the necklace.

"I will not leave Eagan alone to take three females through dangerous territory."

Eagan turned a reddish shade but didn't say anything.

Kat crossed her arms over her chest. "The necklace—"

"Is secure for the time being," he finished. "Once they are safe at Craignish, we will find the necklace."

"What necklace?" Eagan asked.

Kat and Toren stared at one another without answering. Toren's duty was to his family first. She could almost hear him yelling it in his head.

Very well, she understood. He would protect his family just like she would do anything to find that necklace and go home to hers. She continued to stare unblinking into his eyes until they began to sting.

"Then let's go." She turned to find the horses.

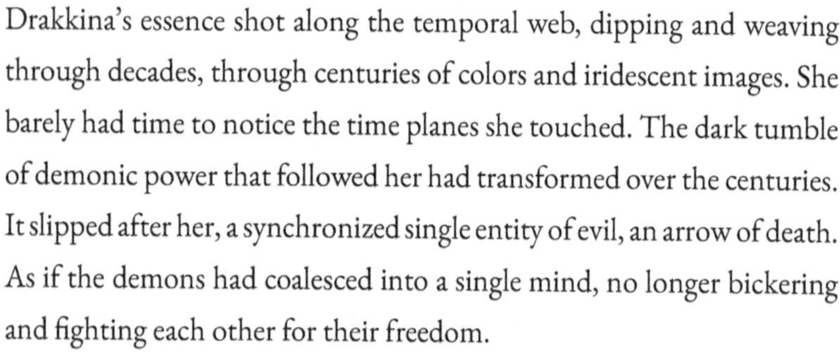

Drakkina's essence shot along the temporal web, dipping and weaving through decades, through centuries of colors and iridescent images. She barely had time to notice the time planes she touched. The dark tumble of demonic power that followed her had transformed over the centuries. It slipped after her, a synchronized single entity of evil, an arrow of death. As if the demons had coalesced into a single mind, no longer bickering and fighting each other for their freedom.

Drakkina had bound them thousands of years ago to hinder them. She, in essence, tied their hands together, tethering them, to slow their malicious intentions. It was what Semiazaz deserved after he'd killed someone very important to Drakkina. She had hoped that the group's constant squabbling would keep them impotent and drained of power. But the arrow chasing her was far from impotent. She hadn't been powerful enough in her spirit form to avenge her love nor to protect Gilla and Druce. Now that they were acting in concert, they were deadlier than they'd ever been.

Drakkina wrapped herself in glamour magic so that she looked, smelled, and vibrated like young Kat. As long as Kat didn't use her own magic to confuse the demons, they should follow Drakkina, thinking that Kat had somehow obtained the ability to cross times. But how long could she stay ahead of them?

Drakkina darted and dove, twisted and turned back on herself, yet they trailed. "My dragonfly," Drakkina breathed tightly as she tore along an ancient line of gritty brown, diving into the dust storm around a half-completed pyramid. The powers surrounding the sacred place radiated outward, obscuring Drakkina's magic signature, camouflaging her within its own magic. She panted as she laid her essence within the cracks around each block of chiseled stone. *I need my dragonfly.* Kat's mate had put a binding spell on it. Only he could release it to Drakkina.

Craignish Castle faced west towards the sea. The stone fortress boasted two tower houses, a wall walk, a thousand arrow slits, and a curtain wall guarded by a toothy portcullis. *Home.* Toren hadn't seen it for five long years of fury-filled panic that it was forever lost. But here he stood among the pines staring out across the glossy surface of Loch Beag. Toren listened to the horses as they slurped mouthfuls of fresh lake water. Toward the center of the magnificent freshwater pool a large fish flopped.

"Right out of one of my favorite Scottish novels," Kat whispered. The sound of her breath between those lovely lips washed over Toren, and he closed his eyes for a moment. He felt her next to him as if she hummed with life or some magical resonance. Cool fingers grazed his hand but then fell away. "Your home is unreal."

He glanced at her, gaze trailing the lush landscape of hair as it fell behind her ear and down her back.

"I mean of course it's real," she said as if needing to explain. "It's just so...majestic, so full of history."

Toren's gaze slid back to the castle. It was safer to look at the hard lines of granite and mortar than the soft lines of Kat's lips. Although the contrast made Kat even more alluring. "Aye, majestic," he repeated without thinking. *Focus.* "But 'tis also full of drafts and mice." He looked at her. "No hot showers and toilets within those solid walls."

Kat gave him a quirky smile. "I suppose there are tradeoffs for pollution, traffic, and modern craziness," she whispered. "I can withstand it for a short time."

Toren's lips clenched tight. *She plans to go back.* Of course. Kat had responsibilities, her children. The ache in the back of Toren's head tightened. *She could get used to life here.* But he didn't say it out loud. Toren turned toward his horse. "Let's ride."

He helped her mount Apollo and climbed on behind her. Kat didn't hold herself apart but rested easily in the saddle against his splayed thighs. He inhaled and caught the smell of fresh wind, woodsmoke, and the remnants of her floral shampoo that she'd carried with her from her century. Pressing Apollo into a canter, the wind blew away Kat's scent, and they rode across the moor that led to the village squatting before the castle like mushrooms around a towering tree.

"Lordy," Kat said when they slowed. "Majestic doesn't do it justice."

The horse clopped along the winding trail through the thatch-roofed cottages. He'd never thought of the place as quaint or charming, but after facing twenty-first century London, his village was filled with peacefulness and quiet beauty. Fresh, cool spring air mixed with the odors of smoking meat with an undercurrent of animal dung. Women beat rugs and worked butter churns. Young children scurried between the cottages laughing and brandishing wooden swords. Dogs barked and chased the children.

People stopped their labors as they rode along. "Laird Toren! Master Eagan! Lady Briana!" The villagers waved and called greetings. Toren breathed deeply. *Aye, 'tis good to be home.*

Kat pulled the woven blanket she'd been using as a shawl over her head like a hood, so the right side of her face was hidden.

Och but she still felt the need to hide her lovely face. He leaned near her ear. "They may think ye're a leper if ye cover up completely."

"Nice, MacCallum," she said with sarcasm and pulled the fabric down.

"The walls are six feet thick," Eagan said. "The water is clean, and we have three wells." Margaret smiled over Sara's head at him.

Their party stopped before a tall set of steps that led to two gigantic doors. Two young boys ran out of the nearby barn and grabbed the reins.

"Thank ye, Will and Bart," Toren said with a nod. The lads hadn't grown at all in the time he'd been gone. It was as if he'd never left 1588. For them anyway. To Toren, the differences between centuries were vast. It must be even more disturbing to Kat. He lowered her to the ground.

People stared at Kat but also Margaret and Sara. Toren caught Kat's gaze with his. "They are but curious."

"Of course," Kat said but still pulled her hair around to swing along the sides of her face. Somewhat camouflaged, she walked with the others up the steps.

A small group of villagers gathered below to watch them ascend. "Welcome, Laird," several called. "Is there news from London?"

"I will hold a town hall meeting as soon as we've recovered from our travels," he said. What would he say then? *I've been in the twenty-first century for five years and brought back a witch who is being chased by a pack of demons and a crone?* That Kat possessed more magic than his mother and grandmama but couldn't use it without bringing the destruction of the world down upon them.

Toren blew a gust as an exhale and strode inside the keep.

⚫

"'Tis good to see ye, Cameron," Eagan said, grabbing the forearm of one man with the end of his sleeve tied closed. Was he missing a hand?

Kat stood with Margaret and Sara as Briana, Eagan, and Toren greeted their people inside. Everyone seemed happy to see them. The homesickness that knotted in Kat's chest tightened.

A middle-aged woman wearing an apron walked up to Toren, her round face cracked in a smile. "We thought ye'd be away longer."

Toren pulled her into a hug. "Oh my, what's this?" she asked with a laugh, her eyes wide.

"I missed ye, Fiona." He set her back with a smile and walked to the table where tankards had been set out. "In answer," he said, "we had business that took us away from Hampton Court." He took several swallows of refreshment, set his tankard down, and took up two more.

Toren dodged several of Briana's friends who were hugging her. "Ye look a sight," a modest-looking lady said, brushing at the dirt on Briana's petticoat. Perhaps she was Briana's lady's maid. She had smallpox scars across her face.

"We ran into..." Briana glanced at Toren, and he gave a slight shake of his head.

Briana turned back to her friend. "Some trouble with the horses. And I had to sleep on the ground last night."

Kat felt Sara's hand brush her own and then push into her palm. Kat squeezed the child's hand.

"Here," Toren said, stopping before them. "Small ale, mild enough for the lass." He handed one to Margaret to share with Sara and one to Kat.

"Thank ye, milord," Margaret said, bowing her head with formality. Sara curtsied. The two stood pale and watchful. Margaret and Sara were refugees and related to the hated enemy. Their lives depended on the forgiveness and acceptance of these people. There were no women's shelters or restraining orders in the sixteenth century. They could be thrown out to the wolves, literally.

"Thank you," Kat said. "Shall I also curtsey?"

Toren's tight lips relaxed. "If ye feel inclined."

Kat just stared without bending an inch and took a sip from the cool ale. It had just enough alcohol to give the water a bready beer taste. She kept Toren's gaze the whole time. The corners of his mouth turned upward as if he found her lack of curtsey amusing.

"A smile?" she asked. "Be careful, Toren, or your chiseled face might crack." Her words sounded terse.

Toren took her elbow and led her closer to the hearth, away from Sara and Margaret. She looked over her shoulder at them. "I'll be right back."

Eagan walked over, his boots clicking on the stone floor. He took Margaret's arm. Bless that man!

Toren stopped near the mantle. "Ye are angry."

She was, but she couldn't pinpoint why. "Well…you said I look like a leper."

He exhaled through his nose. "I did not. I merely said others would wonder what ye were hiding behind yer hood."

"Margaret and Sara are terrified to be here," she said.

Toren motioned to Eagan. "I believe my gregarious brother is starting to remedy that."

"Lady Maxwell saved Briana and all of us by revealing her father's plan," Eagan said and continued the story. Apparently, he hadn't heard that they were keeping things quiet.

Kat held her palms out to the flames in the hearth. "We have come north when we are supposed to be getting the dragonfly amulet back."

"Like I said before, I needed to get the ladies to safety first."

And I don't like the way you make me feel. She couldn't say that of course. He made her both warm and weak. After hours of riding before him in the saddle, smelling his mix of man, leather, and fresh air, he'd worked his way under her skin. Their kiss kept playing through her head, making her stomach tighten with hope that it would happen again. And then he'd frown or stride away or not meet her gaze. The man was as complicated and difficult as one of those iron brain teaser puzzles given away in tourist shops.

She crossed her arms over her chest. "I just want to go home. My people need me."

He nodded slowly. "That is a feeling I've known for five long years, Kat."

Eagan called out toward them. "Bring Kat, Mistress Diciadain, over."

Before she could consider if she'd go over or mutely frown at Toren, he placed her hand on his bent arm and led her over. If she'd tried to stop, she was fairly sure he'd drag her.

Kat bowed her head slightly to the small group before the long table. After all she wasn't even wearing a gown. Curtsying in pants would look ridiculous.

"Please call me Kat," she said, not certain what was allowed.

Eagan raised his goblet like he was making a toast to her. "Mistress Kat risked her life by sneaking into Fergus Campbell's camp and freeing our sister."

"It was amazing!" Briana said and then lowered her voice. "I owe Kat my life."

Smiling faces surrounded Kat, and all she could do was smile back. No one stared at her cheek and jaw, they just smiled into her eyes.

"Lady Margaret and Mistress Kat helped us save Briana," Eagan continued. "We offer them and Lady Margaret's daughter our protection in gratitude."

Eyes turned to Toren as if approval was needed. This was definitely not a democracy. Toren stood tall next to Eagan. "Eagan's words are my words," he said, and the room was filled with wide gazes. Even Eagan looked surprised.

Kat heard whispers behind. "Aye, that's what he said. 'Eagan's words are mine own.'"

Toren thumped his hand down on Eagan's shoulder and nodded toward Margaret. "Ye are welcome Lady Margaret." His eyes moved to Sara, and he bowed slightly. "As are ye, Lady Sara."

Briana looked at the middle-aged woman. "Some food perhaps, Mistress Fiona? In celebration."

Fiona, who Kat assumed was in charge of running the domestic side of the castle, clapped twice, her smile wide. "Janet, Anne, some food."

Several women who had been listening from the periphery bustled toward an alcove that must lead to the kitchens. Warrior-looking men came up to Eagan and clapped him on the back and spoke with Toren. Kat let her gaze run over the plaid wrapping around their hips and sashes and leather belts and scabbards. The swords would be worth so much to a museum.

Heaven help her, she was still thinking of stealing money for the children's home. Even after getting caught up in this... Well, it wasn't exactly a nightmare. She was thrilled to see history come to life around her: sounds, smells, bright colors, and authentic means of living. And there was Toren. He was more a dream than a nightmare, an outlandish Highlander dream. But being stuck here and missing her children was clouding everything.

Women brought out platters of bread and meat and what looked like some sort of mush. Briana directed another woman, pointing to curving steps in a dark alcove. How many rooms did Craignish have?

Briana walked over, ushering them to take seats along the table. She seemed to fit easily into the role of lady of the castle. "Do eat a bit and then ye can refresh above stairs."

"I hope we're not putting you out," Kat said. Briana tilted her head, her eyes squinting. "I mean," Kat explained, "I hope there is room for us and that we're not intruding."

Briana smiled and shook her head. "Father had many rooms built in hopes of a large family. Mother got tired of birthing after I came along."

"And your father was put off?" Margaret asked and then blushed. "Pardon, Lady Briana."

Briana's brows rose. "Oh, I know how odd it sounds, but my mother had a way about her that brooked no refusal."

"A blessing," Margaret said. What had the woman witnessed or endured under her father's rule?

Kat inhaled the delicious rosemary aroma from the steaming beef, and her stomach growled. Margaret, Sara, and Kat sat at the long wooden table while more food was brought out. The homecoming seemed to warrant a celebration with rolls, root vegetables, fish, roast beef, and chicken pies. Tarts with some type of berry in them were brought out for dessert.

Throughout the meal, Kat felt curious eyes on her, and she pulled her hair forward on the right side. So far no one had mentioned her scars nor showed any revulsion to Sara's large birthmark. Perhaps the MacCallums were more accepting.

One woman came forward with a pitcher. "Mistress wishes some light wine?" Kat turned and paused. The woman had puckered skin down her cheek and neck. It was a burn scar, just like Kat's. Kat nodded, and the woman poured. Her smile stretched the taught skin of the burn.

"Thank you," Kat murmured and turned her attention across the table. A man talked with Eagan. He reached forward to stab a slice of venison with his knife. Three fingers on his right hand ended at the first knuckle.

Kat scanned the room. One lady brought in a platter of pheasant or small chickens. A sleeve inched up, revealing a nasty-looking scar on her wrist and forearm —perhaps a water burn. An elderly man at the end of the table stood up to wave at another who had just walked in. The elderly man's right leg ended at the knee. Then there was the man Eagan had clasped forearms with earlier who didn't have a hand.

Kat kept looking around so she wouldn't be caught staring. Her gaze stopped on Toren and connected. He nodded slowly. Thank goodness breathing was a mostly autonomic response or she might have forgotten to as her mind raced. Kat looked down at the buttered bread.

Sara leaned into her and cupped her small hand at Kat's ear and whispered. "Many people here have scars. Did you notice?"

Kat turned to her. "We fit in."

Sara smiled broadly and politely bit a piece of chicken.

Odd that Toren hadn't mentioned that his household was filled with imperfect people. Kat's stomach clenched. Was he orchestrating this scenario to put her at ease? Her face flushed. Could he or his well-meaning sister have asked all those who had scars or deformities in the village to come play the part of normal Craignish Castle attendants? Kat chewed the dissolving bite of bread as she considered the possibility.

"Usually Lizzie's bread makes people smile, not frown so," Briana said from across the table.

Kat's attention rose to Briana's joyful eyes. Sincerity shined there like a beacon, bringing out her own smile. "It is wonderful," she said around a swallow. Even if Briana had hired scarred and disabled people to act as servants and guests in her house, she did it out of friendship.

"Aye, it is most delicious," Sara said. Kat's heart warmed. It was the first time Sara had spoken to another adult without answering a direct question. If the actors had made the child feel as if she fit in, it was a good idea.

"Then what had ye frowning so ferociously?" Briana asked, her sharp gaze on Kat.

"I'm just tired," Kat said and looked down at her dusty clothes. "And very dirty."

Briana looked down at her own clothes. "Och, but we will have to do something about that."

CHAPTER SEVENTEEN
IMPERFECT

"This room will be yours," Briana said, indicating a sparse yet functional room made of white plastered stone walls with two skinny windows, a medium-sized hearth in the wall, and a low bed with cheery yellow curtains surrounding it. A large tapestry graced one wall, and several portraits were spread about, hanging from the molding that ran above. And they were of course all originals. Kat held a hand to her heart, her eyes scanning the lovely chamber.

"Margaret," Briana said, turning to mother and daughter. "I thought ye would like to have Sara with ye."

"Aye," Margaret agreed and clasped Sara's hand.

"Ye will be in the room three doors farther down then, as the bed is larger." The three continued down the hall, leaving Kat standing in the doorway. "Winifred will be up shortly with yer bath, Kat, and then Mary with some gowns," Briana called back.

"Thank you." Kat walked farther into the room. She shivered and took the fire poker to the coals to revive them. She set another dried peat square in the middle and blew until it caught. Standing, she rested a hand on the stone arch above the hearth. Real, hard, cold granite. *Amazing!*

"Will the room do?" a familiar voice yanked Kat around. Toren stood in the doorway.

Kat nodded and drew in a breath. "Yes, it's beautiful."

Toren looked at the tapestry along the wall. "Not our best, but something for a historian to enjoy. I hope ye find it comfortable here," he said with a slight frown. Just what that meant, Kat wasn't sure, but she was having a hard time thinking in the confined space.

"There's no loo or shower here," he continued. "Instead, we have close stools and wooden bathing tubs."

"Perfect for a historian," she said and waved a hand.

He took a step inside the room. "I studied the mechanics of plumbing while I was trapped in yer time, and I plan to create a flush toilet and pipes to bring in water."

Kat's eyes widened. "You can't do that. Flushing toilets and showers won't be in common use for another three hundred years."

His eyes narrowed. "Are ye accusing me of altering the development of good hygiene?"

"Yes. People were just starting to see connections between throwing their excrement in the streets and the rise of disease. Good hygiene wasn't publicized until the mid-eighteen hundreds."

"I'll keep it hidden and swear everyone who knows about it to secrecy," he said, the ghost of a grin on his lips. "I'll be the oddly clean chief."

She frowned at him and opened her mouth to speak, but he started first. "I looked in yer great library, and Queen Elizabeth's godson is creating a toilet-like contraption that he'll present in 1592 to the queen. I will figure one out too."

She huffed. "Do not alter history, Toren MacCallum. There will be repercussions."

"I already have." His smile faded to a straight line, and his eyes went cold. "I rescued my sister from Fergus Campbell." He inhaled fully. "Without doing so, Craignish would be taken by the Campbells and Maxwell, and my bloodline would disappear from history."

It certainly explained why he hadn't even considered going after the amulet when his sister was missing. And his concern that all three of them— Eagan, Briana, and Toren—could be killed facing off against the Campbells. It meant more than their deaths. It meant the erasure of their clan.

"Well..." She stared, unsure what to say.

"I want ye to be comfortable."

His presence filled the room. Toren was tall, broad, and full of muscle. For days Kat had only viewed him in God's grand outdoors. In the shadow of mountains and open sky and soaring trees, Toren seemed of normal large stature, but inside the room, he felt like a giant.

She swallowed. "Comfortable here," she repeated. "Is that why you brought in so many"—she hesitated—"scarred and maimed people?" She indicated the open door and lowered her voice. "So I would feel comfortable with not being able to use my magic?"

Confusion drew Toren's brows in. "I don't understand what ye're saying." He made the same gesture toward the door to mimic her.

Kat walked to one of the windows, the glass thick and wavy. "Really, it's okay, sweet in fact. It made Sara feel much better seeing some other people with scars and physical limitations."

"Those people work in the castle. The others were seasoned warriors." Toren followed her. "No one brought in people to make ye feel more comfortable."

Kat turned so that her good cheek faced him. "But so many of them were scarred or hurt in some way."

"Life is hard in this century. Ye know that, lass."

She ignored the flush she felt rising. "But at court I didn't see anyone—"

"Court won't allow imperfection, at least not on the outside." Toren's hand reached for the bit of hair resting over her right cheek. "But in real life, outside the court many people have scars, imperfections. And they don't have to hide them."

At that Kat's chin rose. "I'm not hiding."

"Good." He smiled. "Because scars show that a person is strong. That they survived."

Kat watched him, frozen, as he ran his finger down her right cheek.

"That something battled against them and they won because they lived, whether it was illness or from a sword or from a burn."

"I guess I never thought of it that way," she murmured.

"Of course, ye haven't." He dropped his hand and turned. "Not living in yer world of face paint, supermodels, plastics, buutox."

"Botox," Kat corrected.

"Whatever foolishness," he said. "I watched a lot of yer television and almost every picture shows a way to look younger and smoother and more like a wee lass, rather than a full-grown woman." He shook his head. "Scars show strength and wisdom."

"My scars just show how stupid I was," Kat said, her gaze on the floor, but then she forced it up. She wouldn't look pitiable in front of Toren.

"Ye were a young lass, right?"

Kat nodded.

"Curious, headstrong."

She nodded again.

He caught her chin and tilted it so he could look in her eyes. "Perfect qualities in a leader and a warrior. And ye survived and learned from it. Ye know the feel of pain, ye lived through it and came out the stronger." Toren tilted his head. "It has added interest and strength to yer beauty."

Kat's breath was held captive by Toren's deep hazel eyes. He let her chin go and stepped back. Kat nearly fell forward, his pull like that of a small moon sucking in an orbiting object.

In one swipe he pulled off his tunic and stood naked from the waist up. She almost choked on her inhale. "Most of my scars were earned in battle," he said.

Kat blinked, letting her gaze slide along the nicks and little puckers of skin of Toren's muscled torso and chest. The fire glowed on his skin, making it look warm. He turned then. "But not all of them."

Kat stopped the gasp she knew would sound like pity or horror as she surveyed the deep lash marks across Toren's back. He'd been whipped terribly, probably within an inch of his life. The scars looked old, healed but not forgotten. Never forgotten.

Kat reached out and touched one with her fingertip. Toren remained still, like a scarred statue.

"You've known pain, too," Kat whispered. "A lot of pain."

Toren turned and pulled on his tunic. A hollow feeling of regret collected in Kat's chest.

He grinned slightly, but it was brittle. "Briana says that the scars on the inside are more painful, which is why my sister continually tries to get me to talk about them."

Kat thought about her children at home. Some of them had come to Lisa and her in so much emotional pain that all they could do was stare or cry. It had taken months to reach Clara and her brother. "Your sister is a wise woman," Kat said.

"She would agree with ye, lass." He grinned. This time the smile reached his eyes, warming them with a flirtatious spark.

Toren looked toward the door, and Kat could hear the faint footsteps far off down the hallway. "Even though we are not at court," he said, "ye should bar yer door at night."

"Should I?" Kat asked, although the words sounded more like a passionate whisper. She cleared her throat and tried to smile.

"If ye wish to keep someone out," Toren replied and took a step closer.

"Is there someone I should keep out?" Kat continued, as if her tongue was apart from her brain. Was she actually flirting? Lisa would be so proud.

Toren stood close enough that she could feel the energy within him. He was full of humming power. Did he realize that he possessed magic? He'd talked of the gift his mother had.

He turned his gaze to the flames. "Fire gives off heat, draws people to it," Toren said. She followed his gaze to the dancing flames but didn't say anything. "But when the fire is fed," he looked at her, "it can consume ye."

Kat swallowed. "Am I being warned?"

Toren paused. "I lived in yer century for five years, Kat." Toren's gaze washed down her body, still clad in the tunic and tight-fitting pants. His face grew serious. The man's emotions could change with the wind. Within a heartbeat he'd gone from flirtatious to dangerous. "I figured out quickly," he said, "that women do not wait for marriage to let a man into their beds."

Normal women, perhaps. Not a twenty-six-year-old virgin who didn't want anyone touching her right cheek. Where was he going with this? "I suppose so," she answered.

His eyes reflected the flame as he stared into her face. "We started something at court, something we could finish," he said and looked at her sideways.

Kat's eyes grew wide under raised eyebrows. She forced herself to blink because the fire's heat was drying them out. A loud rap on the door frame made her jump.

A maid stuck her head around the corner to look at Kat. "Pardon, milady, I am Winifred." Her gaze fell on Toren. "Oh! Many pardons, Chief, I but..." She flapped her hand toward the hallway. "The bath water and tub are coming up now."

Toren leaned closer to Kat's ear. "Ye're playing with fire, Kat," Toren said low. "Embrace it and ye may be consumed." His gaze bored into her own. "Otherwise, squelch it quickly else it burn ye."

She pulled back to stare into his eyes. "I thought pain made one strong."

He raised one eyebrow. "As long as ye survive it."

Kat's tongue went dry and stuck to the roof of her mouth.

Was that his answer to whether she should bar the door? A giddy restlessness flipped in Kat's stomach.

Men marched in with buckets of steaming water for her warm bath. At the moment, a cold shower would serve her better. Too bad that wouldn't be possible for nearly three hundred years.

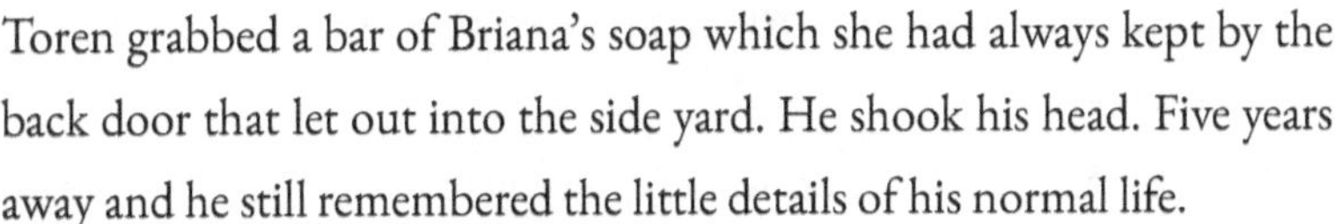

Toren grabbed a bar of Briana's soap which she had always kept by the back door that let out into the side yard. He shook his head. Five years away and he still remembered the little details of his normal life.

Normal life. His grin was more like a sarcastic sneer. Normal life was over the moment he'd been sucked out of his time, forced to live as a twenty-first century man, and thrown back home again. And now he had an auburn-haired temptress messing with his loyalties. Toren strode across the bailey, nodded to one of the guardsmen, and jogged toward Loch Beag.

It had been five years since he'd bathed in the icy mountain runoff of Aonach Beag. It was April, far enough into spring that the ice had melted on the top of the loch. As he neared the familiar shoreline, Toren unbelted his plaid, unraveling it as he slowed. Last off, his tunic. Completely naked, Toren dove through the glassy surface. The frigid water slammed against his skin, and his muscles contracted. Even his heart gave a start.

He surfaced. "Bloody hell!" *'Tis foking ice!* "Damn twenty-first-century hot showers," he cursed and threw himself into a broad stroke. Five years of hot showers and central heat had thinned his Highland blood. *Time to toughen back up.*

Toren pumped arms and kicked long legs across the loch. Turning, he headed back for the soap. Perhaps he should start with short, daily swims to recondition himself. At least the cold had cooled the blood that simmered close to boiling whenever he found himself near Kat.

Toren grabbed the soap and lathered its pine scent into the hair across his chest and down between his narrow hips. Ahh—good old pine and lye, no moisturizers and aloe extract. None of the strawberry and candy-smelling scents he'd accidentally bought early in his exile. He squelched a shiver as wind whipped across the lake, raising the hairs across his body.

"Her century makes men weak," he growled and dove back under the water to rinse the soap and dirt away. He pushed off the bottom, surfacing, and threw wet, shaggy hair back with a flick of his head. "Foking cold." He willed his leg muscles not to cramp and walked out of the lake.

Toren wrapped the dry tartan loosely and grabbed his shirt and soap. He glanced up at the window of Kat's room. How did he know exactly where she was without counting them? He stopped to count. Aye, it was her window, but he'd known immediately, as if she was a beacon. Or like the binding he'd placed on the dragonfly necklace.

Frowning, he walked toward the gates of Craignish and saw a flicker beyond the slit window of her room. Kat should have finished her warm bath by now. She'd have sat in the tub of hot, steaming water up to her lush breasts, her hair over the back rim. Briana would have given her some flower-smelling soap. Kat's skin would smell of honeysuckle or lilac. It would be soft after years of pampering in her century, not rough and wind-parched.

He'd have to find a way to import some lotions and oils from France to protect her skin, especially during the winter months. And he'd have to find the warmest clothing for her. If she grew sick here without the medicine of her time... Toren's stomach tightened. He'd read about resistance to invisible creatures, called germs, when he'd been so sick that first year in Kat's century. His immune system wasn't used to the onslaught of new germs that were unseen but everywhere. And Kat's body wouldn't have any resistance to the unsanitary conditions of his century. "Daingead," he murmured, drying his hair with a small towel. He'd talk to the cook about washing and cooking Kat's food longer than typical and he'd speak to Winifred about boiling water to wash Kat's underclothes.

"Bloody cold to be bathing in the loch," Eagan called down from the wall.

Toren frowned and trudged forward. He nodded to a few other men as he walked up the path. For a moment he paused outside the keep, his hand resting on the rough gray stone. Craignish needed him. The history books in the twenty-first century had barely a word about his family's demise after he'd left.

True, he'd returned and saved his sister from a deadly marriage, but was that enough to save his clan? To keep them in the history books? His eyes moved upward, straight toward the tower Kat inhabited with flower-smelling warm skin. "I'm sorry, lass," he said and ducked inside. "I must stay here, and I'm not letting ye go."

CHAPTER EIGHTEEN
OILS FROM THE EAST

Kat sat on the edge of the bed, unable to fully breathe. The water had felt wonderful, and the flowery soap was pure bliss. The heat had worked to unkink her muscles and soothe her bruises. But then she'd stepped out, wrapped herself in a yellow bathing sheet, and suddenly felt turmoil roll through her. It was like a tug of war and then regret and resolve.

She closed her eyes, fingers touching the dragonfly birthmark on her upper arm. There was no tingling. She touched her right jaw line and felt the puckered skin. "I'm not using any magic, not even thinking about it," she murmured. Yet somehow she was picking up on emotions, strong ones.

"Toren," she said and clutched the bathing sheet tighter around herself. The emotions she felt were hard, as hard as the walls the Highlander built around himself, rugged yet beautiful in their sharp lines. Kat closed her eyes, letting the feelings float along her consciousness. She held a hand fisted against her chest. *Sadness, longing, anger, regret.* And then like that, the feelings dissolved like the minute bubbles along the surface of the water.

A rapping on the door jerked her eyes open. Winifred walked in with her sunny smile and a sleeping garment. The sun had set, and Kat hadn't slept well on the hard ground the night before. Perhaps it would be best to just go to sleep. *After all, tomorrow is another day.*

Outside the watery glass windowpane, Kat saw the full moon rising. Would the full moon have as much effect on her cycle in the sixteenth century as it did back home? That's why her abdomen kept cramping. It wasn't the venison; it was her period. And not a tampon in sight.

<hr>

For three days after the full moon, Kat was held prisoner in her room with a cloth Winifred told her to hold between her legs. Food was brought up and Briana, Margaret, and Winifred came in and out for entertainment.

What would have happened if the moon had been full during their journey? Kat was torn between irate annoyance at the sexist world she'd been thrown into and the pure pleasure of studying the tapestry and paintings around the room and the gloriously authentic gowns Winifred kept bringing by for her inspection.

With legs clenched together to prevent the cloth from slipping since there were no knickers to be had, Kat stood while Winifred pinned and gathered and cut old seams from a beautiful Elizabethan day gown. There were almost no examples of this type of gown left in her century. Only a few costly court gowns remained. One of Elizabeth's bodices would be taken apart sometime in the next century and used as an altar cloth until it would be identified properly in 2015. Otherwise, none of the queen's gowns still existed in Kat's time.

Kat smoothed her hand down the soft woolen weave of medium blue. Small flowers and of all things, butterflies, were stitched in yellow and green threads. "Was this one of Briana's dresses?" she asked Winifred.

She shook her capped head. "Nay, it was made for her mother, though the Lady MacCallum never wore it."

"Why is that?"

"She always said it belonged to someone else." Winifred smiled past the two pins perched between her teeth. "The lady had a touch of sight," she whispered as if the walls could hear.

Kat ran her finger over the yellow threads stitched into a butterfly. "Toren's mother?"

"Aye, milady, but she was a good Christian woman." She nodded vigorously. "She just knew things that would happen sometimes. And she said this dress belonged to another lady who would come one day."

Kat felt the chill of prophecy creep up her spine.

"Perhaps that lady is ye," Winifred said, and looked down, her fingers flitting along the hem with a tiny, flashing needle.

Toren's mother had magic of her own. Was that why he was so accepting of Kat's powers? Was that why her magic didn't work on him? He'd used a binding spell for the necklace, so apparently he knew something of magic. Kat's arm tingled and she scratched through the fabric.

A breeze blew through the room, making the flames in the hearth lie flat and then surge. Winifred frowned at the fire and then at Kat. Kat shrugged and Winifred bent her head again just as Drakkina's misty image coalesced above the stone mantel. Kat gasped softly.

Winifred jumped. "Did I prick ye with the needle?"

Kat watched as the witch's image hovered, her long finger drawn to her lips. "No, I..." Kat looked down at the anxious maid. She smiled. "I just had a cramp." She cupped her abdomen where the dress's outer layer opened to show a green forepart.

Winifred frowned. "I've pushed ye too much," she said, and stood up. "Let me help ye from the gown. I can finish the hem in my rooms and let ye rest."

Kat nodded her thanks and stood while Winifred removed the outer parts of the gown. "It will be done on the morrow," the maid said. "I would think yer courses would be finished by then too.

Kat only nodded, trying hard not to glance at Drakkina's floating image. As soon as the door shut behind Winifred, Kat turned. "Drakkina."

Drakkina's body floated down until she nearly touched the floor. Her hair moved as if a gentle wind blew, and several dragonflies flitted about, alighting on the veil that sat on her shoulders. "You look well, child," Drakkina said. Her voice seemed much too solid to be coming from her ethereal form.

What to say to a great Wiccan spirit that was obviously there for something you didn't have? The dragonfly amulet was miles away in another country. This woman or whatever she was could transport her back to her children. Kat bit her lower lip, wishing that Toren was there to help answer any questions about the amulet.

Drakkina narrowed her eyes. "Silence? What is wrong with your tongue?"

Kat had to say something. "Do you happen to have a tampon?"

Her face pinched. "A what?"

"Never mind." She plopped down on the stuffed tick laid out on tight rope cords to serve as a mattress, which was fascinating in books but not so much when one had to sleep on its lumpy surface.

"Have you wed your Highlander yet?"

"What?"

"That frowning, rugged brute of a man who's your soul mate, child."

Kat didn't answer.

"Have you at least mated with him?"

"You've only been gone for a week." Kat stood and propped her hands on her hips, although it was difficult to look like a woman with attitude in a loose sixteenth-century lace-edged nightgown with a rag clenched between her legs.

Drakkina waved a hand in the air, scattering the little dragonflies. "Yes, yes, I've learned that it takes time. Frustrating, that part." Drakkina's eyes seemed to solidify more, giving them an odd, disembodied look. "Did he retrieve my necklace? I don't feel it here, but he'd probably cloak it. He's most likely still angry about me sending him to your century."

Irritation made Kat's hands fist. "Of course he's angry, furious, as he should be," Kat said in her best lecture tone. "You have no right to pick people up from their lives and fling them to other times."

"I have every right," Drakkina said with calm precision. "Saving the worlds from the evil that stalks you is more important than any individual lives."

"You could have at least given him directions to me, not just let him wander around for five years building hatred towards you."

"I've been told I meddle too much," Drakkina said. "I thought I'd let you two find one another." She smiled. "And you did."

Kat ran her hands down her face and sat back on the bed.

"So does he have it?" Drakkina asked, floating along the floor to stand before Kat.

Kat swallowed down the nervous tension and cleared her throat. "No, but he knows where it is and we'll get it. Give us some time."

"Don't *you* retrieve it," Drakkina said. "You can't touch it and don't use your magic. I've just returned from flying around the temporal web to confuse those bloody demons. Don't call them back here by using magic."

"I know," Kat said, her hand absently touching her right jaw line.

Drakkina's gaze followed her hand. "Your sister, Merewin, could heal those. Make your skin smooth and perfect."

"Really?" Kat's gaze snapped up to Drakkina's, her chest pounding. "My sister? She could make these go away?"

Drakkina nodded. "I've seen her heal worse."

"How...when? Can I meet her now? Why didn't you tell me this before?"

Drakkina propped hands on her hips. "I just said I was busy luring demons away."

Kat could hardly draw in a full breath of air. The thought of forever ridding herself of the scars, being normal, was more than enticing, it was life-altering. Never to hide again, never to worry if someone could feel the roughness when she allowed them to touch her. "Can she do it right now?"

Drakkina shook her head. "Not now, child. I can't risk magic around you here. When I have the dragonfly, I'll take it far from you and then the demons won't notice the magic vibrations the healing will cause. It's your proximity to the dragonfly that allowed them to find you now."

Kat's heart sank, but she wasn't finished trying. "I could catch my soul mate better if my skin was flawless." It was a last-ditch effort. Toren seemed to appreciate her scars, but still...Kat had always wished them away, and one conversation wouldn't change her mind. She'd like herself better without the scars and one must love oneself before luring anyone else to love them. Or at least that was what the self-help books said.

"Hmmm." Drakkina considered, her eyes soft. It wasn't pity in them, but something else, something almost motherly, like concern. "Perhaps if we go to the stone circle." Her lips tightened. "Yes, the ancient magic there would shield us."

Kat's heart rate jumped into a run. "Where?"

"The stone circle where you were born."

"Is it near?"

Drakkina smiled and the dragonflies danced as if they were an outward show of the priestess's cheerfulness. "Do you not feel my pull?"

Kat had felt it forever, wondered about it forever. "I feel it." She pointed to the west.

"This far into the Highlands, it should be very strong," Drakkina reflected.

"It's increased the farther we've come. I even found myself sleepwalking last night. I woke up standing with my nose against the west wall of my room."

"Your older sister had to tie herself to her bed not to roam."

"Really? Which sister? The one who can heal me?"

"No. The oldest sister, Serena." She waved away Kat's next question before she could ask it. "The circle has a beacon, meant to draw you and your sisters. It's your origin and your safe haven. It's the place where one day you will battle with your sisters to save the world."

"That doesn't sound so safe," Kat said, but her mind was already throwing together a plan to escape Craignish.

"Right now it is. And I will call Merewin there to heal your face when you arrive."

Drakkina's form started to fade.

"Wait, when will you be there?"

Drakkina smiled. "I'm there now," she said. She snapped her fingers and disappeared. *I'll be waiting.* Drakkina's words echoed in Kat's mind even though the witch was no longer in the room.

I have to find a saddled horse. Kat didn't know anything about putting one on. Could she ride a horse without a saddle? She'd seen it done in movies.

Kat took a deep breath. "I can't do it tonight." Even if the pull of the stone circle would lead her there, she wouldn't be able to use her magic to hide if wolves or marauders lurked in the forest. Even in her own century, Kat wouldn't want to be in the woods at night. Alone and without protection. She glanced at the window where the sun was already beginning its descent. "I'll go tomorrow during daylight." But she could still scout out the best exit.

Kat shimmied into the stiff pair of Wednesday underwear she'd washed out the night before and hid hanging on a nail at the back of her clothes press. The scratchy material made her hesitate, but she hadn't become comfortable going commando. Plus there was the rag to secure. Her period was at an end, but she didn't want to risk staining the smock.

If she didn't return home soon, she'd have to find another set of knickers. To heck with stopping undergarments from becoming a thing over a hundred years too soon. She'd sew some herself if she must, although they'd be a far cry from Victoria Secret's stretchy satin.

Kat stepped into the corridor wearing the day dress Winifred had finished, a simple gown of blue. She tread lightly to the end of the hall where she'd seen a guard go up a flight of steps, hopefully to the roof. She'd be able to see the whole bailey from up there and which road out of the village would take her west.

She pulled open the heavy oak door, and a gust of wind pushed her back. She should have brought a cloak, but she'd be quick before daylight was completely gone. Without streetlamps, seeing the roads around the village would be impossible in the dark. Kat climbed the steps and poked her head up so that her eyes were level with the walkway around the roof of the keep. She stopped at the sight of Toren and Eagan looking out over the wall.

"While I'm away in the south," Toren said, "send word to Morton in the east that I want the things on this list." Toren handed Eagan a piece of paper. "As many as can be had."

Eagan looked down at it and laughed. "Oil for the body? Why would anyone want to become slippery?"

"It protects skin against the cold and wind," Toren replied. Kat could hear his frown even though his back was turned.

"I did not know that the wind parched ye so much, Brother," Eagan said, laughter still edging his voice.

"'Tis not for me, 'tis for Kat," Toren said, and Kat froze. He was ordering body oils while they were gone to get the necklace. *As many as can be had?*

"Aye, her skin does look soft." Eagan held up hands in defense, the list fluttering in the breeze. "Not that I'm staring at yer woman, just hard not to notice one so bonny."

A mix of unease and anger prickled under Kat's skin, and she leaned against the wall at the bottom of the steps leading to the roof.

"A shame her face was burned," Eagan said, casually. "Amazing one so delicate could survive it." Kat repeated the comment in her head, searching for the telltale sneer or pity that fed her insecurities. Eagan's words were kind, simple observation.

Toren continued to look out on his territory. "What would ye do, Eagan, about Campbell's treachery?"

Eagan turned toward his brother even though Toren kept his gaze outward.

"Well…I…" Eagan stood taller and moved his gaze outward. "I would send word that they are considered an enemy to all MacCallums. I would fortify MacCallum Castle and bring our people closer, expecting a challenge. Set the watch like ye've done. I'd probably also raid their cattle to show how serious we are. They are in league with Maxwell, too, so we must watch the politics of England."

Toren nodded. "Ye have the thoughts of a leader, Eagan."

"But not the birthright," Eagan answered.

"Pardon, milady," a guard said behind Kat as he ran up the steps from the doorway behind her.

Kat grabbed the rock wall to keep from falling down the short stairwell into the guard's chest. "I was just coming up for fresh air," she said with a casual voice and walked up the remaining steps, stopping at the top as if surprised to see the brothers. "Good evening, Toren." She looked at Eagan. "And Eagan."

Eagan nodded, a grin on his face. Toren neither nodded nor grinned. "I think I will go check how the men are doing on the north wall," Eagan said and moved past Kat.

"The cattle have been brought back in from the fields like ye ordered," the guard said to Toren.

"Good," Toren said, but his gaze had gone to Kat. "Watch for any unusual movement on the moors." The guard nodded and strode around the wall to the other side.

Kat walked over to Toren and looked out over the hills and woods. To the right was a forest where the stones must sit, because the invisible string pulled so hard that Kat nearly leaned that way, right into Toren's chest.

She purposely looked outward and breathed deeply. "I've been cooped up for days. Needed some air," she said, but couldn't keep the anger from her voice. The man thought she would stay here a long time. Kat supposed she should be happy that he thought of her comfort with the oils. What else was on that list? Tampons? Ibuprofen? Knickers?

Kat turned a narrowed stare to him. "So when do we leave? For the necklace? Drakkina wants it now, and I can't wait to get home."

"Ye've spoken with the witch?" He turned completely toward her.

"She was just in my room."

"Fok." Toren ran a hand through his hair. The side of his jaw clenched. "I will stay with ye."

"Why?"

"To protect ye. I've found some ancient spells that may keep her power from touching ye or me. They're from a book of my mother's."

A Highland warrior protecting her? Her twenty-first century feminist confidence wanted to spurn his sixteenth-century manly need to protect his female, but he was the one accustomed to the lawlessness of the century. "Drakkina doesn't want to hurt me or you," she said.

"Bloody hell she does!" Toren lowered his voice. "She took me without warning, away so that my family was destroyed." He looked over the small village at the feet of the great keep. "I will find a way that she cannot just pick us up at will again." The quiet vehemence caught in Kat's chest.

Her words were equally low. "So you plan to keep me here by making Drakkina unable to send either of us back to my home." She waited for him to deny it. And waited. And waited.

Toren turned back to watch the darkening landscape. He inhaled fully. "Yer world is polluted, overpopulated, and full of artificial ingredients and terrorists."

Kat's anger welled. "The Thames isn't an open sewer in my century."

"Yer century also has nuclear bombs, pistols, artificial food, and light beer."

"You have a problem with light beer?"

"It tastes like piss."

She crossed her arms. "Well I could point out things like smallpox, and no showers, tampons, ibuprofen, or phones." Her voice had risen in strength.

"Give it another decade or so with nuclear bombs and none of that will remain. It will all end up floating in your melted icecaps with the drowning polar bears." Toren was so close that he glared down at her.

"The meat here is foul with fat and gristle. And people don't bathe nearly enough."

"My century has organic food without the expense since we don't have pesticides."

"You know what my world also has?" Kat took a full breath, her voice dropping out of yelling mode. "My world has"—she pursed her lips—"Fairy Princess Clara. And her twin brother, the one with strep throat. He didn't even speak when he first came to the orphanage. He'd held his sister so she couldn't see their father kill their mother. I held him for weeks until one day he said his favorite cookie was chocolate chip."

Kat felt the tears well up. "And then there is Margie, she's twelve and awkward. She was so angry about coming to the children's home that she was a first-rate bully until Lisa and I put her to work scrubbing the dishes and cutting the little one's toenails. Little Jeremiah talked so much to her while she tried to cut his wiggly toes that she actually started to laugh."

The memory was still sharp in her mind, beyond her teary view. "After that, Jeremiah stuck to her and suddenly she wasn't alone in the world, she had a little brother to watch out for.

"Then Sophie and Tim came from a terrible foster home. Neither of them could sleep soundly for weeks. Lisa and I took turns sitting with them in their rooms, watching over them, promising we wouldn't let the bad people hurt them again." Tears swelled out of her eyes now.

"Cece came to us as a baby, so she thinks Lisa and I are her two mothers. We've told her we aren't, but she still calls us 'Mom' and 'Mama'." She poked a finger in her chest. "I'm Mama. I think her school mates think we are married lesbians." She shrugged.

Toren watched her in silence as she continued to detail each of the children in her care. Once, he tried to reach for her, but Kat put up a hand. If she let him comfort her, she'd fall apart into a puddle of pain.

Her throat began to ache while night had grown around them and thousands of stars twinkled above. "And Mary-Sue is almost fifteen. She's been abandoned over and over." Kat looked up into Toren's eyes. "She can't withstand abandonment again at such an age. I won't abandon any of my kids, Toren MacCallum." Her voice grew as anger poured liquid steel into her spine.

Toren didn't say a word. His hand moved to her arm, but Kat stepped backward along the wall.

"So make sure, MacCallum, that if you conjure any more of your binding spells, you don't try to bind me to you." Anger made her sneer as the emotion of her justifications pumped through her. She pointed at him as she backed toward the steps. "If you are bound to me, you will find yourself living in the twenty-first century away from your glorious castle and unpolluted air."

Kat whirled around and retreated back down into the dark stairwell to the oak door. The tears washed down her cheeks as she hurried to her room. Homesickness engulfed her like a ten-foot wave as more memories swamped her. "By God in Heaven," she swore amidst her anguish. "Somehow I'm getting home!"

CHAPTER NINETEEN
SO CLOSE

Toren frowned, grunted, and growled through the rest of the night and next day. The castle staff and the warriors gave him a wide berth. He swam in the icy water, rode to the edges of his borders, and swung his practice sword without mercy while sparring with the men. After one match that ended up with an unconscious warrior, Eagan approached him.

"What in bloody hell has ye spitting bees and stomping around like a poked bull?" Eagan spoke low, a hand on Toren's stiff shoulder. "Ye're skilled enough that yer fury isn't hindering yer fight, but it's hindering yer judgment."

Toren's eyes met Eagan's with a dull chill. "Kat wants to go home." Toren released the words like they were poison he must spit out.

Eagan signaled the men to continue their training while he and Toren walked toward the keep. "Does that mean ye won't need oils for her skin?" Eagan joked and then murmured an apology when Toren's gaze sliced frozen steel through him. Eagan rubbed his chest. "Brother, she's just a lass ye met not too long ago. If she doesn't feel the same way about ye—"

"She does," Toren interrupted. At least he thought she did. He'd felt it in the heat of her kiss, the way she'd wrapped delicate fingers in his hair. Or did all uninhibited twenty-first-century women do that? The thought infuriated him even more.

And how exactly did he feel about her? Besides the need to bed her, and the anger that swelled against the limits of his control when he thought of her leaving him?

"Well then handfast with her," Eagan said. "Then she has to stay for a year and a day."

"The old ways are not legal. I cannot make her stay." Toren shook his head. "Even if I could. She has…" He breathed deep. How could he tell his brother that Kat had twelve children waiting for her to return? "She has people at home depending on her."

"Ahh," Eagan said as if he understood though he couldn't possibly. "Then go home with her."

Toren's eyes met Eagan's. "I may not be able to return." He paused. "Ever."

"Why the hell not?"

Toren looked away. The sun was climbing toward noon. He glanced at the top of the keep. Would Kat be walking up there? He hadn't seen her since she'd strode away from him with tears and determination clouding her eyes the night before. He'd knocked on her door that morning, but she hadn't answered, and he hadn't seen her in the Great Hall all morning. "'Tis complicated."

"I am considered bright, Tor." Eagan followed him as he walked away from the training field toward the small drawbridge. They walked in silence under the portcullis and inside the keep.

The change from the coolness to the warmth inside made Toren sweat. If Kat was above on the wall walk, maybe she would talk to him.

"Tor?" Eagan said right behind him, but he kept walking and climbed the steps without breaking stride.

Toren reached the door to the roof and pushed back out into the fresh air. "Daingead," he murmured when a quick glance showed that Kat wasn't there.

"There's something else," Eagan said, jogging up behind him. Toren stopped near the wall to look out over the bailey and village. Maybe he'd spot the blue cloak she liked to hide within.

"I want...well, I mean." Eagan hesitated, and Toren looked over his shoulder at his younger brother. He stood straight, his broad shoulders back, chest out. "I want yer blessing. I'm going to ask Margaret Maxwell to wed with me."

Toren turned toward his brother, his stare hard. "Ye do not know her, Eagan." He shook his head and looked away. "Ye should marry to strengthen our alliances," Toren said, falling back on the words they'd both heard a thousand times while growing up. Life was all about duty to one's clan. Wasn't it?

"Ye sound like Da," Eagan said, low. "And ye were the one to stop him from forcing me to wed the Maclean lass. He took out his fury on ye instead of me."

"I could handle fury." Toren glanced across the bailey, but he didn't see Kat. "I lived under Maxwell's whip for years. I was stronger than ye. It made sense."

"I'm not weak, Brother, and I know who I love."

"Ye do not know her enough to bind yerself to her."

"I know her as well as two people need to before they wed. Some know less about each other," Eagan said, defensiveness edging his tone.

Toren closed his eyes. What could he say? He looked at Eagan, his little brother, full grown, a man in his own right. "Talk with her first. Ask Margaret about..." he hesitated. "Ask her about her brother's death."

"The night of the fire?" Eagan asked, brows drawing together in question.

"Aye, ask Margaret about the fire." Toren watched the sun drop below the tree line. "People will do anything to survive. And some"—he looked at Eagan—"some do absolutely nothing to survive."

Eagan's frown made him look older. His younger brother had grown up suddenly. How was that possible? In Eagan's time, it had only been a month since they'd stood here planning their visit to court to prove their goodwill towards Elizabeth.

Maybe Toren was the one who had changed during his five-year exile, changed enough to see that his brother had grown into a fierce, intelligent MacCallum leader.

"Just talk to her first, Eagan," Toren said, his gaze diverted by a reflected glow along the southern border of their territory. "Before ye ask her to wed."

Toren leaned forward. Eagan followed his gaze. "Shite," Eagan said, as they watched the flash of a flame reflected by a glass mirror, their warning beacon.

"Hughe Maxwell comes," Toren said. "Ye best have yer talk with Margaret now. It will be easier to keep her if she's already a MacCallum." Eagan opened his mouth but then closed it again. Perhaps he realized that was Toren's blessing on the subject.

Eagan turned and jogged down the steps. Toren spied the guards along the wall who had also spotted the fire. Just as planned, the warning bell tolled. People in the village would prepare to leave their homes. They'd come into the keep if the bell tolled a second time.

Men and women came out onto the streets. Their movements were organized, no panic. A tremor of pride beat with his pulse as he watched them prepare for possible war. They'd been trained to survive before the witch had taken him, yet the MacCallums had still been annihilated in the future he'd read about helplessly from the twenty-first century. He felt the weight of responsibility like a shroud around his strong shoulders.

Toren hailed one of the warriors on the roof and spoke with him about alerts to the rest of the warriors. Then he turned toward the steps. He must talk to Kat now, whether she liked it or not. She had to know what was coming. He reached for the door just as Eagan yanked it open. Toren's stomach gripped at the sight on Eagan's face. Margaret stood behind, hands clasped as if she could start praying any moment.

"What's happened?" Toren asked.

"Kat's gone," Eagan said. "Briana went with her."

"Where?" Toren's voice boomed out.

Eagan reached his hand back to Margaret, who obviously had information.

"Did ye see them go, Margaret? Or did they just disappear?" Toren asked.

Eagan looked confused but rushed on anyway. "She saw them leave together on one horse an hour ago."

Toren pushed past them down the corridor.

"Why? Where are they going?" Eagan called from behind as they followed.

Toren threw Kat's door open. All looked normal. He strode through, heart pounding. No note, all her clothes still there, although she might not consider them hers to take. He turned toward Margaret. "What do ye know, woman? This time speak up." His eyes bored into her.

She straightened but her eyes were still round with fear. "Kat said she wanted to visit a circle of stones to the west of here. She said it was close."

"And ye let her go?" Toren rubbed a hand over his face, trying to keep from yelling.

"She was already on her way out when Briana and I came upon her in the back courtyard. She'd found some door in the wall that Briana didn't even know about."

Toren looked at Eagan who shrugged. "I'll check it out."

"Briana wouldn't let her go alone," Margaret continued. "Kat said they'd be back by nightfall."

They had no idea an army of Maxwells was near. *The fool women!* She and Briana were out there, possibly already in Maxwell's hands. Possibly in Fergus Campbell's grimy hands. Toren strode past them. "Ye're in charge, Eagan. If Maxwell comes, tell him I'll be back soon."

"What should I do if he demands Margaret and Sara?" Eagan asked. "If he carries a royal order?"

"That's up to ye," Toren said and yelled for two warriors near the door. "We ride!"

"Winifred," Eagan yelled. "Prepare the Lady Margaret. There's going to be a handfasting."

⚬

Kat rode behind Briana. Her companion knew more about handling the horse than she did. Kat pointed west and Briana steered them through the budding birch trees and pines.

"I know the way, Kat," Briana said.

"You do?"

"Aye. My brothers and I played in the ten stones many times growing up before Tor was sent away. 'Tis quite close."

"Why was Toren sent away?" Toren hadn't talked again about his time living with the Maxwells, but she'd seen his scars.

"Sons of Highland chiefs are to be schooled for some years in the Lowlands to learn English ways and court etiquette," Briana said, and pushed a low pine branch out of their way. "Our father believed that Queen Elizabeth would name our King James as her heir since she has no children. So Toren was to learn the ways of the English court under Maxwell."

"Toren lived with Hughe Maxwell and Margaret?"

"And Margaret's brother, Edward. He still lived while Toren was there."

"How did he die?" Margaret hadn't talked about her brother.

Briana hesitated. "There was a fire in the stables six years ago, the last time Da made us visit. Edward died in it."

"How horrible," Kat said. "Was Toren there when it happened?"

"Aye," a man's voice called out as he stepped from behind a tree trunk. Briana's back stiffened, and she yanked back on the reins. He was middle-aged, possibly older, with gray in his hair and neat, tailored English clothing. But it was his eyes that caused a chill to prick down Kat's back. They were like beads of blue ice, so cold, so hard.

Fergus Campbell jogged out of the woods and grabbed their horse's bridle. He *tsk*ed. "Do not ye know the dangers of riding alone in the woods?"

"These are MacCallum woods, MacCallum land," Briana yelled. "And ye will die for trespassing."

The man with the icy stare walked forward. "To answer your question, Toren MacCallum was there at the fire." Those frozen orbs pierced Kat, making her want to disappear. "Which is why I am here."

"Tor had nothing to do with Edward's death, Lord Maxwell," Briana said. Kat felt a tremor run through Toren's sister even if her voice held nothing but hostile reproof.

Lord Maxwell? This was the man who'd sliced Toren's cheek, who'd probably beaten him as a young boy. Rage grew rapidly inside Kat, and she met the icy stare.

"Toren MacCallum set that fire and left Edward to die in it after Edward walked in on him and Margaret fornicating," Maxwell said. His statement was calm, but checked fury held it aloft like wind under still-lit ash. "And now he will learn what it means to suffer from losing one of his family members." His gaze rested on Briana before sliding to Kat. "And someone he cares for."

"Ye think Toren MacCallum cares for a woman who resembles a monster?" Fergus asked and chuckled.

Kat's stomach contracted so hard she thought she might be sick. Briana's hand slid behind her, seeking Kat's but Kat could only sit in rigid pain.

Maxwell shrugged. "If he covers her face, the rest of her looks good enough to ride."

A breeze blew through the branches making them sway. The pine needles rattled softly against each other, releasing their scent. The smell of the sea mixed with the pine to infuse Kat's inhales. She breathed it in, trying to let the cruel words exhale out of her, but they stuck. She was suddenly back in the hall of the orphan's home being compared to a Halloween monster. The echoes of the two teens laughing scratched open unhealed wounds.

The stones were just on the other side of the rise. They were so close to Drakkina and the sister who could fix her face. "Drakkina!" Kat yelled with only her voice since she couldn't use her magic.

"Drakkina?" Fergus said, glancing around with a smirk.

"My brothers will not stand for this!" Briana had a backbone even though Kat felt her quake. At least ten other men came from behind trees to surround them.

Kat looked back over one shoulder, but Toren wasn't riding to the rescue. She turned around, her eyes trained on the path to the stones. "Drakkina!"

"Toren!" Briana yelled, but there was no way he'd be able to hear her an hour's ride away.

"Yer brothers are not here," Fergus sneered and yanked the reins from Briana's fingers. He pulled their horse along behind him and mounted another.

"Where are ye taking us?" Briana demanded.

"Somewhere we can have a little discussion," Maxwell said.

"And if ye jump off that pretty mare," Fergus said, "I'll slice its throat."

Kat's heart hammered. "I'm so sorry," she whispered to Briana. To be back in the same devious hands as before must be terrifying, and Kat had been the one to insist on this journey.

Briana reached back for Kat's hand. "Any butterflies around?"

"I don't know how to call them," Kat whispered against Briana's ear.

"Butterflies?" Fergus sneered. "I lost good men that day to foking butterflies." Fergus thumped a hand on the blanket tied to his horse. "We all carry blankets now, nice thick ones. Unless yer butterflies can eat through wool, they're no threat to us." Several of the surrounding men nodded and others made the sign of the cross before their jerkins.

They rode away from the coast to the south for an hour, the sky clear above in contrast to the dire situation playing out below. The whole time, Kat called out to her butterflies in her mind as well as to Drakkina, but she didn't dare use magic.

Maxwell turned to Fergus. "Have the men we left south of the lake ride to your holding. Now that we have *guests*," he said stressing the word, "we will change our strategy."

Fergus motioned to one of his men, and the rest of them continued on through a valley.

Kat felt Briana's shoulders fall as she exhaled. "We're no longer on MacCallum land," she whispered. "This is Campbell dirt beneath us now." Kat rubbed her hands up and down Briana's arms.

"They will come for us," Kat said near Briana's ear and squeezed her in a warm.

Turmoil and worry twisted through Kat but also pangs of fierce anger. The first emotions she'd assumed were just her own, but the intensity of the fury that had begun piercing her soon after Maxwell's kidnapping were something else. *Toren.*

"What is it?" Briana asked, having noticed her stiffening.

Kat rubbed her chest. Fury and bloodlust swirled with worry and fear. It had to be Toren.

"Toren knows we're gone," she whispered to Briana.

"How do ye know?"

"Ye two, shut yer pretty lips," Fergus commanded, riding close. Both women stared straight ahead. Fergus reached out and caught a slip of Kat's hair. He ran it through thick fingers. "Shorter than most, but soft." He twisted it over his fist, forcing Kat to bend toward him. "Smells nice, too." He lowered his voice, releasing her. "Hmmm, now what should I do with a lovely lass who happens to be Toren's woman?" His smile was a leer. How could Toren have ever thought to marry Briana to this monster?

"Watch out. I may be a witch," Kat said.

Fergus opened his eyes wide in mock worry. "Well, well, the Mistress Kat has claws." He smiled. "I think I can handle yer butterflies, witch." Fergus kicked his horse and trotted toward the front of the line.

"Can you handle them biting your knob right off?" she said. Butterflies could do no such thing, but these were magic butterflies, and the arse had no idea what they could or couldn't do.

Fergus's eyes widened slightly when she glanced at his crotch. "Right off," she said and bared her teeth.

The man looked wary and glanced about. Without a word he rode toward the front of their procession.

"Not sure what that meant, but you scared him for certain," Briana whispered.

Fergus remained up front with Maxwell until their group rode together under the pointed jaws of the gate into the bailey of another castle. The bars lowered after they entered, grinding until they sank into the ground like teeth into a fettered lip. With the sound, Kat's breath hitched. She swallowed against the terror and almost turned invisible right in front of everyone. But she stopped herself. Which enemy was worse, the Campbells and Maxwell or the demons bent on killing her, stripping her magic, and destroying the world? *Well heck.*

Kat breathed deeply. She'd need oxygen to make her brain work. And she definitely needed her brain since she couldn't use magic.

"Dismount," Maxwell said, "unless you want Fergus to help you."

Briana scrambled down, and Kat tried to make her dismount look casual. They were ushered into the keep by two large, silent warriors in well-worn kilts. "Stay there," one said after walking them to a corner before joining some other men who ate and drank at a long table. The design of the fortress was comparable to the keep at Craignish, but the similarity stopped there. The rushes were dirty, the few tapestries on the walls held a layer of dust, and the servants seemed to prefer the shadows.

"There has not been a lady of the house in years," Briana whispered.

"I can tell."

"To think I almost became the lady of this keep," Briana said, her hand pressed to her heart.

A timid woman wearing an apron smeared with some yellow substance brought over two trenchers of bread and thick stew.

"Thank you," Kat said, while Briana nodded her thanks. The woman gave them a timid smile and receded into the darkness. Kat barely ate the chunky pieces of meat and some sort of root vegetable in the thick gravy.

"Eat more," Briana said. "We will need our strength to get home."

Home? Where was that? The thought of not seeing Toren knotted in Kat's stomach like the homesickness she'd felt for her kids. Was she destined to always have that gnawing feeling no matter what century she lived in?

The timid lady brought them some watered wine. "Is there a way out of here?" Kat asked. "Can you help us?"

The servant's eyes froze like a badger caught in front of a lorry. Frightened, not sure which way to run, perhaps in denial that she was about to be roadkill.

"If ye will be harmed by answering, do not," Briana offered and smiled. "I'm Lady Briana and this is Mistress Kat."

"I know who ye are." The small voice breathed from dry, thin lips.

"And you can come with us when we leave, if you want," Kat said. "I'm sure the MacCallums will take you in if you're mistreated here."

Kat smiled, then shook her head. "No one deserves to be mistreated." The woman looked amazed.

Thankfully Briana nodded to confirm Kat's words. The wrongness of domestic violence was a new concept for the sixteenth-century peasant woman.

"Do you have anyone else here, parents, children, siblings?" The woman shook her head, scattering coarse dreadlocked hair around bent shoulders. Kat smiled. "Then you're coming with us."

"What's yer name?" Briana asked.

"Alyce! Get back here," Fergus yelled from the table. The woman jumped and ran to refill goblets.

Kat huffed. "She's like a puppy who never knows when it will be kicked." She had seen it before in some of her children when they first arrived.

Alyce darted around filling mugs and struggling under large platters of food. Kat began to rise to help her, but Briana placed a hand on her arm. "It will see ye both abused even more," she said softly.

It was awful to watch people bump Alyce without apologizing. One man even pinched her. During the entire painful meal, Alyce's eyes continued to flit toward Kat and Briana.

"She wants to go with us," Kat said.

"I'm not sure we will be going anywhere." Briana took a sip from her mug. "At least not before we look like her."

CHAPTER TWENTY
COURAGE TO ACT

Kat's face hardened as she watched Alyce. *I will never look like that.* And she couldn't abandon someone who did.

Kat's gaze roamed the keep's structure. The kitchens would be where Alyce brought out the food. A set of curving stairs twisted higher, most likely leading to the bedrooms. Another set curved downward, probably to the dungeons. Kat had never visited a true, rat-infested dungeon, but it would be a preferred resting spot over the bedrooms above if rape was on the minds of their captors.

As if cued into her thoughts, Fergus glanced over at her, leering. "I think a scarf or pillow over her face will do just fine." The man next to him glanced at Kat and chuckled. Fergus adjusted himself openly with a hand under his kilt.

Just one butterfly, Kat wished deeply. Just one fluttering around the room would wipe that smirk from his cocky face.

Maxwell glanced in their direction and began to talk, but Kat couldn't hear him. He seemed calm enough, like a man who held all the cards.

"Come!" Fergus called out to them.

"Are we hounds then," Briana whispered, but rose. Kat followed, and they walked arm in arm across the hall.

Maxwell motioned for them to sit, and Kat and Briana did as one. "I assume that my daughter and her child are at Craignish." It was a statement, but he waited for an answer.

"Lady Margaret has sought refuge for herself and her daughter," Briana answered. "And we are honoring that request."

Maxwell's face hardened, his eyes turning to ice. "Refuge? Why would she need to seek refuge in a holding where she is to be married? I freely give her to Toren MacCallum. He shall marry her to right his wrong."

"Then you have no need to retain us," Kat said.

"Oh, but I do," Fergus said, and his eyes moved to Briana. "I've long since had a heart full of love for the Lady Briana." His gaze moved to Kat. "And an interest now in her lady friend."

"Fergus Campbell," Briana said, "I swear before God that I will never wed with ye. If ye so much as touch me or Mistress Kat, ye will be acting against God, and the MacCallums will not rest until ye are smashed into the ground." So, she was not going with a subtle strategy.

Fergus looked at Kat. She shrugged. "I think she said it all quite well."

Maxwell glared, his eyes raking down Kat's body in a way that made Kat feel like he might order Fergus to stay off her only to keep her for himself. "And who exactly *are* you?"

Kat crossed her arms and raised her chin. "I am Mistress Katell Diciadain."

Fergus chuckled. "Mistress Wednesday."

"I know your bloody name," Maxwell said, "but why are you involved with the MacCallums?"

Fergus set his tankard on the table. "It's said that Toren will marry her instead of yer daughter."

Maxwell wet his thin lips. "Tonight will put an end to that." He smoothed back his neatly cropped, graying hair. Kat swallowed down the bile rising up from her stomach with the stew. Even though the man was older, he looked quite strong.

"I've long since wanted to remarry," Maxwell said with thinly veiled lust. The hard stare, as if he were assessing her weaknesses and attributes, made Kat's skin crawl. "I will take you despite your scars, Mistress Diciadain."

"You're old enough to be my father," Kat said, her face tightening in a look of disgust.

"That hardly matters," he said, with a vicious glower that showed the tips of browning teeth.

Fergus frowned. "But Maxwell..." he hesitated. "I was going to teach this lass a thing or two, perhaps with my future bride."

Holy Mother Mary! They were arguing over who was going to rape and marry who.

"This is ridiculous, and you two are absurd, perverted criminals," Kat blurted out. "Neither of us is marrying either of you. Nor doing anything else with you."

Everyone looked at her like she was insane. "You"—she pointed to Fergus—"are an enemy to the MacCallums. If you force yourself on either one of us, you will bring the entire horde of MacCallums down on you. They'll just kill you and take Briana and me home." Kat wiped her hands in the air as if the deed was easily accomplished.

Kat turned to Maxwell. "And I don't know why you insist Toren killed your son and slept with your daughter when he didn't, but raping and marrying his woman isn't going to accomplish anything except putting a target on your chest. He'll just kill you and take me home. Or do you plan to stay locked in this castle forever?"

"You mistake your worth," Maxwell ground out, his words calm, chilling. "Toren will marry Margaret, or I will take her home."

"She's not going anywhere," Kat continued. "She's going to wed Eagan."

A red flush of fury rushed up Maxwell's neck and across his face. With luck he would have a stroke right here.

"Never!" Maxwell yelled, shattering his self-restraint. "She will wed with the chief of the MacCallums."

"If ye hate Toren so much, why would ye want yer daughter to marry him?" Briana asked.

Maxwell took a moment to calm himself, and his voice lowered to a steely, determined precision. "The child is his, not his brother's." The man was like a malevolent beast who was shackled but holding its own leash.

The hairs on Kat's nape rose in sickening suspicion. "Sara is not Toren's child, and you know it," Kat said, her eyes narrowing as she studied the man. He stood with hands fisted at his sides.

Maxwell stared her down, but she refused to look away. "Who is the father?" Kat asked. The question hung in the air, ignored, shunned. Kat knew victims. Many of her children in the orphanage were taken away from incestuous homes. Margaret was a woman but treated much like a child in this time. She had no rights of her own, forced to live with her father. And now that she had a daughter who was growing up, she'd sought refuge.

Maxwell's eyes veiled over with dark apathy, or was it denial?

"She looks so much like you." Kat pushed a little harder, unable to keep the condemnation from her eyes.

"Take them upstairs now," Maxwell said, his eyes never leaving Kat's. "Do with them what you like. When you've taught this one a lesson"—he looked at Kat—"send for me. I want an obedient wife."

"Anything I like?" Fergus said.

"Take the whole bloody troop with you if you want," Maxwell said. The barely controlled fury in Maxwell's eyes told Kat that her questions had hit home. Several men at the table stood up, ready to be called. Kat swallowed hard, fear working its way up her throat. Perhaps the stew would make a second appearance.

She should have paid more attention in the self-defense classes Lisa dragged her to. Kat had always just assumed she'd turn invisible or into a giant if she was ever attacked.

Drakkina! Kat screamed in her head. *Toren! God, help us!* Her legs felt leaden as she climbed the staircase. Kat had visited castle ruins in the twenty-first century. She'd stood at window remains looking out on the moors, wondering who had once stood there watching for their love to return. She'd trailed her hands along walls as she climbed chipped stairways, wondering who had touched the same places. But she'd never thought about what poor soul may have been forced to climb the stairs toward brutality without hope for escape.

They reached a cold room of plastered stone with a small sagging bed against one wall. The man called Thomas pulled his shirt off over his head.

Fergus snorted. "Ready are ye?"

"Since I saw them walk in." Thomas laughed, while grabbing himself under his kilt. He all but pummeled his chest in anticipation. Kat's stomach gurgled. Would vomit deter them?

"Start a fire." Fergus pointed to the cold hearth. "I don't want to freeze my ballocks."

Briana's grip started to make Kat's arm go numb. Kat's stomach gurgled again around the thick chunks of stew she'd forced herself to eat. She grabbed her stomach. "I don't feel good," Kat said and doubled over.

"Ye'll feel good soon enough," Thomas said from where he crouched before the hearth.

"Ye take Briana first," Fergus said, walking closer to Kat. "I'll take a taste of Toren's woman."

"Ye want me to take the maidenhead of The MacCallum's sister?" Thomas asked, his words falling upon each other. He straightened, turning wide eyes on Briana and then Fergus. "That's asking to die," he said, and threw the dried peat square on the rapidly growing flames. "Ye're going to wed her so he can't kill ye."

"Oh but he will," Briana said low. "He will kill ye both." Briana looked up and met Thomas's stare. "He'll slice ye from yer ballocks to yer skull until yer insides fall out for ye to look at while ye die." Now that was a picture.

"I need to use the bathroom," Kat said, not entirely lying.

Fergus turned to Kat. "No time to bathe. If ye survive the night, perhaps ye can have one on the morrow."

"No I mean I need to use the...the chamber pot. I need some privacy." Kat tried again.

Fergus pointed at a clay pot in the corner. "Piss in that."

Kat looked him in the face. "I might have food poison," she said and her stomach gurgled for emphasis.

"There was no poison in the food," Thomas said, frowning.

"The stew didn't agree with me," Kat said, doubling over and groaning.

The three people in the room stared at her, Briana confused, and the two men suspicious. "Food," Fergus said, "cannot agree with a person. 'Tis food."

Kat huffed but made it sound like a groan. "I'm about to have diarrhea from that food you served us. The flux." She ran toward the chamber pot. "Do you wish to watch?"

Thomas's eyes grew round. "I'll wait down the corridor. No need to hear that."

"Bloody hell," Fergus growled and pointed to the window on the far wall. "Open that when ye're done. Damn lass will stink up the room." He headed for the door.

"I'll need some"—Kat paused to groan—"time."

"We'll give ye some, but be naked when we return," Fergus grumbled and walked out. A key turned in the outside lock. Footsteps clipped down the stone corridor.

"Are ye ill, Kat?" Briana asked.

Kat shook her head but groaned loudly. "Help me block the door from the inside."

"Ye were very convincing," Briana said, as they wedged a broom across the doorway in two wooden slats meant for a bar of some sort.

"Now something heavy." Kat's gaze darted around.

"We'll be trapped in here," Briana said.

"Better trapped than ravished." Kat motioned toward a trunk at the end of the bed, and they lifted it together. "We can wait until they're asleep and..." Kat's words trailed off with the sound of stone brushing stone, and she spun around. "Alyce?"

The maid peeked out of a tunnel in the stone wall next to the fireplace. She waved them to her. "I listened for ye to be alone."

They slid through the crack in the wall, and Kat closed the tunnel door, setting the latch in place before following Alyce's lantern light downward. The tunnel was more like a hole. It smelled of mildew and rot. Kat's fingers slipped along the wet, moss-covered walls. Her skirts caught, but her boots and desperate grip on the wall kept her from slipping on the moist steps.

"Holy Mother," Kat whispered, feeling as if the darkness had taken on the heaviness of the granite walls pressing in on her.

"Not too much farther," Alyce said.

"Breathe slower, Kat," Briana whispered, glancing back. "Else ye will fall and tumble us all down." Her words were lighter than the dark situation, and it helped Kat keep going. *In, two, three. Out, two, three.* She had never liked close quarters.

Above them, pounding and a muffled roar made Kat jump, and they all turned in the passage.

"Hurry!" Alyce called.

Kat's hands braced against both sides of the wall as she flew down the dark steps toward Alyce's only light. Down they went and around a corner to where a door sat.

Kat followed Alyce and Briana out into the night that had descended while they were inside. A light drizzle deepened the cold, but Kat didn't care. They were on the outside of the wall surrounding the bailey and keep.

"You did it, Alyce. You saved us." Kat rested hands on knees through the heavy dress. She pulled in gulps of air and considered sitting, but Briana dragged her upright.

"We have a long way to run before they realize we're not in the keep," Briana urged.

Kat nodded and began to follow the two onto the dismal moor stretching before them. "A horse would be helpful about now," she murmured.

Bending low, the three women ran through the darkness, holding their skirts. Kat held hers above her knees to stop the rustling as much as she could. Kat was thankful she'd worn the boots that Winifred had brought for her as she tried not to twist her ankle on the uneven ground.

"Oh dear Lord," Briana said. "Look."

They all crouched low, Kat clutching the peat before her to balance on the balls of her feet. At the edge of the woods at the far end of the moor rode a person on horseback.

The horse was too pale to be Apollo, making Kat's hope drop.

"'Tis a woman," Alyce breathed softer than a whisper.

CHAPTER TWENTY-ONE
TRUTH SET FREE

Kat watched the horse halt near the gate. She gasped and tried to rise, but Briana still held her hand. "That's Margaret. What is she doing here?"

Briana craned her neck next to Kat. Only Alyce stayed hunched as if wishing to dig down into the ground. "And that's one of our stable boys with her," Briana said. Stunned, they watched Margaret dismount, pulling her hood back as she walked forward. The boy wheeled the horse around.

"No, no, no," Kat whispered. "He's leaving her there. Does she think to trade herself for us?"

"How would she know we were in there?" Briana asked breathlessly and called out to the stable boy as he rode straight toward them. The boy spotted them and brought the horse to a stop.

"Lady Briana," he said. "Mistress Kat. They've been searching for ye both." His eyes flicked to Alyce, but he didn't ask who she was.

"Henry, what is Lady Margaret doing here?" Briana asked.

Maxwell's daughter walked toward the castle in a long cape, shoulders slumped as the rain pelted her.

"She paid me to bring her here. Said her da was here and this is where she belongs," Henry said. "Who's the little lass?"

"Alyce, Henry. Henry, Alyce," Kat said still looking at Margaret's lone figure. "What is she going to—"

"Campbells!" Margaret yelled out, her voice small against the void of night weighing in on her slight form. She'd stopped about fifty yards from the gates.

"Bloody hell," Briana cursed. "She'll give us away."

Kat noticed Alyce hopping up and down. "The three of you go." Kat didn't need to repeat it for the mistreated maid. Alyce ran to the horse. Kat pushed her up behind Henry. She weighed about the same as a child. "Briana, get Toren," Kat said. "Tell him...tell him I need him."

"I will not leave ye," Briana insisted, her eyes going to Margaret.

"Something's happened to make her come here." Kat shook her head. "I can't let her go back to that man, those men."

Briana stared at her. "Do ye think he—"

"Even if Hughe Maxwell isn't the father of his own granddaughter, I'm sure he will kill Margaret if she goes back to him. Have you seen Toren's back?" Kat tugged Briana to the horse. "There isn't even room for me up there. Go. Find Toren. I'll get Margaret."

"Campbells!" Margaret hollered again, her voice squeaking at the end. "Tell Lord Maxwell that his daughter is here."

Briana nodded at Kat. "Let her know she is welcome at Craignish." She mounted the very back of the horse, and it walked rapidly into the woods. Their form was swallowed in the mist and Kat ran to Margaret as men gathered on the wall walk. *No! No! No!* If they found Kat before the others had put enough distance between them, Fergus would send men after them. Kat stepped up directly behind Margaret, hiding behind her form.

Margaret jumped and screeched, but Kat held her by the shoulders. "Don't move, or they'll see me," Kat whispered in her ear. "Margaret, come away from here."

Margaret kept her body facing forward. "Kat, they've been looking for you."

"Long story, but Briana just rode home on your horse."

"You should have gone with her," Margaret said.

"Hail, daughter," Maxwell called from above the gate, his eyes scanning the mist-enshrouded night. "All alone? Where's your husband?"

"I have no husband, Father," she called back.

Maxwell held up a torch, its light casting a glow down. It nearly reached them. "Lady Briana said you were going to wed Eagan MacCallum," Maxwell called.

"Nay, Father!" Margaret said, her words tearing out of her.

"Briana is here, preparing for her wedding. You can tell her she lies."

Kat saw Fergus's face appear in the splash of torchlight, and he said something to Maxwell. They both frowned outward, and Kat nearly turned invisible, but stopped herself.

"Margaret," Kat whispered in her ear. "I know."

Margaret stiffened. "Know?"

Kat hesitated. "Hughe Maxwell... Is he Sara's father?"

Margaret gasped softly, her body going rigid. Her head sagged forward. "Nay... but..." her refusal broke with a little sob. She took a shallow breath and swallowed. "Edward, my brother...was not in control when lust overtook him," she whispered. "Father says I am to blame."

"Why have you come here?" Maxwell called. "Alone. Do you foolishly wish to trade yourself for Lady Briana?"

"No father. I...I am a Maxwell and should return to you since I am unwed."

Her own brother had attacked her, and her father said it was her fault. Kat hugged onto the back of Margaret, wishing to turn her around to pull her into her arms. Kat's stomach tightened with the trauma this woman had endured, helpless and used by those who were supposed to protect her. "The night of the fire?" she guessed.

Margaret drew in a rattling breath. "I...ran from the barn after...Edward had finished and passed out with drink." Her words were full of shame and fear. "I...I kicked over the lantern into the hay. It was an accident." She almost turned around, but Kat held her straight, still hiding behind her. "I just ran...I was...naked. Father said...I lured Edward."

Kat had to concentrate on not gripping Margaret too hard. She'd never wanted to exact revenge on anyone as much as Hughe Maxwell.

"Even the second son rejected you," Maxwell called, his words crushing down upon Margaret. Kat felt her sway and held her steady.

"Did you tell Eagan?" Kat whispered. Margaret's head flopped forward in a nod. "He does not hold you responsible," Kat said, hoping her words were true.

"If the MacCallums sent ye away, why would we want ye?" Fergus yelled, his words meant to pierce, and Kat felt Margaret flinch.

"The MacCallums will take you in," Kat insisted.

"You didn't see the look in his eyes," Margaret said softly and almost turned, but checked herself. "The pain on his face, the..."

Maxwell interrupted her trailing words. "I certainly won't take you back after you told them which way Laird Campbell had taken their sister."

"Briana knows that a crime has been done against you, and she wants you to come home to the MacCallums. She doesn't hold your family's crime against you."

"I cannot face her, face Eagan," Margaret said. "My own brother—"

"You're not at fault, Margaret. Your father is wrong about you being to blame." The man was worse than wrong, he was complicit. "Come away from here."

Maxwell yelled something to the guards in the bailey and male laughter echoed inside the walls. Fury and frustration meshed inside Kat. If she only had a rifle. *And knew how to fire one.* She'd blast a hole in Hughe Maxwell.

Maxwell looked back down. "Nothing to say? I should make you march your worthless arse back across that moor and marry one of the MacCallums," Maxwell said and raised the torch higher. He squinted. "Who is that behind you?"

"Bugger," Kat said and tried to make herself as small as possible.

"No one, Father. I came alone."

"You abandoned the abomination?" Maxwell said, referring to Sara.

"She remains with the MacCallums." Margaret trembled, choking out the words. Her hands were clasped together before her heart as if it were dying inside her.

Maxwell frowned at her standing in the dark mist. "You may enter. I will figure out what to do with you in the morn." The portcullis began to rise.

Margaret stood rooted to the mud. Kat's fingers dug into her shoulders. "Don't go inside," Kat pleaded.

"Father," Margaret called but didn't move. "I lied when you asked me if I saw Toren set the fire that killed Edward. I kicked over the lantern. It was an accident."

Kat's breath caught. Maxwell stared down at her as judge, jury, and probably executioner.

Margaret shook her head, her words once again soft. "'Tis why my father hates him so much. I've brought ruin on the MacCallums."

"Traitor against yer own." Maxwell cursed. Even in the distance, Kat could see the man's fury, as if he'd hardened to rock. "Come inside, girl."

"Don't," Kat said, knowing the woman would never come out again. "Don't abandon Sara."

Margaret shook on a sob. "I'm leaving her with you, with people who will care for her."

"She needs her mother." Kat stopped, thinking of all those children she'd taken in who had horrible mothers. "Believe me, Margaret, I've seen children who were better off without their mothers. Sara is not one of them."

Maxwell squinted at Margaret and raised his torch higher. "Who are you talking to? There is someone behind you. Lady Briana, Mistress Kat? We've been looking for you." Maxwell turned. "Fergus, our brides are outside the walls!"

Kat pulled hard on Margaret's shoulders. "Come now with me. If you don't, they'll catch both of us and maybe Briana." *And poor Alyce.*

Margaret took a step backwards, and Kat moved with her. Then another step until she turned to look Kat in the eyes. In the muted moonlight, Kat saw tears streaming down Margaret's cheeks. Desperation and trauma contorted her face into pure anguish.

"Come with me," Kat said and pulled her into the mist.

"Stop!" Hughe Maxwell yelled.

Kat held tightly to Margaret's hand as they raced through the increasing rain. Their feet slipped on the mud, and Margaret fell. Kat pulled her upright. "Keep running!"

Horses clopped out of the gates behind them. Kat would have to use glamour magic to escape. Would it call the demons? *Drakkina needs me alive.* And she'd only use a touch of magic, hardly any was needed in the thick fog that settled around them, a cloud descending from the heavens. Water fueled her magic, and she was surrounded by it.

They ran together, tripping and lunging over the spongy moor. Their gowns, sopping wet, tangled around their legs. *Toren, where are you?* If any duo needed a knight in shining armor to come riding up over the moors of Scotland now, it was Kat and Margaret.

"There," Margaret called, and they ducked behind a boulder. Kat grabbed Margaret's dark wool cloak and threw it over them as they hunkered down to hide.

Horses' hooves thudded against the earth. Bridles jingled.

"Find them!" Maxwell's voice called from horseback. "They went to the right. There will be three of them." They were closing in.

Dear Holy Mother, please don't let this be too much magic. Kat pulled her power from the mist around them. She allowed a sliver of magic to cover them, reflecting their outward appearance as rock and mist.

Hooves pounded, closing in as a horse leapt over the boulder. Margaret gasped under the cloak and pressed in closer to Kat and the rock. The horse circled on the other side but then continued into the night. Kat uncloaked them, one ear trained on the surrounding hunt. She'd make them invisible again if any others came near. Next to her, Margaret started to pray in whispers. Kat joined in her mind and sent a desperate plea to Toren.

Toren paced in the bailey before Craignish Castle. Kat's need for help was a physical boulder in his chest. "We must ride now!" he yelled as Eagan ran out of the keep. They'd followed the trail into the forest where it was apparent from tracks that a small army had taken Kat and Briana south. They'd returned to Craignish to gather more warriors.

"Margaret's gone, too!" Eagan yelled, jogging out of the castle. "Left Sara with Fiona."

Toren swore and looked hard at his brother. "Is she trying to get herself killed?"

Eagan's eyes closed, then opened. "I asked her about the fire. She admitted to me that she let everyone think ye started it even though it was she."

"I knew that," Toren replied impatiently and motioned to a group of men who harnessed themselves, ready for battle.

"'Tis why Maxwell hates ye."

Toren nodded.

"Tor..." Eagan walked closer to him, his voice low. "She told me...her brother attacked her that night, forced himself on her. That he had before, more than once." Toren's eyes met the pain in Eagan's. "That Sara..." Eagan lowered his voice. "Edward is Sara's father, was her father. Foking Hughe blamed Margaret for enticing her own brother." He spit on the ground.

"Damn him," Toren murmured, regret heavy in his exhale. Had the abuse been happening while he'd been living with the Maxwells as a lad? He'd been so caught up in his own selfish misery that he hadn't wondered about the timid, forever hiding lass.

They mounted their horses, and Toren looked at his tormented brother. "What did ye say when she told ye?"

Eagan cursed low, a mournful curse that sounded like it was against himself. "Nothing." He looked across at Toren. "Tor, I bloody hell said nothing."

Toren didn't need to tell his little brother how wrong that had been. Eagan looked like guilt, death, and revenge mixed up into a single form of anguish. The sound of their horses clopping over the drawbridge were as hollow as Eagan must feel. "We will find her too," Tor said. "Then ye can tell her what ye should have said."

Toren glanced at the band of twenty MacCallums mounted behind them. "We ride!" With a guttural cry, the men leaned forward, and their mounts leaped into a run across the moor into misty darkness. They trained on these fields and knew the safest paths over the hilly ground.

Piercing need. Drowning sorrow. Roaring fury.

Kat's jeopardy felt like a punch to Toren's chest. It radiated through him, a pulsing cry for help. Every warrior instinct he had sent lightning through his blood. He spurred Apollo into a gallop. The horse's hooves flew, barely touching the ground. Rain began, mist at first, then small pelting drops.

"I'm coming," Toren said as they raced onward. He was certain Maxwell had Kat, and probably Briana and now Margaret. They'd be at the Campbell holding. It was the closest fortified refuge. Toren cursed again and pushed his mount harder. Without Kat's magic, the women would be at the mercy of Hughe Maxwell and Fergus Campbell.

He shouldn't have let Kat hide away. He could have gone to her rooms, kissed her again, told her that if she left, there would be a hole in him. He could have made her understand, somehow, she had to understand. He couldn't let her leave him to return to the twenty-first century.

Thunder rumbled in the distance, a slow, spreading wave of sound. Ahead, a glow formed into the ghostly figure of the witch, Drakkina.

Horses screeched as their riders pulled up hard. Grunts and gasps surrounded Toren. "Bloody olc witch," he swore, and Drakkina's form morphed into the figure of the Virgin Mary. What was she up to?

She spoke, though her lips only smiled. Her words were in Toren's mind. *I know where she is.* Drakkina's tense words were at odds with the serene appearance of an angelic Madonna.

"At the Campbell's holding," Toren said out loud and added "olc witch" in his head. The Madonna's image frowned slightly at him. "Why do ye appear like this?" he asked.

The transformed Drakkina smiled at him and answered silently. *I should look like the god, goddess, or saint to your people if I want them to follow what I need them to do. Otherwise I just scare them and they run away.*

"My men would never run away," Toren said, but she spoke over him, her voice breaking through the rumbling thunder.

"Go to the women. They need you," Mary's image said.

"Suithad!" he yelled and pressed the sides of his horse. *Try to keep up, witch.* He rode past her misty image. His men, regaining their wits, followed.

Toren. The witch flew along as a little glow up ahead. *I know exactly where she is.* She floated beside him. *Because she's using her magic.*

Thunder rumbled again, this time a bit closer. "Kat must not have a choice," Toren yelled and leaned over his horse's neck. "Go to her, help her." Drakkina's light faded out of sight. If he couldn't make it to Kat in time, at least Drakkina could defend her against the demons. Couldn't she?

Toren pushed Apollo to his limit. Rain drops pelted Toren's face like stones. A sideways glance told him that Eagan charged ahead, their horses neck and neck. They pushed through the night, using the scant moonlight and instinct to guide them south.

They slowed when they neared the Campbell fortress that was lit with torches. "The gates are open," Eagan said.

Horses trotted out of the open gates, but the riders weren't keeping in line. They spread outward. *They're searching.*

There was no mistaking Maxwell, sitting on his white horse, nor Fergus Campbell, pointing and yelling orders to his men. They were undoubtedly hunting. Either way, they would feel his revenge. Revenge against the history he'd learned about his clan in the twenty-first century that Toren hoped would not repeat itself. Revenge for taking his sister twice, for making Margaret feel shame for being a victim, and for stealing Kat.

Images of brutality fueled Toren's bloodlust. As they broke from the forest, he raised his sword in the air and yelled the MacCallum war cry. "Fuil air son buaidh! Blood for victory!"

Next to him Eagan also yelled out, his arm raised. Toren looked at his brother as they flew toward the chaotic scene. Eagan's face was stone, his lips peeled back in fury. His eyes narrowed as he spied Maxwell.

"Maxwell is mine!" Eagan ground out. With those words Toren saw his little brother as if for the first time. Before Toren's eyes, his brother grew into a leader of men.

She is here, a familiar voice whispered in his head. Off to the left, Drakkina's ethereal Holy Mother Mary image hovered near a large boulder.

Toren broke away from Eagan. His labored horse covered the distance in less than three heartbeats. Toren pulled back on the reins and threw his leg over, jumping off before the beast could stop. "Kat!" he called and dashed around the boulder.

There was movement under a cloak. "Kat," he called again, and the cloak pushed back as two drenched women clung to each other.

"Toren," Kat said, her face too pale.

He reached down to help her stand, his hands under her arms to lift her. She shook with cold or emotion or both. Relief, like a tidal wave, crashed over Toren as he pulled her into his chest. He ran his hands down her hair to her shoulders and closed his eyes, drinking in the feel of Kat's body warming against his. "Are ye hurt?"

"No."

Thank God or the devil, he didn't care which.

"What took you so long?" she asked against the beat of his heart.

Toren heard the battle behind him, heard his brother's war cry, and his commands to their men. Eagan had things well under control.

Toren's eyes moved to the other figure. It wasn't Briana. Margaret stood alone, drenched, shivering. She held her cloak around her rounded shoulders.

"Where is Briana?" he asked and turned toward the castle. "Is she still—"

"No," Kat said. "She's riding home on Margaret's horse, with Henry, one of your stable boys, and a mistreated woman named Alyce who helped us escape." Kat pointed. "That way."

Toren's whistle pierced the noise with two short blasts. Two of the closest MacCallums turned to ride towards them. Toren started yelling at them before they stopped. "Briana and two others are riding a single horse through the night that way. Find them," he said. The two trusted men nodded and tore off into the darkness. They would get his sister home.

"This storm is not natural," Drakkina said, appearing suddenly as the Holy Mother Mary once again.

Margaret gasped and dropped to her knees, head bowed. "Dearest Holy Mother," she whispered and began reciting prayers for help in the smallest but most urgent whispers.

"Drakkina?" Kat asked. "Why?" She indicated her form.

"It's easier to look this way in this century," Drakkina answered. Hard eyes in the angelic face stared into Kat's. "You used magic."

"I had to, or we'd be dead or on our way there."

"You need to get away," Drakkina said.

"I'll take her with me to get the dragonfly necklace," Toren ground out through his teeth as he pulled Kat against him again. There was no way he'd let the crone just snatch Kat away, hurling her through time to some other place. Thunder rumbled on the horizon. Drakkina looked at the veined splits of lightning along the mountains.

"They have her scent now," Drakkina said. "I need to hide you." The wind swirled, tugging Kat's hair and making Toren's kilt fly up around his legs.

"Do not send us anywhere in time, crone," Toren yelled above the wind.

"There is nowhere I can send you two in this time where—"

"The meadow," Kat said. "I warded it with the magic that was already there, tied into the earth by the trees and rocks around it. Send us there."

Drakkina frowned, her gaze sliding to the storm-ridden sky and then back. "There was a time when I couldn't feel our link but then you were there again."

"Yes, the meadow," Kat said.

Drakkina raised her hands and the area behind the boulder quavered as if a vertical sheet of water flowed over the darkness. "'Tis a temporal bridge that should get you south to where the demons and I first felt your magic, Kat. Go through and ride upon the bridge to the end." Bits of Drakkina's hair pulled free of her long braid to fly about her head like serpents, reminding Toren of Medusa. "I will pretend to be you and lead them away. Again." Suddenly the Holy Virgin Mary turned into Kat upon a horse.

Margaret gasped as Drakkina tore off in another direction, passing Eagan as he rode toward them.

"Kat?" Eagan asked, his head swiveling to watch the rider and then to look at Kat who was jamming her foot into the stirrup of Toren's horse.

"'Tis the witch," Toren said. "Take Margaret back to Craignish." His gaze fell on the wide-eyed woman, still clutching the cloak around her. "'Tis where she belongs. With her daughter."

"I..." she began, but Toren continued, staring at her.

"I am heartily sorry." He shook his head. "I should have seen what was happening under that devil's roof."

Margaret looked down at her hands. "You were just a boy when it started."

"And ye were just a lass," Toren answered. "Ye and Sara are now under the protection of the MacCallums."

"I am sorry," she said, looking back up, "about the fire and not explaining."

Toren nodded, accepting her apology, and mounted. "Ye are safe with us, ye and Sara."

"Is Briana still in there?" Eagan asked. He'd dismounted and stood before Margaret.

"Nay," Toren answered. "Kieven and Connor are riding after her. She's on Margaret's horse headed home."

The toothed gate crunched closed, leaving the MacCallums yelling insults at them from the outside. Hughe and Fergus had escaped inside, but there was no time to go after them.

Eagan maneuvered his horse up to Margaret and held out a hand. "Let me take ye home, Margaret." Tears flowed down her face. She accepted Eagan's hand, and he pulled her to sit on his horse. Toren knew there would need to be many more words between them, but it was a good start.

"Eagan," Toren said. "Kat and I must...leave, now." Toren nudged Apollo close to his brother and reached out to grasp his forearm. "While I am away, ye are The MacCallum, the chief."

Eagan frowned but then nodded and squeezed Toren's forearm. "I will take care of everyone until ye return, Brother."

Toren nodded, their eyes locked. They unclasped arms, and Toren wrapped his around Kat's middle. With a tap of his heels, Apollo leaped into a run toward the wavering sheet pushing her body into his chest. Where she belongs.

Lightning splintered across the sky, illuminating the moor as if something still hunted Kat. Apollo neighed, not liking the strangeness of the wavering air. Toren agreed, but there wasn't another choice. From the lightning, it didn't seem as if the demons were fooled by the witch. "Apollo," Toren said, "Siuthad!" The horse flattened his ears, and the three hurtled into the blur.

CHAPTER TWENTY-TWO
BLACKBERRY HAVEN

The horse's hooves sounded different, dulled, as if the noise lay flat in the swirl instead of rising into the air as sounds normally should. Darkness pressed in on them, and Kat stared out over the horse's head. Some sort of luminescence lit the straight path before them.

"Can you even see?" Kat called back to Toren.

"Enough," he said, his voice over her head.

"Do you think we can fall off?" she asked.

His arms tightened around her until she felt almost pulled into his chest. The horse cantered, the smooth waves of movement surreal under Kat in this strange tunnel.

"I don't know," he said near her ear. "But we aren't going to find out."

Kat caught glimpses of hills and lochs, farms and manor houses rushing by on both sides, moonlight shining down. Did they run over or through objects?

"So weird," Kat called. Even her voice didn't sound normal to her. She glanced up at a dark swirling ceiling. This was a tunnel more than a bridge.

They rode for what felt like an hour when the horse's ears flicked and he snorted. "Slow," Toren said.

"What is it?" Kat asked.

"Apollo senses something, and I trust him." Toren patted the beast's neck.

"Maybe he's tired."

As if a giant hand pushed them from the back, they were thrown forward over Apollo's neck. The charger's back legs flew out behind them but found ground immediately. It was like going from sixty to ten miles per hour on the roof of a truck.

"Whoa!" Kat yelled and grabbed hard onto the pummel before her. The dull thuds of the horse's hooves hitting the temporal bridge changed to a natural clop against thick meadow grass. A gentle rain sprinkled over them as warm night air breezed by.

"Are we at the clearing?" Kat asked.

"I think." He pointed toward brambles of ripe blackberries. "And 'tis warm. We may have landed in summer."

"Did Drakkina draw the demons away?" She watched fireflies light up in the darkening forest.

Toren guided his horse toward the thick brambles. "They could follow the witch's magic probably the same way they could follow yers. I think she sent us months into the past or future."

They sat atop Apollo for a moment, listening, feeling the air around them. Thunder rumbled in the distance and Kat swiveled in her seat. "That could be the demons."

Tor nudged his horse around the edge of the brambles. Trees were toppled like a tornado had dropped down into the forest. Could the demons have followed them? That could be why Drakkina had shifted their time. Kat rubbed one hand across her forehead. It was too confusing to contemplate.

Apollo stepped over fallen storm debris and branches. Kat pointed. "There, I think."

"No magic," Toren warned.

"I feel its hum without any magic on my part," she answered and glanced up. "Don't you?" He had never admitted his magic to her openly.

"Aye." He guided Apollo to the invisible path in the darkness. They pushed through the sweet-smelling brambles. Toren plucked off a ripe blackberry and passed it to Kat. "Seems summer is in its fullness."

Kat ate the berry. It was sweet and reminded her of Lisa's tarts. A tendril of homesickness coiled through her. She glanced behind Tor's side, back at the path, and in the light of the fleeting moon she watched the path disappear, leaving only a thorny hedge. The Earth magic was strong here.

"The berries were just as ripe before, but the air is definitely warmer," she said.

Apollo shook his mane and stood still in the clearing. The lightning blinked far off.

"It could be a natural storm," Kat said, searching the night sky.

Toren dismounted and helped Kat down. "Do ye feel the warding? Is it still set?" he asked, sliding his hand along her cheek to push her hair back from her face. The touch smoothed a calmness through her.

Kat breathed deep, careful not to open even a crack around her magic. The natural energy of the place resonated against her body, seeking the core of her own power. She felt the tethered wards she'd left intertwined with the ancient magic of the place. Pray God the demons didn't feel anything more than what was already there.

She turned in a tight circle to view the giant oaks and boulders that stood sentry around them. This was either the safest place on earth, or they'd just walked into the ring of a bull's eye.

"It's still warded."

"They can't sense ye here? Even if they find this time period?"

"We'll find out soon enough," Kat said glancing at the distant flashes.

"Just in case—"

"No magic," Kat finished. "I know. I wouldn't have done so before, but Maxwell's men were upon us."

Toren threw a blanket over Kat's shoulders. "Why did ye and Briana leave Craignish?"

Because I don't want to look like a monster anymore. The thought flipped around in her stomach before she shoved it into submission. She met his gaze in the filtered moonlight. "The standing stones near the coast call to me, pull me from my birthmark. It never ceases to tug, and Briana said she knew how to get there. That you three used to play amongst them."

Toren rested a hand on her shoulder. "The one on yer arm that's shaped like a dragonfly?"

She nodded and clasped the blanket closed before her. Even though it was a summer night, the wet dress and frantic ride coupled with sheer physical exhaustion made her shiver.

"I would have taken ye."

She frowned up at him. "If you'd been with us that day, they'd have killed you and taken us." And her heart would have been torn in two.

He frowned back, but clouds covered the moon above, cutting off much of the light. The rain increased, large drops pelting down, wetting her face. Toren lifted the blanket over her head. She glanced up at a flash of distant lightning. *Please let it be a natural thunderstorm.*

Toren turned, walking toward his horse. "Don't leave me," Kat called, standing alone in the dark. *Ugh. That sounded pathetic.* "I mean, don't go out of the circle. The storm could be them."

Lightning slapped jagged shards of white across his features. Rain streamed down, running off the rugged lines of his brow and nose. "I go nowhere without ye, lass."

Guilt, twisted and heavy, pooled in the pit of Kat's stomach. Because of her, Drakkina had stolen Toren from his world and then threw them back in where Kat brought demons upon them and walked his sister into a deadly trap.

Toren paced the perimeter. He dragged large branches that had dropped into the clearing, some of them small trees.

Kat walked over to Toren's horse and leaned into Apollo's warmth. She patted the animal. "Thank you," she said to the beast while her gaze followed Toren. "Thank you," she whispered at the hulking warrior who easily pulled branch after branch toward the center of the clearing. He jogged back through the slanting sheets of rain and grabbed rope tied in loops to the back of his saddle.

Kat watched in fascination as he strapped the branches together in some type of framework similar to a teepee. *As good as any Eagle Scout.* Toren would definitely win on *Naked and Afraid*, the reality show about people left to survive in the wilderness.

"The blanket," he said and pulled its weight from her shoulders. "'Tis wet so I can use it on the shelter. I have another that's dry."

The wind died to a gentle breeze although the clouds above still raced. Kat followed Toren to the small arched fort. He threw the blanket over the limbs, securing them with the ends of the ropes. "Go inside and strip out of yer wet clothes."

Kat crouched down and duckwalked into the structure to squat on another blanket he'd put on the ground like a rug. She shivered. "Just strip and—" Her words cut off as a folded blanket was tossed in from the opening.

"Wrap up in this," Toren said from outside.

"How the hell am I supposed to get out of this costume?" Ah hell, she'd said 'hell.' She blamed it on Toren. Sister Susanna would raise her left eyebrow and make her walk around the Stations of the Cross until she calmed down. Kat's eyes teared up. "I miss you," she whispered in the dark and yanked at the ties that the rain had welded shut. "Hell!" she cursed again and pushed up her skirts to take off the grimy petticoat beneath. Luckily her period had ended.

Kat listened to Toren breaking sticks outside and peeked out to see him starting a fire under another small tent he'd fashioned. "He'd definitely win *Naked and Afraid*," she murmured. And Lord help her, she wanted to see him naked, and never afraid.

Kat gave up on her wet ties and pulled her knees to her half-undone bodice to keep her body heat circulating under the dry blanket he'd tossed in. She heard Toren's footfalls. He pushed into the small enclosure with a lit lantern. She blinked at the assault to her eyes.

"Ye're still dressed," he said.

Kat covered her eyes. "I'm blind now. Thank you."

He mumbled an apology and came all the way inside. "Why are ye still in wet clothes?"

"I can't get the damn thing off." Hell, now she was saying 'damn.' A fresh tear stung her eyes. She blinked as if the action could pull the proof of her weakness back inside.

Toren's large body crowded next to her. His fingers worked at the ties at the back of the gown for several minutes, their soft tickle comforting.

"See," Kat said when he grunted in frustration.

"Hold still." He slid his dagger from his boot.

"You're cutting them?"

"The costume is irreparable." He sliced each tie, releasing the tight hold around Kat's middle. "No dry cleaners in my world." Was that a joke? Kat would take even a hint of humor right now.

Kat pulled the bodice away from her clammy skin. "What I wouldn't do for a hot shower," she said and shimmied the once lovely stays down the smock, leaving her in only the thin white gown. The smock was transparent when wet, but Toren covered her with the wool blanket.

"Ye should take off that wet smock," he said. "No hot showers at present," he added, the slight tinge of humor gone.

Kat stared at his large shape in the flickering darkness. There was subdued anger in his voice.

"Toren," she started. I'm—"

"The storm seems to be moving off and ye need sleep."

"But I—"

Toren crawled out of their hut. "I'll keep watch to make certain everything is safe."

"I'm sorry," Kat whispered to the muted sound of his footfalls on the moss. She scrunched the smock up and off, then curled into a tight ball under the heavy blanket. She even covered her head like she used to when she was little and alone in the darkest part of the night.

Kat ran cold fingers along the puckered skin of her face. Tears ached behind her eyes as guilt over Briana's abduction twisted in her stomach. She should have asked Toren to take her to the stones, but she hadn't wanted to tell him that she sought her sister to smooth away her scars. He would have said something ridiculous about them making her more interesting. But she was tired of hiding them from a world that just saw her as a monster.

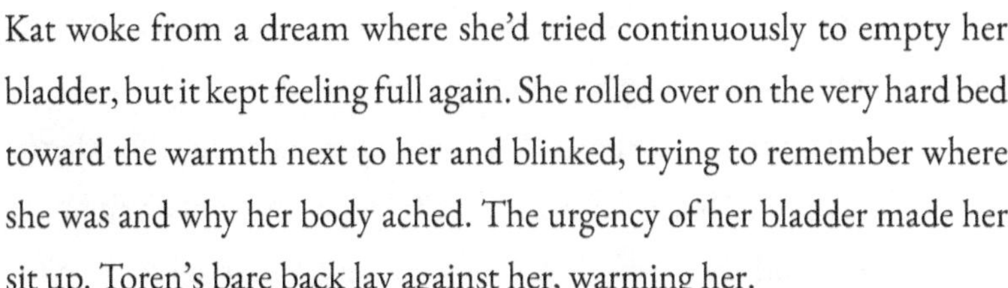

Kat woke from a dream where she'd tried continuously to empty her bladder, but it kept feeling full again. She rolled over on the very hard bed toward the warmth next to her and blinked, trying to remember where she was and why her body ached. The urgency of her bladder made her sit up. Toren's bare back lay against her, warming her.

Kat grabbed her somewhat dry smock from where it hung on the ends of some sticks that made up the opening of their shelter. Holding it against herself like a blanket, she crept out into the predawn mist. Standing, she threw it on over her head, the cold clinging to it making her shiver. All lay quiet, muted, only a few bird calls breaking the morning stillness. Kat stepped well away from the hut but remained in the circle and squatted behind a bush near the perimeter. *Much better.* She straightened, turning back to the hut.

Toren stood outside, legs braced apart, arms crossed over his bare muscled chest. A kilt lay hastily wrapped around his narrow hips.

Kat walked back. "I had to wee," she said and ducked back inside. The smock was cold and damp, so she threw it back off and wiggled between the two layers of blanket that still held their heat.

Toren ducked back in, his kilt gone. Kat closed her eyes, but the sight of his heavy member and powerful legs flashed like neon lights in her mind.

Toren stepped over her and found his warm spot under the blanket. Their two naked bodies were a mere inch apart. Kat rubbed a hand down her sensitive skin, wishing she could wipe away the passion building in all the right places. She sighed, her eyes opening.

Toren pushed up on an elbow and looked at her. Kat could just make out the faint lines of his features in the deep shadows. He studied her in the stillness. "Ye just left." His voice was low, but strong. There was vulnerability in the words, yet he didn't allow any pain to seep into his tone. "Without a word of goodbye, ye just left Craignish."

Kat stared up at him, feeling the pain through their connection that he would never admit. It caught at her breath and brought out a full press of tears she could not stop. All the remorse, all the fear, all the conflict that warred inside poured out with the tears, wetting her cheeks.

"I was coming back," she said and tried to breathe.

His stare felt almost smothering. "Ye were going to the stones. If the witch had been there, she could have taken ye away, and I would never see ye again."

"She wouldn't do that since we are supposed to be...fated mates or something." She tucked the blanket under each arm to hold it up over her breasts.

"But you would have asked to return home, to yer children and friend."

"Not without saying goodbye." Yet the thought of that goodbye twisted in her stomach, making her nauseous.

"Why were ye going to the stones then, if not to convince the witch to send ye home?"

She exhaled. He wouldn't believe anything but the truth. "Drakkina said that if I came to the stone circle it would be safe enough there for her to bring one of my sisters to meet me." That was definitely true.

"And ye raced off when we knew Maxwell and Fergus Campbell were on their way? To meet yer sister? For what reason?"

"I...just wanted to meet her."

"A dangerous time for that." His raised brow asked further questions.

An ascending sun brightened the inside of the hut. Kat could see the creases in Toren's brow, the hardness of his jaw, the distrust in his eyes. She pulled her hair absently over the right side of her face and glanced down at the muscles of his chest. "My sister is a healer. Apparently a very talented one." Kat let her statement lie flat between them as the silence roared. She twisted the ragged end of the blanket between her fingers.

"Are ye ill?"

"No."

Kat jerked slightly when she felt Toren's warm fingers push back her hair, but she remained still. His thumb gently traced the puckered skin along her jaw line. Kat barely breathed.

"Ye went to smooth these away," he said, his voice a low rumble in the close space. "Ye risked so much for so little."

Kat looked up to his eyes. "So little?" She pulled back and threw her hand out indicating his face and body. "What do you know of suffering through stares and whispers when you have a gorgeous face and scars you can hide?"

He stared into her smoldering gaze. "I do not hide my scars," he said simply. "They are a part of me, make me who I am."

"So I am an ugly, stupid girl."

"Nay. Ye were a curious little girl who learned that life is full of challenges."

Kat dropped her gaze to her lap. "What I learned was to hide," she whispered.

Toren leaned forward and edged closer so he could easily cup her face. His hands were large, rough from swordplay, but also warm and gentle, just like the rest of him. Kat looked back up, unable to hide the tears blurring her vision.

Toren's lips touched hers. "Do not hide from me." His hot breath, broken by the gentle graze of his lips, moved along her right cheek and down the scars to her collarbone. "Every sweet part of ye, lass, makes ye who ye are. A strong, clever, courageous woman." His hand slid across the dragonfly mark on Kat's upper arm, and she felt a sizzle jump between them. Passion flooded her, languid, hot, sinking passion. It could be coming from Toren or from her, but it didn't matter. Its building strength was the same in them both. They were alone and naked, cocooned in a cozy shelter in a magical clearing. When would there be a better time to give in to her curiosity and passion?

Kat released the blanket, and it slid down, exposing her sensitive breasts, the nipples hard. "Will we finish what we started?" she murmured when his eyes came back to her face.

He inhaled, and she could imagine him catching the scent of her desire. "Aye, if ye will have me." He kissed her then, a deep, languid kiss, full of sensual power. His hand slid along her neck, over her shoulder and down to cup one breast.

Kat moaned against his mouth, losing herself in the tantalizing sweep of sensation. Wet heat slid through her to drench the juncture of her legs.

Toren lowered her into the blankets. His flat palm swept down her stomach, brushing along the curves of her waist and hips. The blanket rested just over the curls hiding her sex. He squeezed her hip bone. "I've wanted ye so bloody much, ye distracting siren," he said and stared into Kat's eyes.

His words made her heart speed, and the tone caused her stomach to feel full of butterflies. Toren's mouth descended to suck in a taut nipple with such exquisite pressure that Kat arched off the makeshift bed. Her toes literally curled into the blanket under them. She moaned softly as his hand moved to the other breast while his tongue swirled the erect bud of its twin.

Kat threaded fingers through Toren's thick wavy hair. *More.* She wanted more. Kat pushed upward with her hips, grinding her pelvis against Toren's stomach. He broke free and looked at her face. The dark passion in his green-brown eyes turned his grin into a promise, and a chill of desire shivered through Kat's flushed body.

"I can smell yer need, lass. I can feel it." He pressed his fist to his chest. "Here." He slid the fist down his own body to the obvious erection under the blanket. "And here."

"I feel yours too." Kat pulled the blanket to the side and felt his gaze devour her. The desire in his eyes and the small growling noise he made sent her fingers stroking down her heated body while he watched. Without the effort or worry to conceal her scars, Kat's body revved with anticipation. She parted her legs, fingers brushing down through her curls to the slick folds below.

"You like this," she whispered. Kat dipped her fingers into her heat, her other hand wrapping around one breast to squeeze and pinch.

Toren growled, his gaze following her hands. The muscles in his torso were ridges like waves of power that led to his large cock. A new surge of anticipation rushed through her, and she reached for him, touched him. It was Toren's turn to choke on an inhale as Kat worked her hand along his long, thick shaft.

Toren leaned forward and captured Kat's lips in a kiss that sent her spiraling away from all thoughts save one. She must feel him inside her or she'd die from the throbbing ache.

Toren's fingers replaced her own as he found her heat. Kat moaned against his lips and ground into his hand as his fingers pushed inside. He pushed back with the heel of his palm against the bundle of nerves of her clit, setting off another string of electric tingles.

"Ye're so tight, lass," he said as he moved his fingers in her flesh. "As if ye were—"

"I need you Toren," Kat cut off the words with a moan as she released all holds on herself. "In me. Please."

Kat opened her legs wide, spreading herself. Instead of pushing into her, he dropped his mouth to her sex. Kat gasped at the wet heat as he tasted and tongued her. "Oh my God," she said, pressing upward against his mouth. She felt the brush of his short beard against her thighs and his tongue moving against her clit, so fast. Looking down her writhing body, the sight of him loving her so intimately was the final push, and Kat orgasmed.

"Yes! Oh God!"

As her body contracted, spiraling over into the abyss, Toren shifted, and she felt him at her entrance. "Kat?" he said through shallow breaths, his cock hard and ready.

"Yes," she breathed.

Toren sank inside her open, flooded, hot body, filling her, breaking through. The smallest pain pierced Kat as he buried himself completely, and she wrapped her arms around his back.

Toren froze, his features tight as he stared down at her. Confusion warred with passion in his eyes. "Ye're a virgin?"

"Not anymore." She raised her legs, wrapping them around his tight ass as if trapping him to her.

"But...ye're from the twenty-first century."

Kat smiled, passion still heating her words. "Apparently I was waiting for my sixteenth-century soul mate."

A slow grin spread across Toren's lips, and his hand moved to her curls, easily finding the sensitive bundle. Kat's eyes closed with the flood of sensation, her channel still clenching around him.

He moaned and trailed hot kisses down Kat's neck and ear. "Mine," he whispered huskily, sending goosebumps along her skin. "Ye are mine, now and forever."

The words sizzled through Kat like the hum of magic. Was he binding her to him? Kat didn't care. She was his, no matter where or when they were.

Kat thrust upward, moaning as it pushed him higher inside her. "Time to move, Highlander."

"By yer command, mo ghràdh."

Kat's moonstone translated his rugged Gaelic. *My love.* Her smile morphed into a moan as he pulled back to thrust in again. And again. And again, starting a rhythm in and out of her heat. He kissed her, his forearms braced on either side of her head. Moving higher on her body, the angle changed within her so that he hit a sensitive spot inside as well as her clit outside. The man was a sexual wizard.

"Oh God! Toren!"

Toren kept their rhythm going. "Open yer eyes, lass. I want ye to see who brings ye such pleasure."

Kat hadn't realized she'd closed them. She opened her eyes and stared into his hazel orbs. They were bright with sexual intensity, like a beast exploring her inside and out, devouring her with passion. Whatever bond tethered them accentuated the incredible feelings racing through their bodies. Her body pulsed, and she felt his animal excitement, his need to mate, his possession of her.

"I'm going to fill ye, make ye part of me." Toren's raw words pushed her over the edge of control, and her body crashed into another orgasm.

Kat cried out while focusing on Toren's tight features, and he roared his own pleasure, pumping into her.

His mouth found hers, and they thrust over and over against each other, Kat's legs rising to hook around his pumping arse. His strokes continued to push pleasure into her until her passion began to slow. It took many minutes for their bodies to descend, wrapped together in heat and the scent of their combined desire.

Toren rolled them to their sides, still joined, legs intertwined. Kat's hot body began to cool, and she nuzzled closer to Toren. He wrapped her in his arms and pulled the blanket back over them.

Dawn blazed warm sunlight onto the hut. Kat caught the chirps of birds and the faint gurgle of the rain-fed creek nearby. Her right cheek lay contentedly against Toren's chest where she heard the deep glub-dup of his heart. She sighed and he hugged her closer.

"Mmmm, ye smell wonderful," Toren said into her hair. Toren nuzzled against her ear. "Like warm woman and sex." He pulled in an exaggerated inhale. "And ye smell like me."

Kat smiled into his chest. "You've marked me."

Toren tipped her chin up and kissed her. "Completely, inside and out."

Kat took a deep inhale. Was marking like binding? Right that moment, she didn't care if it was as long as it meant she could stay in Toren's warm embrace.

CHAPTER TWENTY-THREE
TOGETHER

Toren kept to the shade as much as possible along the winding southeast road. The sun beat down with full summertime strength. Sweat beaded against his brow, and he reached for the flask of cold creek water. He took a gulp and handed the flask to Kat, who rode with her skirts pulled up to her knees. Quite unseemly for the sixteenth-century gentlewoman.

He smiled as his eyes traveled along one shapely calf, remembering how his mouth had followed the same trail just that morning. Once Kat had reawakened, they'd feasted on roast hare and blackberries in the magical glade. And then they'd feasted on one another.

"I can't believe we are traveling to Tilbury in August 1588," Kat said with open enthusiasm. She twisted in the seat, which pushed her breasts almost out of the hastily obtained dress. "Elizabeth will be there waiting for the Armada! The gosh darn bloody Spanish Armada!" She breathed deeply, making her pale flesh rise higher along the neckline, and Toren nearly steered Apollo into a tree. The horse whinnied and sidestepped back to the center of the road. Toren refocused his eyes on the path ahead.

"The merchant said it was August seventh, right?" Kat asked but didn't wait for an answer. "That would be in the Julian Calendar and the seventeenth in the Gregorian Calendar that won't be used until 1752 in England. We know Elizabeth will give her famous speech to boost her navy on the nineteenth of the Gregorian Calendar which was the ninth in the current calendar, or two days from now."

Toren smiled at the exuberance in Kat's voice. "Yer love of history is showing, lass. Best not give it away to anyone else or ye'll be accused of witchery."

Kat glanced back toward the village they'd left. "No one's out here." They had stopped in the small village an hour's ride from the glade to find a clean dress for Kat and information. The witch had sent them four months into the future. Toren frowned over Kat's head at the thought of his family. Was all well at Craignish? He breathed deeply, remembering Eagan's strength. His brother thought he was taking Kat home. Would Briana's rescue be enough to change his clan's history?

"Will we make it to Tilbury in two days?" she asked, twisting, which spread a feast of smooth flesh before Toren's eyes.

"Not if ye keep distracting me," he said.

"Distracting you?"

Toren looked pointedly toward Kat's ample display. The deep well between her breasts where her moonstone nestled begged for his exploration. A delicate flush feathered upwards along Kat's collarbone and neck, and into her cheeks.

Toren's gaze moved back to her face. Despite the flush, she smiled. She dipped her fingers into the well. Toren made a half-groan, half-growl sound. Kat squealed, yanked the gown higher, and turned back around. "I will endeavor not to distract you." She laughed but then tilted her head back. "At least not while on horseback."

They slept in an abandoned cabin that night. After a full day of riding, the lass was plain worn out. Toren cradled Kat against him after she fell into an instant sleep. He inhaled her fresh scent and listened to her gentle breaths. Every once in a while, she whistled on an exhale. Toren smiled into the darkness. He'd never tire of hearing Kat's sounds, soft and loud…very loud. He closed his eyes and settled in for an uncomfortable night.

The next day Kat continued to rattle on about the details of Elizabeth's win over the Spanish general whom Philip had placed in charge after Santa Cruz died. "His name is Medina Sidonia. He's a duke." She shook her head. "The man even gets seasick."

"Aye, I've heard of the general."

"And there were these ships, eight of them, that were packed with dry wood that the English lit on fire and sent into the Spanish crescent." She looked back at Toren. "They call it a crescent because that is how the ships sail, the whole navy in a crescent shape which is impenetrable."

Toren was well-versed in Spanish attack positions. Anyone would be after an evening listening to talk at court in the last year. But he just nodded, too entranced by the spark dancing in Kat's blue eyes to say anything. It was the same spark he'd seen when she'd playfully thrown a handful of blackberries at him the previous morning before they left the magic glade. He smiled, even though he was thinking more about the surprised squeal she'd made when he'd stalked her in full retaliation.

"Hell Burners," she said.

"What?"

"The ships that they lit, I mean light, on fire and maneuver out into the Spanish fleet," she said.

"They are called Hell Burners." He grunted. "Sounds appropriate."

"I can't believe I'll be here to witness it." Kat turned around and relaxed into his chest.

Toren let the comment sit for a long moment and then very softly replied. "Ye could witness firsthand the next sixty-odd years of history, Kat."

Birds sang overhead in the summer breeze. Small animals fled Apollo's feet. The hot sun filtered down through a thick canopy of oak leaves. It was as if the whole world continued, uncaring what her answer would be. He hadn't even asked the question, just laid out the issue.

Tightness entered Toren's chest, a panicky flutter in his torso, and his breath sucked in rapidly. What malady was this? This ache through his body, pooling into the pit of his stomach? It was similar to the dread he'd felt as a child, scared, torn from his family, alone. And it was coming from his connection with Kat. Toren closed his eyes and let the feeling roll around inside. He sensed the war within as she rode silently in his arms. He pulled her body into him and rubbed her arm with one hand. He felt her pain, the pain of guilt of wanting to see history but also needing to go home to her children. They depended on her. And the pain of missing them filled her heart, heavy as stones.

"I'm sorry, lass," he breathed into her soft, wavy hair that she twisted over one shoulder. He kissed the side of her face. "I don't wish to bring ye pain, but we need to decide what we will do once we return the necklace to the witch."

"If she gives us a choice," Kat whispered.

Was there some small hope that they wouldn't be given a choice? Aye. "No matter what, we stay together," he said, and practically held his breath.

Kat reached down and squeezed his hand and the nauseous tight grip on his stomach abated. That was agreement, wasn't it? She wanted to stay with him. Now he just had to convince her that his century was the wisest choice. He frowned as his mind twisted, looking for hard reasons to stay.

⸺◆⸺

They reached Tilbury on August eighth. With the gold coins he'd begun carrying on him, Toren commissioned a court gown to be made from a partially stitched costume. He replaced his rugged shirt and kilt with court hose and doublet. Most of Elizabeth's navy was stationed in tents dotting the hills near the shore, leaving the inns for the commanders. Toren found one room and secured it for the two of them as a wedded couple.

"Elizabeth has planned plays and a masquerade for tomorrow night after she addresses her troops," Toren said to Kat where she sat cross-legged on the small mattress in her smock. He tossed his jacket on the one rickety chair in the room and sat to pry off his boots.

"There are so many people moving in and around that I think it would be best for us to blend in, pretend we've been near the whole time. We need to get close to Elizabeth to see if she still wears the dragonfly."

Kat nodded and nibbled at the wedge of white cheese Toren had brought up with bread and wine.

"Perhaps there will be news of what's happening at Craignish," Kat said, her eyes serious.

Toren nodded. "I must tell Elizabeth about Margaret withdrawing her claim that I am Sara's sire."

"You won't tell her the truth." Kat shook her head.

"Not outright, but Elizabeth has a way of finding out every truth in her realm if she has a heart to."

Toren watched Kat cover a yawn with her hand. The lass was tired from the ordeal and the constant moving. And there were also their late nights together. "Ye should sleep."

"You should, too."

He nodded and eyed the small mattress. "Either we take turns, or I sleep under ye." His eyebrows shot up. "Or on top of ye."

Kat laughed and scooted over, patting the gray tick. "If we hold tight to each other, we shouldn't roll off." She brushed at the bedding. "I'm trying to ignore what is probably living in these blankets."

Toren yanked at the top cover. Kat jumped up and he stripped the linens, replacing them with the blankets they'd been using on their journey.

"They might be road dusty, but they don't bite."

"This inn would definitely not make Frommer's," Kat said. Toren didn't know what Frommer's was, but her twenty-first-century cleanliness preferences wouldn't be found near Tilbury or anywhere on any continent at present. She leaned way over the edge of the bed and smiled. "There's plenty of room."

Toren tossed the rest of his clothes over the chair, momentarily wondering if the brittle bed would crumble under his weight. Kat's gaze moved leisurely over his naked chest, torso, and below as he secured the door and laid out his short sword and long sword within reach of the bed. He climbed under the rough blanket and up against Kat's softness. Catching the end of her smock, he lifted and tugged it up over her head.

"There isn't room for this," he said and tossed it with his clothes on the chair. Kat laughed softly and wiggled her backside into his groin as he spooned up against her. Toren ran one arm under her head and the other over her middle, reaching up to casually cup her wonderfully ample breast.

"Mmmm," she sighed as he kneaded her warm flesh.

Toren growled low and inhaled Kat's hair. She scrunched her shoulder as if it tickled but he persisted. His thumb strummed against her nipple as he feathered kisses along her hairline. "Och, but ye are soft and warm everywhere."

Kat pushed back, grinding into him. "I'm hotter and softer in certain places, MacCallum," she breathed. The edge of impatience in her tone made him chuckle.

"No longer the timid virgin," he said.

Kat turned so that she looked up at him. "No longer the virgin perhaps, but I was never timid."

His smile turned lusty, reflecting the thoughts of their last two days together. Indeed, Kat was not timid. Her hand snaked along her bare hip to duck below the globe of her perfect arse. Her fingers were cool against his heat as she wrapped around him, stroking.

"Nay, lass, never timid," he murmured as he pushed her back flat on the bed. Her wee hand tugged out and found him once again.

Toren leaned in, his weight and power all around her slender frame. Shielding, protecting, exuding strength but never overpowering. His lips descended, hot, fierce, consuming. Her luscious mouth slanted naturally against his, her hands brushing a path back up across his chest and over his shoulders. She tried to push him over, but he didn't move. His tongue mated with hers as his fingers found that hot spot. She groaned against his mouth as he moved them rapidly.

He paused and she pressed against one shoulder. "Over." The word came out in a rush. "I want to be on top." Toren raised an eyebrow. "I may have been a virgin two days ago, but I've read extensively." She smirked.

No further explanation needed. In one fluid movement, Toren tucked Kat against him and lifted her so that her soft curves lay across and over the hard planes of his heated body. Her breasts pushed against him, and she straddled his hips. He groaned as he felt her slick heat, her two glorious globes hanging before his face. Toren feasted on one swell as his hand found her pleasure below. Kat moaned and wrapped her hand around him, rubbing until Toren thought he'd lose all control. He lifted her hips and slowly slid her open, wet body down over him.

Kat huffed softly out from parted lips, passion flooding her eyes. She held herself over his face as she moved back and forth, building fast, grinding her pelvis against him where she was impaled completely. He sucked on one sweet nipple and then the next. She circled her hips, and the pleasure was so intense that Toren groaned with no care if those on the other side of the thin walls could hear. He was enthralled, captured in the most exquisite way.

Kat's hands splayed across his solid chest as she found her rhythm, and a scorching tempest built, a swirling need of heat. Toren's hand slid along her spine and sweet flexing arse, holding onto her, knowing he would never let go of this incredible woman that he'd found across centuries. His equal in courage and passion.

Their bodies moved as one toward a goal of overwhelming pleasure. Reaching in front, he thrummed her sensitive nub, gently with persistent pressure. His breath came in gusts as he watched her ride him, using her body to stroke along his length. His thumb moved faster with his breath as he thrust upward into her, over and over, following her rhythm.

"Oh God," Kat huffed, and he felt her body squeeze around him. He captured the back of her neck, guiding her face down to him as she cried out against his lips with her climax. The pulsing heat and her uninhibited response threw him over the edge into his own glory. He filled her as she shuddered, and both of them rode the waves of molten pleasure until they ebbed, and coherent thought returned.

Toren pulled her down upon him, their arms and legs intertwined. He cradled her and flung one of the blankets across Kat's cooling back.

Her exhale tickled against his chest. "If only demons didn't hunt me to destroy the world..." she said, her voice soft. It held a note of humor but more regret. "If I didn't miss my children so much it physically hurt." Toren caressed along her spine, rubbing, soothing. "If we didn't have to steal a cursed artifact from the most powerful queen in history and give it to a floating, dragonfly witch." She huffed softly and her voice grew soft. "If we didn't need to choose whose life to forfeit in order to stay together."

Kat pushed up on her elbows and looked into his face. "If we were just any girl and boy born in the same century." A sad laugh broke from her lips, and Toren reached up to run his thumb over her chin. "Just Toren and Kat." She sighed heavily and kissed the palm of his hand. "Now, that would be wonderful."

Toren pulled her back down to lay across his heart. "Aye, how wonderful," he agreed and stroked her hair as his mind moved to his family. Was saving Briana from Fergus enough, or would Clan MacCallum of Craignish still disappear from the pages of history?

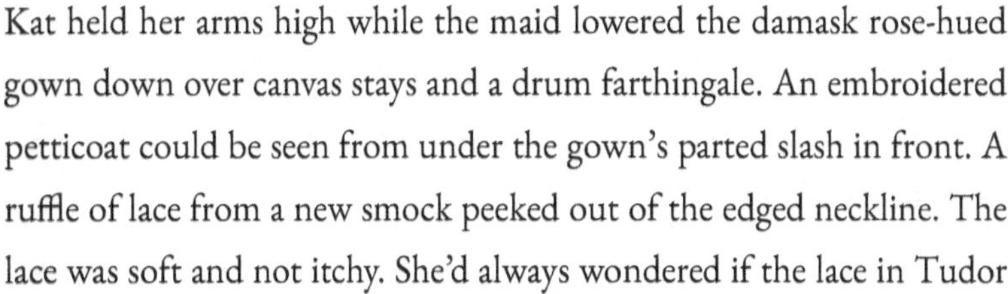

Kat held her arms high while the maid lowered the damask rose-hued gown down over canvas stays and a drum farthingale. An embroidered petticoat could be seen from under the gown's parted slash in front. A ruffle of lace from a new smock peeked out of the edged neckline. The lace was soft and not itchy. She'd always wondered if the lace in Tudor times itched. She ran a finger just under it, marveling at the exquisite work.

Kat stood before a polished mirror made from Venetian glass that the proprietor of the inn had boasted incessantly about when he'd had two strong men carry it into her room for her fitting. The maid, whose name was Abigail, set the large, flat belt around Kat's middle. Kat smoothed it with her hands and smiled. It made her waist look narrower than any set of Spanx, probably because the bottom of the gown flared out so much. Gold thread danced along the belt, stitched into butterflies.

Toren had given Kat several small bobbles to hang from the belt as was the fashion: a gold cross, a sweet-smelling pomander filled with cloves, a blue butterfly, and a gold heart which opened. The only piece of jewelry she wore was her moonstone that lay outward on her bodice. Kat's hand slid from the moonstone to the heavy heart on her belt. Inside was a scrap of MacCallum plaid. No explanation, just a kiss, was all Toren had given her when she'd asked.

"You look lovely, milady, and your hair is dry now after your bath," Abigail said, and secured the deep rose-colored French hood to Kat's head. Her hair flowed in waves under the thin veil of cobweb lawn that fell from the headdress pinned far back on Kat's forehead as was the fashion.

Kat wiggled her toes in the satin pumps and smiled. She ran her hand down the fabrics, fingers sliding along the gold thread and pearls sewn into braids and hems. *Exquisite.* Since his abduction by Drakkina, Toren had carried coins on his person, and they'd certainly come in handy.

Kat breathed past the wild thumping in her heart. "It is lovely. Thank you, Abigail," she said. "I couldn't have donned it without you." Kat passed her a silver threepenny.

"Thank you, milady." The beaming woman smiled as she curtsied and left Kat alone in the rented room.

Kat turned back to the polished glass mirror. She did look lovely. Even her skin seemed smoother. Kat stepped up to the glass and ran cool fingers over the right side of her cheek and jaw. The skin seemed less puckered, less red and angry. And she wasn't using any magic to hide the scars. Were they fading?

Kat studied her face a long while. "No," she said to herself in the mirror. "They just aren't as bad as I remember." She absently rubbed a spot on her upper arm. When was the last time she'd really looked at her true face? Years perhaps. In her mind she'd always seen them at their worst, but now they didn't seem quite as noticeable. Especially when she was decked in genuine Elizabethan elegance.

"I'm glad to see you aren't using your glamour." Drakkina's voice made Kat jump inside the heavy frame of the gown. She whirled, hand to her chest which made the petticoats bell outward.

"You could use some make-up on those scars," the witch continued. "Until we get you and Merewin to meet." The misty figure of the crone glanced around. "I don't suppose my dragonfly is here." Her ethereal, spirit dragonflies hovered about the room as if searching.

"No," Kat said, "but Toren is working on a plan to get it. It's here in this town, with Queen Elizabeth."

"Humph!" Drakkina snorted. "Stupid to give it to her in the first place."

"He didn't have another choice since you stuck us in her castle ready to walk in to gift her with something. The only other gift he could have given her was me."

Drakkina's frown mellowed into something of a grin. Her icy blue eyes twinkled. "Defending the Highlander? That's good." She peered closer at Kat and tapped her bottom lip with one finger. "I'd say you two have bonded or at least bedded."

"What?"

"Married or mated or given your hearts to one another." She shrugged. "Or all three. Doesn't matter. I can spot love."

"You can spot love? What exactly are your credentials? Have you been in love? Married and mated? Bonded and bedded?"

Drakkina frowned at her. "I don't need to do all that to know a loved woman when I see one. I've seen it in your sisters."

Kat's sly smile flattened. "How many sisters do I have?"

"Three," she waved her hands around. "You can meet them after my amulet is back and the demons have lost your trail. Then Merewin can smooth your face, and the Highlander will love you even more."

Could Toren love her? She turned back to her reflection. "The scars don't bother him."

"Nonsense, a perfect face will solidify his love."

Kat turned toward the apparition. "You truly don't know anything about relationships or love, do you?"

Drakkina huffed. "I know about a lot of things, things you couldn't even comprehend, uppity girl."

Kat tilted her head and stared at her. "About warm, in-your-bones, toes-curling, fluttery middle, true love?"

Drakkina flapped her hand. "I don't know about bones and toes and fluttery such. But I do know love heals hurt hearts and broken souls. But it doesn't heal scalding oil scars."

Kat turned back to the mirror and peered closer. "I think they look better."

"They haven't changed since you were a teenager."

"Hmmm," Kat said to her reflection and then turned back to Drakkina. "So you've been watching me since I was a child? Where do you live, anyway?" Kat moved her hand in the air. "Up there in the ether or something? Anyone up there with you to bed and wed?"

Drakkina gave her a fierce frown. "'Tis my duty to watch Gilla's children, help them find their soul mates. And yes, I live"—she moved her hands around—"out there in the ether. By. My. Self." She punctuated each word.

"Why?"

"Why what?" Drakkina snapped.

"Why do you live in the ether? Why not move on to heaven or somewhere to rest? I mean...you are dead."

"My body is dead, but I'm still trying to save this blasted world and Gilla's ungrateful daughters."

Kat shook her head. She wasn't getting very far with her questions. She spoke slowly as if to a child. "But why are you still trying to save this world? Why not just move on and leave the saving up to those who are still alive?"

"Well for one thing, you couldn't do it without me." Drakkina rubbed a hand down a face that suddenly looked tired. "And...I suppose I'm a bit responsible for putting it in danger."

"How?"

The old woman seemed to fade and then return, and her lips curled inward as she looked overhead, thinking. "I bound the demons together, thirteen of them." She waved a hand. "It was long ago. I was trying to stop them, reduce their power, but I haven't succeeded. And I'm afraid that by binding them, well, they may be getting stronger."

"What were you trying to stop them from doing?"

Drakkina began to pace in the confines of the room. She wrung her hands together and looked at Kat. "I did love once." Her timeless visage seemed to age some as if the memory taxed her. "'Twas a very long time ago. He was strong and sound, a master of magic." She paused to look out the window. "He had a very kind heart." Drakkina's voice hitched in her throat. This was the first emotion Kat had seen in the woman other than anger and impatience.

Drakkina stared out for a long moment, but then whirled around, scattering the dragonflies that had flown closer to her. "The demons seduced him," she said, her words succinct and full of venom. "They taught him things to make his magic more powerful. Little by little they worked at him, feeding him information until the quest for knowledge overrode the purity of his heart." She closed her pale blue eyes. "It...it corrupted him, killed him."

"I'm sorry," Kat whispered, not sure what else to say. It was hard to think of the witch who was holding her hostage as having a story of her own, but everyone did. Kat certainly knew that after having heard the stories of her children. Every soul had baggage. "So...you stay here or in your ether, seeking revenge."

Drakkina's body seemed to inflate a bit more, making her larger in the room. "My fight is for much more than simple revenge. I fight for this world because there is still goodness here. If the demons win, evil will rule, and your God of Light will have no more influence in this realm."

Kat felt her stubborn nature seize on a very good cause. "Then we will win."

"Not without my dragonfly." Drakkina threw her arms out to the sides, making her robes billow in an invisible breeze. "The strange storms that have been plaguing the Spanish on their journey to take England are the demons. They know the amulet is around here somewhere. They are hunting...and waiting for you to show up again. Then they will strike." Drakkina started to fade.

"Where are you going?"

"Your Highlander comes. I will return when you have the dragonfly. Meanwhile I'll consult the oracle." Drakkina's last words drifted to Kat on the breeze through the window.

CHAPTER TWENTY-FOUR
TILBURY

Rap. Rap. "'Tis me."

Kat recognized the deep brogue and smiled. "You may enter." She sounded every bit the queen in her costume.

"Elizabeth is about to leave for—" Toren's words cut off as his eyes fastened onto Kat. His mouth hung open as if waiting for the next word to come out. "Ye look..." Toren's eyes met Kat's. "Ye're exquisite, Kat."

She smiled broadly. "Thanks to your negotiating skills for the dress."

"Are ye wearing the knickers I had made?"

Her smile turned wicked as she thought of the lacy shorts under her petticoats. She nodded slowly. "Thank you for that."

His gaze narrowed into something much more smoldering. He took a step closer and pulled Kat into a kiss. When he began to tug on the belt at her waist, she pulled back. "It took me over an hour with a maid who knew what she was doing to get this gown on me."

"I can get ye out of it in two minutes," he growled.

Kat planted her hands on Toren's chest. "I don't have another hour to put it back on." She put several steps between them, despite the voice in her head saying 'just lift the skirts.'

"You said Elizabeth was leaving. For Tilbury Hill?" she asked.

Toren's erection was a heavy bulge in the Elizabethan breeches. "Aye," he said with a roll of his brogue, making it sound like a growl. "We best get moving else ye find yerself ravished, milady."

The heat of his kiss and his gaze had lit a smoldering want inside Kat, but she turned to the door. "Where did Abigail put my fan?"

"Och, I almost forgot." Toren stopped her. "To wear, it matches yer costume." Toren pulled from a folded piece of cloth an intricate gold and rose-colored mask held on a ribbon-wrapped stick.

Kat's stomach dropped. "You want me to hide my face." She went from heated giddiness to nauseously numb in two seconds. Maybe Drakkina was right.

Toren frowned, his gaze locking with hers as if in confusion. "Elizabeth is having a masquerade later, for the court, to lighten the mood of impending war. All the ladies and many of the men will be holding a mask."

Kat watched his eyes, his face for any indication that there was more to his explanation.

He returned her direct gaze, questioning. "Ye look pale suddenly, upset." Toren touched her arm. He pulled out a black leather mask and held it briefly before his own face. "The masks will help us blend in so we can approach Elizabeth easier."

His explanation made sense. Kat nodded. "Of course, yes, we will be just another glittery couple behind masks."

Toren tossed his mask on the bed and bent slightly to stare into her eyes. He ran his large, warm palm down the right side of her face. Kat tried not to cringe. "Kat, I would never hide ye. Ye are strong and cunning and exquisite." He kissed her. A long slow kiss filled with conviction that he spoke the truth. When he drew back Kat gave him a weak smile. Old insecurities were hard to release.

"I..." she started. "Thank you...for the mask. It does match perfectly."

His frown relaxed into his neutral serious look. "Let's go hear some history, then." He steered her to the door and grabbed a light cloak. "'Tis windy and looks like rain."

They stepped into the hallway, and she rested her hand on his arm. "Drakkina says it's the demons," Kat whispered. Toren's gaze snapped around the landing.

"Is the witch back?"

"She was just here before you came in. She wants the dragonfly and said that the demons are circling, waiting to find me." Kat's finger curled into his sleeve. "I can't use a flicker of magic."

"Did she try to take ye, send ye somewhere?" Toren's arm wrapped around Kat's, pulling her closer to him as they took the stairs.

"No, she just seems to want the...she called it an amulet. You know, I don't think she even cares about the necklace. She just wants the dragonfly off it." They landed at the bottom and Toren threaded them through the chairs and men in the common room until they were outside. "That necklace, without the dragonfly on it." She stopped and looked at Toren. "I knew I recognized it."

"What?" he asked as they fell into the small crowd striding toward a knoll near the shore.

"The pearl and ruby necklace with the onyx medallion in the middle is seen in a couple of Elizabeth's portraits." Kat squeezed Toren's hand. "It even has the tear-shaped pearl hanging from it," she whispered. "But there is no dragonfly in the center of the medallion. That's why I didn't recognize it." Kat tugged until Toren looked down. "She wears the necklace in the Armada picture. She's supposed to have it, just without the dragonfly."

Kat's pulse quickened. "So we will be successful in getting it back. We already know she'll wear it without Drakkina's amulet." Relief bloomed inside her chest, making it easier for her to breathe in the warm, damp air.

Above, the sun battled dark clouds racing in. Kat's legs stretched under the wide hoop of her farthingale to keep up with Toren's strides. Her breath caught on an inhale as a white warhorse carried a royally bedecked Elizabeth through the throng to the knoll. "Oh God," she breathed. Here was history, unfolding before her.

Kat shot ahead as fast as she could walk in the heavy costume, holding the layers before her so her slippered feet could move just under a run. The grand monarch wore a white gown made of velvet, shot through with gold thread, the virgin queen. Kat's heart beat fast, and she wished she had her phone or a camera. A few artists along the road had set up easels and were busily sketching.

Over the white gown, Elizabeth wore a silver cuirass that covered her chest and back. She was the epitome of warrior queen. A page walked behind her steed carrying a silver helmet with a white ostrich plume. A man in full court regalia carried a bejeweled sword before her while her favorite, Robert Dudley, led the horse by the bridle.

Toren maneuvered the two of them through the growing crowd until they stood only four layers away. Elizabeth's red hair blew with the snap of the banners above her head. Guards in metal pointed helmets and breast plates surrounded her horse. Kat's eyes scanned the crowd. Many were nobles, courtiers coming out to hear the queen speak on the dawn of war, a war many didn't think she'd win. The rest were guards and working men, the ones who would fight the war for her, the ones who needed to hear their queen's words.

The queen's voice pierced the air, slicing through the jumble of murmurs. Kat held her breath and Toren's arm as she sucked in every word, every nuance of Elizabeth's stature and face. This was no BBC rendition of the famous Armada speech on Tilbury. This was the genuine, how-it-really-happened, amazing speech.

Kat took it all in like a historian. The rapture of the crowd, the growing force of Elizabeth's voice as she spoke her heart, the heart of a woman king. Elizabeth Tudor was at her best. She loved her people, it was obvious. She loved England and would, if needed, dive into the fight herself to see it safe, as she had done her entire life. The crowd held their collective breath with Kat. Not a fidget, not a whisper, nothing but rapt enthrallment.

Red lips in an ivory face full of strength and character, Elizabeth spoke her final words. "In the meantime, my lieutenant general shall be in my stead, than whom never prince commanded a more noble or worthy subject; not doubting but by your obedience to my general, by your concord in the camp, and your valor in the field, we shall shortly have a famous victory over those enemies of my God, of my kingdom, and of my people." She ended with her fist in the air.

The crowd cheered and raised their weapons and fists. Kat whooped, hands cupped around her mouth as if she were at a football game, until Toren tugged her arm. He gave a small shake of his head even though a grin softened his mouth. Kat inhaled, nodding, but she couldn't tone down her smile.

Women waved banners, children threw flowers from open windows nearby, men hurrahed. Elizabeth bowed her head to her subjects. The guards easily opened a path, and Elizabeth rode slowly through the throng, touching many, taking small bunches of posies, nodding with a serious smile. This was no pageant, this was war. Kat would love to tell her that it would work out in England's favor but knew that would go against all advice on fictional time travel.

As the queen rode by, Kat touched the edge of the white and gold skirts that draped down along the horse. The buzz of magic instantly raced up Kat's arm to her dragonfly birthmark. Elizabeth gasped softly and looked down, blue eyes wide. Kat snatched back her hand as a rumble of thunder sounded far off. Elizabeth clutched the dragonfly amulet in her palm as Kat curtsied low.

"Laird MacCallum," Elizabeth said, and Kat stood straight again. Elizabeth looked forward but spoke to Toren. "So you have not disappeared off the face of this earth."

"Nay, Yer Majesty."

"Come see me when we reach Dover." She continued through the crowd, her words coming back to them on the wind. "And bring your lady wife."

"She thinks we're married," Kat said as they rode horses side by side along the wide pathway to Dover.

Toren pulled Apollo closer to the gentle mare he'd secured for Kat. He took her cold hand. "She would have heard that we were staying as husband and wife at the inn," Toren said, his voice low so those riding around them wouldn't overhear. The whole battalion plus the queen had packed up and headed toward Dover as soon as Elizabeth's speech was over. Despite her advisors' council, she insisted on seeing her enemy with her own eyes. So the whole court rode along the Thames behind the queen. Toren caught a glimpse of one of the eight Hell Burner ships that sailed along up ahead.

"When I touched her dress," Kat murmured, "magic hummed up my arm even though I didn't open myself to it."

Toren wove the slender fingers through his own, his mind working through discarded plans to retrieve the dragonfly. "The amulet calls to ye, just like it did at my show when ye took it."

"But I can't touch it, not even to give to Drakkina."

Toren nodded.

"And you need to release it to her. How does that work anyway?" she asked.

"I have to hold it and say that I release it," he answered, his eyes scanning around them for any eavesdroppers. Most of the riders laughed and talked in small groups or charged up ahead to be near the queen. "There's more to it than that, but that's all anyone would see."

Kat grinned. "I didn't know I was married to a wizard."

Toren snorted. "I apparently know enough magic to cause trouble. My mother had greater gifts than I."

Once settled at an inn in Dover, Kat and Toren made their way to Elizabeth's lavish tents. Garlands and silken ribbons adorned the white canvas sides. Luxurious carpets covered the dirt, weeds and stones, and two guards stood with pikes at the tent opening.

Kat glanced up at the gray clouds. "The storm clouds are unnatural."

"Aye, time grows short. I can feel it." Time had never been such an enemy as it was now.

"Laird Toren MacCallum of Craignish Castle and his wife Mistress Kat MacCallum."

Kat squeezed Toren's arm as they walked through the slash in the curtained door. Toren dodged a hanging candlelit chandelier as they entered a large tented room filled with courtiers. Guards with pikes stood at regular intervals around the perimeter, guarding their queen. It was said that Elizabeth's advisors had pleaded with her not to attend Tilbury or journey to Dover for her safety, but this queen would be what England needed. She was their lioness, their strength, and she would be seen.

Many of the people in the room already wore ornate masks. Kat raised her own to cover her face as they walked through the curious throng. Toren left his off.

"Yer Majesty," Toren said and bowed low before Elizabeth. Kat sunk into a deep curtsey like she had on the knoll.

"Rise MacCallum," Elizabeth spoke. She was irritated. "I have heard that you have decided to throw your sword in with the Spanish, that your wife here is a witch from Spain who has bespelled you to turn traitor on your queen and country. That you disappeared months ago to take her home and have helped Medina Sidonia prepare for this attack. That even now you spy for him."

Toren felt Kat's grip tighten on his arm, but he stood firm, unmoving. If Elizabeth really believed the reports they would already be on their way to the Tower. No, she was giving him a chance to refute the allegations.

"And who would burden ye with these lies?" he asked but already knew the answer.

"Lord Maxwell." Elizabeth called out. It had the sound of a summons not an answer. The man next to Elizabeth lowered his mask and Hugh Maxwell met Toren's gaze with narrowed eyes. Beside him, Fergus Campbell also lowered his mask. The master and his attack dog.

Where was Eagan? Did he know Maxwell and Campbell were worming their way into Elizabeth's court and into her head?

"So you've returned from Spain," Maxwell said, with the smugness of a cat before a bowl of cream.

"I haven't been to Spain. After ye abducted my sister and Kat, I took Kat away to wed."

"Ye could have wed in London," Fergus Campbell said, his voice a sneer.

Daingead. He'd almost forced Briana to marry the monster. Toren kept silent for a moment. "Kat, remove yer mask."

Kat lowered the ornate piece and several people next to Elizabeth gasped.

Elizabeth studied Kat, her long auburn hair and fair complexion. "What has become of her face?" Elizabeth asked.

"Kat was injured the night Maxwell and Campbell took her, a burn," Toren said.

Fergus sputtered next to Elizabeth. "A lie!"

Elizabeth held up a beringed hand and Fergus clamped his mouth shut.

"I took her to heal away from prying eyes."

"Is this true?" Elizabeth asked, her eyes boring into Kat's.

"Yes, Your Majesty. Toren helped me heal." The words were so full of sincerity that Toren nearly believed them himself.

"She's a witch herself," Fergus said. "I told ye of the butterflies."

Maxwell just stared, his gaze calculating, while his attack dog sputtered.

Elizabeth waved a hand in the air as if dismissing a crazy tale. "Look at her," Fergus continued. "She's a witch, scarred by heaven's fire, a monster."

The crowd around Elizabeth murmured, nodding and condemning. No wonder witch hunts were so easily started.

Elizabeth held up a hand and the judgment calmed. Her people waited for her assessment. Toren watched her clasp the amulet on the necklace around her neck. How was he going to get it from her? He had to hold the bloody thing to release the binding spell. And he couldn't very well leap onto her lap and grab something snuggled against her bosom.

"Are you a witch?" Elizabeth addressed Kat.

"Your Majesty, I hold only the power of a natural woman, not with magic but by using my wits. These men would condemn a strong woman who uses cleverness to escape their schemes."

Kat was clever, alright. Elizabeth knew full well about scheming men, and how dangerous they could be to a woman.

"But look at her," Fergus said again and pointed.

Elizabeth tilted her head, studying Kat. "I see nothing that would indicate she is of Spanish blood nor evil. She wears our Savior's cross," she said and eyed the gold cross tied to Kat's belt.

"But the scars, which she did not get from my hands," Fergus insisted. "They just appeared on her. From working her dark magic. Tell her, Maxwell."

Hughe Maxwell cleared his throat. Could he see that his lies hadn't taken firm enough root to be believed? "We did not burn the lady. We merely sought to find the truth of her plots against you." He raised one beringed hand to gesture toward Lord Walsingham, Elizabeth's spy master. "Our loyalty to you, your majesty, demands we bring attention to anyone who may be of danger."

Elizabeth sat back in her throne. She looked at Toren who stood silent. He wouldn't beg, nor defend, knowing she would judge him as she saw fit. The woman usually weighted silence and stance more than words and defense. All around them people peered at Kat and whispered. Even though the scars were faded, several ladies acted as if they were ghastly. Toren reached to shield Kat, pull her closer, but she resisted. She stood tall, her eyes trained on the queen.

"It seems to me," Elizabeth said. "That in my years of rule and before, the monsters I have met, who have sought to thwart me, were smooth of skin and most beautiful to the eye." The room sat in muffled silence as every ear strained to hear her firm words. "I have found that monsters"—she stressed Fergus's word—"conceal their scars inside. Their ugliness and perfidy hide behind masks of perfection. That those who survive vicious outward attacks and live with visual scars are not the ones I must guard against."

She turned to Hughe Maxwell who stood in his velvet finery, his smooth features likening him to the devil. "What ugliness sits in your heart, Lord Maxwell?" Her sharp gaze lifted to Fergus Campbell. "And yours, Laird Campbell? I would be a fool to ignore the threat."

"I am no threat to yer Majesty," Fergus murmured and bowed, backing up.

Toren felt Kat relax into him, leaning against his arm. The murmurs and curious gazes of the crowd had turned to Campbell and Maxwell.

A guard leaned into Elizabeth's ear and whispered something. She nodded. "There will be no more accusations made," she said strongly. She turned her eyes to Toren. "I will have no more disappearing, Highlander."

"Aye, yer Majesty." He bowed slightly. Hopefully the witch wouldn't snatch him away again. Queen Elizabeth's wrath would be worse than a plague attacking his family.

"I must change for my portrait." Elizabeth turned to one of her ladies. "And have my necklace polished. The dust clouds the pearls."

"Ye honor my clan by wearing my gift," Toren said as she descended the two steps. Kat curtsied low before her.

"I am fond of the necklace, but the winged bug is odd." She frowned. Toren watched the necklace as the lady removed it. "I would prefer a bee."

"I could remove the dragonfly from the necklace," Toren suggested in a casual tone. "May I?" He was within inches of it. If he could just hold it for five seconds, a moment to release the spell. His hand itched to grab it. Time and mere inches hung between them.

"Not now," Elizabeth said and shooed the lady away with it. "After the portrait perhaps. Time is short before we send our first wave of Hell Burners toward the Spanish crescent."

Toren's fingers curled into a tight fist. *So foking close.* He bowed and stepped back.

"But Highlander," Elizabeth said, pausing, "There are rumors of Lady Maxwell and her child being abducted by your brother, Eagan MacCallum."

Campbell murmured something, but Maxwell yanked his arm, stopping him. Elizabeth ignored them, but Toren saw the pinching of her lips. The woman noticed everything.

"Truth mixed with lies," Toren said.

"Follow then," she called. "I would hear your truth, Highlander, while I walk."

Kat leaned into Toren's ear. "Go with her. I will try to get the amulet." The exchange looked like a sweet farewell.

He brushed her lips with his. "Whatever ye do, don't touch it."

CHAPTER TWENTY-FIVE
THE DEPTHS OF TROUBLE

Kat waited until Elizabeth and Toren left the tent before she began to walk through the curious throng. People stared and whispered. Twice Kat raised the mask but then let it fall beside her skirts. Head held high, shoulders back, she glided among the people. Elizabeth had defended her, Toren thought she was beautiful, and she even had a last name besides the one the orphanage had assigned her. So what if it was just borrowed, so was the dress. At the moment, both were hers. Kat nodded to several courtiers and left the tent, determination adding steel to her spine.

Colorful banners snapped in the charged wind, and three minstrels played their instruments to the delight of the crowd. The threat of war had people looking toward the sea, but the English people had faith enough in their queen to make this waiting into a festival of sorts.

Along the docks, dilapidated fishing boats were being stuffed with flammable items like straw and splintered crates covered in pitch. These were the Hell Burners, being prepped to ram into the Spanish ships, lighting them on fire. "Professor Willcock would poop himself if he were here," she whispered, thinking of her uni history professor. She walked in the other direction, toward the inn, just in case anyone watched. Lord Walsingham always had spies about, watching for any threats against his queen.

When she reached the inn, she walked out the back door through the kitchens and stuck to the sides of houses as she meandered toward Elizabeth's tent. Kat held the mask before her face and walked behind a larger group of laughing courtiers as they made their way up the hill. When they passed Elizabeth's tent, Kat veered off. A back entrance allowed servants to move in and out. Only one guard stood near the door.

Out of the corner of her eye, Kat saw a woman beating a quilted blanket behind a home. After a few minutes the woman went back inside, leaving the blanket to air in the wind. *I'll just borrow it.* Kat grabbed the blanket and folded it hastily, walking toward the back tent entrance.

"Halt," the guard said and peered at Kat who held the mask before her face.

"A gift for her majesty from the keeper of that inn." She tilted her head in the inn's direction.

"Why would a lady be running an errand for an innkeeper?"

Bugger. She was dressed in court clothes. "I did not want anyone as low as she to step into the queen's chambers." Hopefully that sounded authentically prejudiced against the poor.

The guard grabbed the blanket and shook it out. When no poison or weapon could be found, he balled it back up and pushed it into Kat's arm.

"Leave it in there." He held the door flap. "And refold it."

Kat moved through the tent into one of Elizabeth's back rooms. A small bed had been set up with curtains hanging around it. Kat smiled softly. Elizabeth had insisted that she tent out like her troops, but Kat very much doubted that her troops slept with silk and satin draped around them.

Kat heard voices in the front tents and quickly refolded the blanket, placing it on a large leather trunk at the end of the bed. As her fingers brushed the dark leather a shock of magic raced up her arm to her birthmark. Startled, she jumped back. The dragonfly must be inside. Kat glanced around. No one was there, and there were no security cameras to avoid. She tried the lid, and it opened. There on a bed of black velvet sat the necklace, clean and awaiting its mistress.

Kat stared at the dragonfly as it hummed with energy. The delicately carved wings shifted, lifted, and stretched upwards. Kat blinked hard and the image collapsed back down into the two-dimensional etching.

A woman's gasp made Kat whip around, but the room was still empty.

"I said the black and gold gown with red ribbons, not this gown," the woman said from behind the thin tent partition in the next room.

Kat grabbed a scarf that lay next to the necklace and scooped it up. Toren would have to take the dragonfly amulet off the necklace since she couldn't touch it without bringing the demons down on their heads. Kat shoved the rolled scarf and necklace into a concealed pocket in her skirts. They'd have to act fast if she was going to return it before the Armada picture was sketched. And before the demons felt the vibration of the amulet so close to her.

Kat whisked out the back opening past the guard without a backwards glance. Now where to go? Somewhere Toren could find her easily, somewhere private so he could release the binding spell and return the amulet to Drakkina. Kat walked once again behind a group of courtiers, her mask in place, until she veered off to the inn. She walked with anonymous dignity up the stairs and turned the knob of their small, rented room. Stepping in she released the breath she'd been holding. As she inhaled, a trickle of awareness set the hairs up the back of her neck on end.

An iron-like arm wrapped around her stomach as a rag covered her mouth, stifling her scream. The ornate mask clattered to the floor as Kat was hauled back against a powerful body.

"Bloody witch," Fergus Campbell hissed in her ear. "Ye think ye can ruin all my work, all my scheming to take MacCallum land." His foul breath surged along Kat's cheek, and she fought for air. "Ye kill my men with yer dark magic, ye steal my bride, and ye escape my walls. And now just when Maxwell and I have Elizabeth's ear, the two of ye show up and she's meeting with Toren instead of Maxwell."

Fergus's hand snaked through Kat's hair, yanking out the intricate weave. He sniffed along her neck, and Kat swore he left a line of snot. "Ye smell nice, nice enough to taste." He laughed and Kat could feel him fumbling with his codpiece. The window stood open. Could she fling herself toward it? Perhaps a passerby would see the struggle and report it. The hand on her mouth fell to her breasts as Fergus squeezed.

"Let go of me!" she screamed. "Help!"

"Ye bitch!" Fergus hissed, grabbing her wrist and reaching over to slam the window shut. "Shite!" he cursed, and Kat glimpsed Toren striding across from the queen's tents.

Toren!

Kat felt the buzz of the amulet pressed against her skirts and a clap of thunder echoed closer.

Fergus dragged her toward the door. "We're leaving, lass."

"Oh no we're not!" Kat yelled. *Never let someone take you to a second location.* She *had* been listening during her self-defense class despite what Lisa said.

Kat kicked her foot toward Fergus's groin, but the man grabbed it, twisted it, and in one quick lunge punched her in the face. Pain arced through Kat's skull upon contact. As the room tunneled out to blackness she recalled another of Lisa's self-defense rules, one she was breaking. Never lose consciousness.

Kat was rocking as if in a swinging cradle. The sound of lapping water filled her ears, and the smell of oil made Kat's nose wrinkle. She groaned softly at the dull ache in her face and blinked, slowly focusing on the wooden slats before her. She tried to move her hands but couldn't. She lay on her side and listened. The boards beneath her creaked, and a strong breeze blew her loose hair around her face. *I'm outside.* With her wrists tied with rope before her, she slowly pushed herself into a sitting position. It was dusk.

I'm on a boat. She glanced around. *A boat with no captain or crew.*

Kat spied the edge of the sun descending behind the trees backing the small village of Dover.

"Ye'll die by fire or by water, witch!" Fergus yelled from somewhere far off. Kat's head whipped around toward the shore, eyes searching as the wind picked up the sails and fed the fire smoldering below deck. *Holy Mother Mary!* She was on a Hell Burner!

Kat screamed into the gag in her mouth. She pressed her body against some brittle wooden crates stuffed with musty hay and worked her feet under her to stand. Fergus had wedged her there, probably to stop people from seeing her. Two soldiers approached Fergus, but he ran, drawing them away. Kat dug her fingers at her gag until she was able to pull it down. "Help! Fire!" But the Hell Burner had sailed too far away with the strong wind pulling it by its sails.

The thin line of orange sun cut a curve over the trees as the sun set. *Toren!* Kat screamed in her mind, praying with all her heart as she heard flames snapping below deck. She tried to take a step to the side of the small ship and nearly tripped. Looking down she saw the rope tied around her waist. She squinted to see where it ended. Had the bastard tied her to a burning ship? Her hands banded together at the wrists twisted around the rope, pulling. A rough, dragging scrape sounded from the shadows.

Kat tugged with her whole body to move the small barrel at the end of the rope. A keg of gunpowder! The man was truly insane.

Kat inched her way to the side of the ship. She glanced down at the black water lapping beneath as the wind tipped the boat on an angle, pulling the Hell Burner toward the Spanish crescent far from the harbor. Kat coughed on the black smoke sifting up through the cracks in the boards and pouring up out of the steps below deck.

"Drakkina!" she screamed and looked back at the darkening shore. "Toren!" The wind grabbed her words and hurled them through the gloaming. Kat swallowed against the acrid dryness of smoke in her throat and nose. She tugged on the rope with her tied hands but couldn't break the rope nor the many knots tying her to the barrel.

An explosion beneath threw Kat against the gunwale. *I'm going to die. No! No! No!* Her internal scream broke from her lips. "No! No! No!!" The firmness in her voice bolstered her courage. Kat moved her wrist over to her pocket. Perhaps the amulet could add to her magic. Drakkina had never mentioned what power it held.

Kat pushed through the skirts while she coughed against the hazy gray smoke. *Nothing.* She felt no fizzle, no hum like before. She clawed at the material until she managed to wiggle her fingers into the pocket. "Fricking, fricking bastard!" It was empty. Fergus must have taken the amulet.

The smoke rose thick until it nearly blocked her view of the harbor torches. Kat leaned over the gunwale and tried to suck in clean air, but the ship was becoming engulfed. Heat licked at her back.

"I'll end up in the water either way," she said and yanked on the barrel. How deep was the English Channel? What animals lived in its depths? Because the heavy barrel of gunpowder tied around her waist would sink her to the bottom.

She heaved with her tied hands until she balanced the barrel on the rim of the ship. It had to go into the water first or she'd just hang from it until the ship exploded. The heat of the fire scorched her back, and the smoke choked every breath. She stepped up on a crate and was about to jump when she saw the small stopper in the side of the barrel. Could she empty it? Would it help her float? But it was full of gunpowder. Would it explode? The thought of sinking all the way to the bottom of the channel was possibly worse than blowing up.

Kat balanced the barrel on the side of the ship and wiggled the cork loose. It popped out and for an instant she almost lost it in the murk below. Her fingernails dug into it, holding it as the gunpowder poured into the water. *Hurry!* Another tug of wind tilted the ship, almost pushing her overboard. *Hurry!*

As the dark grainy powder poured out, Kat kicked off her shoes and began to yank with her toes on her farthingale and petticoats. She managed to get one petticoat off but the ties holding the bell-shaped farthingale wouldn't budge.

Kat plugged the barrel and held it to her chest. The sun was gone, the shore too. The only thing that remained was the haze of the smoke, the blaze behind her, and the dark water below. Tears slipped out of Kat's stinging eyes. She had to jump. Roaring, snapping, the sounds of hell swirled behind Kat as she balanced on the edge of the ship.

"I am not going to die!" she yelled at the water, as if it were the grim reaper, and jumped.

For an instant the wind caught the billows of her skirts as if she floated on the fierce breeze. But then cold water slammed into Kat, both cooling and burning the scorch marks on her back. Salt water went up Kat's nose. She snorted out underwater and kicked, kicked as hard as she could. The skirts wrapped around her legs like tentacles, dragging her down. The pressure of the water crushed the drum farthingale. Kat felt the rope on the barrel grow taut as she continued to descend into the pitch black of the sea. She kicked but the heavy fabric pulled at her until she felt the tug of the barrel floating on the surface. Would she pull it under?

Kat's cheeks felt like bursting, and she let out the bubbles. She closed her eyes and released her hold on the magic at her core. She opened her mouth...and breathed in the salty wash of water. It stung her throat, her lungs. She exhaled the remaining bubbles caught inside the little airway ducts as they filled. Magic throbbed through Kat, and she inhaled the water again, in and out while she kicked. The barrel remained overhead, but Kat couldn't tell if she dragged it below water or not.

Maybe the magic would bring Drakkina. Kat's eyes blinked open, and she stared at the dark water surrounding her, above, below, on all sides. The pressure of it sent her heart racing. Far off in the distance an occasional flash of fire could be seen hitting what must be the surface.

A large explosion made Kat jerk where she hovered in the salty water. Fire dotted the surface, quickly extinguishing into nothingness. *In and out, in and out.* How long would she have to wait here? Something rubbed against her toes, and Kat yanked her foot up into her twisting skirts. A shark? A barracuda? What swam in the English Channel? Kat turned invisible. She was already calling the demons with her magic, might as well add a little more.

"Toren!" she screamed in the water. "Drakkina! Holy Mother Mary! Dearest God of Light!" Bloody hell, she needed light. Kat had never liked the dark, nor small places. The weight of the water over her felt as if it were pressing down. The darkness pushed in from all sides, nothingness had swallowed her. *In and out, in and out, not too fast.* Sparks danced in front of Kat's eyes, and she forced herself to slow her breathing. If she lost consciousness, she'd lose hold of her magic and drown. *In and out, in and out.* She closed her eyes and imagined an open sky, wide-open lands around her.

Kat felt another bump against her leg. Her eyes snapped open to the same black nothingness. *In and out, in and out.* The big fish couldn't see her. Kat squeezed her eyes shut.

Her shoulders ached from holding her bound hands overhead. Her legs were numb as she continued to kick against the water and her skirts. The salt and grime from the sea bit into the soft flesh of her mouth and throat. She floated there in limbo, waiting. What would happen first? Would Drakkina find her or the demons? Would she kick all night long or lose consciousness and drown? *In and out, in and out.* She hovered in a state of near panic.

Katell! Drakkina's voice filled Kat's head. Kat blinked against the salt water. She tilted her head back and stared at the glow hovering way up high, illuminating the rope hanging down from the barrel. The waves overhead were choppy, but the barrel seemed to be on the surface. Kat kicked, relief renewing her strength.

"Drakkina!" she warbled in the muting water and released her invisibility.

Drakkina's light descended through the murk, illuminating the pitch blackness. Large fish circled. Kat coughed on the water, floundering and kicking with all her might.

"Get me out of here!"

Drakkina came level with Kat. She threw her hands this way and that, pushing back the curious fish. Drakkina's face was white in the darkness, her eyes round, her hair floating like some nightmarish mermaid. Fear and worry etched deep lines into Drakkina's face. Not what Kat wanted to see.

"Get me out of here!"

I can't. Drakkina spoke in her mind. The crone moved below Kat and tried to push up against her legs to lift, but her body moved through Kat, making Kat's birthmark sizzle on her arm.

This is bad. Kat watched with horror-filled eyes as something as large as her flipped its tail and swam off into the darkness.

The demons are coming, and you're stuck underwater with your Highlander on the shore. Aye, this is bad.

In and out, in and out. Kat continued to breathe despite the increasing weight of terror pressing in on all sides. "Toren!" The word came out garbled in the water.

I will get him, Drakkina said and began to ascend.

"No!" Kat yelled as darkness crept back in. *Don't leave me!* She screamed in her mind, and Drakkina seemed to hear.

The ethereal woman floated back down to stare into Kat's face. Her eyes were soft, gentle as she nodded. *I will not leave you, Katell.* Drakkina placed her hands along Kat's cheeks. Kat felt the soft sizzle of her touch. *Relax, Katell, I will keep the beasties away. Save your strength. Your*

Highlander can feel your magic. He will find you, and I will stay with you until he does.

Kat let out a sob and nodded at Drakkina. *Talk to me. Tell me anything so that I don't think about where I am right now, please.*

What should I tell you?

Anything, something interesting. Tell me about you, when you were young. Kat closed her eyes, imagining the open field, and she heard Drakkina's words in her mind.

It was so long ago, thousands of years.

You were a child once? Kat opened her eyes to see the spirit's glow.

Of course. Drakkina smiled. *A precocious little brat to be sure.*

Sisters, brothers?

Neither. Drakkina threw her light out toward a long-nosed fish with pointy little teeth. The fish diverted.

Mother, father?

I suppose, but they died early. I lived with an aunt.

Was she a witch? Kat tried to keep her thoughts on the questions she asked and Drakkina's answers, but fear kept pressing in.

Aye, and she was very busy, too busy for me until I was older. Then she showed me some things I hadn't already picked up on my own.

Kat watched sadness shadow Drakkina's face. She'd seen it before in the children who came to Sister Susanna's Home with slacked jaws and downcast eyes. Neglect.

"I'm sorry," Kat warbled through the water, and Drakkina's eyes focused sharply on hers.

For what?

No child should be alone.

Drakkina stared at her for a long moment. *You make sure those children in your home are never alone, don't you?*

Tears squeezed out of Kat's eyes to add to the saltwater embracing her. She nodded. *I love them.*

More than your Highlander?

Kat closed her eyes and concentrated on filtering oxygen out of the water. *In and out, in and out.*

CHAPTER TWENTY-SIX
BEACON IN THE DARK

Wind pushed the waves against the shoreline. Thunder clapped and lightning crackled in the north. Toren turned from the sky to watch the Hell Burners breaking into the fleet of Spanish ships anchored across the channel in Gravelines. From the glow of the fire, it was apparent that the crescent was breaking. But that didn't matter much to him. Where was Kat?

Toren stood watching history unfold, but his mind was elsewhere. Kat was afraid. He could feel her panic. "Where are ye?" he murmured. She hadn't been back at the inn when he returned. Only her discarded mask had been on the floor, broken as if someone had crushed it underfoot.

Toren heard the sound of a sword being unsheathed behind him, and he pulled his free, swiveling on instinct to meet the thrust.

"Foking menace!" Hughe Maxwell cursed and twisted his sword to slide along Toren's. Toren easily deflected it, staring into the face of his childhood tormentor and accuser. Even his own daughter had suffered at his hands.

Fergus Campbell ran up, out of breath and sweaty as if he'd been chased. He pulled his sword to join in the fight.

Toren sidestepped a lunge from Campbell and turned to stab, but the huffing man met the blow. "Ye foking interfering bastard," Campbell said. "I'd have Briana wed to me by now if ye hadn't broken the betrothal."

"And she'd be tied to a brutal husband who would lay claim to Clan MacCallum," Toren said and advanced, turned and lunged again. *Twist, lunge, pull back.* His sword hit Maxwell's and then curved downward as he turned to strike Fergus's shoulder. A dark spot of blood spread on the man's white shirt. Toren had all his warriors practice against one, two, and even three attackers at once. The dance was different for each number.

"Clan MacCallum will be mine," Maxwell said as he parried Toren's press. "Recompense for the loss of my son."

Maxwell knew as well as Toren that it was Margaret who'd set fire to the barn as she escaped after her brother's attack. "Ye are at fault for Edward's death," Toren said. "Not I. Ye raised a raping bastard. Yet ye take yer guilt out on yer daughter and granddaughter and me."

"Shut your bloody gob!" Maxwell yelled, spittle flying from his mouth. He lunged toward Toren who easily sidestepped the wild attack.

"My family knows the truth, Maxwell, and I've let Elizabeth know of the foulness ye allowed under yer roof, yer neglect of yer daughter and the apprentices trapped in yer care."

'Twas almost as if the old man wanted to die. With a howl of fury, he ran to Toren, his sword raised. Toren sliced across his middle, cutting through clothing, skin, muscle, and bone. Maxwell dropped to his knees, his sword clattering on the pebbled ground. His eyes were wide, unbelieving.

"Meet yer son in Hell, Hughe Maxwell," Toren said and turned in time to see

Fergus's sword coming down in an arc. The momentum would be too strong to deflect, so Toren dropped and rolled, popping up behind Fergus who spun around. His eyes were wide. Perhaps he realized that without Maxwell his chances of survival had dropped dramatically.

"She's probably dying right now." Fergus huffed as he staggered back. "While ye waste time with me."

Toren kept his sword raised. He felt the hum of the binding he'd placed on the amulet. "Ye have the dragonfly amulet," he said calmly.

Fergus's laugh was like a rabid bark. "Ye care more about the amulet than yer wife. Now I know why ye left her alone to saunter around the camp. First ye lose yer sister and now yer wife. Can ye not protect anyone?"

Toren drew his sword back, his eyes assessing the grinning monster before him. "Where is Kat?" he roared at Fergus.

For an instant, uncertainty flashed across Fergus's features, fear. Toren rushed toward him, but Fergus retreated. The man's sword pointed out over the black water beyond Toren's shoulder.

"There. But ye better hurry for I think she's dying. In fact," he said, his face smug, "I'm certain of it."

Toren's gaze shot back and forth between the man that must die and the black water. Fergus had the dragonfly amulet, but Toren only cared about Kat. He opened his mind up as he tried to force his breaths to stay calm, his mind to work, the magic within him to work.

Help me! Toren! Kat's pain washed through Toren. He felt her soaring panic, felt her terror.

Toren could finish Fergus here and now, stop the bastard from threatening his family ever again. But every second wasted could cost Kat her life.

"Ye will die by MacCallum sword," Toren said, his eyes searching the shore. A rowboat rested near the edge. "Tonight or tomorrow." He shrugged. "It doesn't matter. Ye're still a dead man."

Toren ran to the boat and flipped it. His whole being hummed with power. Kat was near death. Fergus had sworn it, and Kat's terror confirmed it. What was happening to her? Where was she?

Toren pushed the boat out against the growing waves, splashing water up his body with each hasty step, and jumped into the hull. He grabbed the oars, turned his back to the dark sea and heaved, his shoulder muscles working, hurtling the dinghy out into the choppy waves.

He glanced over his shoulder. "Kat! Where are ye!" All he could see were the flames of the Hell Burners exploding near the Spanish fleet. Cheers came from the men down the shore who watched fire lick up a Spanish ship's sails. Lightning splintered against the night, blinding him. He cursed into the growing wind.

"Kat!" His roar reached across the waves, through his skull, through his heart, an arrow to her. If only he'd bound her to him like the amulet. It would have been simple, they were halfway there already. She'd given him her maidenhead, her part of the binding, even without words, a binding of the flesh. He'd given her his colors, his tartan, in the little hollow orb she wore on her belt. All he had to do was utter the words. But he hadn't wanted to do it without asking her first. They needed more time.

"Bloody crone," he yelled into the dark sky. "Where is Kat?"

In the glow of the distant fires, Toren's eyes picked up a cloud moving toward him. It changed shape. He blinked hard against the sting of sweat and salt water in his eyes, but the cloud still grew and...sparkled? Unnatural lightning cut jagged lines across the sky. The lass was using magic.

Something brushed against his cheek pulling his gaze. His breath froze. Butterflies, hundreds of them, sat along the rim of the rowboat. He looked up and the cloud of fluttering wings hovered above him.

"Kat's in danger! Find her!" he demanded. The iridescent wings rose from the rowboat to join the swarm. The butterflies moved, spreading out into something of a straight path, out into the center of the channel.

"Kat! I'm coming," he roared and put his back and powerful thighs against the black waves. *Pull! Pull! Pull!* Every so often he'd check the mass of fluttering wings to make certain he was on course.

A jolt of panic and fear gripped Toren's chest. Kat's fear. "Hold on, love, I'm coming," he gritted out with each pull, his rhythm smooth, hard, full of desperate determination. "God!" Toren yelled up into the stormy sky. "God, help her!"

Highlander! The voice ripped through his head.

"Witch!" Toren yelled. "Kat's in danger!"

I'm with her, but I can't help her. Look for my light.

Toren's head rotated around, north, west, east, south, but the only light he saw came from the burning boats and the lightning above. The lights of Dover sputtered in and out against the shore as the waves grew to block them.

"Where!"

Look down, Highlander.

Down? Down!

The cloud of butterflies now sat on the water, drowning against the soft glow of light coming up from the depths. Their wings fluttered against the wet pull, sacrificing themselves to show him the way.

Toren stopped rowing over the glow and dropped the oars. He kicked off his boots and prepared to jump in. Then he saw the barrel, floating with butterflies covering it.

"Kat? Love?"

She's tied to the rope on the barrel. Drakkina's voice brushed again through his brain, softer now as if her power faded.

Toren grabbed an oar and snagged the barrel, capturing it in a cloud of butterflies that fluttered upward to be blown away by the increasing wind. Hand over hand, he pulled the thick cord up and into the boat. He didn't know how she was attached. Could he yank it from her hands? Smoothly, up, up through the cold dark water, he pulled. Lightning splintered the sky and thunder cracked. Ships burned and popped. Spanish curses from over the water caught on the rushing wind and rising waves.

Kat, Kat, my love! How long had she been under there?

Drakkina's light surfaced with her, but Toren barely noticed. "Find my dragonfly amulet, quickly," she said and faded.

Kat's head broke the water, long hair flat against her pale face. Wide eyes stared up at him.

"Kat!" he yelled and reached for her hand. He grasped her cold fingers and realized her wrists were bound. "I've got ye, love."

She didn't say anything, but her face tightened with a silent sob. He grabbed her under the arms and pulled her over the edge of the dinghy as her butterflies encircled them, delicate wings fighting against the wind. His dagger swiftly cut the rope from her wrists and waist.

"Kat," he breathed against her face and pushed her hair back. Kat turned her head and vomited. Swiftly he held her over the edge of the boat as water poured from her mouth. She coughed, the first sound she'd made. And took a breath of air.

She turned her face to him. "Toren!" she sobbed. Wretched pain creased the beauty of her face and Toren's chest clenched. He pulled her into his arms and held her in his warmth while she shuddered against him.

"I've got ye."

"Fergus. He tied me up on a Hell Burner. I...I had to jump or be burned alive."

He kissed her forehead while she rambled. "I am so sorry."

She pushed up from his chest as Toren steadied them on the tossing boat.

"I used magic," Kat confessed. "A lot of it, to...to stay alive." Guilt engulfed her words as wide worried eyes gazed up at the sky.

Toren placed her in the bottom of the boat, draping her with his wet, yet warm, coat. He grabbed up the oars. "Of course ye did." He met her gaze and pulled hard on the oars. "A warrior stays alive to fight another day."

She sat huddled with her knees bent under her sopping, misshapen gown, fingers white and thin against the rails of the boat. Toren threw his muscles into each pull, back to the shores of Dover. He had to release that amulet and somehow give it to the witch. The damn thing just pulled the demons closer to Kat. Thunder cracked as lightning sparked.

"We need to get that amulet."

"Fergus has it," Kat said. "I had it. He took it from me when he knocked me out."

"He struck ye?" Toren peered closer at her face in the dark. Anger surged at the bruising on her jaw. "I'll peel his skin from his bones."

A small grin played on Kat's lips at his adamant curse. "The man tied me to a Hell Burner and sent me to burn or drown. But it's a bruise on my face that makes you want to skin him alive?"

She teased, he knew, but the fury ran so strong that he could only growl. Kat reached forward and touched Toren's fist on the oar handle.

"I'm okay, Toren. Let's just get that darn dragonfly back to Drakkina, and we'll worry about Fergus later."

"If I see him again tonight, he's dead tonight," Toren said, his eyes dark and full of bloodlust.

"All right, but together," Kat said as if bracing herself for another ordeal. "I don't want to be alone again for a good long while." She held his gaze until he nodded.

"Together," he said as if sealing a pledge. The words, he should say the words, locking them together for eternity, binding them as one. Simple words said with a surge of magic, *I bind you to me for all time. I bind you to this world with me.* But she should know first. "Together," he said again, the words on the tip of his tongue, the hum of magic buzzing with his adrenaline. "I…"

She smiled, waiting, trusting. He could bind her to him, to his century, keep her safe with him forever. Simple words said with simple magic and a sincere heart. She'd already done her part whether she knew it or not. "I…I love ye, Kat."

Her eyes grew round and then crinkled as her smile overtook shock. She blinked. "I love you too." Her words sank into him, dousing his magic, and filling him with another feeling. A buzz of warmth spread through him, a magic of a different kind.

"Guards, arrest that man and his woman!" Elizabeth's voice reached him as he felt the boat hit bottom.

CHAPTER TWENTY-SEVEN
TORN ASUNDER

Kat shivered, her hands wrapped under the hard wooden seat of the boat. Queen Elizabeth's face was lit by torchlight, fury cutting into the lines she tried to hide with makeup.

Toren's boots splashed as they hit the water. He turned and lifted Kat against him despite her being soaked. He growled at the guards in their armor and stalked with her through the water to the shore. Climbing upon the bank, he set her down. She leaned into him, needing his support after fighting against the water for so long.

Fergus stood beside Elizabeth, a bandage over his shoulder. "You," Kat yelled. "You terrible person." Her gaze went to the queen. "He knocked me unconscious and put me on a Hell Burner with a barrel of gunpowder tied around my middle."

"Liar," Fergus said and pointed out toward the Spanish fleet fighting against the wind, waves, and burning ships. "They return from trying to aid the Spanish," Fergus called. "Traitors, both of them. Hughe Maxwell tried to stop them, and Toren MacCallum killed him."

Wind whipped at the banners held by four men around Elizabeth. Her cape flew out from behind her like the wings of a mythic Valkyrie.

Amulet. Hidden pocket inside his doublet. Drakkina's voice wafted like whispery wings against Kat's mind.

"Ye will die today, Campbell," Toren said. "For striking my wife and lying to the queen."

"Why else would ye be rowing in this growing storm?" Fergus asked. His body swelled with smugness. "Ye see the Spaniards are losing and are trying to return."

"I was rowing to rescue my wife," Toren said, his tone rough. He began to pull away as if he truly were going to rip the man in half. "Ye tried to kill her, but ye failed, again, Campbell." Kat held tightly to his arm.

Fergus's boasting smile faltered, and he looked at Elizabeth. The monarch stood silent, assessing, staring at Toren and then Kat.

"I haven't even seen the Lady MacCallum until now. And heavens, why would I try to kill her?" Fergus asked innocently.

Even with Elizabeth staring her down, Kat found her voice and pushed it up from her raw lungs. "Because I saw you take her dragonfly necklace, the one Toren gifted her," she rasped.

"What?" Fergus's eyes threatened, promised worse than death if she continued, but Kat ignored it.

"I saw you take it. I said that I would reveal your treachery, and you struck me." Kat's fingers touched the bruise she knew stood on her jaw.

"Outrageous tale!" Fergus yelled but Elizabeth held up one hand to silence him.

"I had to jump overboard to save myself from the flames." Kat fought to keep the shudder of fear down. She held her chin high. "But Toren saved me before my strength was completely gone."

Elizabeth's eyes raked Kat, taking in her appearance. "Turn," she ordered, and Kat pivoted slowly around, dropping Toren's coat from her chafed shoulders. Kat couldn't see them, but she knew the fire had burned her.

Several grunts sounded behind her and Toren's hand lay gentle on Kat's back. "Och love, yer back." The cool wash of wind told her that the dress had been burned away in places and blisters must sit on her red puckered skin.

"Burnt trying to reach the enemy," Fergus said, trying to dismiss her agony. "Serves her right," he murmured and Toren lunged. Kat wobbled around. Toren held Fergus by the throat, choking him with one solid fist, his face within an inch of Fergus's pinched features.

"Ye will die now!" Toren seethed.

"Release him, MacCallum," Elizabeth ordered, but Toren continued to hold.

"Toren, I am okay. Toren." Kat stepped up and touched Toren's shoulder.

Toren's grip relaxed, and Fergus pulled in a rush of air.

"I'll ignore, for the moment"—Elizabeth stressed—"that you stepped down by order of your wife and not me."

"Your Majesty," Kat said and bowed her head. "You can see the damage Fergus Campbell has inflicted on me. He is a lying, vindictive man who will do anything to make you believe lies against us. Talk about treachery. He even stole from Your Majesty."

"False accusations!" Fergus yelled.

"I saw him slip the necklace into a hidden pocket inside his doublet."

"Guards," Elizabeth ordered while Fergus sputtered. They removed his jacket and turned it inside out.

"She lies," Fergus insisted.

"I saw him slide it into some hidden pocket on the inside," Kat repeated, and a guard probed along the material.

"Here," he called and split the satin lining. Out fell the necklace into the guard's hand.

Quickly, release it to me! Drakkina's words whirled on the wind that tugged Kat's drying hair across her face.

Toren must have heard the crone's words, because he grabbed the necklace from the startled guard's hands.

He closed his eyes for the briefest of moments. "I cut yer tether." Kat felt the tickle of magic vibrate in the air, an awareness that glanced off to mix with the wind. It felt like a release, a knot loosened in a child's stubborn shoelace.

Kat watched Toren's fist around the circle holding the dragonfly. It tensed, white knuckles in the torchlight. The wind buffeted them. Elizabeth's skirts flapped high, her red ringlets snaking free of the intricate weave, the pearls in her hair dropping amongst the Dover pebbles.

"Toren MacCallum," Elizabeth called above the howling wind. She held out a hand, her long fingers stretched for the necklace.

Give me my dragonfly! Drakkina screeched from above. *The demons are upon us!*

A gust of gravelly wind tore along the thatched rooftops of the fishermen's small cottages behind. An entire roof lifted up as if a hand slid along the eaves. Guards rushed for Elizabeth, blocking her body from flying debris.

Kat backed against a building, her eyes moving to the swirling sky. The moon had been obliterated, the stars swallowed, the soft black of the night mutated into an oily dark mass. Lightning flashed in the depths of the thundercloud, and in the silence following the crackling clap of thunder, Kat heard voices. Keening, growling, gnashing like animals, yet with words.

The hairs along her body rose in defense. She couldn't use her magic to hide. Instead she gently pressed her back against the brick side of a building, grimacing with the burn, and held tightly to her mother's moonstone that still rested against her chest.

Torch flames flattened, some blowing out. "Your Majesty!" the captain of the guard yelled. "Come away!"

Elizabeth thrust her hand to Toren. He let the necklace slide through his fingers, the chain catching on the ends of his digits.

"Yer Majesty."

Elizabeth snatched it from his hand. Glanced at it and back at him. Her hair streamed around her pale face and crimson lips. "The dragonfly?"

Kat's gasp was swallowed by the noise around them as Toren held up the amulet.

"It fell off." He stared at her. "The piece is better without it."

"Your Majesty, 'tis not safe in this storm!" The guards formed a perimeter around Elizabeth, ever queenly despite the world crashing down around her.

"With Spain at my doors, I cannot bring myself to fear the wind," she said against the howl, but tipped her head to Toren and turned on her heel, necklace in hand.

Kat rushed to Toren, careful not to touch the amulet. A tree in a churchyard creaked and groaned as it fell, its long roots bursting out of the earth like gnarled, dirt-dripping fingers from the grave.

Toren anchored Kat against him, the two of them facing the swirling mass above. The voices grew louder. "Kill, rip, slice away the magic! Freedom! Strip the powers! Kill! Break! Tear! Drakkina! My Drakkina!"

The last word came like a wail through the chaotic swirl of hate and vengeance. The demons' hate felt very personal which made it all the more powerful. They wanted to kill Drakkina and anyone associated with her white magic.

Kat clung to Toren's arm. Drakkina materialized before him, her hands outstretched.

Give it to me. She spoke, her lips moving, but the sound was only heard in their minds.

"I don't trust ye, witch," Toren said above the dissonance of cries.

"You have no choice, Highlander," she said, and her face showed calm determination. "They will kill us all if you don't."

Toren squeezed Kat to him as if he were afraid that she'd be ripped away, tossed up into the jaws of the wind. With his free hand he laid the amulet in the crone's ethereal cupped hands. The amulet quivered on contact, the wings of the dragonfly fluttering, accepting and then settling into her palms, becoming a part of her.

Drakkina's image intensified, solidified into a real body, standing before them. Even the dragonflies that flitted about her thickened into life and adhered to her hair before they were sucked away. Drakkina ducked as a cart flew by, hay and early fall apples shooting out in all directions.

The cloud loomed lower and lower as if it would lay upon them like a wet blanket and smother them.

"What do we do?" Kat called.

"You can't stay here," Drakkina said. "They know you're here. They know your smell, your power."

Drakkina's eyes shifted to Toren. "You know that, Highlander. She cannot stay. Katell will die here."

"Fergus Campbell still lives," Toren said, his whole body stiff, solid, and strong against the attack that crept closer.

"I cannot keep them away forever," Drakkina said, "even with my amulet."

A warding, of course. Kat could feel it now. An invisible shield that kept out the evil ink raining down from the skies. It dripped around the ward, sizzling as it sank into the wet ground. Grass shriveled where it touched as if burnt by flames. Kat shivered against the scorched rawness of her shoulders and neck. The heavy leather basque, although it nearly towed her to the bottom of the ocean, had protected her skin from the blaze on the Hell Burner. But the skin above the corset burned even as she shivered with the icy cold of the demons' collective breath.

A tree limb ripped from an oak and hurled through the darkness, through Drakkina's warding. Toren threw Kat to the ground as the ragged javelin ricocheted off the brick wall just over her head. Mud and pebbles rained down on Kat. She opened her eyes and stared over the scratchy twigs now separating her from Toren. She stood, her hands reaching for him.

"My warding only stops the demons, not what they can throw," Drakkina answered. The ground began to rumble and quake.

"Toren!" Kat yelled. Another tree flew through the air as a tornado bore down around them, swirling along the perimeter of Drakkina's shield. The ground beneath Kat began to split. She screamed and dropped to the cold mud, dirt and gravel pushing under her fingernails. She pressed backwards along the side of the brick building. The crevice grew into a gaping maw before her. The heavy wet court gown dragged in the mud as the brick wall crumbled away, falling into the crevice. Kat crawled backwards, sharp pebbles slicing her palms as she fought to hold onto a tilting, breaking edge of an abyss. It was as if the mouth of hell was opening before her.

"Send her!" Toren yelled above the chaos and deep gravelly sound of churning earth. "Send her, now!"

Drakkina floated slightly above them, her hands outspread as if damming back the demonic press. "On the currents of my blood, on the currents of my renewed power, send her now, Earth Mother—"

"No!" Kat yelled. "Toren!"

Toren's strong body stood solid on the other side of the chasm that had opened. Through the steam misting up from the earth, Kat watched Toren's face waver as if through water. "No!" she screamed. "Together, we stay together."

Kat watched Toren's lips move but she couldn't hear his voice. His lips mouthed the words she felt radiating from him as she melted into a thin blue line. *I love you too!* Kat screamed in her mind for words were useless without a mouth.

I must send you somewhere else first, before you can go home. Drakkina's words whispered through Kat's mind as the thread shot off into the night, up through a break in the dank black clouds.

Kat's thread soared, guided by Drakkina's magic. Dodging, piercing, diving, hiding, it flew. Kat's consciousness lay helpless upon the thread, watching the sun and moon chase each other across the sky, faster and faster until they blended into a whirling flash. There was no time, just flashing, just pulsing power that was Kat's consciousness. Could she unravel, disperse into the space between seconds, dissolve away?

Toren! Together! Kat railed at the flashing.

Fullness enveloped her essence and the thread expanded. The flashing turned into a bright noon sun, beating down on Kat's filling body. She shot down upon a hot desert, into the shadow of a pyramid. Kat glanced down her body. Besides her own blue moonstone that she wore around her neck, only the thin smock under her Elizabethan dress remained, wet and sucking against her skin. What had happened to the ruined court gown? With the expansion of Kat's body, the burns on her back screamed as the dry heat bit at the angry flesh like sand scratching against it.

Kat grimaced and glanced around, her mind whirling through ancient history. A young boy with a shaved head stood before her wearing nothing but a loincloth. His eyes were round as moons. He dropped, flattening himself on the sand before her feet.

"Goddess, you bless me," he called, lips in the hot grains. The words were foreign and heavily accented, but the stone at her neck translated them. The boy had obviously seen her expand and descend.

Kat looked up at the towering pyramid, gleaming like a huge triangular mirror. "Toto, we're not in Kansas anymore," she murmured. "Drakkina, where have you sent me?"

"I worship you, my goddess," the boy said, keeping his face in the hot sand.

What type of goddess would have serious burns across her back?

Use your magic here, Katell. Then I will thread you again. Drakkina's voice hummed like a tickle through Kat's head as if from far away. *We're leaving trails for them to follow, trails that will lead nowhere.*

"Toren?" Kat called as she opened her magic, cloaking herself in the golden splendor of an Egyptian queen. But the vibration of Drakkina's voice had flattened and disappeared. The boy looked up and then slammed his face back to the sand, not daring to look at a now golden Kat. In that brief glance Kat had seen ferocious fear and doubt. Such a young child for so much worry. Just like one of her boys back at the orphanage.

Kat knelt to the boy and touched his little head. She felt her body start to melt inside again and yanked back her hand in case touching him would bring him with her. "You will do great things, child. Stand. You are blessed," she said and straightened.

Once again her body elongated into a single thread and shot up into the cloudless sky. She watched the boy stand, head held high, determination marking his young features.

Next she landed in a jungle, then a Victorian train station. Kat stopped interacting with those who happened to see her. Instead, as soon as she felt herself expand, she released her water magic, cloaking herself with invisibility. A city teeming with horses and carriages and a few ancient cars at the turn of the century, a medieval castle under siege, a flooded rice crop with the Great Wall of China in the distance, a Native American sweat lodge among huge red rocks.

Kat landed once more outside a small cottage inside a circle of ten tall stones. The smell of bread baking wafted from an open window. Laughter bubbled from within along with a long, low chuckle. Kat's heart pounded with a sudden clenching in her expanded chest. She moved with invisible steps to the window and peeked in, drawn by the familiarity.

A woman, large with child, hummed as she pulled bread from a stone oven. She turned to the window and smiled, a curious tilt to her head. Kat threw herself to the side of the house and released her cloak. If this was her family, there was no way she was leading the demons here. *Drakkina, don't bring them here!*

You are safe within the stones. They hide you. Sit and wait. Drakkina's voice vibrated through her head. Still uncloaked, Kat crept up to the corner of the window so that only one eye could take in the domestic scene. A tall man with auburn hair and strong features sat near the hearth, carving a piece of flat wood. Pieces of a half-made cradle lay beside him. Two older girls helped their mother punch and mold several mounds of soft dough. Two toddlers rolled a leather ball between them near their father. Twins?

"Katell, not too close to the fire," the man said and put down his carving. He pulled one of the girls up onto his lap and tickled her until she giggled helplessly. Kat stared at her young self, so happy and safe in her father's arms.

Tears wet her cheeks, and she blinked to clear her watery sight. She watched the older girls, one with dark hair and the other with flaming red hair. Which one was Merewin, the healer?

Kat's gaze shifted to her twin, one she knew nothing about. They both had red-blond hair like their father, but her sister had dolls lined up to instruct. Where Kat giggled with her father, her sister seemed serious in her apron that matched the one their mother wore.

How many times had Kat felt that part of her was missing? How many times had she wished for a family? So many. She swallowed against the pain in her raw throat. Kat had created her own with Lisa and her children, and they waited for her in the future. She had Toren unless... Could he survive battling brutal vengeful demons? A small sob escaped Kat, and she sank to the ground, the scene no longer giving her any solace. Home, where was home? Here in the stone circle? With her children in the twenty-first century? *No*, she cried against her knees and wiped the back of a hand across her runny nose. *My home is with Toren.*

The low vibration of Drakkina's magic began to soften Kat's core, liquefying her from the inside out. It wasn't painful, merely strange. Kat released a breath and stood, eyes peering through the window once more before the scene began to waver. Her mother hummed as she worked, her hand sliding over the baby who must be pressing within her womb. Drakkina hadn't mentioned a fifth sibling.

No magic now, Drakkina said, and Kat shot off into the sky.

"Where is Toren?" Kat yelled, but her words garbled into nothing but a strange howl of wind as her face dissolved completely into Drakkina's thread.

The flickering light once more took over, drowning Kat's essence in nothing but bursts of light and dark mixed with speed. Was she moving or was time? It didn't matter, nothing mattered. Her body gone, Kat was pure thought and emotion. Despair enveloped her, sucking her strength. She didn't have a heart but knew it was broken, crushed under the weight of fear and loss. *Together.* They had decided to stay together, wherever that was, whenever that was. He was part of her now and without him, Kat would be broken.

The sun and moon slowed until Kat could clearly see the celestial bodies moving across the light and dark skies. East to west, right to left, arcing high over her thread until they stopped. Kat hung suspended, not expanding, under a hot sun and blue sky. Then the sun moved left to right, west to east, followed by the moon as if time backed up, adjusting, pushing her thread back into a dark, inky night.

Kat's thread swelled. *No magic right now*, Drakkina's breezy voice instructed. *I've brought you home.*

Kat descended into the night, rain drops pelting her as she expanded, down through the roof of a huge building, through floors, her half-filled body sliding through the stone and metal like a straw penetrating Jell-O. She alighted on a soft rug in darkness. Sparks of lightning outside illuminated a familiar hallway. Somerset House. Wind roared and the building shook. Kat flattened herself against the wall. Swirling voices clipped with hatred and anarchy accompanied the howl of the wind. The demons were hunting her.

She watched as a woman ran past the opening of the hallway, through a door into the catering kitchen. She wore nothing but a black bra and hot pink knickers that Kat knew read *Wednesday* across the bum.

Toren ran out of the dining rooms. "Ye won't get away this time."

"Toren," Kat whispered.

He strode through her path of vision, paused, and turned toward her form in the dark hall as if he sensed her there. Should she say something? Every part of her ached to run to him, grab hold and never let go. But what would that do to everything they'd accomplished in his time? Would it stop him from saving his sister? His clan? She barely breathed.

The door slammed in the kitchen, pulling Toren's gaze away from the pitch blackness hiding her. He pushed through the swinging side door. Within seconds he would find her former self, wet and cold in the gazebo on the terrace.

Kat sank to the floor, wrapping her arms around her knees. "Toren." She held tight for several long minutes, not letting herself move. The thunder ebbed, and tears slid down her cheeks. Toren and her other self must be gone. Lights flickered on in the open dining rooms. A small overhead light in the hall illuminated an Oriental rug, dark wet spots beneath her feet. "They're gone," she whispered.

"Kat?" Lisa's voice came from the end of the hallway. Several people stood beside her, dessert plates in hand. Lisa's feet thudded closer to where Kat huddled, soaked and in pain in the thin ankle-length smock.

Kat pushed her face up from her knees and Lisa gasped. *That's right, no magic.*

"Kat, what's happened to you?" Lisa knelt and tenderly pushed back wet, tangled hair. "Your face," she said and looked over Kat's shoulder.

"Oh my God, Kat, your back. It's burnt." Kat saw Robert from the bank staring wide-eyed down the hall. "Someone call an ambulance!" Lisa yelled with authority. She looked into Kat's watery eyes. "What happened?"

Kat just shook her head and let the tears fall.

CHAPTER TWENTY-EIGHT
BINDING

"I don't understand, Kat," Lisa said next to Kat's shiny metallic hospital bed. Flowers sat on the sliding side table and a multitude of handmade cards lay amongst the balled-up snotty tissues all over Kat's bed. "You were supposed to be sick at the orphanage last night. Then you show up at the charity ball, take a new job from a man I thought you'd never met before, and then got burnt from lightning in that ancient-looking..." Lisa moved her hands around as if searching for words.

"Smock," Kat provided, her cheek pressed into the overly white hospital pillowcase that smelled like diluted bleach. She lay on her stomach with nonstick Telfa dressing covering her shoulder blades.

"Yes, smock. Where the hell did you get it? You were wearing a gold cocktail dress an hour before. A gorgeous one that hadn't been in your closet earlier because I checked. And somehow it changed into an ancient, filthy smock that smelled like fish." Lisa didn't pause long enough for Kat to attempt an answer. "And then big fearsome Toren MacCallum disappears from his own charity ball along with that gaudy necklace he put on you."

Tears welled in Kat's eyes, and she squeezed them shut. She had cried most of the previous night after Lisa had left to check on the children and get some sleep. Cried and pleaded with God to bring Toren to her. She'd even cried out to Drakkina during the night, hoping to convince her to steal him again, rip him from his family, destroy his clan. Kat had cried all the more when she realized she couldn't ask it. Thus, the mountain of scratchy, hospital-generic tissues grew.

The burn specialists at the Royal London Hospital were keeping her for a couple of nights, treating Kat's second-degree burns with ointments and antibiotics. The pain of her back was minimized by prescription pain killers administered through the steady drip of an IV. Even though she could go home the next day, she would need to watch the burns for infection. Kat sighed and sniffed back the tears. She might have some scars but at least they were on her back, unlike her face.

"And then the doctors say the burn on your face is from when you were a kid." Lisa stood and paced across the narrow room. She might consider herself short, but Lisa had a powerful stride, and her hands flipped around as she talked. "I remember your burn then. It was terrible, but it healed. It went away, little by little until it was gone. I remember."

Lisa stooped down and swept the hair back from the right side of Kat's face that was turned upward on the pillow. "I don't understand, Kat."

Kat blinked hard but couldn't stop the tears from rolling out and down her nose. "It's a secret I kept for so long. I hid them." She stared into her friend's eyes. "I'm sorry. You're my best friend and..." A sob bubbled out.

Lisa put her face close to Kat's. "Shhh...now," she soothed. "Whatever...doesn't matter. You've always had secrets, like where the money came for the new bathrooms." She held a finger against Kat's lips when she tried to speak. "And I still love you. I'm just glad you're going to be okay."

Lisa's cell phone rang, and she straightened. Kat rubbed a hand over her stinging eyes and pinched her nose with a tissue. She rammed her face back into the thin pillow. No more hiding the scars. She didn't care what people thought. She didn't care about anything at the moment. Eventually she'd have to get back on two feet, plaster a smile on a scarred face and head back to her kids. They needed her and she would find solace in their love.

"What did he look like?" Lisa asked someone who was speaking very fast on the phone. "Big, fierce, huh...by chance did he have a Scottish accent?"

Kat turned her head out of the pillow to stare at Lisa. "Who is it?"

Lisa pressed the speaker icon, and Miss Edith spoke quickly. "He had a sword and was wearing a skirt tied around him. He looked wild. I made the children all hide in their bedrooms and lock the doors."

Kat pushed up from the pillow, ignoring the tight burning sensation across her shoulders as her bare feet slid over the side of the bed. "Holy Mother Mary," she whispered.

"Her name is Katell MacCallum!" The voice came from the hospital hallway, and Kat and Lisa both turned to look at the door, the phone forgotten. "She's my wife, and ye will tell me where she is, now!"

A nurse's stern voice met the brutal growl. "I'm sorry sir, but there is no MacCallum listed, and you're not allowed to carry a sword into a hospital. I'm calling security."

"Toren?" Kat choked, her heart thumping into a wild race. Kat grabbed Lisa's arm. "Toren!" she croaked past the raspy pain still in her throat. Kat slid her feet in fuzzy socks to the floor.

"Toren MacCallum!" Lisa yelled much louder. "In here!"

I love that woman. Kat clutched the IV pole like it was a cousin she hadn't wanted to bring along to a party, and it was time to go. She pulled it with her out of the room, Lisa at her elbow.

Toren stood in the sterile hallway, garbed in some sort of sheet wrapped like a kilt around his hips. An Oxford T-shirt stretched near to breaking across his broad chest. He held his sword in one hand but had turned toward them, his breaths coming in and out like that of a rampaging animal.

"Toren!" Kat yelled. Two security guards ran onto the scene. Wide-eyed and holding their batons, they must wonder what they'd do up against an enraged lunatic swinging a sword.

Lisa ran toward them. "All is well," she called. "He is Kat's boyfriend...uh...husband."

It took only two strides for Toren to meet Kat. They stood face to face, tears brimming in Kat's eyes, a stupid grin full of amazement and joy on her numb lips. Toren sheathed his sword and gently took Kat's face in his large hands.

"Where have you been?" Kat asked, as she stared into his hazel eyes.

"Olc witch sent me back to yer university, the one in Oxford. And she sent me back naked. Took some explaining and...creativity to get here."

Kat's hand twisted in the tight Oxford shirt as she pulled him closer. They breathed in each other, foreheads touching. "I'm so sorry, Toren." He looked confused. "For her tearing you away from your family again. I...I..."

Toren ran his thumb over Kat's lips as he stared into her eyes. "Ye're my family, love. I chose to come. I love ye, Kat."

Kat half bit back a sob. "I love you too," she breathed. "I thought I lost you."

"Nay" he said. "We stay together as one."

Kat nodded, blinking away her tears. "Together. Forever."

A relieved smile melted the tension in his features. He touched his nose to hers half a second before his lips captured Kat's in a slow, deep kiss.

Toren pulled back just enough to allow breath. "I bind ye to me for all time," he said and closed his eyes for a moment. "Forever."

A sizzle of magic tingled from Toren's hands into her own, making Kat suck in a quick breath. He wrapped his arms around her, careful to avoid her burns across her shoulder blades. They held each other for a moment. Behind them, Kat heard Lisa talking quickly.

"They met at a Highland games up in Scotland," she said. "It was magical. I think he just got carried away with the sword thing. Of course, he'd never use it on a person. It's just a replica. He uses it to slice haggis at the games. I know it doesn't look like it, but he's brilliant when he's splitting haggis."

Toren helped Kat back to her room with the IV pole. She sat on the hospital bed. "That was it? All you had to do was say those words and we're bound forever? Like a magic spell?"

"Aye." He kissed her lightly on the lips. "Ye did yer part back in the hidden glade when ye gave me yer maidenhead," he said. "I but needed to complete the binding."

Kat's brows pinched. He'd asked his brother to find oils and lotions for her in the sixteenth century as if he'd planned to keep her there. "You could have bound me at any time, keeping me with you?"

"'Twas honorable to ask ye first."

A smile softened her mouth. "And you are the most honorable man I've ever met."

His jaw was tight with conviction. "But I'm not losing ye again. If ye hadn't agreed, I would have remained by yer side until ye did."

"So not only do you know Toren MacCallum, but you're married to him," Lisa quipped from the doorway, hands propped on her tilted hips.

Toren's eyes remained fixed on Kat's. "We are bound through eternity," he said.

Excitement sizzled within Kat along with complete joy. Her smile spread across her face as she stared back at Toren.

"Bound through eternity?" Lisa asked and then blinked rapidly. "Is that a yes, you are married?" Lisa began a rapid-fire interrogation. "You're really married, like he wasn't just saying that to get in to see you? When did that happen? Sweet Jesus, he's only been in town for a week."

"Just let her talk." Kat smiled. "She doesn't usually expect a reply."

"And where was I when you were binding yourselves for eternity? Was it a church wedding?" Lisa looked stricken. "I wasn't there to hold your bouquet or straighten your dress or cry. The kids didn't see it."

Kat cupped Toren's face, gazing into his eyes. She never wanted to look away.

"We need a do-over." Lisa said. "We're having a wedding. I'll plan the whole thing. We'll do a Scottish theme." Lisa nodded at the white cloth tied around Toren's hips that he'd managed to pleat. "We can get you a real kilt."

"Where did you get that thing?" Kat whispered.

"'Tis a linen from a bed I saw at a house with Greek letters on it. The inhabitants were into their cups. They won't miss it."

⚬

"We could expand yer children's home," Toren said as Kat curled against his side. Visiting hours would end soon, and she didn't want to let go of him. His public relations manager had brought over a change of clothes.

He wore soft faded jeans and a light blue cambric shirt over his hard chest.

Kat laid her cheek against his strong beating heart. "Expand it? I just thought to fix it up. New appliances would help so much."

Toren kissed her forehead. "We will need a nursery for our own children."

Kat lifted her gaze up and smiled at him. The gleam in his eyes matched her own. As soon as she was released from the hospital and found some privacy, they might start on that family immediately. Her heart swelled with joy. "Sounds like a wonderful idea," she said.

"Perhaps we should move the whole children's home onto a larger area of land so they have room to run. Children should run," Toren said. "And swim. We will find land with a loch so I can swim each morning, even in winter."

Kat rubbed a finger over his frown lines. "Just like a Highlander."

"Aye." Toren rolled Kat on top of him, his hand splayed against her knicker-clad backside showing through the slit of the hospital gown. His other hand tangled in her hair, bringing her mouth down toward his own. The kiss was soul melding and perfect.

The mark on Kat's arm tingled.

"See now," a familiar voice called. "You *are* soul mates."

Kat felt Toren's body tense beneath her, but he continued the kiss as if they had all the time in the world.

"Katell," Drakkina called. "I know you and your mate hear me."

Kat smiled against Toren's lips at the sound of Drakkina's annoyance. She pulled back reluctantly.

"There now," Drakkina said. "You have visitors."

Visitors? Kat looked over her shoulder while spread across Toren, her bum hanging out. She inhaled quickly and stared at the two images hovering near Drakkina's. Toren rolled her gently to the side and stood in front of Kat in one swift protective move.

"Stand down, Highlander," Drakkina said. "These are Katell's older sisters." Drakkina floated around Toren and looked at Kat. "I promised I would bring Merewin to heal you, and I thought you would like to meet Serena, the eldest of Gilla's daughters."

Kat caught Toren's strong arm, edging to the side of the bed. The two women smiled at her.

"He's quite protective," the woman with lush red hair said. "But I promise, Toren MacCallum, we will not take her away."

"Serena can read minds," Drakkina said.

Serena frowned slightly. "I also block a lot of thoughts, because 'tis rude to eavesdrop." But she nodded to Kat. "And we don't trust Drakkina either. You should hear how she interfered with us."

"She dumped me naked in the square of a college campus," Toren growled.

"I left your clothes, and Katell's, back in your century so Elizabeth would think you were sucked out of them by the tornado and not just turning traitor to Spain."

Toren snorted.

"No gratitude," Drakkina murmured.

The sister's lavender eyes turned back to Kat, ignoring Drakkina's huff, and she smiled. "I am so pleased to meet you."

"I am Kat, although you know that." She smiled timidly, wishing she wasn't wearing a hospital gown. "And...where do you live or when do you live?"

"Eighteenth century, with the Macleans of Kylkern on the west coast of Scotland," Serena said.

"Are you close to the circle of stones then?" Kat asked.

"Yes," Serena answered. "It was our home once, when we were little."

Kat remembered the happy scene she'd watched for mere minutes during her trip back to this century. "There were four of us girls?"

Serena nodded.

"Was there a fifth?"

Serena's brow furrowed, and she looked at Drakkina.

"And this is your second sister," Drakkina said, her arm out toward the tall woman with lovely green-gold eyes and honey-brown hair.

"I am Merewin, and I live in tenth-century Denmark with the barbaric Norsemen." She laughed lightly. "Fierce and passionate," she added with a twinkle in her eye. It was then that Kat realized Merewin stood naked with a fur wrapped around her body. "Aye, the crone has terrible timing." Merewin glared at Drakkina.

"You and your warrior are constantly mating, Merewin. It's hard to find a time when you are fully dressed," Drakkina said and turned back to Kat, ignoring Merewin's little growl. "I promised to bring Merewin to heal you. Now that the demons are lost along our trails and tired of hunting for a while I was able to bring her."

"So I can use my magic again?" Kat asked, looking at the ethereal version of the dragonfly necklace that hung around Drakkina's neck.

Drakkina nodded and fingered the piece. "I keep the real amulet far away, saved for the final battle. It would be...inappropriate to use its magic now."

Toren looked down at Kat. "But ye have no need for your magic now," he said with a frown. "My investments and artifacts will keep the children clothed, fed, and well cared for. Ye have no need to steal to survive."

"And Merewin will heal your scars," Drakkina added.

Kat watched Toren's eyes. "The doctors say my back will have some scars, but not as bad as my face."

"I can take the pain away," Merewin said.

"She can also smooth the scars on your face," Drakkina said. "Isn't that what you've craved since you were a child?"

Kat turned from her sisters to Toren. Strong acceptance, respect, and love sat heavy in the lines and planes of Toren's face. He said nothing, letting her decide.

Kat cleared her tight throat and spoke slowly. "There is a child in the room next to me." Kat looked at Merewin. "She's burnt terribly, a house fire. They brought her in yesterday. Could you heal her?"

"How old is the child?"

"Perhaps ten, maybe older."

Merewin nodded. "I can heal her, but I won't have enough energy to heal you too," she said, her image wavering. "Not on this trip. It is difficult to heal across temporal planes."

Kat bit down on her bottom lip. "That's okay."

"Oh-kay?" Merewin repeated.

"You don't need to heal away my scars."

"But the point of me bringing her here was to heal your face, child," Drakkina said. "Don't you want to be free of the scars?" Her visage moved between young and old, fresh and then world-weary. Her dragonflies scattered as if sensing her confusion and zipped around the ceiling of the crowded room.

No one said anything. Kat turned to the mirror that stood against the bathroom door. The scars she'd hidden since childhood puckered along her cheek and jaw, feathering out and smoothing into her neck. She touched them lightly. Years of crying over them, smoothing them by pulling them tight over her face, and then ignoring and hiding them with glamour magic. So much energy and pain. Then Kat's eyes focused on Toren's face standing behind her image. His gaze was full of love.

Ye are a survivor. Kat heard the words he'd spoken in the past. His support remained in his eyes.

Drakkina tapped her foot silently in the mist at her feet. "Merewin, heal her."

"She is already healed," Serena said, a soft smile touching her lips. Kat's eldest sister tilted her head, studying Kat. "The scars inside are healed. The ones on the outside are no matter."

Serena came forward and hugged Kat. Even though Kat couldn't quite feel a warm body, she felt a shift of air, a tingle of magic, the essence of sisterly love in the embrace. Merewin was right on Serena's heels and hugged her, too.

"We will visit again," Merewin said. "My time grows short so I will find the child in the next room."

"I will come again too," Serena said. "To the wedding." She smiled brightly.

Merewin moved through the walls connecting the rooms, and Serena began to fade.

Drakkina floated close to Kat, her confused look smoothing into a smile. "I suppose you are a beauty no matter what's on your face." She winked a sparkling blue eye. "Stay out of dark water, Katell." She stepped back, fading away with Serena. *Call me if you need me.* Drakkina's words whispered through Kat's mind.

Toren stood in front of Kat. He ran his hand through her hair, cupping the right side of her face. Passion and happiness lurked in his eyes as he pulled her closer, a promise filled with love. "Och my love, yer loveliness shines out of yer eyes." He touched her face. "Out of yer smile." His gaze dropped down her body. "And along yer form." He ran his hands down the sides of her body. Kat ached for his touch. He leaned in, his lips brushing her own. "And when I get ye home I'm going to taste every single inch of ye."

"Home," Kat whispered, smiling as she held his gaze. "You are my home, Toren." She closed her eyes as he kissed her, feeling the greatest magic of all twine them together, the magic of love.

EPILOGUE

Six months later

Royal London Hospital Pediatric Burn Unit

"And the cruel knight lunged." Toren huffed while thrusting his polished sword toward the brightly painted wall. The children in the burn unit stared silently, their eyes wide. Some had bandages covering most of their faces. Some had burns on other parts of their young bodies. One boy lay on a gurney the nurse had rolled him in on, all but his face covered in sterile white bandages.

"But the honorable knight blocked the attack," Toren continued.

"Don't forget about the princess," Chelsea, a little girl with dark hair, called from her position on the floor. She tried to stand but the bandages wrapped around her hands made it difficult.

Kat scooped her up, settling the light weight on her lap. "Don't worry, Toren would never forget the princess." Kat smiled behind the little head as she watched Toren perform the medieval tale he said his father had told him and Eagan when they were young boys.

Out of the corner of her eye, Kat spotted Lisa quietly swinging through the burn unit's double doors, clipboard in hand. Lisa caught

Kat's eye and pointed at her watch. Kat nodded and mouthed back *when he's finished.* Lisa rolled her eyes but leaned against the wall, waving at several kids who had seen her.

"And the honorable knight rode through the dark forest to the castle where the princess..." he looked at Kat, and she nodded. They'd talked about how important it was for girls to learn about female empowerment. "Where the princess had already broken free of the dungeon by cleverly using the pins in her hair."

"Yes!" one of the older girls said.

"What was the princess's name?" Chelsea asked from Kat's lap.

"Princess Chelsea," Toren said.

The little girl bobbed up and down in Kat's lap with excitement, knocking Kat's chin. "Yay!"

"The knight slew the terrible Fomorian monster with his sword and found Princess Chelsea already on his horse in the courtyard. He mounted and they rode away together."

"To marry each other in a gorgeous ceremony in the forest," one of the older girls piped up and several nodded and sighed. The boys groaned and the children giggled.

Lisa pointed at her watch, her brows arched high. "Toren and Kat have to catch a train, now."

"So they can go get married," another girl called out.

"That's right," Lisa said and smiled. "The twelve flower girls and ring bearers are already on their way to the station." Lisa huffed as if the exertion was too much for her. "When I said a Scottish theme, I had no idea you'd want it actually in Scotland. Luckily Toren's family has a castle there. At least that part was easy."

Conquering Maxwell and thwarting Fergus Campbell's plans in order to protect Craignish Castle had been far from easy. Finding that it was still standing had lit Toren's face with joy, and he'd swung her around in celebration.

"But we'll be back, lads and lasses. In a couple weeks with more tales of Craignish," Toren said.

Chelsea turned in Kat's lap and touched the right side of her face with her bandaged hand. "You will be so beautiful as a bride."

Another girl named Jenny stood close. She looked to be about twelve, maybe thirteen, a critical age for self-esteem. She had burns healing on her face. "I hope I can find someone who will want to marry me someday," she said looking down. Her blond hair fell in front of her face, hiding the angry skin. "It's hard when you're a monster," she mumbled.

Kat's breath caught, and she noticed several other children looking down, having heard Jenny's pain-filled words. Kat let Chelsea slide off her lap.

Lisa apparently heard Jenny too because she plopped down in a chair. "Edith and two others are with the children. We can catch the next train if we miss it."

Kat turned to the girl. "Jenny," she said and bent to catch her eyes. "A very wise woman, a queen in fact, a real queen, once told me that it's the scars on the inside that make a person a monster. That many beautiful people are the true monsters because they have scars on the inside that make them bitter and angry."

Jenny looked up. "No one will love me because of the way I look." Such despair glittered in Jenny's eyes, mirroring Kat's own all those years before. Kat glanced at Toren. "When someone loves you, they don't look on the outside, they look on the inside."

Sadness still weighed down the girl's shoulders. Kat gave her a hug though the girl remained stiff.

An older boy across the room with bandages on his back and shoulders stared at the squares of white and gray linoleum, his slippered feet sliding back and forth. "Hold this," Toren said and pulled his sheathed sword off his back and handed it to him.

"Oh," the boy said. "Sure."

In one tug, Toren yanked his shirt out of his kilt and pulled it off over his head. He turned around, displaying the deep scars across his back from the beatings he'd endured at Maxwell's hands. Kat's heart clenched every time she thought of him as a boy, suffering alone.

"What do ye see?" Toren asked the boy holding his sword.

"One hell of a scarred up back," the kid replied.

"That's not from a burn," another boy called out.

"It looks more like...sword slashes."

Toren turned around and threw his shirt back on. "Doesn't matter what caused it or what caused yer scars. What matters is what it means."

Toren had the kids' rapt attention. Kat held her breath with them. "It means," Toren said, standing tall, "that I survived." He pointed at the boy holding his sword. "Yer scars mean that ye survived. Ye are stronger than the flames." He pointed at Jenny. "It means ye faced death and won." He pointed to the other boy. "It means ye are a warrior."

Kat watched as the kids in the room seemed to swell with Toren's words. Their little bodies stood taller, their heads lifted, their shoulders straightened.

Toren's finger moved about the room, pointing to each child. "Ye are all strong of heart because ye faced something terrible and lived. Ye won against the monster."

His words sent chills along Kat's arms. Toren looked at her and nodded. Hadn't he said such words to her before, words that he meant with true conviction?

"Okay kids," the nurse standing at the door called, her eyes a bit glassy with unshed tears. "It's time to let them leave. The train waits for no one, not even a Highland laird."

The kids yelled goodbye. Even Jenny looked happier, at least for the moment. The scars inside these kids, just like the ones inside Kat, would take time to heal.

"We'll be back soon," Kat called and took Toren's arm. "And I'll bring biscuits!" The kids cheered.

As they walked through the automatic sliding glass doors of the hospital, Kat pulled back on Toren's arm. Lisa ran ahead to get Toren's SUV. Kat smiled up into Toren's eyes. "Thank you," she said. "You are..." She floundered for words.

"Sexy as hell," he said, repeating Lisa's description of him.

Kat laughed. "Absolutely." She smiled warmly. "And amazingly kind."

He pulled her into his warm, strong arms and leaned down to brush her lips with his. "Ye do good things here, Kat. In this century." He nodded. "It is where we belong."

Kat's smile widened. "We...together."

Toren nodded. "Bound forever," he said and stared into her eyes. The intensity in his gaze seemed to stop time when she looked into it.

The chauffeur-driven SUV pulled up to the curb, and Lisa yelled from the lowered window. "Save it for Scotland, you two."

Toren pulled back reluctantly.

"Craignish awaits," Kat said. "I wonder how much it's changed." They slid into the back of the SUV.

"It is not in ruins," Toren said. "That's all that matters."

"It's amazing that your ancestral castle is still standing," Lisa said from the passenger seat up front. "I looked it up online. They say it was built in the fourteenth century."

Toren squeezed Kat's hand, with reined in excitement, and pulled her up against him in the cushioned leather seat. The MacCallums hadn't died out leaving nothing but ruins. They had prospered through Eagan and Margaret's offspring as well as Briana's. Fergus Campbell, on the other hand, had disappeared from the pages of history.

Kat kissed Toren softly and smiled back. "It's like you're going home."

Toren grinned at her, pulling her tighter against his side. "I already am."

***

Continue the Dragonfly Chronicles with Kat's twin sister, Kailin, in Victorian era Egypt as she hunts the Orb of Life amongst the pyramids and learns to control her immense power. Will the American treasure hunter find it before her, stealing it like he's stolen her heart?

***

Subscribe to my Newsletter

Be the first to know when Eleri Drake/Heather McCollum has a new cover reveal, release, sale, or giveaway! You will be able to choose how much or how little you hear from me.

Newsletter

Did you love Kat and Toren's slow burn romance and epic adventure? The message that scars show how strong you are? **If you did, please leave a review wherever you purchased this book or on Goodreads.** Writing a review and telling others that you loved a book is the #1 way to thank an author. Thank you! Eleri

About the Author

Eleri Drake is the penname of Heather McCollum, a *USA Today* and *Publishers Weekly* bestselling author of Scottish historical romance. Books written under the pseudonym Eleri Drake contain fantasy and paranormal elements to make the adventure and passion even more fun.

Growing up, Eleri/Heather dreamed of fairies and magic. She would swim in her family pool with her legs together, hoping they'd fuse, and she'd become a mermaid. Her favorite television show was *Bewitched* where she wished to be Tabitha, the playful, trouble-making little witch child. Now she can funnel all her whimsy into these romantasies set back in time.

Acknowledgements

Thank you to my wonderful readers, those who know me as Heather McCollum and those who have found me as Eleri Drake. When you read, you bring our characters to life. Being able to give adventure and a happily-ever-after to another person makes me so happy!

Thank you to my lovely editor, Melinda DeJongh, who finds all the inconsistencies, keeps me in the 16th century, polishes my story, and corrals errant commas. And who manages all my quick turn around times. You are golden!

Also…

At the end of each of my books, I ask that you, my awesome readers, please remind yourselves of the whispered symptoms of ovarian cancer. I am now a fourteen-year survivor, one of the lucky ones. Please don't rely on luck. If you experience any of these symptoms consistently for three weeks or more, go see your GYN.

· Bloating

· Eating less and feeling full faster

· Abdominal pain

· Trouble with your bladder

Other symptoms may include indigestion, back pain, pain with intercourse, constipation, fatigue, and menstrual irregularities.

OTHER SERIES BY HEATHER MCCOLLUM

HIGHLAND HEARTS

First Book – Captured Heart
Enemies to Lovers

Set in the early 16th century Highlands. A Scottish Historical Romance series, spanning generations, with a touch of magic. The women in the Macbain Clan have the power to heal, a "gift" that gets passed down through family lines. Those with the gift must evade witch hunters and deal with suspicion. They harness herbal lore and learn to use their magic to help those they love.

HIGHLAND ISLES

First Book – The Beast of Aros Castle
Marriage of Convenience

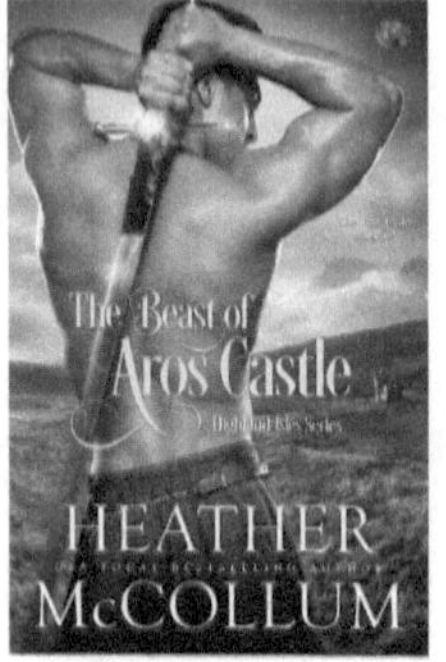

Set in the mid-16th century on the western isles off Scotland. Fun banter and laugh-out-loud adventures with the broody chiefs of the clans and the feisty women who find their way into their lives. Mysteries and secrets abound!

THE CAMPBELLS

First Book – The Scottish Rogue
Enemies to Lovers

Set in the 17th century in Scotland. Two English sisters journey to Scotland to start a school for the local people in a castle that their brother bought (or so he thought). They quickly realize that on top of learning to read, cipher numbers, and serve tea, the girls need to learn how to defend themselves against both Scottish and English villains. The school becomes a self-defense school, and the pupils are called the Roses (beautiful but with dangerous thorns).

SONS OF SINCLAIR

Enemies to Lovers
First Book – Highland Conquest
Enemies to Lovers

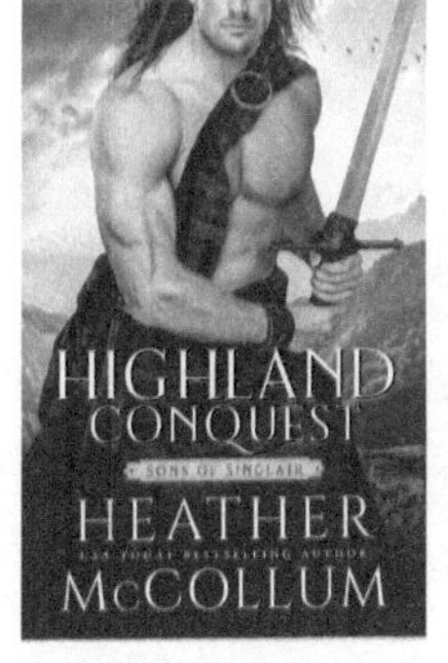

Set in the late 16th century northern Scotland. Four brothers were raised by a mad, war-loving father to be the biblical four horsemen of the apocalypse. They are mere flesh and bone, but they were raised to be Conquest, War, Judgement, and Death. Learning to love, the most powerful prize of all, challenges all their beliefs.

BROTHERS OF WOLF ISLE

First Book – The Highlander's Unexpected Proposal
Marriage of Convenience

Set in the 16th century off the west coast of Scotland. Five brothers are trying to rebuild their clan on their ancestral isle, but the isle is said to be cursed. To break the curse, they must learn truths about love. The original idea for this series was loosely based on the musical *Seven Brides for Seven Brothers*.

THE QUEEN'S HIGHLANDERS
First Book – The Highlander & the Queen's Sacrifice
Secrets, Body Guard, Tudor

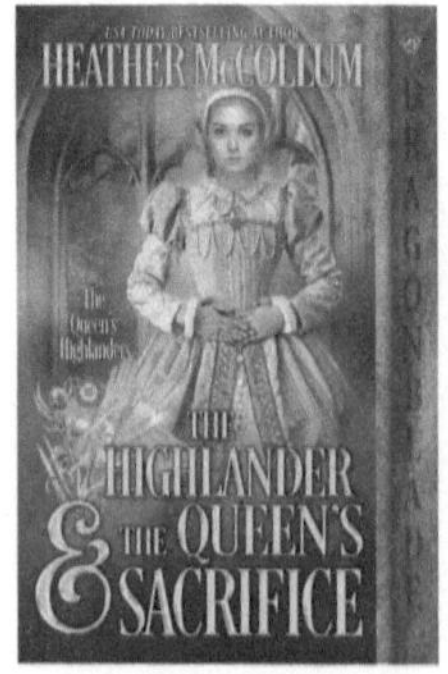

Set in 16th century London at Queen Elizabeth's court. Three of the queen's ladies get mixed up with visiting Highlanders to expose assassination plots. Poisoned gowns, a chastity belt, and masquerade fun!

BROTHERHOOD OF SOLWAY MOSS

First Book – The Highlander's Wild Flame
Enemies to Lovers

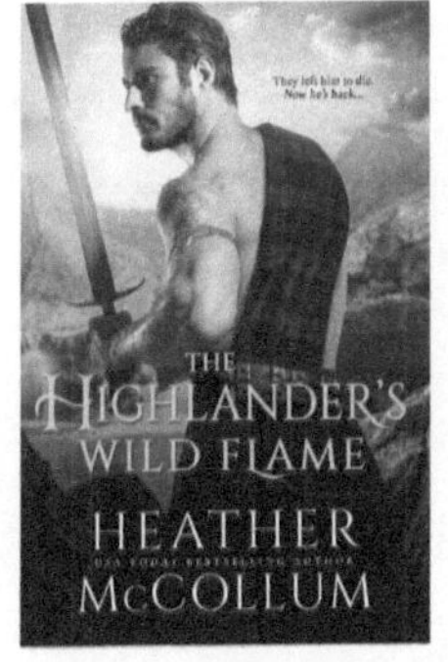

Set in the mid 16th century Highlands. Four Highlanders, who were raised as enemies, escape an English dungeon by working together. When they return to the Isle of Skye, they pledge to convince their feuding families to unite to strengthen Scotland. Alliances are only as strong as the emotions behind them, love being the most powerful. Strong women and a witch work to bring elements of fire, air, water, and earth together to strengthen their isle.

◆◇◆

Support a Small Business
Buy Print Books Directly from Heather's Online Store

Heather/Eleri
Website

www.ingramcontent.com/pod-product-compliance
Lightning Source LLC
Chambersburg PA
CBHW021414310726
48971CB00005B/1337